The Second Leonaur Book
of Supernatural Detectives

The Second Leonaur Book of Supernatural Detectives

Investigations of Ghosts and Strange Occurrences Including 'Door into Infinity', 'The Mark of the Beast', 'The Spectre House', 'The Telepather,' 'The Mystery of the Circular Chamber', 'The Haunted Homestead' and Eight Other Short Stories

Morgan Tyler

LEONAUR

The Second Leonaur Book of Supernatural Detectives
Investigations of Ghosts and Strange Occurrences Including 'Door into Infinity', 'The
Mark of the Beast', 'The Spectre House', 'The Telepather,' 'The Mystery of the Circular
Chamber', 'The Haunted Homestead' and Eight Other Short Stories
By Morgan Tyler

FIRST EDITION

Leonaur is an imprint
of Oakpast Ltd

ISBN: 978-1-78282-441-1 (hardcover)
ISBN: 978-1-78282-442-8 (softcover)

http://www.leonaur.com

Publisher's Notes

The views expressed in this book are not necessarily
those of the publisher.

Contents

Carnacki, the Ghost Finder:
The Whistling Room
William Hope Hodgson

Carnacki shook a friendly fist at me as I entered, late. Then he opened the door into the dining room, and ushered the four of us—Jessop, Arkright, Taylor and myself—in to dinner.

We dined well, as usual, and, equally as usual, Carnacki was pretty silent during the meal. At the end, we took our wine and cigars to our usual positions, and Carnacki—having got himself comfortable in his big chair—began without any preliminary:—

"I have just got back from Ireland, again," he said. "And I thought you chaps would be interested to hear my news. Besides, I fancy I shall see the thing clearer, after I have told it all out straight. I must tell you this, though, at the beginning—up to the present moment, I have been utterly and completely 'stumped.' I have tumbled upon one of the most peculiar cases of 'haunting'—or devilment of some sort—that I have come against. Now listen.

"I have been spending the last few weeks at Iastrae Castle, about twenty miles northeast of Galway. I got a letter about a month ago from a Mr. Sid K. Tassoc, who it seemed had bought the place lately, and moved in, only to find that he had bought a very peculiar piece of property.

"When I got there, he met me at the station, driving a jaunting car, and drove me up to the castle, which, by the way, he called a 'house shanty.' I found that he was 'pigging it' there with his boy brother and another American, who seemed to be half-servant and half-companion. It seems that all the servants had left the place, in a body, as you might say, and now they were managing among themselves, assisted by some day-help.

"The three of them got together a scratch feed, and Tassoc told me all about the trouble whilst we were at table. It is most extraordinary, and different from anything that I have had to do with; though that Buzzing Case was very queer, too.

"Tassoc began right in the middle of his story. 'We've got a room in this shanty,' he said, 'which has got a most infernal whistling in it; sort of haunting it. The thing starts any time; you never know when, and it goes on until it frightens you. All the servants have gone, as you know. It's not ordinary whistling, and it isn't the wind. Wait till you hear it.'

"'We're all carrying guns,' said the boy; and slapped his coat pocket.

"'As bad as that?' I said; and the older boy nodded. 'It may be soft,' he replied; 'but wait till you've heard it. Sometimes I think it's some infernal thing, and the next moment, I'm just as sure that someone's playing a trick on me.'

"'Why?' I asked. 'What is to be gained?'

"'You mean,' he said, 'that people usually have some good reason for playing tricks as elaborate as this. Well, I'll tell you. There's a lady in this province, by the name of Miss Donnehue, who's going to be my wife, this day two months. She's more beautiful than they make them, and so far as I can see, I've just stuck my head into an Irish hornet's nest. There's about a score of hot young Irishmen been courting her these two years gone, and now that I'm come along and cut them out, they feel raw against me. Do you begin to understand the possibilities?'

"'Yes,' I said. 'Perhaps I do in a vague sort of way; but I don't see how all this affects the room?'

"'Like this,' he said. 'When I'd fixed it up with Miss Donnehue, I looked out for a place, and bought this little house shanty. Afterward, I told her—one evening during dinner, that I'd decided to tie up here. And then she asked me whether I wasn't afraid of the whistling room. I told her it must have been thrown in *gratis*, as I'd heard nothing about it. There were some of her men friends present, and I saw a smile go 'round. I found out, after a bit of questioning, that several people have bought this place during the last twenty-odd years. And it was always on the market again, after a trial.

"'Well, the chaps started to bait me a bit, and offered to take bets after dinner that I'd not stay six months in the place. I looked once or twice to Miss Donnehue, so as to be sure I was "getting the note" of the talkee-talkee; but I could see that she didn't take it as a joke, at all. Partly, I think, because there was a bit of a sneer in the way the men were tackling me, and partly because she really believes there is something in this yarn of the Whistling Room.

"'However, after dinner, I did what I could to even things up with the others. I nailed all their bets, and screwed them down hard and safe. I guess some of them are going to be hard hit, unless I lose; which I don't mean to. Well, there you have practically the whole yarn.'

"'Not quite,' I told him. 'All that I know, is that you have bought a castle with a room in it that is in some way "queer," and that you've been doing some betting. Also, I know that your servants have got frightened and run away. Tell me something about the whistling?'

"'Oh, that!' said Tassoc; 'that started the second night we were in. I'd had a good look 'round the room, in the daytime, as you can understand; for the talk up at Arlestrae—Miss Donnehue's place—had made me wonder a bit. But it seems just as usual as some of the other rooms in the old wing, only perhaps a bit more lonesome. But that may be only because of the talk about it, you know.

"'The whistling started about ten o'clock, on the second night, as I said. Tom and I were in the library, when we heard an awfully queer whistling, coming along the East Corridor—The room is in the East Wing, you know.

"'That's that blessed ghost!' I said to Tom, and we collared the lamps off the table, and went up to have a look. I tell you, even as we dug along the corridor, it took me a bit in the throat, it was so beastly queer. It was a sort of tune, in a way; but more as if a devil or some rotten thing were laughing at you, and going to get 'round at your back. That's how it makes you feel.

"'When we got to the door, we didn't wait; but rushed it open; and then I tell you the sound of the thing fairly hit me in the face. Tom said he got it the same way—sort of felt stunned and bewildered. We looked all 'round, and soon got so nervous, we just cleared out, and I locked the door.

"'We came down here, and had a stiff peg each. Then we got fit again, and began to think we'd been nicely had. So we took sticks, and went out into the grounds, thinking after all it must be some of these confounded Irishmen working the ghost-trick on us. But there was not a leg stirring.

"'We went back into the house, and walked over it, and then paid another visit to the room. But we simply couldn't stand it. We fairly ran out, and locked the door again. I don't know how to put it into words; but I had a feeling of being up against something that was rottenly dangerous. You know! We've carried our guns ever since.

"'Of course, we had a real turn out of the room next day, and the whole house place; and we even hunted 'round the grounds; but there was nothing queer. And now I don't know what to think; except that the sensible part of me tells me that it's some plan of these Wild Irishmen to try to take a rise out of me.'

"'Done anything since?' I asked him.

"'Yes,' he said—'watched outside of the door of the room at nights, and chased 'round the grounds, and sounded the walls and floor of the room. We've done everything we could think of; and it's beginning to get on our nerves; so we sent for you.'

"By this, we had finished eating. As we rose from the table, Tassoc suddenly called out:—'Ssh! Hark!'

"We were instantly silent, listening. Then I heard it, an extraordinary hooning whistle, monstrous and inhuman, coming from far away through corridors to my right.

"'By G—d!' said Tassoc; 'and it's scarcely dark yet! Collar those candles, both of you, and come along.'

"In a few moments, we were all out of the door and racing up the stairs. Tassoc turned into a long corridor, and we followed, shielding our candles as we ran. The sound seemed to fill all the passage as we drew near, until I had the feeling that the whole air throbbed under the power of some wanton Immense Force—a sense of an actual taint, as you might say, of monstrosity all about us.

"Tassoc unlocked the door; then, giving it a push with his foot, jumped back, and drew his revolver. As the door flew open, the sound beat out at us, with an effect impossible to explain to one who has not heard it—with a certain, horrible personal note in it; as if in there in the darkness you could picture the room rocking and creaking in a mad, vile glee to its own filthy piping and whistling and hooning. To stand there and listen, was to be stunned by Realisation. It was as if someone showed you the mouth of a vast pit suddenly, and said:—That's Hell. And you knew that they had spoken the truth. Do you get it, even a little bit?

"I stepped back a pace into the room, and held the candle over my head, and looked quickly 'round. Tassoc and his brother joined me, and the man came up at the back, and we all held our candles high. I was deafened with the shrill, piping hoon of the whistling; and then, clear in my ear, something seemed to be saying to me:—'Get out of here—quick! Quick! Quick!'

"As you chaps know, I never neglect that sort of thing. Sometimes it may be nothing but nerves; but as you will remember, it was just such a warning that saved me in the 'Grey Dog' Case, and in the 'Yellow Finger' Experiments; as well as other times. Well, I turned sharp 'round to the others: 'Out!' I said. 'For God's sake, *out* quick.' And in an instant I had them into the passage.

"There came an extraordinary yelling scream into the hideous whistling, and then, like a clap of thunder, an utter silence. I slammed the door, and locked it. Then, taking the key, I looked 'round at the others. They were pretty white, and I imagine I must have looked that way too. And there we stood a moment, silent.

"'Come down out of this, and have some whisky,' said Tassoc, at last, in a voice he tried to make ordinary; and he led the way. I was the back man, and I know we all kept looking over our shoulders. When we got downstairs, Tassoc passed the bottle 'round. He took a drink, himself, and slapped his glass down on to the table. Then sat down with a thud.

"'That's a lovely thing to have in the house with you, isn't it!' he said. And directly afterward:—'What on earth made you hustle us all out like that, Carnacki?'

"'Something seemed to be telling me to get out, quick,' I said. 'Sounds a bit silly, superstitious, I know; but when you are meddling with this sort of thing, you've got to take notice of queer fancies, and risk being laughed at.'

"I told him then about the 'Grey Dog' business, and he nodded a lot to that. 'Of course,' I said, 'this may be nothing more than those would-be rivals of yours playing some funny game; but, personally, though I'm going to keep an open mind, I feel that there is something beastly and dangerous about this thing.'

"We talked for a while longer, and then Tassoc suggested billiards, which we played in a pretty half-hearted fashion, and all the time cocking an ear to the door, as you might say, for sounds; but none came, and later, after coffee, he suggested early bed, and a thorough overhaul of the room on the morrow.

"My bedroom was in the newer part of the castle, and the door opened into the picture gallery. At the east end of the gallery was the entrance to the corridor of the East Wing; this was shut off from the gallery by two old and heavy oak doors, which looked rather odd and quaint beside the more modern doors of the various rooms.

"When I reached my room, I did not go to bed; but began to un-pack my instrument trunk, of which I had retained the key. I intended to take one or two preliminary steps at once, in my investigation of the extraordinary whistling.

"Presently, when the castle had settled into quietness, I slipped out of my room, and across to the entrance of the great corridor. I opened one of the low, squat doors, and threw the beam of my pocket searchlight down the passage. It was empty, and I went through the doorway, and pushed-to the oak behind me. Then along the great passageway, throwing my light before and behind, and keeping my revolver handy.

"I had hung a 'protection belt' of garlic 'round my neck, and the smell of it seemed to fill the corridor and give me assurance; for, as you all know, it is a wonderful 'protection' against the more usual *Aei-irii* forms of semi-materialisation, by which I supposed the whistling might be produced; though, at that period of my investigation, I was quite prepared to find it due to some perfectly natural cause; for it is astonishing the enormous number of cases that prove to have nothing abnormal in them.

"In addition to wearing the necklet, I had plugged my ears loosely with garlic, and as I did not intend to stay more than a few minutes in the room, I hoped to be safe.

"When I reached the door, and put my hand into my pocket for the key, I had a sudden feeling of sickening funk. But I was not going to back out, if I could help it. I unlocked the door and turned the handle. Then I gave the door a sharp push with my foot, as Tassoc had done, and drew my revolver, though I did not expect to have any use for it, really.

"I shone the searchlight all 'round the room, and then stepped in-side, with a disgustingly horrible feeling of walking slap into a waiting danger. I stood a few seconds, waiting, and nothing happened, and the empty room showed bare from corner to corner. And then, you know, I realised that the room was full of an abominable silence; can you understand that? A sort of purposeful silence, just as sickening as any of the filthy noises the Things have power to make. Do you remember what I told you about that 'Silent Garden' business? Well, this room had just that same *malevolent* silence—the beastly quietness of a thing that is looking at you and not seeable itself, and thinks that it has got you. Oh, I recognised it instantly, and I whipped the top off my lan-tern, so as to have light over the *whole* room.

"Then I set-to, working like fury, and keeping my glance all about me. I sealed the two windows with lengths of human hair, right across, and sealed them at every frame. As I worked, a queer, scarcely perceptible tenseness stole into the air of the place, and the silence seemed, if you can understand me, to grow more solid. I knew then that I had no business there without 'full protection'; for I was practically certain that this was no mere *Aeiirii* development; but one of the worst forms, as the *Saiitii*; like that 'Grunting Man' case—you know.

"I finished the window, and hurried over to the great fireplace. This is a huge affair, and has a queer gallows-iron, I think they are called, projecting from the back of the arch. I sealed the opening with seven human hairs—the seventh crossing the six others.

"Then, just as I was making an end, a low, mocking whistle grew in the room. A cold, nervous pricking went up my spine, and 'round my forehead from the back. The hideous sound filled all the room with an extraordinary, grotesque parody of human whistling, too gigantic to be human—as if something gargantuan and monstrous made the sounds softly. As I stood there a last moment, pressing down the final seal, I had no doubt but that I had come across one of those rare and horrible cases of the *Inanimate* reproducing the functions of the *Animate*, I made a grab for my lamp, and went quickly to the door, looking over my shoulder, and listening for the thing that I expected. It came, just as I got my hand upon the handle—a squeal of incredible, malevolent anger, piercing through the low hooning of the whistling. I dashed out, slamming the door and locking it. I leant a little against the opposite wall of the corridor, feeling rather funny; for it had been a narrow squeak.

Theyr be noe sayfetie to be gained bye gayrds of holieness when the monyster hath pow'r to speak throe woode and stoene.

So runs the passage in the Sigsand MS., and I proved it in that 'Nodding Door' business. There is no protection against this particular form of monster, except, possibly, for a fractional period of time; for it can reproduce itself in, or take to its purpose, the very protective material which you may use, and has the power to '*forme* wythine the pentycle'; though not immediately. There is, of course, the possibility of the Unknown Last Line of the *Saaamaaa* Ritual being uttered; but it is too uncertain to count upon, and the danger is too hideous; and even then it has no power to protect for more than 'maybee fyve beats of the harte,' as the Sigsand has it.

13

"Inside of the room, there was now a constant, meditative, hooning whistling; but presently this ceased, and the silence seemed worse; for there is such a sense of hidden mischief in a silence.

"After a little, I sealed the door with crossed hairs, and then cleared off down the great passage, and so to bed.

"For a long time I lay awake; but managed eventually to get some sleep. Yet, about two o'clock I was waked by the hooning whistling of the room coming to me, even through the closed doors. The sound was tremendous, and seemed to beat through the whole house with a presiding sense of terror. As if (I remember thinking) some monstrous giant had been holding mad carnival with itself at the end of that great passage.

"I got up and sat on the edge of the bed, wondering whether to go along and have a look at the seal; and suddenly there came a thump on my door, and Tassoc walked in, with his dressing gown over his pyjamas.

"'I thought it would have waked you, so I came along to have a talk,' he said. 'I can't sleep. Beautiful! Isn't it!'

"'Extraordinary!' I said, and tossed him my case.

"He lit a cigarette, and we sat and talked for about an hour; and all the time that noise went on, down at the end of the big corridor.

"Suddenly, Tassoc stood up:—

"'Let's take our guns, and go and examine the brute,' he said, and turned toward the door.

"'No!' I said. 'By Jove—no! I can't say anything definite, yet; but I believe that room is about as dangerous as it well can be.'

"'Haunted—really haunted?' he asked, keenly and without any of his frequent banter.

"I told him, of course, that I could not say a definite yes or no to such a question; but that I hoped to be able to make a statement, soon. Then I gave him a little lecture on the False Re–Materialization of the Animate–Force through the Inanimate–Inert. He began then to see the particular way in the room might be dangerous, if it were really the subject of a manifestation.

"About an hour later, the whistling ceased quite suddenly, and Tassoc went off again to bed. I went back to mine, also, and eventually got another spell of sleep.

"In the morning, I went along to the room. I found the seals on the door intact. Then I went in. The window seals and the hair were all right; but the seventh hair across the great fireplace was broken.

This set me thinking. I knew that it might, very possibly, have snapped, through my having tensioned it too highly; but then, again, it might have been broken by something else. Yet, it was scarcely possible that a man, for instance, could have passed between the six unbroken hairs; for no one would ever have noticed them, entering the room that way, you see; but just walked through them, ignorant of their very existence.

"I removed the other hairs, and the seals. Then I looked up the chimney. It went up straight, and I could see blue sky at the top. It was a big, open flue, and free from any suggestion of hiding places, or corners. Yet, of course, I did not trust to any such casual examination, and after breakfast, I put on my overalls, and climbed to the very top, sounding all the way; but I found nothing.

"Then I came down, and went over the whole of the room—floor, ceiling, and walls, mapping them out in six-inch squares, and sounding with both hammer and probe. But there was nothing abnormal.

"Afterward, I made a three-weeks search of the whole castle, in the same thorough way; but found nothing. I went even further, then; for at night, when the whistling commenced, I made a microphone test. You see, if the whistling were mechanically produced, this test would have made evident to me the working of the machinery, if there were any such concealed within the walls. It certainly was an up-to-date method of examination, as you must allow.

"Of course, I did not think that any of Tassoc's rivals had fixed up any mechanical contrivance; but I thought it just possible that there had been some such thing for producing the whistling, made away back in the years, perhaps with the intention of giving the room a reputation that would ensure its being free of inquisitive folk. You see what I mean? Well, of course, it was just possible, if this were the case, that someone knew the secret of the machinery, and was utilizing the knowledge to play this devil of a prank on Tassoc. The microphone test of the walls would certainly have made this known to me, as I have said; but there was nothing of the sort in the castle; so that I had practically no doubt at all now, but that it was a genuine case of what is popularly termed 'haunting.'

"All this time, every night, and sometimes most of each night, the hooning whistling of the room was intolerable. It was as if an intelligence there knew that steps were being taken against it, and piped and hooned in a sort of mad, mocking contempt. I tell you, it was as extraordinary as it was horrible. Time after time, I went along—tiptoeing noiselessly on stockinged feet—to the sealed door (for I always kept the room sealed). I went at all hours of the night, and often the whistling, inside, would seem to change to a brutally malignant note, as though the half-animate monster saw me plainly through the shut door. And all the time the shrieking, hooning whistling would fill the whole corridor, so that I used to feel a precious lonely chap, messing about there with one of Hell's mysteries.

"And every morning, I would enter the room, and examine the different hairs and seals. You see, after the first week, I had stretched parallel hairs all along the walls of the room, and along the ceiling; but over the floor, which was of polished stone, I had set out little, colourless wafers, tacky-side uppermost. Each wafer was numbered, and they were arranged after a definite plan, so that I should be able to trace the exact movements of any living thing that went across the floor.

"You will see that no material being or creature could possibly have entered that room, without leaving many signs to tell me about it. But nothing was ever disturbed, and I began to think that I should have to risk an attempt to stay the night in the room, in the Electric Pentacle. Yet, mind you, I knew that it would be a crazy thing to do; but I was getting stumped, and ready to do anything.

"Once, about midnight, I did break the seal on the door, and have a quick look in; but, I tell you, the whole room gave one mad yell, and seemed to come toward me in a great belly of shadows, as if the walls had bellied in toward me. Of course, that must have been fancy. Anyway, the yell was sufficient, and I slammed the door, and locked it, feeling a bit weak down my spine. You know the feeling.

"And then, when I had got to that state of readiness for anything, I made something of a discovery. It was about one in the morning, and I was walking slowly 'round the castle, keeping in the soft grass. I had come under the shadow of the East Front, and far above me, I could hear the vile, hooning whistle of the room, up in the darkness of the unlit wing. Then, suddenly, a little in front of me, I heard a man's voice, speaking low, but evidently in glee:—

"'By George! You Chaps; but I wouldn't care to bring a wife home in that!' it said, in the tone of the cultured Irish.

"Someone started to reply; but there came a sharp exclamation, and then a rush, and I heard footsteps running in all directions. Evidently, the men had spotted me.

"For a few seconds, I stood there, feeling an awful ass. After all, *they* were at the bottom of the haunting! Do you see what a big fool it made me seem? I had no doubt but that they were some of Tassoc's rivals; and here I had been feeling in every bone that I had hit a real, bad, genuine case! And then, you know, there came the memory of hundreds of details, that made me just as much in doubt again. Anyway, whether it was natural, or ab-natural, there was a great deal yet to be cleared up.

"I told Tassoc, next morning, what I had discovered, and through the whole of every night, for five nights, we kept a close watch 'round the East Wing; but there was never a sign of anyone prowling about; and all the time, almost from evening to dawn, that grotesque whistling would hoon incredibly, far above us in the darkness.

"On the morning after the fifth night, I received a wire from here, which brought me home by the next boat. I explained to Tassoc that I was simply bound to come away for a few days; but told him to keep up the watch 'round the castle. One thing I was very careful to do, and that was to make him absolutely promise never to go into the room, between sunset and sunrise. I made it clear to him that we knew nothing definite yet, one way or the other; and if the room were what I had first thought it to be, it might be a lot better for him to die first, than enter it after dark.

"When I got here, and had finished my business, I thought you chaps would be interested; and also I wanted to get it all spread out clear in my mind; so I rung you up. I am going over again tomorrow, and when I get back, I ought to have something pretty extraordinary to tell you. By the way, there is a curious thing I forgot to tell you. I tried to get a phonographic record of the whistling; but it simply produced no impression on the wax at all. That is one of the things that has made me feel queer, I can tell you. Another extraordinary thing is that the microphone will not magnify the sound—will not even transmit it; seems to take no account of it, and acts as if it were nonexistent. I am absolutely and utterly stumped, up to the present. I am a wee bit curious to see whether any of your dear clever heads can make daylight of it. I cannot—not yet."

He rose to his feet.

"Goodnight, all," he said, and began to usher us out abruptly, but without offence, into the night.

A fortnight later, he dropped each of us a card, and you can imagine that I was not late this time. When we arrived, Carnacki took us straight into dinner, and when we had finished, and all made ourselves comfortable, he began again, where he had left off:—

"Now just listen quietly; for I have got something pretty queer to tell you. I got back late at night, and I had to walk up to the castle, as I had not warned them that I was coming. It was bright moonlight; so that the walk was rather a pleasure, than otherwise. When I got there, the whole place was in darkness, and I thought I would take a walk 'round outside, to see whether Tassoc or his brother was keeping watch. But I could not find them anywhere, and concluded that they had got tired of it, and gone off to bed.

"As I returned across the front of the East Wing, I caught the hooning whistling of the room, coming down strangely through the stillness of the night. It had a queer note in it, I remember—low and constant, queerly meditative. I looked up at the window, bright in the moonlight, and got a sudden thought to bring a ladder from the stable yard, and try to get a look into the room, through the window.

"With this notion, I hunted 'round at the back of the castle, among the straggle of offices, and presently found a long, fairly light ladder; though it was heavy enough for one, goodness knows! And I thought at first that I should never get it reared. I managed at last, and let the ends rest very quietly against the wall, a little below the sill of the larger window. Then, going silently, I went up the ladder. Presently, I had my face above the sill and was looking in alone with the moonlight.

"Of course, the queer whistling sounded louder up there; but it still conveyed that peculiar sense of something whistling quietly to itself—can you understand? Though, for all the meditative lowness of the note, the horrible, gargantuan quality was distinct—a mighty parody of the human, as if I stood there and listened to the whistling from the lips of a monster with a man's soul.

"And then, you know, I saw something. The floor in the middle of the huge, empty room, was puckered upward in the centre into a strange soft-looking mound, parted at the top into an ever changing hole, that pulsated to that great, gentle hooning. At times, as I watched, I saw the heaving of the indented mound, gap across with a queer, inward suction, as with the drawing of an enormous breath; then the thing would dilate and pout once more to the incredible melody. And suddenly, as I stared, dumb, it came to me that the thing was living. I was looking at two enormous, blackened lips, blistered and brutal, there in the pale moonlight. . . .

"Abruptly, they bulged out to a vast, pouting mound of force and sound, stiffened and swollen, and hugely massive and clean-cut in the moon-beams. And a great sweat lay heavy on the vast upper-lip. In

the same moment of time, the whistling had burst into a mad screaming note, that seemed to stun me, even where I stood, outside of the
window. And then, the following moment, I was staring blankly at the
solid, undisturbed floor of the room—smooth, polished stone flooring, from wall to wall; and there was an absolute silence.

"You can picture me staring into the quiet room, and knowing
what I knew. I felt like a sick, frightened kid, and wanted to slide *quietly* down the ladder, and run away. But in that very instant, I heard
Tassoc's voice calling to me from within the room, for help, *help*. My
God! but I got such an awful dazed feeling; and I had a vague, bewildered notion that, after all, it was the Irishmen who had got him in
there, and were taking it out of him. And then the call came again, and
I burst the window, and jumped in to help him. I had a confused idea
that the call had come from within the shadow of the great fireplace,
and I raced across to it; but there was no one there.

"'Tassoc!' I shouted, and my voice went empty-sounding 'round
the great apartment; and then, in a flash, *I knew that Tassoc had never
called*. I whirled 'round, sick with fear, toward the window, and as I did
so, a frightful, exultant whistling scream burst through the room. On
my left, the end wall had bellied-in toward me, in a pair of gargantuan lips, black and utterly monstrous, to within a yard of my face. I
fumbled for a mad instant at my revolver; not for *it*, but myself; for the
danger was a thousand times worse than death. And then, suddenly,
the Unknown Last Line of the *Saaamaaa* Ritual was whispered quite
audibly in the room. Instantly, the thing happened that I have known
once before. There came a sense as of dust falling continually and mo-
notonously, and I knew that my life hung uncertain and suspended for
a flash, in a brief, reeling vertigo of unseeable things.

"Then *that* ended, and I knew that I might live. My soul and body
blended again, and life and power came to me. I dashed furiously at
the window, and hurled myself out head-foremost; for I can tell you
that I had stopped being afraid of death. I crashed down on to the ladder, and slithered, grabbing and grabbing; and so came some way or
other alive to the bottom. And there I sat in the soft, wet grass, with
the moonlight all about me; and far above, through the broken window of the room, there was a low whistling.

"That is the chief of it. I was not hurt, and I went 'round to the
front, and knocked Tassoc up. When they let me in, we had a long
yarn, over some good whisky—for I was shaken to pieces—and I explained things as much as I could, I told Tassoc that the room would

have to come down, and every fragment of it burned in a blast-furnace, erected within a pentacle. He nodded. There was nothing to say. Then I went to bed.

"We turned a small army on to the work, and within ten days, that lovely thing had gone up in smoke, and what was left was calcined, and clean.

"It was when the workmen were stripping the panelling, that I got hold of a sound notion of the beginnings of that beastly development. Over the great fireplace, after the great oak panels had been torn down, I found that there was let into the masonry a scrollwork of stone, with on it an old inscription, in ancient Celtic, that here in this room was burned Dian Tiansay, Jester of King Alzof, who made the Song of Foolishness upon King Ernore of the Seventh Castle.

"When I got the translation clear, I gave it to Tassoc. He was tremendously excited; for he knew the old tale, and took me down to the library to look at an old parchment that gave the story in detail. Afterward, I found that the incident was well-known about the countryside; but always regarded more as a legend than as history. And no one seemed ever to have dreamt that the old East Wing of Iastrae Castle was the remains of the ancient Seventh Castle.

"From the old parchment, I gathered that there had been a pretty dirty job done, away back in the years. It seems that King Alzof and King Ernore had been enemies by birthright, as you might say truly; but that nothing more than a little raiding had occurred on either side for years, until Dian Tiansay made the Song of Foolishness upon King Ernore, and sang it before King Alzof; and so greatly was it appreciated that King Alzof gave the jester one of his ladies, to wife.

"Presently, all the people of the land had come to know the song, and so it came at last to King Ernore, who was so angered that he made war upon his old enemy, and took and burned him and his castle; but Dian Tiansay, the jester, he brought with him to his own place, and having torn his tongue out because of the song which he had made and sung, he imprisoned him in the room in the East Wing (which was evidently used for unpleasant purposes), and the jester's wife, he kept for himself, having a fancy for her prettiness.

"But one night, Dian Tiansay's wife was not to be found, and in the morning they discovered her lying dead in her husband's arms, and he sitting, whistling the Song of Foolishness, for he had no longer the power to sing it.

"Then they roasted Dian Tiansay, in the great fireplace—probably from that selfsame 'galley-iron' which I have already mentioned. And until he died, Dian Tiansay ceased not to whistle the Song of Foolishness, which he could no longer sing. But afterward, 'in that room' there was often heard at night the sound of something whistling; and there 'grew a power in that room,' so that none dared to sleep in it. And presently, it would seem, the king went to another castle; for the whistling troubled him.

"There you have it all. Of course, that is only a rough rendering of the translation of the parchment. But it sounds extraordinarily quaint. Don't you think so?"

"Yes," I said, answering for the lot. "But how did the thing grow to such a tremendous manifestation?"

"One of those cases of continuity of thought producing a positive action upon the immediate surrounding material," replied Carnacki. "The development must have been going forward through centuries, to have produced such a monstrosity. It was a true instance of *Saiitii* manifestation, which I can best explain by likening it to a living spiritual fungus, which involves the very structure of the Aether-fibre itself, and, of course, in so doing, acquires an essential control over the 'material substance' involved in it. It is impossible to make it plainer in a few words."

"What broke the seventh hair?" asked Taylor.

But Carnacki did not know. He thought it was probably nothing but being too severely tensioned. He also explained that they found out that the men who had run away, had not been up to mischief; but had come over secretly, merely to hear the whistling, which, indeed, had suddenly become the talk of the whole countryside.

"One other thing," said Arkright, "have you any idea what governs the use of the Unknown Last Line of the *Saaamaaa* Ritual? I know, of course, that it was used by the Ab-human Priests in the Incantation of *Raaaee*; but what used it on your behalf, and what made it?"

"You had better read Harzan's *Monograph*, and my addenda to it, on Astral and Astral Co-ordination and Interference," said Carnacki. "It is an extraordinary subject, and I can only say here that the human vibration may not be insulated from the astral (as is always believed to be the case, in interferences by the Ab-human), without immediate action being taken by those forces which govern the spinning of the outer circle. In other words, it is being proved, time after time, that there is some inscrutable protective force constantly intervening between the human soul (not the body, mind you,) and the Outer

21

Monstrosities. Am I clear?"

"Yes, I think so," I replied. "And you believe that the room had become the material expression of the ancient Jester—that his soul, rotten with hatred, had bred into a monster—eh?" I asked.

"Yes," said Carnacki, nodding, "I think you've put my thought rather neatly. It is a queer coincidence that Miss Donnehue is supposed to be descended (so I have heard since) from the same King Ernore. It makes one think some curious thoughts, doesn't it? The marriage coming on, and the room waking to fresh life. If she had gone into that room, ever . . . eh? *It* had waited a long time. Sins of the fathers. Yes, I've thought of that. They're to be married next week, and I am to be best man, which is a thing I hate. And he won his bets, rather! Just think, *if* ever she had gone into that room. Pretty horrible, eh?"

He nodded his head, grimly, and we four nodded back. Then he rose and took us collectively to the door, and presently thrust us forth in friendly fashion on the Embankment and into the fresh night air.

"Goodnight," we all called back, and went to our various homes. If she had, eh? If she had? That is what I kept thinking.

Door into Infinity

By Edmond Hamilton

1. THE BROTHERHOOD OF THE DOOR

(An amazing weird mystery story, packed with thrills, danger and startling events).

"Where leads the Door?"

"It leads outside our world."

"Who taught our forefathers to open the Door?"

"They Beyond the Door taught them."

"To whom do we bring these sacrifices?"

"We bring them to Those Beyond the Door."

"Shall the Door be opened that They may take them?"

"Let the Door be opened!"

Paul Ennis had listened thus far, his haggard face uncomprehending in expression, but now he interrupted the speaker.

"But what does it all mean, inspector? Why are you repeating this to me?"

"Did you ever hear anyone speak words like that?" asked Inspector Pierce Campbell, leaning tautly forward for the answer.

"Of course not—it just sounds like gibberish to me," Ennis exclaimed. "What connection can it have with my wife?"

He had risen to his feet, a tall, blond young American whose good-looking face was drawn and worn by inward agony, whose crisp yellow hair was brushed back from his forehead in disorder, and whose blue eyes were haunted with an anguished dread.

He kicked back his chair and strode across the gloomy little office, whose single window looked out on the thickening, foggy twilight of London. He bent across the dingy desk, gripping its edges with his hands as he spoke tensely to the man sitting behind it.

23

"Why are we wasting time talking here?" Ennis cried. "Sitting here talking, when anything may be happening to Ruth!

"It's been hours since she was kidnapped. They may have taken her anywhere, even outside of London by now. And instead of searching for her, you sit here and talk gibberish about Doors!"

Inspector Campbell seemed unmoved by Ennis' passion. A bulky, almost bald man, he looked up with his colourless, sagging face, in which his eyes gleamed like two crumbs of bright brown glass.

"You're not helping me much by giving way to your emotions, Mr. Ennis," he said in his flat voice.

"Give way? Who wouldn't give way?" cried Ennis. "Don't you understand, man, it's Ruth that's gone—my wife! Why, we were married only last week in New York. And on our second day here in London, I see her whisked into a limousine and carried away before my eyes! I thought you men at Scotland Yard here would surely act, do something. Instead you talk crazy gibberish to me!"

"Those words are *not* gibberish," said Pierce Campbell quietly. "And I think they're related to the abduction of your wife."

"What do you mean? How could they be related?"

The inspector's bright little brown eyes held Ennis'. "Did you ever hear of an organisation called the Brotherhood of the Door?"

Ennis shook his head, and Campbell continued, "Well, I am certain your wife was kidnapped by members of the Brotherhood."

"What kind of an organisation is it?" the young American demanded. "A band of criminals?"

"No, it is no ordinary criminal organisation," the detective said. His sagging face set strangely. "Unless I am mistaken, the Brotherhood of the Door is the most unholy and blackly evil organisation that has ever existed on this earth. Almost nothing is known of it outside its circle. I myself in twenty years have learned little except its existence and name. That ritual I just repeated to you, I heard from the lips of a dying member of the Brotherhood, who repeated the words in his delirium."

Campbell leaned forward. "But I know that every year about this time the Brotherhood come from all over the world and gather at some secret centre here in England. And every year, before that gathering, scores of people are kidnapped and never heard of again. I believe that all those people are kidnapped by this mysterious Brotherhood."

"But what becomes of the people they kidnap?" cried the pale young American. "What do they do with them?"

Inspector Campbell's bright brown eyes showed a hint of hooded horror, yet he shook his head. "I know no more than you. But whatever they do to the victims, they are never heard of again."

"But you must know something more!" Ennis protested. "What is this Door?"

Campbell again shook his head. "That too I don't know, but whatever it is, the Door is utterly sacred to the members of the Brotherhood, and whomever they mean by They Beyond the Door, they dread and venerate to the utmost."

"Where leads the Door? *It leads outside our world,*" repeated Ennis. "What can that mean?"

"It might have a symbolic meaning, referring to some secluded fastness of the order which is away from the rest of the world," the inspector said. "Or it might——"

He stopped. "Or it might what?" pressed Ennis, his pale face thrust forward.

"It might mean, literally, that the Door leads outside our world and universe," finished the inspector.

Ennis' haunted eyes stared. "You mean that this Door might somehow lead into another universe? But that's impossible!"

"Perhaps unlikely," Campbell said quietly, "but not impossible. Modern science has taught us that there are other universes than the one we live in, universes congruent and coincident with our own in space and time, yet separated from our own by the impassable barrier of totally different dimensions. It is not entirely impossible that a greater science than ours might find a way to pierce that barrier between our universe and one of those outside ones, that a Door should be opened from ours into one of those others in the infinite outside."

"A door into the infinite outside," repeated Ennis broodingly, looking past the inspector. Then he made a sudden movement of wild impatience, the dread leaping back strong in his eyes again.

"Oh, what good is all this talk about Doors and infinite universes doing in finding Ruth? I want to *do* something! If you think this mysterious Brotherhood has taken her, you must surely have some idea of how we can get her back from them? You must know something more about them than you've told."

"I don't know anything more certainly, but I've certain suspicions that amount to convictions," Inspector Campbell said. "I've been working on this Brotherhood for many years, and block after block

I've narrowed down to the place I think the order's local centre, the London headquarters of the Brotherhood of the Door."

"Where is the place?" asked Ennis tensely.

"It is the waterfront *café* of one Chandra Dass, a Hindoo, down by East India Docks," said the detective officer. "I've been there in disguise more than once, watching the place. This Chandra Dass I've found to be immensely feared by everyone in the quarter, which strengthens my belief that he's one of the high officers of the Brotherhood. He's too exceptional a man to be really running such a place."

"Then if the Brotherhood took Ruth, she may be at that place now!" cried the young American, electrified.

Campbell nodded his bald head. "She may very likely be. Tonight I'm going there again in disguise, and have men ready to raid the place. If Chandra Dass has your wife there, we'll get her before he can get her away. Whatever way it turns out, we'll let you know at once."

"Like hell you will!" exploded the pale young Ennis. "Do you think I'm going to twiddle my thumbs while you're down there? I'm going with you. And if you refuse to let me, by heaven I'll go there myself!"

Inspector Pierce Campbell gave the haggard, fiercely determined face of the young man a long look, and then his own colourless countenance seemed to soften a little.

"All right," he said quietly. "I can disguise you so you'll not be recognized. But you'll have to follow my orders exactly, or death will result for both of us."

That strange, hooded dread flickered again in his eyes, as though he saw through shrouding mists the outline of dim horror.

"It may be," he added slowly, "that something worse even than death awaits those who try to oppose the Brotherhood of the Door— something that would explain the unearthly, superhuman dread that enwraps the secret mysteries of the order. We're taking more than our lives in our hands, I think, in trying to unveil those mysteries, to regain your wife. But we've got to act quickly, at all costs. We've got to find her before the great gathering of the Brotherhood takes place, or we'll never find her."

******

Two hours before midnight found Campbell and Ennis passing along a cobble-paved waterfront street north of the great East India Docks. Big warehouses towered black and silent in the darkness on one side, and on the other were old, rotting docks beyond which Ennis glimpsed the black water and gliding lights of the river.

As they straggled beneath the infrequent lights of the ill-lit street, they were utterly changed in appearance. Inspector Campbell, dressed in a shabby suit and rusty bowler, his dirty white shirt innocent of tie, had acquired a new face, a bright red, oily, eager one, and a high, squeaky voice. Ennis wore a rough blue seaman's jacket and a vizored cap pulled down over his head. His unshaven-looking face and subtly altered features made him seem a half-intoxicated seaman off his ship, as he stumbled unsteadily along. Campbell clung to him in true land-shark fashion, plucking his arm and talking wheedlingly to him.

They came into a more populous section of the evil old waterfront street, and passed fried-fish shops giving off the strong smell of hot fat, and the dirty, lighted windows of a half-dozen waterfront saloons, loud with sordid argument or merriment.

Campbell led past them until they reached one built upon an abandoned, mouldering pier, a ramshackle frame structure extending some distance back out on the pier. Its window was curtained, but dull red light glowed through the glass window of the door.

A few shabby men were lounging in front of the place but Campbell paid them no attention, tugging Ennis inside by the arm.

"Carm on in!" he wheedled shrilly. "The night ain't 'alf over yet— we'll 'ave just one more."

"Don't want any more," muttered Ennis drunkenly, swaying on his feet inside. "Get away, you damned old shark."

Yet he suffered himself to be led by Campbell to a table, where he slumped heavily into a chair. His stare swung vacantly.

The *café* of Chandra Dass was a red-lit, smoke-filled cave with cheap black curtains on the walls and windows, and other curtains cutting off the back part of the building from view. The dim room was jammed with tables crowded with patrons whose babel of tongues made an unceasing din, to which a three-string guitar somewhere added a wailing undertone. The waiters were dark-skinned and tiger-footed Malays, while the patrons seemed drawn from every nation east and west.

Ennis' glazed eyes saw dandified Chinese from Limehouse and Pennyfields, dark little Levantins from Soho, rough-looking Cockneys in shabby caps, a few crazily laughing blacks. From sly white faces, taut brown ones and impassive yellow ones came a dozen different languages. The air was thick with queer food-smells and the acrid smoke.

Campbell had selected a table near the back curtain, and now stridently ordered one of the Malay waiters to bring gin. He leaned forward with an oily smile to the drunken-looking Ennis, and spoke to him in a wheedling undertone.

"Don't look for a minute, but that's Chandra Dass over in the corner, and he's watching us," he said.

Ennis shook his clutching hand away. "Damned old shark!" he muttered again.

He turned his swaying head slowly, letting his eyes rest a moment on the man in the corner. That man was looking straight at him.

Chandra Dass was tall, dressed in spotless white from his shoes to the turban on his head. The white made his dark, impassive, aquiline face stand out in chiselled relief. His eyes were coal-black, large, coldly searching, as they met Ennis' bleared gaze.

Ennis felt a strange chill as he met those eyes. There was something alien and inhuman, something uncannily disturbing, behind the Hindoo's stare. He turned his gaze vacantly from Chandra Dass to the black curtains at the rear, and then back to his companion.

The silent Malay waiter had brought the liquor, and Campbell pressed a glass toward his companion. "'Ere, matey, take this."

"Don't want it," muttered Ennis, pushing it away. Still in the same mutter, he added, "If Ruth's here, she's somewhere in the back there. I'm going back and find out."

"Don't try it that way, for God's sake!" said Campbell in the wheedling undertone. "Chandra Dass is still watching, and those Malays would be on you in a minute. Wait until I give the word.

"All right, then," Campbell added in a louder, injured tone. "If you don't want it, I'll drink it myself."

He tossed off the glass of gin and set the glass down on the table, looking at his drunken companion with righteous indignation.

"Think I'm tryin' to bilk yer, eh?" he added. "That's a fine way to treat a pal!"

He added in the coaxing lower tone, "All right, I'm going to try it. Be ready to move when I light my cigarette."

He fished a soiled package of Gold Flakes from his pocket and put one in his mouth. Ennis waited, every muscle taut.

The inspector, his red, oily face still injured in expression, struck a match to his cigarette. Almost at once there was a loud oath from one of the shabby loungers outside the front of the building, and the sound of angry voices and blows.

28

The patrons of Chandra Dass looked toward the door, and one of the Malay waiters went hastily out to quiet the fight. But it grew swiftly, sounded in a moment like a small riot. *Crash*—someone was pushed through the front window. The excited patrons pressed toward the front. Chandra Dass pushed through them, issuing quick orders to his servants.

For the time being the back of the *café* was deserted and unnoticed. Campbell sprang to his feet, and with Ennis close behind him, darted through the black curtains. They found themselves in a black corridor at the end of which a red bulb burned dimly. They could still hear the uproar.

Campbell's gun was in his hand, and the American's in his.

"We dare only stay here a few moments," the inspector cried. "Look in those rooms along the corridor here."

Ennis frantically tore open a door and peered into a dark room smelling of drugs. "Ruth!" he cried softly. "Ruth!"

2. DEATH TRAP

There was no answer. The light in the corridor behind him suddenly went out, plunging him into pitch-black darkness. He jumped back into the dark corridor, and as he did so, heard a sudden scuffle further along it.

"Campbell!" he exclaimed, lunging forward in the black passageway. There was no answer.

He pitched forward through stygian obscurity, his hands searching ahead of him for the inspector. In the dark something whipped smoothly around his throat, tightened there like a slender, contracting tentacle.

Ennis tore frenziedly at the thing, which he felt to be a slender silken cord, but he could not loosen it. It was choking him. He tried to cry out again to Campbell, but his throat could not emit the sounds. He thrashed, twisted helplessly, hearing a loud roaring in his ears, consciousness receding. Then, dimly as though in a dream, Ennis was aware of being lowered to the floor, of being half carried and half dragged along. The constriction around his throat was gone and rapidly his brain began to clear. He opened his eyes.

He found himself lying on the floor of a room illuminated by a great hanging brass lamp of ornate design. The walls of the room were hung with rich, grotesquely worked red silk Indian draperies. His hands and feet were bound behind him, and beside him, tied in

29

the same manner, lay Inspector Campbell. Over them stood Chandra Dass and two of the Malay servants. The faces of the servants were tigerish in their menace, but Chandra Dass' face was one of dark, impassive scorn.

"So you misguided fools thought you could deceive me so easily as that?" he said in a strong, vibrant voice. "Why, we knew hours ago that you, Inspector Campbell, and you, Mr. Ennis, were coming here tonight. We let you get this far only because it was evident that somehow you had learned too much about us, and that it would be best to let you come here and meet your deaths."

"Chandra Dass, I've men outside," rasped Campbell. "If we don't come out, they'll come in after us."

The Hindoo's proud, dark face did not change its scorn. "They will not come in for a little while, inspector. By that time you two will be dead and we shall be gone with our captives. Yes, Mr. Ennis, your wife is one of those captives," he added to the prostrate young American. "It is too bad we cannot take you and the inspector to share her glorious destiny, but then our accommodations of transport are limited."

"Ruth here?" Ennis' face flamed at the words, and he raised himself a little from the floor on his elbows.

"Then you'll let her go if I pay you? I'll raise any amount, I'll do anything you ask, if you'll set her free."

"No amount of money in the world could buy her from the Brotherhood of the Door," answered Chandra Dass steadily. "For she belongs now, not to us, but to They Beyond the Door. Within a few hours she and many others shall stand before the Door, and They Beyond the Door shall take them."

"What are you going to do to her?" cried Ennis. "What is this damned Door and who are They Beyond it?"

"I do not think that even if I told you, your little mind would be able to accept the mighty truth," Chandra Dass said calmly. His coal-black eyes suddenly flashed with fanatic, frenetic light. "How could your poor, earth-bound little intelligences conceive the true nature of the Door and of those who dwell beyond it? Your puny brains would be stricken senseless by mere apprehension of them, They who are mighty and crafty and dreadful beyond anything on earth."

A cold wind from the alien unknown seemed to sweep the lamplit room with the Hindoo's passionate words. Then that rapt, fanatic exaltation dropped from him as suddenly as it had come, and he spoke in his ordinary vibrant tones.

"But enough of this parley with blind worms of the dust. Bring the weights!"

The last words were addressed to the Malay servants, who sprang to a closet in the corner of the room.

Inspector Campbell said steadily, "If my men find us dead when they come in here, they'll leave none of you living."

Chandra Dass did not even listen to him, but ordered the dark servants sharply, "Attach the weights!"

The Malays had brought from the closet two fifty-pound lead balls, and now they proceeded quickly to tie these to the feet of the two men. Then one of them rolled back the brilliant red Indian rug from the rough pine floor. A square trapdoor was disclosed, and at Chandra Dass' order, it was swung upward and open.

Up through the open square came the sound of waves slap-slapping against the piles of the old pier, and the heavy odours of salt water and of rotting wood invaded the room.

"The water under this pier is twenty feet deep," Chandra Dass told the two prisoners. "I regret to give you so easy a death, but there is no opportunity to take you to the fate you deserve."

Ennis, his skin crawling on his flesh, nevertheless spoke rapidly and as steadily as possible to the Hindoo.

"Listen, I don't ask you to let me go, but I'll do anything you want, let you kill me any way you want, if you'll let Ruth——"

Sheer horror cut short his words. The Malay servants had dragged Campbell's bound body to the door in the floor. They shoved him over the edge. Ennis had one glimpse of the inspector's taut, strange face falling out of sight. Then a dull splash sounded instantly below, and then silence.

He felt hands upon himself, dragging him across the floor. He fought, crazily, hopelessly, twisting his body in its bonds, thrashing his bound limbs wildly.

He saw the dark, unmoved face of Chandra Dass, the brass lamp over his head, the red hangings. Then his head dangled over the opening, a shove sent his body scraping over the edge, and he plunged downward through dank darkness. With a splash he hit the icy water and went under. The heavy weight at his ankles dragged him irresistibly downward. Instinctively he held his breath as the water rushed upward around him.

His feet struck oozy bottom. His body swayed there, chained by the lead weight to the bottom. His lungs already were bursting to

A SHOVE SENT HIS BODY SCRAPING OVER THE EDGE, AND HE PLUNGED
DOWNWARD THROUGH DANK DARKNESS.

draw in air, slow fires seeming to creep through his breast as he held his breath.

Ennis knew that in a moment or two more he would inhale the strangling waters and die. The thought-picture of Ruth flashed across his despairing mind, wild with hopeless regret. He could no longer hold his breath, felt his muscles relaxing against his will, tasted the stinging salt water at the back of his nose.

Then it was a bursting confusion of swift sensations, the choking water in his nose and throat, the roaring in his ears. A scroll of flame unrolled slowly in his brain and a voice shouted there, "You're dying!" He felt dimly a plucking at his ankles.

Abruptly Ennis' dimming mind was aware that he now was shooting upward through the water. His head burst into open air and he choked, strangled and gasped, his tortured lungs gulping the damp, heavy air. He opened his eyes, and shook the water from them.

He was floating in the darkness at the surface of the water. Someone was floating beside him, supporting him. Ennis' chin bumped the other's shoulder, and he heard a familiar voice.

"Easy, now," said Inspector Campbell. "Wait till I cut your hands loose."

"Campbell!" Ennis choked. "How did you get loose?"

"Never mind that now," the inspector answered. "Don't make any noise, or they may hear us up there."

Ennis felt a knife-blade slashing the bonds at his wrists. Then, the inspector's arm helping him, he and his companion paddled weakly through the darkness under the rotting pier. They bumped against the slimy, mouldering piles, threaded through them toward the side of the pier. The waves of the flooding tide washed them up and down as Campbell led the way.

They passed out from under the old pier into the comparative illumination of the stars. Looking back up, Ennis saw the long, black mass of the house of Chandra Dass, resting on the black pier, ruddy light glowing from window-cracks. He collided with something and found that Campbell had led toward a little floating dock where some skiffs were moored. They scrambled up onto it from the water, and lay panting for a few moments.

Campbell had something in his hand, a thin, razor-edged steel blade several inches long. Its hilt was an ordinary leather shoe-heel.

The inspector turned up one of his feet and Ennis saw that the heel was missing from that shoe. Carefully Campbell slid the steel blade beneath the shoe-sole, the heel-hilt sliding into place and seeming merely the innocent heel of the shoe.

"So that's how you got loose down in the water!" Ennis exclaimed, and the inspector nodded briefly.

"That trick's done me good service before—even with your hands tied behind your back you can get out that knife and use it. It was touch and go, though, whether I could get it out and cut myself loose in the water in time enough to free you."

Ennis gripped the inspector's shoulder. "Campbell, Ruth is in there! By heaven, we've found her and now we can get her out!"

"Right!" said the officer grimly. "We'll go around to the front and in two minutes we'll be in there with my men."

★★★★★★

They climbed dripping to their feet, and hastened from the little floating dock up onto the shore, through the darkness to the cobbled street.

The shabbily disguised men of Inspector Campbell were not now in front of Chandra Dass' *café*, but lurking in the shadows across the street. They came running toward Campbell and Ennis.

"All right, we're going in there," Campbell exclaimed in steely tones. "Get Chandra Dass, whatever you do, but see that his prisoners are not harmed."

He snapped a word and one of the men handed pistols to him and to Ennis. Then they leaped toward the door of the Hindoo's *café*, from which still streamed ruddy light and the babel of many voices.

A kick from Inspector Campbell sent the door flying inward, and they burst in with guns gleaming wickedly in the ruddy light. Ennis' face was a quivering mask of desperate resolve.

The motley patrons jumped up with yells of alarm at their entrance. The hand of a Malay waiter jerked and a thrown knife thudded into the wall beside them. Ennis yelled as he saw Chandra Dass, his dark face startled, leaping back with his servants through the black curtains.

He and Campbell drove through the squealing patrons toward the back. The Malay who had thrown the knife rushed to bar the way, another dagger uplifted. Campbell's gun coughed and the Malay reeled and stumbled. The inspector and Ennis threw themselves at the black curtains—and were dashed back.

They tore aside the black folds. A dull steel door had been lowered behind them, barring the way to the back rooms. Ennis beat crazily

34

upon it with his pistol-butt, but it remained immovable.

"No use—we can't break that down!" yelled Campbell, over the uproar. "Outside, and around to the other end of the building!"

They burst back out through that madhouse, into the dark of the street. They started along the side of the pier toward the river-end, edging forward on a narrow ledge but inches wide. As they reached the back of the building, Ennis shouted and pointed to dark figures at the end of the pier. There were two of them, lowering shapeless, wrapped forms over the end of the pier.

"There they are!" he cried. "They've got their prisoners out there with them."

Campbell's pistol levelled, but Ennis swiftly struck it up. "No, you might hit Ruth."

He and the inspector bounded forward along the pier. Fire streaked from the dark ahead and bullets thumped the rotting boards around them.

Suddenly the loud roar of an accelerated motor drowned out all other sounds. It came from the river at the pier's end.

Campbell and Ennis reached the end in time to see a long, powerful, gray motor-boat dash out into the black obscurity of the river, and roar eastward with gathering speed.

"There they go—they're getting away!" cried the agonized young American.

Inspector Campbell cupped his hands and shouted out into the darkness, "River police, ahoy! Ahoy there!"

He rasped to Ennis. "The river police were to have a cutter here tonight. We can still catch them."

With swiftly rising roar of speeded motors, a big cutter drove in from the darkness. Its searchlight snapped on, bathing the two men on the pier in a blinding glare.

"Ahoy, there!" called a stentorian voice over the roar of the motors. "Is that Inspector Campbell?"

"Yes. Come alongside," yelled the inspector, and as the big cutter shot close to the end of the pier, its reversing propellers churning the dark water to foam, Ennis and Campbell leaped.

They landed amid unseen men in the cockpit, and as he scrambled to his feet the inspector cried, "Follow that boat that just went down-river. But no shooting!"

★★★★★★

With thunderous drumfire from its exhausts, the cutter jerked forward so rapidly that it almost threw them from their feet again. It shot out onto the bosom of the dark river that flowed like a black sea between the banks of scattered lights that were London.

The moving lights of yachts and barges coming up-river could be seen gliding in that darkness. The captain of the cutter barked an order and one of his three men, the one crouched at the searchlight, switched its powerful beam out over the waters ahead.

In a moment it picked up a distant gray spot racing eastward on the black river, leaving a white trail of foam.

"There she is!" bawled the man at the searchlight. "She's running without lights!"

"Keep her in the searchlight," ordered the captain. "Sound our siren, and give the cutter her head."

Swaying, rocking, the cutter roared on through the darkness on the trail of that distant fleeing speck. As they raced down Blackwall Reach, the distance between the two craft had already begun to lessen.

"We're overtaking him!" cried Campbell, clutching a stanchion and peering ahead against the rush of wind and spray. "He must be making for whatever spot it is in England that is the centre of the Brotherhood of the Door—but he'll never reach it."

"He said that within a few hours Ruth would go with the others through the Door!" cried Ennis, clinging beside him. "Campbell, we mustn't let them get away now!"

Pursuers and pursued flashed on down the dark, broadening river, through mazes of shipping, the cutter hanging doggedly to the motor-boat's trail. The lights of London had dropped behind and those of Tilbury now gleamed away on their left.

Bigger, stronger waves now tossed and pounded the cutter as it raced out of the river mouth toward the heaving black expanse of the sea. The Kent coast was a black blur on their right; the gray motor-boat followed it closely, grazing almost beneath the Sheerness lights.

"He's heading to round North Foreland and follow the coast south to Ramsgate or Dover," the cutter captain cried to Campbell. "But we'll catch him before he passes Margate."

The quarry was now but a quarter-mile ahead. Steadily as they roared onward the gap narrowed, until in the glare of the searchlight they could make out every detail of the powerful gray motor-boat plunging through the tossing black waves.

They saw Chandra Dass' dark face turn and look back at them, and the cutter captain raised his speaking-trumpet to his lips and shouted over the roar of motors and dash of waves.

"Stand by or we'll fire at you!"

"He won't obey," muttered Campbell between his teeth. "He knows we daren't fire with the girl in the boat."

"Yes, blast him!" exclaimed the captain. "But we'll have him in a few minutes, anyway."

The thundering chase had brought them into sight of the lights of Margate on the dark coast to their right. Now only a few hundred feet of black water separated them from the fleeing craft.

Ennis and the inspector, gripping the stanchions of the rushing cutter, saw a white figure suddenly stand erect in the boat ahead and wave its arms to them. The gray motor-boat slowed.

"It's Chandra Dass and he's signalling that he's giving up!" Ennis cried. "He's stopping!"

"By heavens, he is!" Campbell explained. "Drive alongside him, and we'll soon have the irons on him."

The cutter, its own motors hastily throttled down, shot through the water toward the slowing gray craft. Ennis saw Chandra Dass standing erect, awaiting their coming, he and the two Malays beside him holding their hands in the air. He saw a half-dozen or more white-wrapped forms in the bottom of the boat, lying motionless.

"There are their prisoners!" he cried. "Bring the boat closer so we can jump in!"

He and Campbell, their pistols out, hunched to jump as the cutter drove closer to the gray motor-boat. The sides of the two craft bumped, the motors of both idling noisily. Then before Ennis and Campbell could jump into the motor-boat, things happened with cinema-like rapidity. Two of the still white forms at the bottom of the motor-boat leaped up and like suddenly uncoiled springs shot through the air into the cutter. They were two other Malays, their dark faces flaming with fanatic light, keen daggers glinting in their upraised hands.

"'Ware a trick!" yelled Campbell. His gun barked, but the bullet missed and a dagger slit his sleeve.

The Malays, with wild, screeching yells, were laying about them with their daggers in the cutter, insanely.

"God in heaven, they're running amok!" choked the cutter captain.

His slashed neck spurting blood and his face livid, he fell. One of his men slumped coughing beside him, another victim of the crazy daggers.

The man at the searchlight sprang for the maddened Malays, tugging at his pistol as he jumped. Before he got the weapon out, a dagger slashed his jugular and he went down gurgling in death. One of the Malays meanwhile had knocked Inspector Campbell from his feet, his knife-hand swooping down, his eyes blazing.

Ennis' gun roared and the bullet hit the Malay between the eyes. But as he slumped limply, the other fanatic was upon Ennis from the side. Before Ennis could whirl to meet him, the attacker's knife grazed down past his cheek like a brand of living fire. He was borne backward by the rush, felt the hot breath of the crazed Malay in his face, the dagger-point at his throat.

Shots roared quickly, one after another, and with each shot the Malay pressing Ennis back jerked convulsively. With the light of murderous madness fading from his eyes, he still strove to drive the dagger home into the American's throat. But a hand jerked him back and he lay prostrate and still.

Ennis scrambled up to find Inspector Campbell, pale and determined, over him. The detective had shot the attacker from behind.

The captain of the cutter and two of his men lay dead in the cockpit beside the two Malays. The remaining seaman, the helmsman, held his shoulder and groaned.

Ennis whirled. The motor-boat of Chandra Dass was no longer beside the cutter, and there was no sight of it anywhere on the black sea ahead. The Hindoo had taken advantage of the fight to make good his escape with his two other servants and their prisoners.

"Campbell, he's gone!" cried the young American frantically. "He's got away!"

The inspector's eyes were bright with cold flame of anger. "Yes, Chandra Dass sacrificed these two Malays to hold us up long enough for him to escape."

Campbell whirled to the helmsman. "You're not badly hurt?"

"Only a scratch, but I nearly broke my shoulder when I fell," answered the man.

"Then head on around North Foreland!" Campbell cried. "We may still be able to catch up to them."

"But Captain Wilson and the others are killed," protested the helmsman. "I've got to report——"

"You can report later," rasped the inspector. "Do as I say—I'll be responsible."

"Very well, sir," said the helmsman, and jumped back to the wheel.

In a minute the big cutter was roaring ahead over the heaving black waves, its searchlight clawing the darkness ahead. There was no sign now of the craft of Chandra Dass ahead. They raced abreast of the lights of Margate, started rounding the North Foreland, pounded by bigger seas.

Inspector Campbell had dragged the bodies of the dead policemen and their two slayers down into the cabin of the cutter. He came up and crouched down with Ennis beside Sturt, the helmsman.

"I found these on the two Malays," Campbell shouted to the American, holding out two little objects in his spray-wet hand.

Each was a flat star of gray metal in which was set a large oval, cabochon-cut jewel. The jewels flashed and dazzled with deep colour, but it was a colour wholly unfamiliar and alien to their eyes.

"They're not any colour we know on earth," Campbell shouted. "I believe these jewels came from somewhere beyond the Door, and that these are badges of the Brotherhood of the Door."

Sturt, the helmsman, leaned toward the inspector. "We've rounded North Foreland, sir," he cried. "Head straight south along the coast," Campbell ordered. "Chandra Dass must have gone this way. No doubt he thinks he's shaken us off, and is making for the gathering-place of the Brotherhood, wherever that may be."

"The cutter isn't built for seas like this," Sturt said, shaking his head. "But I'll do it."

They were now following the coast southward, the lights of Ramsgate dropping back on their right. The waters out here in the Channel were wilder, great black waves tossing the cutter to the sky one moment, and then dropping it sickeningly the next. Frequently its screws raced loudly as they encountered no resistance but air.

Ennis, clinging precariously on the foredeck, turned the searchlight's stabbing white beam back and forth on the heaving dark sea ahead, but without any sign of their quarry disclosed.

White foam of breaking waves began to show around them like bared teeth, and there was a humming in the air.

"Storm coming up the Channel," Sturt exclaimed. "It'll do for us if it catches us out here."

"We've got to keep on," Ennis told him desperately. "We must come up with them soon!"

The coast on their right was now one of black, rocky cliffs, towering all along the shore in a jagged, frowning wall against which the waves dashed foamy white. The cutter crept southward over the wild waters, tossed like a chip upon the great waves. Sturt was having a hard time holding the craft out from the rocks, and had its prow pointed obliquely away from them.

The humming in the air changed to a shrill whistling as the outrider winds of the storm came upon them. The cutter tossed still more wildly and black masses of water smashed in upon them from the darkness, dazing and drenching them.

Suddenly Ennis yelled, "There's the lights of a boat ahead! There, moving in toward the cliffs!"

He pointed ahead, and Campbell and the helmsman peered through the blinding spray and darkness. A pair of low lights were moving at high speed on the waters there, straight toward the towering black cliffs. Then they vanished suddenly from sight.

"There must be a hidden opening or harbour of some kind in the cliffs!" Inspector Campbell exclaimed. "But that can't be Chandra Dass' boat, for it carried no lights."

"It might be others of the Brotherhood going to the meeting-place!" Ennis exclaimed. "We can follow and see."

Sturt thrust his head through the flying spray and shouted, "There are openings and water-caverns in plenty along these cliffs, but there's nothing in any of them."

"We'll find out," Campbell said. "Head straight toward the cliffs in there where that boat vanished."

"If we can't find the opening we'll be smashed to flinders on those cliffs," Sturt warned.

"I'm gambling that we'll find the opening," Campbell told him. "Go ahead."

Sturt's face set stolidly and he said, "Yes, sir."

He turned the prow of the cutter toward the cliffs. Instantly they dashed forward toward the rock walls with greatly increased speed, wild waves bearing them onward like charging stallions of the sea.

Hunched beside the helmsman, the searchlight stabbing the dark wildly as the cutter was flung forward by the waves, Ennis and the inspector watched as the cliffs loomed closer ahead. The brilliant white beam struck across the rushing, mountainous waves and showed only the towering barriers of rock, battered and smitten by the raving waters that frothed white. They could hear the booming thunder of the raging ocean striking the rock.

Like a projectile hurled by a giant hand, the cutter fairly flew now toward the cliffs. They now could see even the little streams that ran off the rough rock wall as each giant wave broke against it. They were almost upon it.

Sturt's face was deathly. "I don't see any opening!" he yelled. "And we're going to hit in a moment!"

"To your left!" screamed Inspector Campbell over the booming thunder. "There's an arched opening there."

Now Ennis saw it also, a huge arch-like opening in the cliff that had been concealed by an angle of the wall. Sturt tried frantically to head the cutter toward it, but the wheel was useless as the great waves bore the craft along. Ennis saw they would strike a little to the side of the opening. The cliff loomed ahead, and he closed his eyes to the impact.

There was no impact. And as he heard a hoarse cry from Inspector Campbell, he opened his eyes.

The cutter was flying in through the mighty opening, snatched into it by powerful currents. They were whirled irresistibly forward under the huge rock arch, which loomed forty feet over their heads. Before them stretched a winding water-tunnel inside the cliff.

And now they were out of the wild uproar of the storming waters outside, and in an almost stupefying silence. Smoothly, resistlessly, the current bore them on in the tunnel, whose winding turns ahead were lit up by their searchlight.

"God, that was close!" exclaimed Inspector Campbell.

His eyes flashed. "Ennis, I believe that we have found the gathering-place of the Brotherhood. That boat we sighted is somewhere ahead in here, and so must be Chandra Dass, and your wife."

Ennis' hand tightened on his gun-butt. "If that's so—if we can just find them——"

"Blind action won't help if we do," said the inspector swiftly. "There must be all the number of the Brotherhood's members assembled here, and we can't fight them all."

His eyes suddenly lit and he took the blazing jewelled stars from his pocket. "These badges! With them we can pose as members of the Brotherhood, perhaps long enough to find your wife."

"But Chandra Dass will be there, and if he sees us——"

Campbell shrugged. "We'll have to take that chance. It's the only course open to us."

The current of the inflowing tide was still bearing them smoothly

41

onward through the winding water-tunnel, around bends and angles where they scraped the rock, down long straight stretches. Sturt used the motors to guide them around the turns. Meanwhile, Inspector Campbell and Ennis quickly ripped from the cutter its police-insignia and covered all evidences of its being a police craft.

Sturt suddenly snicked off the searchlight. "Light ahead there!" he exclaimed.

Around the next turn of the water-tunnel showed a gleam of strange, soft light.

"Careful, now!" cautioned the inspector. "Sturt, whatever we do, you stay in the cutter. And try to have it ready for a quick getaway, if we leave it."

Sturt nodded silently. The helmsman's stolid face had become a little pale, but he showed no sign of losing his courage.

******

The cutter sped around the next turn of the tunnel and emerged into a huge, softly lit cavern. Sturt's eyes bulged and Campbell uttered an exclamation of amazement. For in this mighty water-cavern there floated in a great mass, scores of sea-going craft, large and small.

All of them were capable of breasting storm and wind, and some were so large they could barely have entered. There were small yachts, big motor-cruisers, sea-going launches, cutters larger than their own, and among them the gray motor-launch of Chandra Dass.

They were massed together here, those with masts having lowered them to enter, floating and rubbing sides, quite unoccupied. Around the edges of the water-cavern ran a wide rock ledge. But no living person was visible and there was no visible source for the soft, strange white light that filled the astounding place.

"These craft must have come here from all over earth!" Campbell muttered. "The Brotherhood of the Door has assembled here—we've found their gathering-place all right."

"But where are they?" exclaimed Ennis. "I don't see anyone."

"We'll soon find out," the inspector said. "Sturt, run close to the ledge there and we'll get out on it."

Sturt obeyed, and as the cutter bumped the ledge, Campbell and Ennis leaped out onto it. They looked this way and that along it, but no one was in sight. The weirdness of it was unnerving, the strangely lit, mighty cavern, the assembled boats, the utter silence.

"Follow me," Campbell said in a low voice. "They must all be somewhere near."

He and Ennis walked a few steps along the ledge, when the American stopped. "Campbell, listen!" he whispered.

Dimly there whispered to them, as though from a distance and through great walls, a swelling sound of chanting. As they listened, hearts beating rapidly, a square of the rock wall of the cavern abruptly flew open beside them, as though hinged like a door. Inside it was the mouth of a soft-lit, man-high tunnel, and in its opening stood two men. They wore over their clothing shroud-like, loose-hanging robes of gray, asbestos-like material. They wore hoods of the same gray stuff over their heads, pierced with slits at the eyes and mouth. And each wore on his breast the blazing star-badge.

Through the eye-slits the eyes of the two surveyed Campbell and Ennis as they halted, transfixed by the sudden apparition. Then one of the hooded men spoke measuredly in a hissing, Mongolian voice.

"Are you who come here of the Brotherhood of the Door?" he asked, apparently repeating a customary challenge.

Campbell answered, his flat voice tremorless. "We are of the Brotherhood."

"Why do you not wear the badge of the Brotherhood, then?"

For answer, the inspector reached in his pocket for the strange emblem and fastened it to his lapel. Ennis did the same.

"Enter, brothers," said the hissing, hooded shape, standing aside to let them pass.

As they stepped into the tunnel, the hooded guard added in slightly more natural tones, "Brothers, you two are late. You must hurry to get your protective robes, for the ceremony soon begins."

Campbell inclined his head without speaking, and he and Ennis started along the tunnel. Its light, as sourceless as that of the great water-cavern, revealed that it was chiselled from solid rock and that it wound downward.

When they were out of sight of the two hooded guards, Ennis clutched the detective's arm convulsively.

"Campbell," he said, "the ceremony begins soon! We've got to find Ruth first!"

"We'll try," the inspector answered swiftly. "Those hooded robes are apparently issued to all the members to be worn during the ceremony as protection, for some reason, and once we get robes and get them on, Chandra Dass won't be able to spot us.

"Look out!" he added an instant later. "Here's the place where the robes are issued!"

The tunnel had debouched suddenly into a wider space in which were a group of men. Several were wearing the concealing hoods and robes, and one of these hooded figures was handing out, from a large rack of the robes, three of the garments to three dark Easterners who had apparently entered in the boat just ahead of the cutter.

The three dark Orientals, their faces gleaming with strange fanaticism, quickly donned the robes and hoods and passed hurriedly on down the tunnel. At once Campbell and Ennis stepped calmly up to the hooded custodians of the robes, and extended their hands.

One of the hooded figures took down two robes and handed them to them. But suddenly one of the other hooded men spoke sharply.

Instantly all the hooded men but the one who had spoken, with loud cries, threw themselves forward on Campbell and Paul Ennis.

Taken utterly by surprise, the two had no chance to draw their guns. They were smothered by gray-robed men, held helpless before they could move, a half-dozen pistols jammed into their bodies.

Stupefied by the sudden dashing of their hopes, the detective and the young American saw the hooded man who had spoken slowly lift the concealing gray cowl from his face. It was the dark, coldly contemptuous face of Chandra Dass.

4. THE CAVERN OF THE DOOR

Chandra Dass spoke, and his strong, vibrant voice held a scorn that was almost pitying.

"It occurred to me that your enterprise might enable you to escape the daggers of my followers, and that you might trail us here," he said. "That is why I waited here to see if you came.

"Search them," he told the other hooded figures. "Take anything that looks like a weapon from them."

Ennis stared, stupefied, as the gray-hooded men obeyed. He was unable to believe entirely in the abrupt reversal of all their hopes, of their desperate attempt.

The hooded men took their pistols from Ennis and Campbell, and even the small gold knife attached to the chain of the inspector's big, old-fashioned gold watch. Then they stepped back, the pistols of two of them levelled at the hearts of the captives.

Chandra Dass had watched impassively. Ennis, staring dazedly, noted that the Hindoo wore on his breast a different jewel-emblem from the others, a double star instead of a single one.

Ennis' dazed eyes lifted from the blazing badge to the Hindoo's dark face. "Where's Ruth?" he asked a little shrilly, and then his voice cracked and he cried, "You damned fiend, where's my wife?"

"Be comforted, Mr. Ennis," came Chandra Dass' chill voice. "You are going now to join your wife, and to share her fate. You two are going with her and the other sacrifices through the Door when it opens. It is not usual," he added in cold mockery, "for our sacrificial victims to walk directly into our hands. We ordinarily have a more difficult time securing them."

He made a gesture to the two hooded men with pistols, and they ranged themselves close behind Campbell and Ennis.

"We are going to the Cavern of the Door," said the Hindoo. "Inspector Campbell, I know and respect your resourcefulness. Be warned that your slightest attempt to escape means a bullet in your back. You two will march ahead of us," he said, and added mockingly, "Remember, while you live you can cling to the shadow of hope, but if these guns speak, it ends even that shadow."

Ennis and Inspector Campbell, keeping their hands elevated, started at the Hindoo's command down the softly lit rock tunnel. Chandra Dass and the two hooded men with pistols followed.

Ennis saw that the inspector's sagging face was expressionless, and knew that behind that colourless mask, Campbell's brain was racing in an attempt to find a method of escape. For himself, the young American had almost forgotten all else in his eagerness to reach his wife. Whatever happened to Ruth, whatever mysterious horror lay in wait for her and the other victims, he would be there beside her, sharing it!

The tunnel wound a little further downward, then straightened out and ran straight for a considerable length. In this straight section of the rock passage, Ennis and Campbell for the first time perceived that the walls of the tunnel bore crowding, deeply chiselled inscriptions. They had not time to read them in passing, but Ennis saw that they were in many different languages, and that some of the characters were wholly unfamiliar.

"God, some of those inscriptions are in Egyptian hieroglyphics!" muttered Inspector Campbell.

The cool voice of Chandra Dass said, behind them, "There are pre-Egyptian inscriptions on these walls, inspector, could you but recognize them, carven in languages that perished from the face of earth before Egypt was born. Yes, back through time, back through medieval and Roman and Egyptian and pre-Egyptian ages, the Brotherhood of the Door has existed and has each year gathered in this place to open the Door and worship with sacrifices They Beyond it."

The fanatic note of unearthly devotion was in his voice now, and Ennis shuddered with a cold not of the tunnel.

As they proceeded, they heard a muffled, hoarse booming somewhere over their heads, a dull, rhythmic thunder that echoed along the long passageway. The walls of the tunnel now were damp and glistening in the sourceless soft light, tiny trickles running down them.

"You hear the ocean over us," came Chandra Dass' voice. "The Cavern of the Door lies several hundred yards out from shore, beneath the rock floor of the sea."

They passed the dark mouths of unlit tunnels branching ahead from this illuminated one. Then over the booming of the raging sea above them, there came to Ennis' ears the distant, swelling chant they had heard in the water-cavern above. But now it was louder, nearer. At the sound of it, Chandra Dass quickened their pace.

Suddenly Inspector Campbell stumbled on the slippery rock floor and went down in a heap. Instantly Chandra Dass and his two followers recoiled from them, the two pistols trained on the detective as he scrambled up.

"Do not do that again, inspector," warned the Hindoo in a deadly voice. "All tricks are useless now."

"I couldn't help slipping on this wet floor," complained Inspector Campbell.

"The next time you make a wrong step of any kind, a bullet will smash your spine," Chandra Dass told him. "Quick—march!"

******

The tunnel turned sharply, turned again. As they rounded the turns, Ennis saw with a sudden electric thrill of hope that Campbell held clutched in his hand, concealed by his sleeve, the heel-hilted knife from his shoe. He had drawn it when he stumbled.

Campbell edged a little closer to the young American as they were hastening onward, and whispered to him, a word at a time.

"Be—ready—to jump—them——"

"But they'll shoot, your first move——" whispered Ennis agonizedly.

Campbell did not answer. But Ennis sensed the detective's body tautening.

They came to another turn, the strong, swelling chant coming loud from ahead. They started around that turn.

46

Then Inspector Campbell acted. He whirled as though on a pivot, the heel-knife flashing toward the men behind them.

Shots coughed from the pistols that were pressed almost against his stomach. His body jerked as the bullets struck it, yet he remained erect, his knife stabbing with lightning rapidity.

One of the hooded men slumped down with a pierced throat, and as Campbell sprang at the other, Ennis desperately launched himself at Chandra Dass. He bore the Hindoo from his feet, but it was as though he was fighting a demon. Inside his gray robe, Chandra Dass writhed with fiendish strength.

Ennis could not hold him, the Hindoo's body seeming of spring-steel. He rolled over, dashed the young American to the floor, and leaped up, his dark face and great black eyes blazing.

Then, half-way erect, he suddenly crumpled, the fire in his eyes dulling, a call for help smothered on his lips. He fell on his face, and Ennis saw that the heel-knife was stuck in his back. Inspector Campbell jerked it out, and put it back into his shoe. And now Ennis, staggering up, saw that Campbell had knifed the two hooded guards and that they lay in a dead heap.

"Campbell!" cried the American, gripping the detective's arm. "They've wounded you—I saw them shoot you."

Campbell's bruised face grinned briefly. "Nothing of the kind," he said, and tapped the soiled gray vest he wore beneath his coat. "Chandra Dass didn't know this vest is bullet-proof."

He darted an alert glance up and down the lighted tunnel. "We can't stay here or let these bodies lie here. They may be discovered at any moment."

"Listen!" said Ennis, turning.

The chanting from ahead swelled down the tunnel, louder than at any time yet, waxing and waxing, reaching a triumphant crescendo, then again dying away.

"Campbell, they're going on with the ceremony now!" Ennis cried. "Ruth!"

The detective's desperate glance fastened on the dark mouth of one of the branching tunnels, a little ahead.

"That side tunnel—we'll pull the bodies in there!" he exclaimed.

Taking the pistols of the dead men for themselves, they rapidly dragged the three bodies into the darkness of the unlit branching tunnel.

"Quick, on with two of these robes," rasped Inspector Campbell.

"They'll give us a little better chance."

Hastily Ennis jerked the gray robe and hood from Chandra Dass' dead body and donned it, while Campbell struggled into one of the others. In the robes and concealing hoods, they could not be told from any other two members of the Brotherhood, except that the badge on Ennis' breast was the double star instead of the single one.

Ennis then spun toward the main, lighted tunnel, Campbell close behind him. They recoiled suddenly into the darkness of the branching way, as they heard hurrying steps out in the lighted passage. Flattened in the darkness against the wall, they saw several of the gray-hooded members of the Brotherhood hasten past them from above, hurrying toward the gathering-place.

"The guards and robe-issuers we saw above!" Campbell said quickly when they were passed. "Come on, now."

He and Ennis slipped out into the lighted tunnel and hastened along it after the others.

Boom of thundering ocean over their heads and rising and falling of the tremendous chanting ahead filled their ears as they hurried around the last turns of the tunnel. The passage widened, and ahead they saw a massive rock portal through whose opening they glimpsed an immense, lighted space.

Campbell and Ennis, two comparatively tiny gray-hooded figures, hastened through the mighty portal. Then they stopped. Ennis felt frozen with the dazing shock of it. He heard the detective whisper fiercely beside him.

"It's the Cavern, all right—the Cavern of the Door!"

✶✶✶✶✶✶

They looked across a colossal rock chamber hollowed out beneath the floor of ocean. It was elliptical in shape, three hundred feet by its longer axis. Its black basalt sides, towering, rough-hewn walls, rose sheer and supported the rock ceiling which was the ocean floor, a hundred feet over their heads.

This mighty cathedral hewn from inside the rock of earth was lit by a soft, white, sourceless light like that in the main tunnel. Upon the floor of the cavern, in regular rows across it, stood hundreds on hundreds of human figures, all gray-robed and gray-hooded, all with their backs to Campbell and Ennis, looking across the cavern to its farther end. At that farther end was a flat dais of black basalt upon which stood five hooded men, four wearing the blazing double-star on their breasts, the fifth, a triple-star. Two of them stood beside a cubical, weird-looking gray metal mechanism from which upreared a spherical web of countless fine wires, unthinkably intricate in their network, many of them pulsing with glowing force. The sourceless light of the cavern and the tunnel seemed to pulse from that weird mechanism.

Up from that machine, if machine it was, soared the black basalt wall of that end of the cavern. But there above the gray mechanism the rough wall had been carved with a great, smooth facet, a giant, gleaming black oval face as smooth as though planed and polished. Only, at the middle of the glistening black oval face, were carven deeply four large and wholly unfamiliar characters. As Ennis and Campbell stared frozenly across the awe-inspiring place, sound swelled from the hundreds of throats. A slow, rising chant, it climbed and climbed until the basalt roof above seemed to quiver to it, crashing out with stupendous effect, a weird litany in an unknown tongue. Then it began to fall.

Ennis clutched the inspector's gray-robed arm. "Where's Ruth?" he whispered frantically. "I don't see any prisoners."

"They must be somewhere here," Campbell said swiftly. "Listen——"

As the chant died to silence, on the dais at the farther end of the cavern the hooded man who wore the triple-jewelled star stepped forward and spoke. His deep, heavy voice rolled out and echoed across the cavern, flung back and forth from wall to rocky wall.

"Brothers of the Door," he said, "we meet again here in the Cavern of the Door this year, as for ten thousand years past our forefathers have met here to worship They Beyond the Door, and bring them the sacrifices They love.

"A hundred centuries have gone by since first They Beyond the Door sent their wisdom through the barrier between their universe and ours, a barrier which even They could not open from their side, but which their wisdom taught our fathers how to open.

"Each year since then have we opened the Door which They taught us how to build. Each year we have brought them sacrifices. And in return They have given us of their wisdom and power. They have taught us things that lie hidden from other men, and They have given us powers that other men have not.

"Now again comes the time appointed for the opening of the Door. In their universe on the other side of it, They are waiting now to take the sacrifices which we have procured for them. The hour strikes, so let the sacrifices be brought."

As though at a signal, from a small opening at one side of the cavern a triple file of marchers entered. A file of hooded gray members of the Brotherhood flanked on either side a line of men and women who did not wear the hoods or robes. They were thirty or forty in number. These men and women were of almost all races and classes, but all of them walked stiffly, mechanically, staring ahead with unseeing, distended eyes, like living corpses.

"Drugged!" came Campbell's shaken voice. "They're all drugged, and don't know what is going on."

Ennis' eyes fastened on a small, slender girl with chestnut hair who walked at the end of the line, a girl in a straight tan dress, whose face was white, stiff, like those of the others.

"There's Ruth!" he exclaimed frantically, his cry muffled by his hood.

He plunged in that direction, but Campbell held him back.

"No!" rasped the inspector. "You can't help her by simply getting yourself captured!"

"I can at least go with her!" Ennis exclaimed. "Let me go!"

Inspector Campbell's iron grip held him. "Wait, Ennis!" said the detective. "You've no chance that way. That robe of Chandra Dass' you're wearing has a double-star badge like those of the men up there on the dais. That means that as Chandra Dass you're entitled to be up there with them. Go up there and take your place as though you were Chandra Dass—with the hood on, they can't tell the difference. I'll slip around to that side door out of which they brought the prisoners. It must connect with the tunnels, and it's not far from the dais. When I fire my pistol from there, you grab your wife and try to get to that door with her. If you can do it, we'll have a chance to get up through the tunnels and escape."

Ennis wrung the inspector's hand. Then, without further reply, he walked boldly with measured steps up the main aisle of the cavern, through the gray ranks to the dais. He stepped up onto it, his heart racing. The chief priest, he of the triple-star, gave him only a glance, as of annoyance at his lateness. Ennis saw Campbell's gray figure slipping round to the side door.

The gray-hooded hundreds before him had paid no attention to either of them. Their attention was utterly, eagerly, fixed upon the stiff-moving prisoners now being marched up onto the dais. Ennis saw Ruth pass him, her white face an unfamiliar, staring mask.

The prisoners were ranged at the back of the dais, just beneath the great, gleaming black oval facet. The guards stepped back from them, and they remained standing stiffly there. Ennis edged a little toward Ruth, who stood at the end of that line of stiff figures. As he moved imperceptibly closer to her, he saw the two priests beside the gray mechanism reaching toward knurled knobs of ebonite affixed to its side, beneath the spherical web of pulsing wires.

The chief priest, at the front of the dais, raised his hands. His voice rolled out, heavy, commanding, reverberating again through all the cavern.

5. The Door Opens

"Where leads the Door?" rolled the chief priest's voice.

Back up to him came the reply of hundreds of voices, muffled by the hoods but loud, echoing to the roof of the cavern in a thunderous response.

"It leads outside our world!"

The chief priest waited until the echoes died before his deep voice rolled on in the ritual.

"Who taught our forefathers to open the Door?"

Ennis, edging desperately closer and closer to the line of victims, felt the mighty response reverberate about him.

"They Beyond the Door taught them!"

Now Ennis was apart from the other priests on the dais, within a few yards of the captives, of the small figure of Ruth.

"To whom do we bring these sacrifices?"

As the high priest uttered the words, and before the booming answer came, a hand grasped Ennis and pulled him back from the line of victims. He spun round to find that it was one of the other priests who had jerked him back.

"We bring them to Those Beyond the Door!"

As the colossal response thundered, the priest who had jerked Ennis back whispered urgently to him. "You go too close to the victims, Chandra Dass! Do you wish to be taken with them?"

The fellow had a tight grip on Ennis' arm. Desperate, tensed, Ennis heard the chief priest roll forth the last of the ritual.

"Shall the Door be opened that They may take the sacrifices?"

Stunning, mighty, a tremendous shout that mingled in it worshipping awe and superhuman dread, the answer crashed back.

"Let the Door be opened!"

The chief priest turned and his up-flung arms whirled in a signal. Ennis, tensing to spring toward Ruth, saw the two priests at the gray

51

mechanism swiftly turn the knurled black knobs. Then Ennis, like all else in the vast cavern, was held frozen and spellbound by what followed.

The spherical web of wires pulsed up madly with shining force. And up at the centre of the gleaming black oval facet on the wall, there appeared a spark of unearthly green light. It blossomed outward, expanded, an awful viridescent flower blooming quickly outward farther and farther. And as it expanded, Ennis saw that he could look *through* that green light! He looked through into another universe, a universe lying infinitely far across alien dimensions from our own, yet one that could be reached through this door between dimensions. It was a green universe, flooded with an awful green light that was somehow more akin to darkness than to light, a throbbing, baleful luminescence.

Ennis saw dimly through green-lit spaces a city in the near distance, an unholy city of emerald hue whose unsymmetrical, twisted towers and minarets aspired into heavens of hellish viridity. The towers of that city swayed to and fro and writhed in the air. And Ennis saw that here and there in the soft green substance of that restless city were circles of lurid light that were like yellow eyes.

In ghastly, soul-shaking apprehension of the utterly alien, Ennis knew that the yellow circles were *eyes*—that that hell-spawned city of another universe was *living*—that its unfamiliar life was single yet multiple, that its lurid eyes looked now through the Door!

Out from the insane living metropolis glided pseudopods of its green substance, glided toward the Door. Ennis saw that in the end of each pseudopod was one of the lurid eyes. He saw those eyed pseudopods come questing through the Door, onto the dais.

The yellow eyes of light seemed fixed on the row of stiff victims, and the pseudopods glided toward them. Through the open door was beating wave on wave of unfamiliar, tingling forces that Ennis felt even through the protective robe.

The hooded multitude bent in awe as the green pseudopods glided toward the victims faster, with avid eagerness. Ennis saw them reaching for the prisoners, for Ruth, and he made a tremendous mental effort to break the spell that froze him. In that moment pistol-shots crashed across the cavern and a stream of bullets smashed the pulsing web of wires!

The Door began instantly to close. Darkness crept back around the edges of the mighty oval. As though alarmed, the lurid-eyed pseudopods of that hell-city recoiled from the victims, back through the dwindling Door. And as the Door dwindled, the light in the cavern was failing.

"Ruth!" yelled Ennis madly, and sprang forward and grasped her, his pistol leaping into his other hand.

"Ennis—quick!" shouted Campbell's voice across the cavern.

The Door dwindled away altogether; the great oval facet was completely black. The light was fast dying too.

The chief priest sprang madly toward Ennis, and as he did so, the hooded hordes of the Brotherhood recovered from their paralysis of horror and surged madly toward the dais.

"The Door is closed! Death to the blasphemers!" cried the chief priest as he plunged forward.

"Death to the blasphemers!" shrieked the crazed horde below.

Ennis' pistol roared and the chief priest went down. The light in the cavern died completely at that moment.

In the dark a torrent of bodies catapulted against Ennis, screaming vengeance. He struck out with his pistol-barrel in the mad *mêlée*, holding Ruth's stiff form close with his other hand. He heard the other drugged, helpless victims crushed down and trampled under foot by the surging horde of vengeance-mad members.

★★★★★★

Clinging to the girl, Ennis fought like a madman through a darkness in which none could distinguish friend or foe, toward the door at the side from which Campbell had fired. He smashed down the pistol-barrel on all before him, as hands sought to grab him in the dark. He knew sickeningly that he was lost in the combat, with no sense of the direction of the door.

Then a voice roared loud across the wild din, "Ennis, this way! This way, Ennis!" yelled Inspector Campbell, again and again.

Ennis plunged through the whirl of unseen bodies in the direction of the detective's shouting voice. He smashed through, half dragging and half carrying the girl, until Campbell's voice was close ahead in the dark. He fumbled at the rock wall, found the door opening, and then Campbell's hands grasped him to pull him inside.

Hands grabbed him from behind, striving to tear Ruth from him, to jerk him back. Voices shrieked for help.

Campbell's pistol blazed in the dark and the hands released their grip. Ennis stumbled with the girl through the door into a dark tunnel. He heard Campbell slam a door shut, and heard a bar fall with a clang.

"Quick, for God's sake!" panted Campbell in the dark. "They'll follow us—we've got to get up through the tunnels to the water-cavern!"

They raced along the pitch-dark tunnel, Campbell now carrying the girl, Ennis reeling drunkenly along.

They heard a mounting roar behind them, and as they burst into the main tunnel, no longer lighted but dark like the others, they looked back and saw a flickering of light coming up the passage.

"They're after us and they've got lights!" Campbell cried. "Hurry!"

It was nightmare, this mad flight on stumbling feet up through the dark tunnels where they could hear the sea booming close overhead, and could hear the wild pursuit behind.

Their feet slipped on the damp floor and they crashed into the walls of the tunnel at the turns. The pursuit was closer behind—as they started climbing the last passages to the water-cavern, the torchlight behind showed them to their pursuers and wild yells came to their ears.

They had before them only the last ascent to the water-cavern when Ennis stumbled and went down. He swayed up a little, yelled to Campbell. "Go on—get Ruth out! I'll try to hold them back a moment!"

"No!" rasped Campbell. "There's another way—one that may mean the end for us too, but our only chance!"

The inspector thrust his hand into his pocket, snatched out his big, old-fashioned gold watch.

He tore it from its chain, turned the stem of it twice around. Then he hurled it back down the tunnel with all his force.

"Quick—out of the tunnels now or we'll die right here!" he yelled.

They lunged forward, Campbell dragging both the girl and the exhausted Ennis, and emerged a moment later into the great water-cavern. It was now lit only by the searchlight of their waiting cutter.

As they emerged into the cavern, they were thrown flat on the rock ledge by a violent movement of it under them. An awful detonation and thunderous crashing of falling rock smote their ears.

Following that first tremendous crash, giant rumbling of collapsing rock shook the water-cavern.

"To the cutter!" Campbell cried. "That watch of mine was filled with the most concentrated high-explosive known, and it's blown up the tunnels. Now it's touched off more collapses and all these caverns and passages will fall in on us at any moment!"

The awful rumbling and crashing of collapsing rock masses was deafening in their ears as they lurched toward the cutter. Great chunks of rock were falling from the cavern roof into the water.

★★★★★★

Sturt, white-faced but asking no questions, had the motor of the cutter running, and helped them pull the unconscious girl aboard.

"Out of the tunnel at once!" Campbell ordered. "Full speed!"

They roared down the water-tunnel at crazy velocity, the searchlight beam stabbing ahead. The tide had reached flood and turned, increasing the speed with which they dashed through the tunnel.

Masses of rock fell with loud splashes behind them, and all around them was still the ominous grinding of mighty weights of rock. The walls of the tunnel quivered repeatedly.

Sturt suddenly reversed the propellers, but in spite of his action the cutter smashed a moment later into a solid rock wall. It was a mass of rock forming an unbroken barrier across the water-tunnel, extending beneath the surface of the water.

"We're trapped!" cried Sturt. "A mass of the rock has settled here and blocked the tunnel."

"It can't be completely blocked!" Campbell exclaimed. "See, the tide still runs out beneath it. Our one chance is to swim out under the blocking mass of rock, before the whole cliff gives way!"

"But there's no telling how far the block may extend——" Sturt cried.

Then as Campbell and Ennis stripped off their coats and shoes, he followed their example. The rumble of grinding rock around them was now continuous and nerve-shattering.

Campbell helped Ennis lower Ruth's unconscious form into the water.

"Keep your hand over her nose and mouth!" cried the inspector. "Come on, now!"

Sturt went first, his face pale in the searchlight beam as he dived under the rock mass. The tidal current carried him out of sight in a moment.

Then, holding the girl between them, and with Ennis' hand covering her mouth and nostrils, the other two dived. Down through the cold waters they shot, and then the swift current was carrying them forward like a mill-race, their bodies bumping and scraping against the rock mass overhead.

Ennis' lungs began to burn, his brain to reel, as they rushed on in the waters, still holding the girl tightly. They struck solid rock, a wall across their way. The current sucked them downward, to a small opening at the bottom. They wedged in it, struggled fiercely, then tore through it. They rose on the other side of it into pure air. They were in the darkness, floating in the tunnel beyond the block, the current carrying them swiftly onward.

The walls were shaking and roaring frightfully about them as they were borne round the turns of the tunnel. Then they saw ahead of them a circle of dim light, pricked with white stars.

The current bore them out into that starlight, into the open sea. Before them in the water floated Sturt, and they swam with him out from the shaking, grinding cliffs.

The girl stirred a little in Ennis' grasp, and he saw in the starlight that her face was no longer dazed.

"Paul——" she muttered, clinging close to Ennis in the water.

"She's coming back to consciousness—the water must have revived her from that drug!" he cried.

But he was cut short by Campbell's cry. "Look! Look!" cried the inspector, pointing back at the black cliffs.

In the starlight the whole cliff was collapsing, with a prolonged, terrible roar as of grinding planets, its face breaking and buckling. The waters around them boiled furiously, whirling them this way and that.

Then the waters quieted. They found they had been flung near a sandy spit beyond the shattered cliffs, and they swam toward it.

"The whole underground honeycomb of caverns and tunnels gave way and the sea poured in!" Campbell cried. "The Door, and the Brotherhood of the Door, are ended for ever!"

Flaxman Low:
The Story of the Moor Road
by E. and H. Heron

(pseud. for Katherine and Hesketh Prichard)

"The medical profession must always have its own peculiar off-shoots," said Mr. Flaxman Low, "some are trades, some mere hobbies, others, again, are allied subjects of a serious and profound nature. Now, as a student of psychical phenomena, I account myself only two degrees removed from the ordinary general practitioner."

"How do you make that out?" returned Colonel Daimley, pushing the decanter of old port invitingly across the table.

"The nerve and brain specialist is the link between myself and the man you would send for if you had a touch of lumbago," replied Low with a slight smile. "Each division is but a higher grade of the same ladder—a step upwards into the unknown. I consider that I stand just one step above the specialist who makes a study of brain disease and insanity; he is at work on the disorders of the embodied spirit, while I deal with abnormal conditions of the free and detached spirit."

Colonel Daimley laughed aloud.

"That won't do, Low! No, no! First prove that your ghosts are sick."

"Certainly," replied Low gravely. "A very small proportion of spirits return as apparitions after the death of the body. Hence we may conclude that a ghost is a spirit in an abnormal condition. Abnormal conditions of the body usually indicate disease; why not of the spirit also?"

"That sounds fair enough," observed Lane Chaddam, the third man present. "Has the colonel told you of our spook?"

The colonel shook his handsome grey head in some irritation.

"You haven't convinced me yet, Lane, that it is a spook," he said drily. "Human nature is at the bottom of most things in this world according to my opinion."

"What spook is this?" asked Flaxman Low. "I heard nothing of it when I was down with you last year."

"It's a recent acquisition," replied Lane Chaddam. "I wish we were rid of it for my part."

"Have you seen it?" asked Low as he relit his long German pipe.

"Yes, and felt it!"

"What is it?"

"That's for you to say. He nearly broke my neck for me—that's all I can swear to."

Low knew Chaddam well. He was a long-limbed, athletic young fellow, with a good show of cups in his rooms, and was one of the various short-distance runners mentioned in the Badminton as having done the hundred in level time, and not the sort of man whose neck is easy to break.

"How did it happen?" asked Flaxman Low.

"About a fortnight ago," replied Chaddam. "I was flight-shooting near the burn where the hounds killed the otter last year. When the light began to fail, I thought I would come home by the old quarry, and pot anything that showed itself. As I walked along the far bank of the burn, I saw a man on the near side standing on the patch of sand below the reeds and watching me. As I came nearer I heard him coughing; it sounded like a sick cow. He stood still as if waiting for me. I thought it odd, because amongst the meres and water-meadows down there one never meets a stranger."

"Could you see him pretty clearly?"

"I saw his outline clearly, but not his face, because his back was toward the west. He was tall and jerry-built, so to speak, and had a little head no bigger than a child's, and he wore a fur cap with queer upstanding ears. When I came close, he suddenly slipped away; he jumped behind a big dyke, and I lost sight of him. But I didn't pay much attention; I had my gun, and I concluded it was a tramp."

"Tramps don't follow men of your size," observed Low with a smile.

"This fellow did, at any rate. When I got across to the spot where he had been standing—the sand is soft there—I looked for his tracks. I knew he was bound to have a big foot of his own considering his height. But there were no footprints!"

58

"No footprints? You mean it was too dark for you to see them?" broke in Colonel Daimley.

"I am sure I should have seen them had there been any," persisted Chaddam quietly. "Besides, a man can't take a leap as he did without leaving a good hole behind him. The sand was perfectly smooth, because there had been a strong east wind all day. After looking about and seeing no marks, I went on to the top of the knoll above the quarry. After a bit I felt I was followed, though I couldn't see anyone. You remember the thorn bush that overhangs the quarry pool? I stopped there and bent over the edge of the cliff to see if there was anything in the pool. As I stooped I felt a point like a steel puncheon catch me in the small of the back. I kicked off from the quarry wall as well as I could, so as to avoid the broken rocks below, and I just managed to clear them, but I fell into the water with a flop that knocked the wind out of me. However, I held on to the gun, and, after a minute, I climbed to a ledge under the cliff and waited to see what my friend on top would do next. He waited, too. I couldn't see him, but I heard him—he coughed up there in the dusk, the most ghastly noise I ever heard. The colonel laughs at me, but it was about as nasty a half-hour as I care to have. In the end, I swam out across the pool and got home."

"I laugh at Lane," said the colonel, "but all the same, it's a bad spot for a fall."

"You say he struck you in the back?" asked Flaxman Low, turning to Chaddam.

"Yes, and his finger was like a steel punch."

"What does Mrs. Daimley say to this affair?" went on Low presently.

"Not a word to my wife or Olivia, my dear Low!" exclaimed Colonel Daimley. "It would frighten them needlessly; besides, there would be an infernal fuss if we wanted to go flighting or anything after dark. I only fear for them, as they often drive into Nerbury by the Moor Road, which passes close by the quarry."

"Do they go in for their letters every evening as they used to do?"

"Just the same. And they won't take Stubbs with them, in spite of advice." The colonel looked disconsolately at Low. "Women are angels, bless them! But they are the dickens to deal with because they always want to know why?"

"And now, Low, what have you to say about it?" asked Chaddam.

"Have you told me all?"

"Yes. The only other thing is that Livy says she hears someone coughing in the spinney most lights."

"If all is as you say, Chaddam—pardon me, but in cases like this imagination is apt to play an unsuspected part—I should think that you have come upon a unique experience. What you have told me is not to be explained upon the lines of any ordinary theory."

After this they followed the ladies into the drawing-room, where they found Mrs. Daimley immersed in a novel as usual, and Livy looking pretty enough to account for the frequent presence of Lane Chaddam at Low Riddings. He was a distant cousin of the colonel, and took advantage of his relationship to pay protracted visits to Northumberland.

Some years previous to the date of the above events, Colonel Daimley had bought and enlarged a substantial farmhouse which stood in a dip south of a lonely sweep of Northumbrian moors. It was a land of pale blue skies and far off fringes of black and ragged pine trees.

From the house a lane led over the wind-swept shoulder of the upland down to a hollow spanned by a railway bridge, then up again across the high levels of the moors until at length it lost itself in the outskirts of the little town of Nerbury. This Moor Road was peculiarly lonely; it approached but one cottage the whole way, and ran very nearly over the doorstep of that one—a deserted-looking slip of a place between the railway bridge and the quarry. Beyond the quarry stretched acres of marshland, meadows and reedy meres, all of which had been manipulated with such ability by the Colonel, that the duck shooting on his land was the envy of the neighbourhood.

In spite of its loneliness the Moor Road was much frequented by the Daimleys, who preferred it to the high road, which was uninteresting and much longer. Mrs. Daimley and Olivia drove in of an evening to fetch their letters—being people with nothing on earth to do, they were naturally always in a hurry to get their letters—and they perpetually had parcels waiting for them at the station which required to be called for at all sorts of hours. Thus it will be seen that the fact of the quarry being haunted by Lane Chaddam's assailant, formed a very real danger to the inhabitants of Low Riddings.

At breakfast next day Livy said the tramp had been coughing in the spinney half the night.

"In what direction?" asked Flaxman Low.

Livy pointed to the window which looked on to the gate and the thick boundary hedge, the last still full of crisp ruddy leaves.

"You feel an interest in your tramp, Miss Daimley?"

"Of course, poor creature! I wanted to go out to look for him the other night, but they would not allow me."

"That was before we knew he was so interesting," said Chaddam. "I promise we'll catch him for you next time he comes."

And this was in fact the programme they tried to carry out, but although the coughing was heard in the spinney, no one even caught a glimpse of any living thing moving or hiding among the trees.

The next stage of the affair happened to be an experience of Livy. In some excitement she told the assembled family at dinner that she had had just seen the coughing tramp.

Lane Chaddam changed colour. "You don't mean to say, Livy, that you went to search for him alone?" he exclaimed half-angrily.

Flaxman Low and the colonel wisely went on eating oyster patties without taking any apparent notice of the girl's news.

"Why shouldn't I?" asked Livy quickly, " but as it happens I saw him in Scully's cottage by the quarry this evening."

"What?" exclaimed Colonel Daimley, "in Scully's cottage. I'll see to that."

"Why? Are you all so prejudiced against my poor tramp?"

"On the contrary," replied Flaxman Low, "we all want to know what he's like."

"So odd-looking! I was driving home alone from the post when, as I passed the quarry cottage, I heard the cough. You know it is quite unmistakable; I looked up at the window and there he was. I have never seen anybody in the least like him. His face is ghastly pale and perfectly hairless, and he has such a little head. He stared at me so threateningly that I whipped up Lorelie."

"Were you frightened, then?"

"Not exactly, but he had such a wicked face that I drove away as fast as I could."

"I understood that you had arranged to send Stubbs for the letters?" said Colonel Daimley with some annoyance. "Why can't girls say what they mean?"

Livy made no reply, and after a pause Chaddam put a question.

"You must have passed along the Moor Road about seven o'clock?"

"Yes, it was after six when I left the Post-Office," replied Livy. "Why?"

"It was quite dark—how did you see the hairless man so plainly? I

61

was round on the marshes all the evening, and I am quite certain there was no light at any time in Scully's cottage."

"I don't remember whether there was any light behind him in the room," returned Livy after a moment's consideration; "I only know that I saw his head and face quite plainly."

There was no more said on the subject at the time, though the colonel forbade Livy to run any further risks by going alone on the Moor Road. After this, the three men paraded the lane and lay in wait for the hairless tramp or ghost. On the second evening their watch was rewarded, when Chaddam came hurriedly into the smoking-room to say that the coughing could at that instant be heard in the hedge by the dining-room. It was still early, although the evening had closed in with clouds, and all outside was dark.

"I'll deal with him this time effectually!" exclaimed the colonel. "I'll slip out the back way, and lie in the hedge down the road by the field gate. You two must chivy him out to me, and when he comes along, I'll have him against the sky-line and give him a charge of No. 4 if he shows fight."

The colonel stole down the lane while the others beat the spinney and hedge, Flaxman Low very much chagrined at being forced to deal with an interesting problem in this rough and ready fashion. However, he saw that on this occasion at least it would be useless to oppose the colonel's notions. When he and Chaddam met after beating the hedge they saw a tall figure shamble away rapidly down the lane towards the colonel's hiding-place.

They stood still and waited for developments, but the minutes followed each other in intense stillness. Then they went to find the colonel.

"Hullo, Colonel, anything wrong?" asked Chaddam on nearing the field gate.

The colonel straightened himself with the help of Chaddam's arm.

"Did you see him?" he whispered.

"We thought so. Why did you not fire?"

"Because," said the colonel in a husky voice, "I had no gun!"

"But you took it with you?"

"Yes."

Flaxman Low opened the lantern he carried, and, as the light swept round in a wide circle, something glinted on the grass. It was the stock of the colonel's gun. A little further off they came upon the Damascus

62

barrels bent and twisted into a ball like so much fine wire. Presently the colonel explained.

"I saw him coming and meant to meet him, but I seemed dazed—I couldn't move! The gun was snatched from me, and I made no resistance—I don't know why." He took the gunbarrels and examined them slowly, "I give in. Low, no human hand did that."

"During dinner Flaxman Low said abruptly: "I suspect you have lately had an earthquake down here."

"How did you know?" asked Livy. "Have you been to the quarry?"

Low said he had not.

"It was such a poor little earthquake that even the papers did not think it worth while to mention it!" went on Livy. "We didn't feel any shock, and, in fact, knew nothing about it until Dr. Petterped told us."

"You had a landslip though?" went on Low.

Livy opened her pretty eyes.

"But you know all about it," she said. "Yes, the landslip was just by the old quarry."

"I should like to see the place tomorrow," observed Low.

Next day, therefore, when the colonel went off to the coverts with a couple of neighbours, whom he had invited to join him, Flaxman Low accompanied Chaddam to examine the scene of the landslip.

From the edge of the upland, looking across the hollow crowded with reedy pools, they could see in the torn, reddish flank of the opposite slope the sharp tilt of the broken *strata*. To the right of this lay the old quarry, and about a hundred yards to the left the lonely house and the curving road.

Low descended into the hollow and spent a long time in the spongy ground between the back of the quarry and the lower edge of the newly-uncovered *strata*, using his little hammer freely, especially about one narrow black fissure, round which he sniffed and pottered in absorbed silence. Presently he called to Chaddam.

"There has been a slight explosion of gas—a rare gas, here," he said. "I hardly hoped to find traces of it, but it is unmistakeable."

"Very unmistakeable," agreed Chaddam, with a laugh. "You'd have said so had you been here when it happened."

"Ah, very satisfactory indeed. And that was a fortnight ago, you say?"

"Rather more now. It took place a couple of days before my fall into the quarry pool."

"Anyone ill near by—at that cottage for instance?" asked Low, as he joined Chaddam.

"Why? Was that gas poisonous? There's a man in the colonel's employ named Scully in that cottage, who has had pneumonia, but he was on the mend when the landslip occurred. Since then he has grown steadily worse."

"Is there anyone with him?"

"Yes, the Daimleys sent for a woman to look after him. Scully's a very decent man. I often go in to see him."

"And so does the hairless man apparently," added Low.

"No, that's the queer part of it. Neither he nor the woman in charge have ever seen such a person as Livy described. I don't know what to think."

"The first thing to be done is to get the man from here at once," said Low decidedly. "Let's go in and see him."

They found Scully low and drowsy. The nurse shook her head at the two visitors in a despondent way.

"He grows weaker day by day," she said.

"Get him away from here at once," repeated Low, as they went out.

"We might have him up at Low Riddings, but he seems almost too weak to be moved," replied Chaddam doubtfully.

"My dear fellow, it's his only chance of life."

The Daimleys made arrangements for the reception of Scully, provided Dr. Thomson of Nerbury gave his consent to the removal. In the afternoon, therefore, Chaddam bicycled into Nerbury to see the doctor on the subject. "If were you, Chaddam," said Low before he started, "I'd be back by daylight."

Unfortunately Dr. Thomson was on his rounds, and did not return until after dark, by which time it was too late to remove Scully that evening. After leaving the doctor's house Chaddam went to the station to inquire about a box from Mudie's. The books having arrived, he took out a couple of volumes for Mrs. Daimley's present consumption, and was strapping them on in front of his bicycle, when it struck him that unless he went home by the Moor Road he would be late for dinner.

Accordingly he branched off into the bare track which led over the moors. The twilight had deepened into a fine, cold night, and a moon was swinging up into a pale, clear sky. The spread of heather, purple in the daytime, appeared jet black by moonlight, and across it he could see the white ribbon of road stretching ahead into the distance. The scents of the night were fresh in his nostrils, as he ran easily along the level with the breeze behind him.

He soon reached the incline past Scully's cottage. Well away to the left lay the quarry pool like a blotch of ink under its shadowing cliff. There was no light in the cottage, and it seemed even more deserted-looking than usual.

As Chaddam flashed under the bridge, he heard a cough, and glanced back over his shoulder.

A tall, loose-jointed form he had seen once before, was rearing itself up upon the railway bridge. There was something curiously un-human about the lank outlines and the cant of the small head with its prick-eared cap showing out so clearly against the lighter sky behind.

When Chaddam looked again, he saw the thing on the bridge fling up its long arms and leap down on to the road some thirty feet below.

Then Chaddam rode. He began to think he had been a fool to come, and he counted that he was a good mile from home. At first he fancied he heard footfalls, then he fancied there were none. The hard road flew under him, all thoughts of economising his strength were lost, his single aim was to make the pace.

Suddenly his bicycle jerked violently, and he was shot over into the road. As he fell, he turned his head and was conscious of a little, bleached, bestial face, wet with fury, not ten yards behind!

He sprang to his feet, and ran up the road as he had never run before. He ran wonderfully, but he might as well have tried to race a cheetah. It was not a question of speed, the game was in the hands of this thing with the limbs of a starved Hercules, whose bony knees seemed to leap into its ghastly face at every stride. Chaddam topped the slope with a sickening sense of his own powerlessness. Already he saw Low Riddings in the distance, and a dim light came creeping along the road towards him. Another frantic spurt, and he had almost reached the light, when a hand closed like a vice on his shoulder, and seemed to fasten on the flesh. He rushed blindly on towards the house. He saw the door-handle gleam, and in another second he had pitched head foremost on to the knotted matting in the hall.

When he recovered his senses, his first question was: "Where is Low?"

"Didn't you meet him?" asked Livy, " I—that is, we were anxious about you as you were so late, and I was just going to meet you when Mr. Low came downstairs and insisted on going instead."

Chaddam stood up.

"I must follow him."

But as he spoke the front door opened, and Flaxman Low entered, and looked up at the clock.

"Eight-twenty," he said, "You're late, Chaddam."

Afterwards in the smoking-room he gave an account of what he had seen.

"I saw Chaddam racing up the road with a tall figure behind him. It stretched out its hand and grasped his shoulder. The next instant it stopped short as if it had been shot. It seemed to reel back and collapse, and then limped off into the hedge like a disappointed dog."

Chaddam stood up and began to take off his coat.

"Whatever the thing is, it is something out of the common. Look here!" he said, turning up his shirtsleeve over the point of his shoulder, where three singular marks were visible, irregularly placed as the fingers of a hand might fall. They were oblong in shape, about the size of a bean, and swollen in purple lumps well above the surface of the skin.

"Looks as if someone had been using a small cupping glass on you," remarked the colonel uneasily. "What do you say to it, Low?"

"I say that since Chaddam has escaped with his life, I have only to congratulate him on what, in Europe certainly, is a unique adventure."

The colonel threw his cigar into the fire.

"Such adventures are too dangerous for my taste," he said. "This creature has on two occasions murderously attacked Lane Chaddam, and it would, no doubt, have attacked Livy if it had had the chance. We must leave this place at once, or we shall be murdered in our beds!"

"I don't think, Colonel, that you will be troubled with this mysterious visitant again," replied Flaxman Low.

"Why not? Who or what is this horrible thing?"

"I believe it to be an Elemental Earth Spirit," returned Low. "No other solution fits the facts of the case."

"What is an Elemental?" resumed the colonel irritably. "Remember, Low, I expect you to prove your theories so that a plain man may understand, if I am to stay on at Low Riddings."

"Eastern occultists describe wandering tribes of earth spirits, evil intelligences, possessing spirit as distinct from soul—all inimical to man."

"But how do you know that the thing on the Moor Road is an Elemental?"

"Because the points of resemblance are curiously remarkable. The occultists say that when these spirits materialize, they appear in grotesque and uncouth forms; secondly, that they are invariably bloodless and hairless; thirdly, they move with extraordinary rapidity, and leave no footprints; and, lastly, their agility and strength is superhuman. All these peculiarities have been observed in connection with the figure on the Moor Road."

"I admit that no man I have ever met with," commented Colonel Daimley, "could jump uninjured from a height of 30ft., race a bicycle, and twist up gunbarrels like so much soft paper. So perhaps you're right. But can you tell me why or how it came here?"

"My conclusions," began Low, "may seem to you far-fetched and ridiculous, but you must give them the benefit of the fact that they precisely account for the otherwise unaccountable features which mark this affair. I connect this appearance with the earthquake and the sick man."

"What? Scully in league with the devil?" exclaimed the colonel bluntly. "Why the man is too weak to leave his bed; besides, he is a short, thick-set fellow, entirely unlike our haunting friend."

"You mistake me, Colonel," said Low, in his quiet tones. "These Elementals cannot take form without drawing upon the resources of the living. They absorb the vitality of any ailing person until it is exhausted, and the person dies."

"Then they begin operations upon a fresh victim? A pleasant look-out to know we keep a well-attested vampire in the neighbourhood!"

"Vampires are a distinct race, with different methods; one being that the Elemental is a wanderer, and goes far afield to search for a new victim."

"But why should it want to kill me?" put in Chaddam.

"As I have told you, they are animated solely by a blind malignity to the human race, and you happened to be handy."

"But the earthquake, Low; where is the connection there?" demanded the colonel, with the air of a man who intends to corner his opponent.

Flaxman Low lit one cigar at the end of another before he replied.

"At this point," he said, "my own theories and observations and those of the old occultists overlap. The occultists held that some of these spirits are imprisoned in the interior of the earth, but may be set free in consequence of those shiftings and disturbances which take place during an earthquake. This in more modern language simply means that Elementals are in some manner connected with certain of the primary *strata*. Now, my own researches have led me to conclude that atmospheric influences are intimately associated with spiritual phenomena. Some gases appear to be productive of such phenomena. One of these is generated when certain of the primary formations are newly exposed to the common air."

"This is almost beyond belief—I don't understand you," said the colonel.

"I am sorry that I cannot give you all the links in my own chain of reasoning," returned Low. "Much is still obscure, but the evidence is sufficiently strong to convince me that in such a case of earthquake and landslip as has lately taken place here the phenomenon of an embodied Elemental might possibly be expected to follow, given the one necessary adjunct of a sick person in the near neighbourhood of the disturbance."

"But when this brute got hold of me, why didn't it finish me off?" asked Chaddam. "Or was it your coming that prevented it?"

Flaxman Low considered.

"No, I don't think I can flatter myself that my coming had anything to do with your escape. It was a near thing—how near you will understand when we hear further news of Scully in the morning."

A servant entered the room at this moment.

"The woman has come up from the cottage, sir, to say that Scully is dead."

"At what hour did he die?" asked Low.

"About ten minutes past eight, sir, she says."

"The hour agrees exactly," commented Low, when the man had left the room. "The figure stopped and collapsed so suddenly that I believed something of this kind must have happened."

"But surely this is a very unprecedented occurrence?"

"It is," said Flaxman Low. "But I can assure you that if you take the trouble to glance through the pages of the psychical periodicals you will find many statements at least as wonderful."

"But are they true?"

"At any rate," said he, "we know this is."

The Daimleys have spent many pleasant days at Low Riddings since then, but Chaddam—who has acquired a right to control Miss Livy's actions more or less—persists in his objection to any solitary expeditions to Nerbury along the Moor Road. For, although the figure has never been seen about Low Riddings since, some strange stories have lately appeared in the papers of a similar mysterious figure which has been met with more than once in the lonelier spots about North London. If it be true that this nameless wandering spirit, with the strength and activity of twenty men, still haunts our lonely roads, the sooner Mr. Flaxman Low exorcises it the better.

The Mark of the Beast
Rudyard Kipling

Your Gods and my Gods—do you or I know which are the stronger?
                                              Native Proverb.

East of Suez, some hold, the direct control of Providence ceases; Man being there handed over to the power of the Gods and Devils of Asia, and the Church of England Providence only exercising an occasional and modified supervision in the case of Englishmen.

This theory accounts for some of the more unnecessary horrors of life in India: it may be stretched to explain my story.

My friend Strickland of the police, who knows as much of natives of India as is good for any man, can bear witness to the facts of the case. Dumoise, our doctor, also saw what Strickland and I saw. The inference which he drew from the evidence was entirely incorrect. He is dead now; he died in a rather curious manner, which has been elsewhere described.

When Fleete came to India he owned a little money and some land in the Himalayas, near a place called Dharmsala. Both properties had been left him by an uncle, and he came out to finance them. He was a big, heavy, genial, and inoffensive man. His knowledge of natives was, of course, limited, and he complained of the difficulties of the language.

He rode in from his place in the hills to spend New Year in the station, and he stayed with Strickland. On New Year's Eve there was a big dinner at the club, and the night was excusably wet. When men foregather from the uttermost ends of the empire, they have a right to be riotous. The Frontier had sent down a contingent o' Catch-'em-Alive-O's who had not seen twenty white faces for a year, and were used to ride fifteen miles to dinner at the next fort at the risk of a

Khyberee bullet where their drinks should lie. They profited by their new security, for they tried to play pool with a curled-up hedgehog found in the garden, and one of them carried the marker round the room in his teeth.

Half a dozen planters had come in from the south and were talking 'horse' to the biggest liar in Asia, who was trying to cap all their stories at once. Everybody was there, and there was a general closing up of ranks and taking stock of our losses in dead or disabled that had fallen during the past year. It was a very wet night, and I remember that we sang 'Auld Lang Syne' with our feet in the Polo Championship Cup, and our heads among the stars, and swore that we were all dear friends. Then some of us went away and annexed Burma, and some tried to open up the Soudan and were opened up by Fuzzies in that cruel scrub outside Suakim, and some found stars and medals, and some were married, which was bad, and some did other things which were worse, and the others of us stayed in our chains and strove to make money on insufficient experiences.

Fleete began the night with sherry and bitters, drank champagne steadily up to dessert, then raw, rasping Capri with all the strength of whisky, took Benedictine with his coffee, four or five whiskies and so-das to improve his pool strokes, beer and bones at half-past two, winding up with old brandy. Consequently, when he came out, at half-past three in the morning, into fourteen degrees of frost, he was very angry with his horse for coughing, and tried to leapfrog into the saddle. The horse broke away and went to his stables; so Strickland and I formed a Guard of Dishonour to take Fleete home.

Our road lay through the bazaar, close to a little temple of Hanuman, the Monkey-god, who is a leading divinity worthy of respect. All gods have good points, just as have all priests. Personally, I attach much importance to Hanuman, and am kind to his people—the great gray apes of the hills. One never knows when one may want a friend.

There was a light in the temple, and as we passed, we could hear voices of men chanting hymns. In a native temple, the priests rise at all hours of the night to do honour to their god. Before we could stop him, Fleete dashed up the steps, patted two priests on the back, and was gravely grinding the ashes of his cigar-butt into the forehead of the red, stone image of Hanuman. Strickland tried to drag him out, but he sat down and said solemnly:

'Shee that? 'Mark of the B—beasht! *I* made it. Ishn't it fine?'

In half a minute the temple was alive and noisy, and Strickland, who knew what came of polluting gods, said that things might occur. He, by virtue of his official position, long residence in the country, and weakness for going among the natives, was known to the priests and he felt unhappy. Fleete sat on the ground and refused to move. He said that 'good old Hanuman' made a very soft pillow.

Then, without any warning, a Silver Man came out of a recess behind the image of the god. He was perfectly naked in that bitter, bitter cold, and his body shone like frosted silver, for he was what the Bible calls 'a leper as white as snow.' Also he had no face, because he was a leper of some years' standing, and his disease was heavy upon him. We two stooped to haul Fleete up, and the temple was filling and filling with folk who seemed to spring from the earth, when the Silver Man ran in under our arms, making a noise exactly like the mewing of an otter, caught Fleete round the body and dropped his head on Fleete's breast before we could wrench him away. Then he retired to a corner and sat mewing while the crowd blocked all the doors.

The priests were very angry until the Silver Man touched Fleete. That nuzzling seemed to sober them.

At the end of a few minutes' silence one of the priests came to Strickland and said, in perfect English, 'Take your friend away. He has done with Hanuman, but Hanuman has not done with him.' The crowd gave room and we carried Fleete into the road.

Strickland was very angry. He said that we might all three have been knifed, and that Fleete should thank his stars that he had escaped without injury.

Fleete thanked no one. He said that he wanted to go to bed. He was gorgeously drunk.

We moved on, Strickland silent and wrathful, until Fleete was taken with violent shivering fits and sweating. He said that the smells of the bazaar were overpowering, and he wondered why slaughterhouses were permitted so near English residences. 'Can't you smell the blood?' said Fleete.

We put him to bed at last, just as the dawn was breaking, and Strickland invited me to have another whisky and soda. While we were drinking he talked of the trouble in the temple, and admitted that it baffled him completely. Strickland hates being mystified by natives, because his business in life is to overmatch them with their own weapons. He has not yet succeeded in doing this, but in fifteen or twenty years he will have made some small progress.

'They should have mauled us,' he said, 'instead of mewing at us. I wonder what they meant. I don't like it one little bit.'

I said that the managing committee of the temple would in all probability bring a criminal action against us for insulting their religion. There was a section of the Indian Penal Code which exactly met Fleete's offence. Strickland said he only hoped and prayed that they would do this. Before I left I looked into Fleete's room, and saw him lying on his right side, scratching his left breast. Then I went to bed cold, depressed, and unhappy, at seven o'clock in the morning.

At one o'clock I rode over to Strickland's house to inquire after Fleete's head. I imagined that it would be a sore one. Fleete was breakfasting and seemed unwell. His temper was gone, for he was abusing the cook for not supplying him with an underdone chop. A man who can eat raw meat after a wet night is a curiosity. I told Fleete this and he laughed.

'You breed queer mosquitoes in these parts,' he said. 'I've been bitten to pieces, but only in one place.'

' Let's have a look at the bite,' said Strickland, 'it may have gone down since this morning.'

While the chops were being cooked, Fleete opened his shirt and showed us, just over his left breast, a mark, the perfect double of the black rosettes—the five or six irregular blotches arranged in a circle—on a leopard's hide. Strickland looked and said, 'It was only pink this morning It's grown black now.'

Fleete ran to a glass.

'By Jove!' he said, 'this is nasty. What is it?'

We could not answer. Here the chops came in, all red and juicy, and Fleete bolted three in a most offensive manner. He ate on his right grinders only, and threw his head over his right shoulder as he snapped the meat. When he had finished, it struck him that he had been behaving strangely, for he said apologetically, ' I don't think I ever felt so hungry in my life. I've bolted like an ostrich.'

After breakfast Strickland said to me, 'Don't go. Stay here, and stay for the night.'

Seeing that my house was not three miles from Strickland's, this request was absurd. But Strickland insisted, and was going to say something when Fleete interrupted by declaring in a shamefaced way that he felt hungry again. Strickland sent a man to my house to fetch over my bedding and a horse, and we three went down to Strickland's stables to pass the hours until it was time to go out for a ride. The man who has a weakness for horses never wearies of inspecting them; and when two men are killing time in this way they gather knowledge and lies the one from the other.

There were five horses in the stables, and I shall never forget the scene us we tried to look them over. They seemed to have gone mad. They reared and screamed and nearly tore up their pickets; they sweated and shivered and lathered and were distraught with fear. Strickland's horses used to know him as well as his dogs; which made the matter more curious. We left the stable for fear of the brutes throwing themselves in their panic. Then Strickland turned back and called me. The horses were still frightened, but they let us 'gentle' and make much of them, and put their heads in our bosoms.

'They aren't afraid of *us*,' said Strickland. 'D'you know, I'd give three months' pay if Outrage here could talk.'

But Outrage was dumb, and could only cuddle up to his master and blow out his nostrils, as is the custom of horses when they wish to explain things but can't. Fleete came up when we were in the stalls, and as soon as the horses saw him, their fright broke out afresh. It was all that we could do to escape from the place unkicked. Strickland said, 'They don't seem to love you, Fleete.'

'Nonsense,' said Fleete; 'my mare will follow me like a dog.' He went to her; she was in a loose-box; but as he slipped the bars she plunged, knocked him down, and broke away into the garden. I laughed, but Strickland was not amused. He took his moustache in both fists and pulled at it till it nearly came out. Fleete, instead of going off to chase his property, yawned, saying that he felt sleepy. He went to the house to lie down, which was a foolish way of spending New Year's Day.

Strickland sat with me in the stables and asked if I had noticed anything peculiar in Fleete's manner. I said that he ate his food like a beast; but that this might have been the result of living alone in the hills out of the reach of society as refined and elevating as ours for instance. Strickland was not amused. I do not think that he listened to me, for his next, sentence referred to the mark on Fleete's breast, and I said that it might have been caused by blister-flies, or that it was possibly a birthmark newly born and now visible for the first time. We both agreed that it was unpleasant to look at, and Strickland found occasion to say that I was a fool.

'I can't tell you what I think now,' said he, 'because you would call me a madman; but you must stay with me for the next few days, if you can. I want you to watch Fleete, but don't tell me what you think till I have made up my mind.'

'But I am dining out tonight,' I said.

'So am I,' said Strickland, 'and so is Fleete. At least if he doesn't change his mind.'

We walked about the garden smoking, but saying nothing because we were friends, and talking spoils good tobacco—till our pipes were out. Then we went to wake up Fleete. He was wide awake and fidgeting about his room.

'I say, I want some more chops,' he said. 'Can I get them?''

We laughed and said, 'Go and change. The ponies will be round in a minute.'

'All right,' said Fleete. 'I'll go when I get the chops—underdone ones, mind.'

He seemed to be quite in earnest. It was four o'clock, and we had had breakfast at one; still, for a long time, he demanded those underdone chops. Then he changed into riding clothes and went out into the verandah. His pony—the mare had not been caught—would not let him come near. All three horses were unmanageable—mad with fear—and finally Fleete said that he would stay at home and get something to eat. Strickland and I rode out wondering. As we passed the temple of Hanuman, the Silver Man came out and mewed at us.

'He is not one of the regular priests of the temple,' said Strickland. 'I think I should peculiarly like to lay my hands on him.'

There was no spring in our gallop on the racecourse that evening. The horses were stale, and moved as though they had been ridden out.

'The fright after breakfast has been too much for them,' said Strickland.

That was the only remark he made through the remainder of the ride. Once or twice I think he swore to himself; but that did not count.

We came back in the dark at seven o'clock, and saw that there were no lights in the bungalow. 'Careless ruffians my servants are!' said Strickland.

My horse reared at something on the carriage drive, and Fleete stood up under its nose.

'What are you doing, grovelling about the garden?' said Strickland.

But both horses bolted and nearly threw us. We dismounted by the stables and returned to Fleete, who was on his hands and knees under the orange-bushes.

'What the devil's wrong with you?' said Strickland.

'Nothing, nothing in the world,' said Fleete, speaking very quickly and thickly. 'I've been gardening—botanising you know. The smell of the earth is delightful. I think I'm going for a walk—a long walk—all night.'

Then I saw that there was something excessively out of order somewhere, and I said to Strickland, 'I am not dining out.'

'Bless you!' said Strickland. 'Here, Fleete, get up. You'll catch fever there. Come in to dinner and let's have the lamps lit. We'll all dine at home.'

Fleete stood up unwillingly, and said, ' No lamps no lamps. It's much nicer here. Let's dine outside and have some more chops—lots of 'em and underdone—bloody ones with gristle.'

Now a December evening in Northern India is bitterly cold, and Fleete's suggestion was that of a maniac.

'Come in,' said Strickland sternly. 'Come in at once.'

Fleete came, and when the lamps were brought, we saw that he was literally plastered with dirt from head to foot. He must have been rolling in the garden. He shrank from the light and went to his room. His eyes were horrible to look at. There was a green light behind them, not in them, if you understand, and the man's lower lip hung down.

Strickland said, 'There is going to be trouble—big trouble—to-night. Don't you change your riding-things.'

We waited and waited for Fleete's reappearance, and ordered dinner in the meantime. We could hear him moving about his own room, but there was no light there. Presently from the room came the long-drawn howl of a wolf.

People write and talk lightly of blood running cold and hair standing up and things of that kind. Both sensations are too horrible to be trifled with. My heart stopped as though a knife had been driven through it, and Strickland turned as white as the tablecloth.

The howl was repeated, and was answered by another howl far across the fields.

That set the gilded roof on the horror. Strickland dashed into Fleete's room. I followed, and we saw Fleete getting out of the window, he made beast-noises in the back of his throat. He could not answer us when we shouted at him. He spat.

I don't quite remember what followed, but I think that Strickland must have stunned him with the long boot-jack or else I should never have been able to sit on his chest. Fleete could not speak, he could only snarl, and his snarls were those of a wolf, not of a man. The human spirit must have been giving way all day and have died out with the twilight. We were dealing with a beast that had once been Fleete.

The affair was beyond any human and rational experience. I tried to say 'Hydrophobia,' but the word wouldn't come, because I knew that I was lying.

We bound this beast with leather thongs of the *punkah*-rope, and tied its thumbs and big toes together, and gagged it with a shoe-horn, which makes a very efficient gag if you know how to arrange it. Then we carried it into the dining-room, and sent a man to Dumoise, the doctor, telling him to come over at once. After we had despatched the messenger and were drawing breath, Strickland said, 'It's no good. This isn't any doctor's work.' I, also, knew that he spoke the truth.

The beast's head was free, and it threw it about from side to side. Anyone entering the room would have believed that we were curing a wolf's pelt. That was the most loathsome accessory of all.

Strickland sat with his chin in the heel of his fist, watching the beast as it wriggled on the ground, but saying nothing. The shirt had been torn open in the scuffle and showed the black rosette mark on the left breast. It stood out like a blister.

In the silence of the watching we heard something without mewing like a she-otter. We both rose to our feet, and, I answer for myself, not Strickland, felt sick—actually and physically sick. We told each other, as did the men in *Pinafore*, that it was the cat.

Dumoise arrived, and I never saw a little man so unprofessionally shocked. He said that it was a heart-rending case of hydrophobia, and that nothing could be done. At least any palliative measures would only prolong the agony. The beast was foaming at the mouth. Fleete, as we told Dumoise, had been bitten by dogs once or twice. Any man who keeps half a dozen terriers must expect a nip now and again. Dumoise could offer no help. He could only certify that Fleete was dying of hydrophobia. The beast was then howling, for it had managed to spit out the shoe-horn. Dumoise said that he would be ready to certify to the cause of death, and that the end was certain. He was a good little man, and he offered to remain with us; but Strickland refused the kindness. He did not wish to poison Dumoise's New Year. He would only ask him not to give the real cause of Fleete's death to the public.

So Dumoise left, deeply agitated; and as soon as the noise of the cart-wheels had died away, Strickland told me, in a whisper, his suspicions. They were so wildly improbable that he dared not say them out aloud; and I, who entertained all Strickland's beliefs, was so ashamed of owning to them that I pretended to disbelieve.

'Even if the Silver Man had bewitched Fleete for polluting the image of Hanuman, the punishment could not have fallen so quickly.'

As I was whispering this the cry outside the house rose again, and the beast fell into a fresh paroxysm of struggling till we were afraid that the thongs that held it would give way.

'Watch!' said Strickland. 'If this happens six times I shall take the law into my own hands. I order you to help me.'

He went into his room and came out in a few minutes with the barrels of an old shot-gun, a piece of fishing-line, some thick cord, and his heavy wooden bedstead. I reported that the convulsions had followed the cry by two seconds in each case, and the beast seemed perceptibly weaker.

Strickland muttered, 'But he can't take away the life! He can't take away the life!'

I said, though I knew that I was arguing against myself, 'It may be a cat. It must be a cat. If the Silver Man is responsible, why does he dare to come here?'

Strickland arranged the wood on the hearth, put the gun-barrels into the glow of the fire, spread the twine on the table and broke a walking stick in two. There was one yard of fishing line, gut, lapped with wire, such as is used for *mahseer*-fishing, and he tied the two ends together in a loop.

Then he said, ' How can we catch him? He must be taken alive and unhurt.'

I said that we must trust in Providence, and go out softly with polo-sticks into the shrubbery at the front of the house. The man or animal that made the cry was evidently moving round the house as regularly as a night-watchman. We could wait in the bushes till he came by and knock him over.

Strickland accepted this suggestion, and we slipped out from a bathroom window into the front verandah and then across the carriage drive into the bushes.

In the moonlight we could see the leper coming round the corner of the house. He was perfectly naked, and from time to time he mewed and stopped to dance with his shadow. It was an unattractive sight, and thinking of poor Fleete, brought to such degradation by so foul a creature, I put away all my doubts and resolved to help Strickland from the heated gun-barrels to the loop of twine—from the loins to the head and back again—with all tortures that might be needful.

The leper halted in the front porch for a moment and we jumped out on him with the sticks. He was wonder fully strong, and we were afraid that he might escape or be fatally injured before we caught him. We had an idea that lepers were frail creatures, but this proved to be incorrect. Strickland knocked his legs from under him and I put my foot on his neck. He mewed hideously, and even through my riding-boots I could feel that his flesh was not the flesh of a clean man.

He struck at us with his hand and feet-stumps. We looped the lash of a dog-whip round him, under the arm- pits, and dragged him backwards into the hall and so into the dining-room where the beast lay. There we tied him with trunk-straps. He made no attempt to escape, but mewed.

When we confronted him with the beast the scene was beyond description. The beast doubled backwards into a bow as though he had been poisoned with strychnine, and moaned in the most pitiable fashion. Several other things happened also, but they cannot be put down here.

'I think I was right,' said Strickland. 'Now we will ask him to cure this case.'

But the leper only mewed. Strickland wrapped a towel round his hand and took the gun-barrels out of the fire. I put the half of the broken walking stick through the loop of fishing-line and buckled the leper comfortably to Strickland's bedstead. I understood then how men and women and little children can endure to see a witch burnt alive; for the beast was moaning on the floor, and though the Silver Man had no face, you could see horrible feelings passing through the slab that took its place, exactly as waves of heat play across red-hot iron—gun-barrels for instance.

Strickland shaded his eyes with his hands for a moment and we got to work. This part is not to be printed.

★★★★★★

The dawn was beginning to break when the leper spoke. His mewings had not been satisfactory up to that point. The beast had fainted from exhaustion and the house was very still. We unstrapped the leper and told him to take away the evil spirit. He crawled to the beast and laid his hand upon the left breast. That was all. Then he fell face down and whined, drawing in his breath as he did so.

We watched the face of the beast, and saw the soul of Fleete coming back into the eyes. Then a sweat broke out on the forehead and the eyes—they were human eyes—closed. We waited for an hour but Fleete still slept. We carried him to his room and bade the leper go, giving him the bedstead, and the sheet on the bedstead to cover his nakedness, the gloves and the towels with which we had touched him, and the whip that had been hooked round his body. He put the sheet about him and went out into the early morning without speaking or mewing.

Strickland wiped his face and sat down. A night-gong, far away in the city, made seven o'clock.

'Exactly four-and -twenty hours!' said Strickland. 'And I've done enough to ensure my dismissal from the service, besides permanent quarters in a lunatic asylum. Do you believe that we are awake?'

The red-hot gun-barrel had fallen on the floor and was singeing the carpet. The smell was entirely real.

That morning at eleven we two together went to wake up Fleete. We looked and saw that the black leopard-rosette on his chest had disappeared. He was very drowsy and tired, but as soon as he saw us, he said, 'Oh! Confound you fellows. Happy New Year to you. Never mix your liquors. I'm nearly dead.'

'Thanks for your kindness, but you're over time,' said Strickland. 'Today is the morning of the second. You've slept the clock round with a vengeance.'

The door opened, and little Dumoise put his head in. He had come on foot, and fancied that we were laying out Fleete.

'I've brought a nurse,' said Dumoise. 'I suppose that she can come in for . . . what is necessary.'

'By all means,' said Fleete cheerily, sitting up in bed. 'Bring on your nurses.'

Dumoise was dumb. Strickland led him out and explained that there must have been a mistake in the diagnosis. Dumoise remained dumb and left the house hastily. He considered that his professional reputation had been injured, and was inclined to make a personal matter of the recovery. Strickland went out too. When he came back, he said that he had been to call on the Temple of Hanuman to offer redress for the pollution of the god, and had been solemnly assured that no white man had ever touched the idol and that he was an in-carnation of all the virtues labouring under a delusion. 'What do you think ?' said Strickland.

I said, '*There are more things . . .*'

But Strickland hates that quotation. He says that I have worn it threadbare.

One other curious thing happened which frightened me as much as anything in all the night's work. When Fleete was dressed he came into the dining-room and sniffed. He had a quaint trick of moving his nose when he sniffed. 'Horrid doggy smell, here,' said he. 'You should really keep those terriers of yours in better order. Try sulphur, Strick.'

But Strickland did not answer. He caught hold of the back of a chair, and, without warning, went into an amazing fit of hysterics. It is terrible to see a strong man overtaken with hysteria. Then it struck me that we had fought for Fleete's soul with the Silver Man in that room, and had disgraced ourselves as Englishmen forever, and I laughed and gasped and gurgled just as shamefully as Strickland, while Fleete thought that we had both gone mad. We never told him what we had done.

Some years later, when Strickland had married and was a church-going member of society for his wife's sake, we reviewed the incident dispassionately, and Strickland suggested that I should put it before the public.

I cannot myself see that this step is likely to clear up the mystery; because, in the first place, no one will believe a rather unpleasant story, and, in the second, it is well known to every right-minded man that the gods of the heathen are stone and brass, and any attempt to deal with them otherwise is justly condemned.

Carnacki, the Ghost Finder:
The Horse of the Invisible

William Hope Hodgson

I had that afternoon received an invitation from Carnacki. When I reached his place I found him sitting alone. As I came into the room he rose with a perceptibly stiff movement and extended his left hand. His face seemed to be badly scarred and bruised and his right hand was bandaged. He shook hands and offered me his paper, which I refused. Then he passed me a handful of photographs and returned to his reading.

Now, that is just Carnacki. Not a word had come from him and not a question from me. He would tell us all about it later. I spent about half an hour looking at the photographs which were chiefly "snaps" (some by flashlight) of an extraordinarily pretty girl; though in some of the photographs it was wonderful that her prettiness was so evident for so frightened and startled was her expression that it was difficult not to believe that she had been photographed in the presence of some imminent and overwhelming danger.

The bulk of the photographs were of interiors of different rooms and passages and in every one the girl might be seen, either full length in the distance or closer, with perhaps little more than a hand or arm or portion of the head or dress included in the photograph. All of these had evidently been taken with some definite aim that did not have for its first purpose the picturing of the girl, but obviously of her surroundings and they made me very curious, as you can imagine.

Near the bottom of the pile, however, I came upon something *definitely* extraordinary. It was a photograph of the girl standing abrupt and clear in the great blaze of a flashlight, as was plain to be seen. Her face was turned a little upward as if she had been frightened suddenly by some noise. Directly above her, as though half-formed and coming down out of the shadows, was the shape of a single enormous hoof.

I examined this photograph for a long time without understanding it more than that it had probably to do with some queer case in which Carnacki was interested. When Jessop, Arkright and Taylor came in Carnacki quietly held out his hand for the photographs which I returned in the same spirit and afterward we all went in to dinner. When we had spent a quiet hour at the table we pulled our chairs 'round and made ourselves snug and Carnacki began:

"I've been North," he said, speaking slowly and painfully between puffs at his pipe. "Up to Hisgins of East Lancashire. It has been a pretty strange business all 'round, as I fancy you chaps will think, when I have finished. I knew before I went, something about the 'horse story,' as I have heard it called; but I never thought of it coming my way, somehow. Also I know *now* that I never considered it seriously—in spite of my rule always to keep an open mind. Funny creatures, we humans!

"Well, I got a wire asking for an appointment, which of course told me that there was some trouble. On the date I fixed old Captain Hisgins himself came up to see me. He told me a great many new details about the horse story; though naturally I had always known the main points and understood that if the first child were a girl, that girl would be haunted by the Horse during her courtship.

"It is, as you can see already, an extraordinary story and though I have always known about it, I have never thought it to be anything more than an old-time legend, as I have already hinted. You see, for seven generations the Hisgins family have had men children for their first-born and even the Hisginses themselves have long considered the tale to be little more than a myth.

"To come to the present, the eldest child of the reigning family is a girl and she has been often teased and warned in jest by her friends and relations that she is the first girl to be the eldest for seven generations and that she would have to keep her men friends at arm's length or go into a nunnery if she hoped to escape the haunting. And this, I think, shows us how thoroughly the tale had grown to be considered as nothing worthy of the least serious thought. Don't you think so?

"Two months ago Miss Hisgins became engaged to Beaumont, a young naval officer, and on the evening of the very day of the engagement, before it was even formally announced, a most extraordinary thing happened which resulted in Captain Hisgins making the appointment and my ultimately going down to their place to look into the thing.

"From the old family records and papers that were entrusted to me I found that there could be no possible doubt that prior to something like a hundred and fifty years ago there were some very extraordinary and disagreeable coincidences, to put the thing in the least emotional way. In the whole of the two centuries prior to that date there were five first-born girls out of a total of seven generations of the family. Each of these girls grew up to maidenhood and each became engaged, and each one died during the period of engagement, two by suicide, one by falling from a window, one from a 'broken heart' (presumably heart failure, owing to sudden shock through fright). The fifth girl was killed one evening in the park 'round the house; but just how, there seemed to be no *exact* knowledge; only that there was an impression that she had been kicked by a horse. She was dead when found. Now, you see, all of these deaths might be attributed in a way—even the suicides—to natural causes, I mean as distinct from supernatural. You see? Yet, in every case the maidens had undoubtedly suffered some extraordinary and terrifying experiences during their various court-ships for in all of the records there was mention either of the neighing of an unseen horse or of the sounds of an invisible horse galloping, as well as many other peculiar and quite inexplicable manifestations. You begin to understand now, I think, just how extraordinary a business it was that I was asked to look into.

"I gathered from one account that the haunting of the girls was so constant and horrible that two of the girls' lovers fairly ran away from their ladyloves. And I think it was this, more than anything else, that made me feel that there had been something more in it than a mere succession of uncomfortable coincidences.

"I got hold of these facts before I had been many hours in the house and after this I went pretty carefully into the details of the thing that happened on the night of Miss Hisgins's engagement to Beaumont. It seems that as the two of them were going through the big lower corridor, just after dusk and before the lamps had been lighted, there had been a sudden, horrible neighing in the corridor, close to them. Immediately afterward Beaumont received a tremendous blow or kick which broke his right forearm. Then the rest of the family and the servants came running to know what was wrong. Lights were brought and the corridor and, afterward, the whole house searched, but nothing unusual was found.

"You can imagine the excitement in the house and the half incredulous, half believing talk about the old legend. Then, later, in the middle of the night the old Captain was waked by the sound of a great horse galloping 'round and 'round the house.

"Several times after this both Beaumont and the girl said that they had heard the sounds of hoofs near to them after dusk, in several of the rooms and corridors.

"Three nights later Beaumont was waked by a strange neighing in the night-time seeming to come from the direction of his sweetheart's bedroom. He ran hurriedly for her father and the two of them raced to her room. They found her awake and ill with sheer terror, having been awakened by the neighing, seemingly close to her bed.

"The night before I arrived, there had been a fresh happening and they were all in a frightfully nervy state, as you can imagine.

"I spent most of the first day, as I have hinted, in getting hold of details; but after dinner I slacked off and played billiards all the evening with Beaumont and Miss Hisgins. We stopped about ten o'clock and had coffee and I got Beaumont to give me full particulars about the thing that had happened the evening before.

"He and Miss Hisgins had been sitting quietly in her aunt's *boudoir* whilst the old lady chaperoned them, behind a book. It was growing dusk and the lamp was at her end of the table. The rest of the house was not yet lit as the evening had come earlier than usual.

"Well, it seems that the door into the hall was open and suddenly the girl said: 'H'sh! what's that?'

"They both listened and then Beaumont heard it—the sound of a horse outside of the front door.

"'Your father?' he suggested, but she reminded him that her father was not riding.

"Of course they were both ready to feel queer, as you can suppose, but Beaumont made an effort to shake this off and went into the hall to see whether anyone was at the entrance. It was pretty dark in the hall and he could see the glass panels of the inner draft door, clear-cut in the darkness of the hall. He walked over to the glass and looked through into the drive beyond, but there nothing in sight.

"He felt nervous and puzzled and opened the inner door and went out on to the carriage-circle. Almost directly afterward the great hall door swung to with a crash behind him. He told me that he had a sudden awful feeling of having been trapped in some way—that is how he put it. He whirled 'round and gripped the door handle, but something seemed to be holding it with a vast grip on the other side.

Then, before he could be fixed in his mind that this was so, he was able to turn the handle and open the door.

"He paused a moment in the doorway and peered into the hall, for he had hardly steadied his mind sufficiently to know whether he was really frightened or not. Then he heard his sweetheart blow him a kiss out of the greyness of the big, unlit hall and he knew that she had followed him from the *boudoir*. He blew her a kiss back and stepped inside the doorway, meaning to go to her. And then, suddenly, in a flash of sickening knowledge he knew that it was not his sweetheart who had blown him that kiss. He knew that something was trying to tempt him alone into the darkness and that the girl had never left the *boudoir*. He jumped back and in the same instant of time he heard the kiss again, nearer to him. He called out at the top of his voice: 'Mary, stay in the *boudoir*. Don't move out of the *boudoir* until I come to you.' He heard her call something in reply from the *boudoir* and then he had struck a clump of a dozen or so matches and was holding them above his head and looking 'round the hall. There was no one in it, but even as the matches burned out there came the sounds of a great horse galloping down the empty drive.

"Now you see, both he and the girl had heard the sounds of the horse galloping; but when I questioned more closely I found that the aunt had heard nothing, though it is true she is a bit deaf, and she was further back in the room. Of course, both he and Miss Hisgins had been in an extremely nervous state and ready to hear anything. The door might have been slammed by a sudden puff of wind owing to some inner door being opened; and as for the grip on the handle, that may have been nothing more than the snick catching.

"With regard to the kisses and the sounds of the horse galloping, I pointed out that these might have seemed ordinary enough sounds, if they had been only cool enough to reason. As I told him, and as he knew, the sounds of a horse galloping carry a long way on the wind so that what he had heard might have been nothing more than a horse being ridden some distance away. And as for the kiss, plenty of quiet noises—the rustle of a paper or a leaf—have a somewhat similar sound, especially if one is in an overstrung condition and imagining things.

"I finished preaching this little sermon on commonsense versus hysteria as we put out the lights and left the billiard room. But neither Beaumont nor Miss Hisgins would agree that there had been any fancy on their parts.

"We had come out of the billiard room by this time and were going along the passage and I was still doing my best to make both of them see the ordinary, commonplace possibilities of the happening, when what killed my pig, as the saying goes, was the sound of a hoof in the dark billiard room we had just left.

"I felt the 'creep' come on me in a flash, up my spine and over the back of my head. Miss Hisgins whooped like a child with the whooping cough and ran up the passage, giving little gasping screams. Beaumont, however, ripped 'round on his heels and jumped back a couple of yards. I gave back too, a bit, as you can understand.

"'There it is,' he said in a low, breathless voice. 'Perhaps you'll believe now.'

"'There's certainly something,' I whispered, never taking my gaze off the closed door of the billiard room.

"'H'sh!' he muttered. 'There it is again.'

"There was a sound like a great horse pacing 'round and 'round the billiard room with slow, deliberate steps. A horrible cold fright took me so that it seemed impossible to take a full breath, you know the feeling, and then I saw we must have been walking backward for we found ourselves suddenly at the opening of the long passage.

"We stopped there and listened. The sounds went on steadily with a horrible sort of deliberateness, as if the brute were taking a sort of malicious gusto in walking about all over the room which we had just occupied. Do you understand just what I mean?

"Then there was a pause and a long time of absolute quiet except for an excited whispering from some of the people down in the big hall. The sound came plainly up the wide stairway. I fancy they were gathered 'round Miss Hisgins, with some notion of protecting her.

"I should think Beaumont and I stood there, at the end of the passage for about five minutes, listening for any noise in the billiard room. Then I realised what a horrible funk I was in and I said to him: 'I'm going to see what's there.'

"'So'm I,' he answered. He was pretty white, but he had heaps of pluck. I told him to wait one instant and I made a dash into my bedroom and got my camera and flashlight. I slipped my revolver into my right-hand pocket and a knuckle-duster over my left fist, where it was ready and yet would not stop me from being able to work my flashlight.

"Then I ran back to Beaumont. He held out his hand to show me that he had his pistol and I nodded, but whispered to him not to be too quick to shoot, as there might be some silly practical joking at work, after all. He had got a lamp from a bracket in the upper hall which he was holding in the crook of his damaged arm, so that we had a good light. Then we went down the passage toward the billiard room and you can imagine that we were a pretty nervous couple.

"All this time there had not been a sound, but abruptly when we were within perhaps a couple of yards of the door we heard the sudden clumping of a hoof on the solid *parquet* floor of the billiard room. In the instant afterward it seemed to me that the whole place shook beneath the ponderous hoof falls of some huge thing, *coming toward the door*. Both Beaumont and I gave back a pace or two, and then realised and hung on to our courage, as you might say, and waited. The great tread came right up to the door and then stopped and there was an instant of absolute silence, except that so far as I was concerned, the pulsing in my throat and temples almost deafened me.

"I dare say we waited quite half a minute and then came the further restless clumping of a great hoof. Immediately afterward the sounds came right on as if some invisible thing passed through the closed door and the ponderous tread was upon us. We jumped, each of us, to our side of the passage and I know that I spread myself stiff against the wall. The *clungk clunck, clungk clunck*, of the great hoof falls passed right between us and slowly and with deadly deliberateness, down the passage. I heard them through a haze of blood beats in my ears and temples and my body was extraordinarily rigid and pringling and I was horribly breathless. I stood for a little time like this, my head turned so that I could see up the passage. I was conscious only that there was a hideous danger abroad. Do you understand?

"And then, suddenly, my pluck came back to me. I was aware that the noise of the hoof beats sounded near the other end of the passage. I twisted quickly and got my camera to bear and snapped off the flashlight. Immediately afterward, Beaumont let fly a storm of shots down the passage and began to run, shouting: 'It's after Mary. Run! Run!'

"He rushed down the passage and I after him. We came out on the main landing and heard the sound of a hoof on the stairs and after that, nothing. And from thence onward, nothing.

"Down below us in the big hall I could see a number of the household 'round Miss Hisgins, who seemed to have fainted and there were several of the servants clumped together a little way off, staring up at the main landing and no one saying a single word. And about some twenty steps up the stairs was the old Captain Hisgins with a drawn sword in his hand where he had halted, just below the last hoof sound. I think I never saw anything finer than the old man standing there between his daughter and that infernal thing.

"I daresay you can understand the queer feeling of horror I had at passing that place on the stairs where the sounds had ceased. It was as if the monster were still standing there, invisible. And the peculiar thing was that we never heard another sound of the hoof, either up or down the stairs.

"After they had taken Miss Hisgins to her room I sent word that I should follow, so soon as they were ready for me. And presently, when a message came to tell me that I could come any time, I asked her father to give me a hand with my instrument box and between us we carried it into the girl's bedroom. I had the bed pulled well out into the middle of the room, after which I erected the electric pentacle 'round the bed.

"Then I directed that lamps should be placed 'round the room, but that on no account must any light be made within the pentacle; neither must anyone pass in or out. The girl's mother I had placed within the pentacle and directed that her maid should sit without, ready to carry any message so as to make sure that Mrs. Hisgins did not have to leave the pentacle. I suggested also that the girl's father should stay the night in the room and that he had better be armed.

"When I left the bedroom I found Beaumont waiting outside the door in a miserable state of anxiety. I told him what I had done and explained to him that Miss Hisgins was probably perfectly safe within the 'protection'; but that in addition to her father remaining the night in the room, I intended to stand guard at the door. I told him that I should like him to keep me company, for I knew that he could never sleep, feeling as he did, and I should not be sorry to have a companion. Also, I wanted to have him under my own observation, for there was no doubt but that he was actually in greater danger in some ways than the girl. At least, that was my opinion and is still, as I think you will agree later.

"I asked him whether he would object to my drawing a pentacle 'round him for the night and got him to agree, but I saw that he did not know whether to be superstitious about it or to regard it more as a piece of foolish mumming; but he took it seriously enough when I gave him some particulars about the Black Veil case, when young Aster died. You remember, he said it was a piece of silly superstition and stayed outside. Poor devil!

"The night passed quietly enough until a little while before dawn when we both heard the sounds of a great horse galloping 'round and 'round the house just as old Captain Hisgins had described it. You can imagine how queer it made me feel and directly afterward, I heard someone stir within the bedroom. I knocked at the door, for I was uneasy, and the captain came. I asked whether everything was right; to which he replied yes, and immediately asked me whether I had heard the galloping, so that I knew he had heard them also. I suggested that it might be well to leave the bedroom door open a little until the dawn came in, as there was certainly something abroad. This was done and he went back into the room, to be near his wife and daughter.

"I had better say here that I was doubtful whether there was any value in the 'Defence' about Miss Hisgins, for what I term the 'personal sounds' of the manifestation were so extraordinarily material that I was inclined to parallel the case with that one of Harford's where the hand of the child kept materializing within the pentacle and patting the floor. As you will remember, that was a hideous business.

"Yet, as it chanced, nothing further happened and so soon as daylight had fully come we all went off to bed.

"Beaumont knocked me up about midday and I went down and made breakfast into lunch. Miss Hisgins was there and seemed in very fair spirits, considering. She told me that I had made her feel almost safe for the first time for days. She told me also that her cousin, Harry Parsket, was coming down from London and she knew that he would do anything to help fight the ghost. And after that she and Beaumont went out into the grounds to have a little time together.

"I had a walk in the grounds myself and went 'round the house, but saw no traces of hoof marks and after that I spent the rest of the day making an examination of the house, but found nothing.

"I made an end of my search before dark and went to my room to dress for dinner. When I got down the cousin had just arrived and I found him one of the nicest men I have met for a long time. A chap with a tremendous amount of pluck, and the particular kind of man I like to have with me in a bad case like the one I was on. I could see that what puzzled him most was our belief in the genuineness of the haunting and I found myself almost wanting something to happen, just to show him how true it was. As it chanced, something did happen, with a vengeance.

"Beaumont and Miss Hisgins had gone out for a stroll just before the dusk and Captain Hisgins asked me to come into his study for a short chat whilst Parsket went upstairs with his traps, for he had no man with him.

"I had a long conversation with the old captain in which I pointed out that the 'haunting' had evidently no particular connection with the house, but only with the girl herself and that the sooner she was married, the better as it would give Beaumont a right to be with her at all times and further than this, it might be that the manifestations would cease if the marriage were actually performed.

"The old man nodded agreement to this, especially to the first part and reminded me that three of the girls who were said to have been 'haunted' had been sent away from home and met their deaths whilst away. And then in the midst of our talk there came a pretty frightening interruption, for all at once the old butler rushed into the room, most extraordinarily pale:

"'Miss Mary, sir! Miss Mary, sir!' he gasped. 'She's screaming . . . out in the park, sir! And they say they can hear the Horse—'

"The captain made one dive for a rack of arms and snatched down his old sword and ran out, drawing it as he ran. I dashed out and up the stairs, snatched my camera-flashlight and a heavy revolver, gave one yell at Parsket's door: 'The Horse!' and was down and into the grounds.

"Away in the darkness there was a confused shouting and I caught the sounds of shooting, out among the scattered trees. And then, from a patch of blackness to my left, there burst suddenly an infernal gobbling sort of neighing. Instantly I whipped 'round and snapped off the flashlight. The great light blazed out momentarily, showing me the leaves of a big tree close at hand, quivering in the night breeze, but I saw nothing else and then the ten-fold blackness came down upon me and I heard Parsket shouting a little way back to know whether I had seen anything.

"The next instant he was beside me and I felt safer for his company, for there was some incredible thing near to us and I was momentarily blind because of the brightness of the flashlight. 'What was it? What was it?' he kept repeating in an excited voice. And all the time I was staring into the darkness and answering, mechanically, 'I don't know. I don't know.'

"There was a burst of shouting somewhere ahead and then a shot. We ran toward the sounds, yelling to the people not to shoot; for in the darkness and panic there was this danger also. Then there came two of the game-keepers racing hard up the drive with their lanterns and guns; and immediately afterward a row of lights dancing toward us from the house, carried by some of the men-servants.

"As the lights came up I saw we had come close to Beaumont. He was standing over Miss Hisgins and he had his revolver in his hand. Then I saw his face and there was a great wound across his forehead. By him was the captain, turning his naked sword this way and that, and peering into the darkness; a little behind him stood the old butler, a battle-axe from one of the arm stands in the hall in his hands. Yet there was nothing strange to be seen anywhere.

"We got the girl into the house and left her with her mother and Beaumont, whilst a groom rode for a doctor. And then the rest of us, with four other keepers, all armed with guns and carrying lanterns, searched 'round the home park. But we found nothing.

"When we got back we found that the doctor had been. He had bound up Beaumont's wound, which luckily was not deep, and ordered Miss Hisgins straight to bed. I went upstairs with the captain and found Beaumont on guard outside of the girl's door. I asked him how he felt and then, so soon as the girl and her mother were ready for us, Captain Hisgins and I went into the bedroom and fixed the pentacle again 'round the bed. They had already got lamps about the room and after I had set the same order of watching as on the previous night, I joined Beaumont outside of the door.

"Parset had come up while I had been in the bedroom and between us we got some idea from Beaumont as to what had happened out in the park. It seems that they were coming home after their stroll from the direction of the West Lodge. It had got quite dark and suddenly Miss Hisgins said: 'Hush!' and came to a standstill. He stopped and listened, but heard nothing for a little. Then he caught it—the sound of a horse, seemingly a long way off, galloping toward them over the grass. He told the girl that it was nothing and started to hurry her toward the house, but she was not deceived, of course. In less than a minute they heard it quite close to them in the darkness and they started running. Then Miss Hisgins caught her foot and fell. She began to scream and that is what the butler heard.

"As Beaumont lifted the girl he heard the hoofs come thudding right at him. He stood over her and fired all five chambers of his revolver right at the sounds. He told us that he was sure he saw something that looked like an enormous horse's head, right upon him in the light of the last flash of his pistol. Immediately afterward he was struck a tremendous blow which knocked him down and then the captain and the butler came running up, shouting. The rest, of course, we knew.

"About ten o'clock the butler brought us up a tray, for which I was very glad, as the night before I had got rather hungry. I warned Beaumont, however, to be very particular not to drink any spirits and I also made him give me his pipe and matches. At midnight I drew a pentacle 'round him and Parset and I sat one on each side of him, outside the pentacle, for I had no fear that there would be any manifestation made against anyone except Beaumont or Miss Hisgins.

"After that we kept pretty quiet. The passage was lit by a big lamp at each end so that we had plenty of light and we were all armed, Beaumont and I with revolvers and Parset with a shotgun. In addition to my weapon I had my camera and flashlight.

"Now and again we talked in whispers and twice the captain came out of the bedroom to have a word with us. About half-past one we had all grown very silent and suddenly, about twenty minutes later, I held up my hand, silently, for there seemed to be a sound of galloping out in the night. I knocked on the bedroom door for the captain to open it and when he came I whispered to him that we thought we heard the Horse. For some time we stayed listening, and both Parset and the captain thought they heard it; but now I was not so sure, neither was Beaumont. Yet afterward, I thought I heard it again.

"I told Captain Hisgins I thought he had better go into the bedroom and leave the door a little open and this he did. But from that time onward we heard nothing and presently the dawn came in and we all went very thankfully to bed.

"When I was called at lunchtime I had a little surprise, for Captain Hisgins told me that they had held a family council and had decided to take my advice and have the marriage without a day's more delay than possible. Beaumont was already on his way to London to get a special license and they hoped to have the wedding next day.

"This pleased me, for it seemed the sanest thing to be done in the extraordinary circumstances and meanwhile I should continue my investigations; but until the marriage was accomplished, my chief thought was to keep Miss Hisgins near to me.

"After lunch I thought I would take a few experimental photographs of Miss Hisgins and her *surroundings*. Sometimes the camera sees things that would seem very strange to normal human eyesight.

"With this intention and partly to make an excuse to keep her in my company as much as possible, I asked Miss Hisgins to join me in my experiments. She seemed glad to do this and I spent several hours with her, wandering all over the house, from room to room and whenever the impulse came I took a flashlight of her and the room or corridor in which we chanced to be at the moment.

"After we had gone right through the house in this fashion, I asked her whether she felt sufficiently brave to repeat the experiments in the cellars. She said yes, and so I rooted out Captain Hisgins and Parsket, for I was not going to take her even into what you might call artificial darkness without help and companionship at hand.

"When we were ready we went down into the wine cellar, Captain Hisgins carrying a shotgun and Parsket a specially prepared background and a lantern. I got the girl to stand in the middle of the cellar whilst Parsket and the captain held out the background behind her. Then I fired off the flashlight, and we went into the next cellar where we repeated the experiment.

"Then in the third cellar, a tremendous, pitch-dark place, something extraordinary and horrible manifested itself. I had stationed Miss Hisgins in the centre of the place, with her father and Parsket holding the background as before. When all was ready and just as I pressed the trigger of the 'flash,' there came in the cellar that dreadful, gobbling neighing that I had heard out in the park. It seemed to come from somewhere above the girl and in the glare of the sudden light I saw that she was staring tensely upward, but at no visible thing. And then in the succeeding comparative darkness, I was shouting to the captain and Parsket to run Miss Hisgins out into the daylight.

"This was done instantly and I shut and locked the door afterward making the First and Eighth signs of the *Saaamaaa* Ritual opposite to each post and connecting them across the threshold with a triple line.

"In the meanwhile Parsket and Captain Hisgins carried the girl to her mother and left her there, in a half fainting condition whilst I stayed on guard outside of the cellar door, feeling pretty horrible for I knew that there was some disgusting thing inside, and along with this feeling there was a sense of half ashamedness, rather miserable, you know, because I had exposed Miss Hisgins to the danger.

"I had got the captain's shotgun and when he and Parsket came down again they were each carrying guns and lanterns. I could not possibly tell you the utter relief of spirit and body that came to me when I heard them coming, but just try to imagine what it was like, standing outside of that cellar. Can you?

94

"I remember noticing, just before I went to unlock the door, how white and ghastly Parsket looked and the old captain was grey-looking and I wondered whether my face was like theirs. And this, you know, had its own distinct effect upon my nerves, for it seemed to bring the beastliness of the thing crash down on to me in a fresh way. I know it was only sheer will power that carried me up to the door and made me turn the key.

"I paused one little moment and then with a nervy jerk sent the door wide open and held my lantern over my head. Parsket and the captain came one on each side of me and held up their lanterns, but the place was absolutely empty. Of course, I did not trust to a casual look of this kind, but spent several hours with the help of the two others in sounding every square foot of the floor, ceiling and walls.

"Yet, in the end I had to admit that the place itself was absolutely normal and so we came away. But I sealed the door and outside, opposite each doorpost I made the first and last signs of the *Saaamaaa* Ritual, joined them as before, with a triple line. Can you imagine what it was like, searching that cellar?

"When we got upstairs I inquired very anxiously how Miss Hisgins was and the girl came out herself to tell me that she was all right and that I was not to trouble about her, or blame myself, as I told her I had been doing.

"I felt happier then and went off to dress for dinner and after that was done, Parsket and I took one of the bathrooms to develop the negatives that I had been taking. Yet none of the plates had anything to tell us until we came to the one that was taken in the cellar. Parsket was developing and I had taken a batch of the fixed plates out into the lamplight to examine them.

"I had just gone carefully through the lot when I heard a shout from Parsket and when I ran to him he was looking at a partly-developed negative which he was holding up to the red lamp. It showed the girl plainly, looking upward as I had seen her, but the thing that astonished me was the shadow of an enormous hoof, right above her, as if it were coming down upon her out of the shadows. And you know, I had run her bang into that danger. That was the thought that was chief in my mind.

"As soon as the developing was complete I fixed the plate and examined it carefully in a good light. There was no doubt about it at all, the thing above Miss Hisgins was an enormous, shadowy hoof. Yet I was no nearer to coming to any definite knowledge and the only thing I could do was to warn Parsket to say nothing about it to the girl for it would only increase her fright, but I showed the thing to her father for I considered it right that he should know.

"That night we took the same precaution for Miss Hisgins's safety as on the two previous nights and Parsket kept me company; yet the dawn came in without anything unusual having happened and I went off to bed.

"When I got down to lunch I learnt that Beaumont had wired to say that he would be in soon after four; also that a message had been sent to the rector. And it was generally plain that the ladies of the house were in a tremendous fluster.

"Beaumont's train was late and he did not get home until five, but even then the rector had not put in an appearance and the butler came in to say that the coachman had returned without him as he had been called away unexpectedly. Twice more during the evening the carriage was sent down, but the clergyman had not returned and we had to delay the marriage until the next day.

"That night I arranged the 'Defence' 'round the girl's bed and the captain and his wife sat up with her as before. Beaumont, as I expected, insisted on keeping watch with me and he seemed in a curiously frightened mood; not for himself, you know, but for Miss Hisgins. He had a horrible feeling he told me, that there would be a final, dreadful attempt on his sweetheart that night.

"This, of course, I told him was nothing but nerves; yet really, it made me feel very anxious; for I have seen too much not to know that under such circumstances a premonitory *conviction* of impending danger is not necessarily to be put down entirely to nerves. In fact, Beaumont was so simply and earnestly convinced that the night would bring some extraordinary manifestation that I got Parsket to rig up a long cord from the wire of the butler's bell, to come along the passage handy.

"To the butler himself I gave directions not to undress and to give the same order to two of the footmen. If I rang he was to come instantly, with the footmen, carrying lanterns and the lanterns were to be kept ready lit all night. If for any reason the bell did not ring and I blew my whistle, he was to take that as a signal in the place of the bell.

"After I had arranged all these minor details I drew a pentacle about Beaumont and warned him very particularly to stay within it, whatever happened. And when this was done, there was nothing to do but wait and pray that the night would go as quietly as the night before.

"We scarcely talked at all and by about one a.m. we were all very tense and nervous so that at last Parsket got up and began to walk up and down the corridor to steady himself a bit. Presently I slipped off my pumps and joined him and we walked up and down, whispering occasionally for something over an hour, until in turning I caught my foot in the bell cord and went down on my face; but without hurting myself or making a noise.

"When I got up Parsket nudged me.

"'Did you notice that the bell never rang?' he whispered.

"'Jove!' I said, 'you're right.'

"'Wait a minute,' he answered. 'I'll bet it's only a kink somewhere in the cord.' He left his gun and slipped along the passage and taking the top lamp, tiptoed away into the house, carrying Beaumont's revolver ready in his right hand. He was a plucky chap, I remember thinking then, and again, later.

"Just then Beaumont motioned to me for absolute quiet. Directly afterward I heard the thing for which he listened—the sound of a horse galloping, out in the night. I think that I may say I fairly shivered. The sound died away and left a horrible, desolate, eerie feeling in the air, you know. I put my hand out to the bell cord, hoping Parsket had got it clear. Then I waited, glancing before and behind.

"Perhaps two minutes passed, full of what seemed like an almost unearthly quiet. And then, suddenly, down the corridor at the lighted end there sounded the clumping of a great hoof and instantly the lamp was thrown with a tremendous crash and we were in the dark. I tugged hard on the cord and blew the whistle; then I raised my snapshot and fired the flashlight. The corridor blazed into brilliant light, but there was nothing, and then the darkness fell like thunder. I heard the captain at the bedroom door and shouted to him to bring out a lamp, *quick*; but instead something started to kick the door and I heard the captain shouting within the bedroom and then the screaming of the women.

"I had a sudden horrible fear that the monster had got into the bedroom, but in the same instant from up the corridor there came abruptly the vile, gobbling neighing that we had heard in the park and the cellar. I blew the whistle again and groped blindly for the bell cord, shouting to Beaumont to stay in the Pentacle, whatever happened. I yelled again to the captain to bring out a lamp and there came a smashing sound against the bedroom door. Then I had my matches in my hand, to get some light before that incredible, unseen monster was upon us.

"The match scraped on the box and flared up dully and in the same instant I heard a faint sound behind me. I whipped 'round in a kind of mad terror and saw something in the light of the match—a monstrous horse-head close to Beaumont.

"'Look out, Beaumont!' I shouted in a sort of scream. 'It's behind you!'

"The match went out abruptly and instantly there came the huge bang of Parsket's double-barrel (both barrels at once), fired evidently single-handed by Beaumont close to my ear, as it seemed. I caught a momentary glimpse of the great head in the flash and of an enormous hoof amid the belch of fire and smoke seeming to be descending upon Beaumont. In the same instant I fired three chambers of my revolver. There was the sound of a dull blow and then that horrible, gobbling neigh broke out close to me. I fired twice at the sound. Immediately afterward something struck me and I was knocked backward. I got on to my knees and shouted for help at the top of my voice. I heard the women screaming behind the closed door of the bedroom and was dully aware that the door was being smashed from the inside, and directly afterward I knew that Beaumont was struggling with some hideous thing near to me.

"For an instant I held back, stupidly, paralyzed with funk and then, blindly and in a sort of rigid chill of goose flesh I went to help him, shouting his name. I can tell you, I was nearly sick with the naked fear I had on me. There came a little, choking scream out of the darkness, and at that I jumped forward into the dark. I gripped a vast, furry ear. Then something struck me another great blow knocking me sick. I hit back, weak and blind and gripped with my other hand at the incredible thing. Abruptly I was dimly aware of a tremendous crash behind me and a great burst of light. There were other lights in the passage and a noise of feet and shouting. My hand-grips were torn from the thing they held; I shut my eyes stupidly and heard a loud yell above me and then a heavy blow, like a butcher chopping meat and then something fell upon me.

"I was helped to my knees by the captain and the butler. On the floor lay an enormous horse-head out of which protruded a man's trunk and legs. On the wrists were fixed great hoofs. It was the monster. The captain cut something with the sword that he held in his hand and stooped and lifted off the mask, for that is what it was. I saw the face then of the man who had worn it. It was Parsket. He had a bad wound across the forehead where the captain's sword had bit through the mask. I looked bewilderedly from him to Beaumont, who was sitting up, leaning against the wall of the corridor. Then I stared at Parsket again.

"'By Jove!' I said at last, and then I was quiet for I was so ashamed for the man. You can understand, can't you? And he was opening his eyes. And you know, I had grown so to like him.

"And then, you know, just as Parsket was getting back his wits and looking from one to the other of us and beginning to remember, there happened a strange and incredible thing. For from the end of the corridor there sounded suddenly, the clumping of a great hoof. I looked that way and then instantly at Parsket and saw a horrible fear in his face and eyes. He wrenched himself 'round, weakly, and stared in mad terror up the corridor to where the sound had been, and the rest of us stared, in a frozen group. I remember vaguely half sobs and whispers from Miss Hisgins's bedroom, all the while that I stared frightenedly up the corridor.

"The silence lasted several seconds and then, abruptly there came again the clumping of the great hoof, away at the end of the corridor. And immediately afterward the *clungk, clunk—clungk, clunk* of mighty hoofs coming down the passage toward us.

"Even then, you know, most of us thought it was some mechanism of Parsket's still at work and we were in the queerest mixture of fright and doubt. I think everyone looked at Parsket. And suddenly the captain shouted out:

"'Stop this damned fooling at once. Haven't you done enough?'

"For my part, I was now frightened for I had a *sense* that there was something horrible and wrong. And then Parsket managed to gasp out:

"'It's not me! My God! It's not me! My God! It's not me.'

"And then, you know, it seemed to come home to everyone in an instant that there was really some dreadful thing coming down the passage. There was a mad rush to get away and even old Captain Hisgins gave back with the butler and the footmen. Beaumont fainted outright, as I found afterward, for he had been badly mauled. I just flattened back against the wall, kneeling as I was, too stupid and dazed even to run. And almost in the same instant the ponderous hoof falls sounded close to me and seeming to shake the solid floor as they passed. Abruptly the great sounds ceased and I knew in a sort of sick fashion that the thing had halted opposite to the door of the girl's bedroom.

"And then I was aware that Parsket was standing rocking in the doorway with his arms spread across, so as to fill the doorway with his body. Parsket was extraordinarily pale and the blood was running down his face from the wound in his forehead; and then I noticed that he seemed to be looking at something in the passage with a peculiar, desperate, fixed, incredibly masterful gaze. But there was really nothing to be seen. And suddenly the *clungk, clunk—clungk, clunk* recommenced and passed onward down the passage. In the same moment Parsket pitched forward out of the doorway on to his face.

"There were shouts from the huddle of men down the passage and the two footmen and the butler simply ran, carrying their lanterns, but the captain went against the side-wall with his back and put the lamp he was carrying over his head. The dull tread of the Horse went past him, and left him unharmed and I heard the monstrous hoof falls going away and away through the quiet house and after that a dead silence.

"Then the captain moved and came toward us, very slow and shaky and with an extraordinarily grey face.

"I crept toward Parsket and the captain came to help me. We turned him over and, you know, I knew in a moment that he was dead; but you can imagine what a feeling it sent through me.

"I looked at the captain and suddenly he said:

"'That—That—That—' and I know that he was trying to tell me that Parsket had stood between his daughter and whatever it was that had gone down the passage. I stood up and steadied him, though I was not very steady myself. And suddenly his face began to work and he went down on to his knees by Parsket and cried like some shaken child. Then the women came out of the doorway of the bedroom and I turned away and left him to them, whilst I over to Beaumont.

"That is practically the whole story and the only thing that is left to me is to try to explain some of the puzzling parts, here and there.

"Perhaps you have seen that Parsket was in love with Miss Hisgins and this fact is the key to a good deal that was extraordinary. He was doubtless responsible for some portions of the 'haunting'; in fact I think for nearly everything, but, you know, I can prove nothing and what I have to tell you is chiefly the result of deduction.

"In the first place, it is obvious that Parsket's intention was to frighten Beaumont away and when he found that he could not do this, I think he grew so desperate that he really intended to kill him. I hate to say this, but the facts force me to think so.

"I am quite certain that it was Parsket who broke Beaumont's arm. He knew all the details of the so-called 'Horse Legend,' and got the idea to work upon the old story for his own end. He evidently had some method of slipping in and out of the house, probably through one of the many French windows, or possibly he had a key to one or two of the garden doors, and when he was supposed to be away, he was really coming down on the quiet and hiding somewhere in the neighbourhood.

"The incident of the kiss in the dark hall I put down to sheer nervous imaginings on the part of Beaumont and Miss Hisgins, yet I must say that the sound of the horse outside of the front door is a little difficult to explain away. But I am still inclined to keep to my first idea on this point, that there was nothing really unnatural about it.

"The hoof sounds in the billiard room and down the passage were done by Parsket from the floor below by bumping up against the panelled ceiling with a block of wood tied to one of the window hooks. I proved this by an examination which showed the dents in the woodwork.

"The sounds of the horse galloping 'round the house were possibly made also by Parsket, who must have had a horse tied up in the plantation nearby, unless, indeed, he made the sounds himself, but I do not see how he could have gone fast enough to produce the illusion. In any case, I don't feel perfect certainty on this point. I failed to find any hoof marks, as you remember.

"The gobbling neighing in the park was a ventriloquial achievement on the part of Parsket and the attack out there on Beaumont was also by him, so that when I thought he was in his bedroom, he must have been outside all the time and joined me after I ran out of the front door. This is almost probable. I mean that Parsket was the cause, for if it had been something more serious he would certainly have given up his foolishness, knowing that there was no longer any need for it. I cannot imagine how he escaped being shot, both then and in the last mad action of which I have just told you. He was enormously without fear of any kind for himself as you can see.

"The time when Parsket was with us, when we thought we heard the Horse galloping 'round the house, we must have been deceived. No one was very sure, except, of course, Parsket, who would naturally encourage the belief.

"The neighing in the cellar is where I consider there came the first suspicion into Parset's mind that there was something more at work than his sham haunting. The neighing was done by him in the same way that he did it in the park; but when I remember how ghastly he looked I feel sure that the sounds must have had some infernal quality added to them which frightened the man himself. Yet, later, he would persuade himself that he had been getting fanciful. Of course, I must not forget that the effect upon Miss Hisgins must have made him feel pretty miserable.

"Then, about the clergyman being called away, we found afterward that it was a bogus errand, or, rather, call and it is apparent that Parset was at the bottom of this, so as to get a few more hours in which to achieve his end and what that was, a very little imagination will show you; for he had found that Beaumont would not be frightened away. I hate to think this, but I'm bound to. Anyway, it is obvious that the man was temporarily a bit off his normal balance. Love's a queer disease!

"Then, there is no doubt at all but that Parset left the cord to the butler's bell hitched somewhere so as to give him an excuse to slip away naturally to clear it. This also gave him the opportunity to remove one of the passage lamps. Then he had only to smash the other and the passage was in utter darkness for him to make the attempt on Beaumont.

"In the same way, it was he who locked the door of the bedroom and took the key (it was in his pocket). This prevented the captain from bringing a light and coming to the rescue. But Captain Hisgins broke down the door with the heavy fender curb and it was his smashing the door that sounded so confusing and frightening in the darkness of the passage.

"The photograph of the monstrous hoof above Miss Hisgins in the cellar is one of the things that I am less sure about. It might have been faked by Parset, whilst I was out of the room, and this would have been easy enough, to anyone who knew how. But, you know, it does not look like a fake. Yet, there is as much evidence of probability that it was faked, as against; and the thing is too vague for an examination to help to a definite decision so that I will express no opinion, one way or the other. It is certainly a horrible photograph.

"And now I come to that last, dreadful thing. There has been no further manifestation of anything abnormal so that there is an extraordinary uncertainty in my conclusions. If we had not heard those last sounds and if Parsket had not shown that enormous sense of fear the whole of this case could be explained in the way in which I have shown. And, in fact, as you have seen, I am of the opinion that almost all of it can be cleared up, but I see no way of going past the thing we heard at the last and the fear that Parsket showed.

"His death—no, that proves nothing. At the inquest it was described somewhat untechnically as due to heart spasm. That is normal enough and leaves us quite in the dark as to whether he died because he stood between the girl and some incredible thing of monstrosity.

"The look on Parsket's face and the thing he called out when he heard the great hoof sounds coming down the passage seem to show that he had the sudden realisation of what before then may have been nothing more than a horrible suspicion. And his fear and appreciation of some tremendous danger approaching was probably more keenly real even than mine. And then he did the one fine, great thing!"

"And the cause?" I said. "What caused it?"

Carnacki shook his head.

"God knows," he answered, with a peculiar, sincere reverence. "If that thing was what it seemed to be one might suggest an explanation which would not offend one's reason, but which may be utterly wrong. Yet I have thought, though it would take a long lecture on Thought Induction to get you to appreciate my reasons, that Parsket had produced what I might term a kind of 'induced haunting,' a kind of induced simulation of his mental conceptions to his desperate thoughts and broodings. It is impossible to make it clearer in a few words."

"But the old story!" I said. "Why may not there have been something in *that*?"

"There may have been something in it," said Carnacki. "But I do not think it had anything to do with this. I have not clearly thought out my reasons, yet; but later I may be able to tell you why I think so."

"And the marriage? And the cellar—was there anything found there?" asked Taylor.

"Yes, the marriage was performed that day in spite of the tragedy," Carnacki told us. "It was the wisest thing to do considering the things that I cannot explain. Yes, I had the floor of that big cellar up, for I had a feeling I might find something there to give me some light. But there was nothing.

"You know, the whole thing is tremendous and extraordinary. I shall never forget the look on Parsket's face. And afterward the disgusting sounds of those great hoofs going away through the quiet house."

Carnacki stood up.

"Out you go!" he said in friendly fashion, using the recognised formula.

And we went presently out into the quiet of the Embankment, and so to our homes.

The Beetle, Book 4: In Pursuit

Richard Marsh

The Conclusion of the Matter is Extracted From the Case-Book of the Hon. Augustus Champnell, Confidential Agent.

Chapter 1: A New Client

On the afternoon of Friday, June 2, 18—, I was entering in my casebook some memoranda having reference to the very curious matter of the Duchess of Datchet's Deed-box. It was about two o'clock. Andrews came in and laid a card upon my desk. On it was inscribed 'Mr. Paul Lessingham.'

'Show Mr. Lessingham in.'

Andrews showed him in. I was, of course, familiar with Mr. Lessingham's appearance, but it was the first time I had had with him any personal communication. He held out his hand to me.

'You are Mr. Champnell?'

'I am.'

'I believe that I have not had the honour of meeting you before, Mr. Champnell, but with your father, the Earl of Glenlivet, I have the pleasure of some acquaintance.'

I bowed. He looked at me, fixedly, as if he were trying to make out what sort of man I was. 'You are very young, Mr. Champnell.'

'I have been told that an eminent offender in that respect once asserted that youth is not of necessity a crime.'

'And you have chosen a singular profession,—one in which one hardly looks for juvenility.'

'You yourself, Mr. Lessingham, are not old. In a statesman one expects grey hairs.—I trust that I am sufficiently ancient to be able to do you service.'

He smiled.

'I think it possible. I have heard of you more than once, Mr. Champnell, always to your advantage. My friend, Sir John Seymour, was telling me, only the other day, that you have recently conducted for him some business, of a very delicate nature, with much skill and tact; and he warmly advised me, if ever I found myself in a predicament, to come to you. I find myself in a predicament now.'

Again I bowed.

'A predicament, I fancy, of an altogether unparalleled sort. I take it that anything I may say to you will be as though it were said to a father confessor.'

'You may rest assured of that.'

'Good.—Then, to make the matter clear to you I must begin by telling you a story,—if I may trespass on your patience to that extent. I will endeavour not to be more verbose than the occasion requires.'

I offered him a chair, placing it in such a position that the light from the window would have shone full upon his face. With the calmest possible air, as if unconscious of my design, he carried the chair to the other side of my desk, twisting it right round before he sat on it,—so that now the light was at his back and on my face. Crossing his legs, clasping his hands about his knee, he sat in silence for some moments, as if turning something over in his mind. He glanced round the room.

'I suppose, Mr. Champnell, that some singular tales have been told in here.'

'Some very singular tales indeed. I am never appalled by singularity. It is my normal atmosphere.'

'And yet I should be disposed to wager that you have never listened to so strange a story as that which I am about to tell you now. So astonishing, indeed, is the chapter in my life which I am about to open out to you, that I have more than once had to take myself to task, and fit the incidents together with mathematical accuracy in order to assure myself of its perfect truth.'

He paused. There was about his demeanour that suggestion of reluctance which I not uncommonly discover in individuals who are about to take the skeletons from their cupboards and parade them before my eyes. His next remark seemed to point to the fact that he perceived what was passing through my thoughts.

'My position is not rendered easier by the circumstance that I am

106

not of a communicative nature. I am not in sympathy with the spirit of the age which craves for personal advertisement. I hold that the private life even of a public man should be held inviolate. I resent, with peculiar bitterness, the attempts of prying eyes to peer into matters which, as it seems to me, concern myself alone. You must, therefore, bear with me, Mr. Champnell, if I seem awkward in disclosing to you certain incidents in my career which I had hoped would continue locked in the secret depository of my own bosom, at any rate till I was carried to the grave. I am sure you will suffer me to stand excused if I frankly admit that it is only an irresistible chain of incidents which has constrained me to make of you a confidant.'

'My experience tells me, Mr. Lessingham, that no one ever does come to me until they are compelled. In that respect I am regarded as something worse even than a medical man.'

A wintry smile flitted across his features,—it was clear that he regarded me as a good deal worse than a medical man. Presently he began to tell me one of the most remarkable tales which even I had heard. As he proceeded I understood how strong, and how natural, had been his desire for reticence. On the mere score of credibility he must have greatly preferred to have kept his own counsel. For my part I own, unreservedly, that I should have deemed the tale incredible had it been told me by Tom, Dick, or Harry, instead of by Paul Lessingham.

CHAPTER 2: WHAT CAME OF LOOKING THROUGH A LATTICE

He began in accents which halted not a little. By degrees his voice grew firmer. Words came from him with greater fluency.

'I am not yet forty. So when I tell you that twenty years ago I was a mere youth I am stating what is a sufficiently obvious truth. It is twenty years ago since the events of which I am going to speak transpired.

'I lost both my parents when I was quite a lad, and by their death I was left in a position in which I was, to an unusual extent in one so young, my own master. I was ever of a rambling turn of mind, and when, at the mature age of eighteen, I left school, I decided that I should learn more from travel than from sojourn at a university. So, since there was no one to say me nay, instead of going either to Oxford or Cambridge, I went abroad. After a few months I found myself in Egypt,—I was down with fever at Shepheard's Hotel in Cairo. I had caught it by drinking polluted water during an excursion with some

Bedouins to Palmyra.

'When the fever had left me I went out one night into the town in search of amusement. I went, unaccompanied, into the native quarter, not a wise thing to do, especially at night, but at eighteen one is not always wise, and I was weary of the monotony of the sick-room, and eager for something which had in it a spice of adventure, I found myself in a street which I have reason to believe is no longer existing. It had a French name, and was called the Rue de Rabagas,—I saw the name on the corner as I turned into it, and it has left an impress on the tablets of my memory which is never likely to be obliterated.

'It was a narrow street, and, of course, a dirty one, ill-lit, and, apparently, at the moment of my appearance, deserted. I had gone, perhaps, half-way down its tortuous length, blundering more than once into the kennel, wondering what fantastic whim had brought me into such unsavoury quarters, and what would happen to me if, as seemed extremely possible, I lost my way. On a sudden my ears were saluted by sounds which proceeded from a house which I was passing,—sounds of music and of singing.

'I paused. I stood awhile to listen.

'There was an open window on my right, which was screened by latticed blinds. From the room which was behind these blinds the sounds were coming. Someone was singing, accompanied by an instrument resembling a guitar,—singing uncommonly well.'

Mr. Lessingham stopped. A stream of recollection seemed to come flooding over him. A dreamy look came into his eyes.

'I remember it all as clearly as if it were yesterday. How it all comes back,—the dirty street, the evil smells, the imperfect light, the girl's voice filling all at once the air. It was a girl's voice,—full, and round, and sweet; an organ seldom met with, especially in such a place as that. She sang a little *chansonnette*, which, just then, half Europe was humming,—it occurred in an opera which they were acting at one of the Boulevard theatres,—"*La P'tite Voyageuse.*" The effect, coming so unexpectedly, was startling. I stood and heard her to an end.

'Inspired by I know not what impulse of curiosity, when the song was finished, I moved one of the lattice blinds a little aside, so as to enable me to get a glimpse of the singer. I found myself looking into what seemed to be a sort of cafe,—one of those places which are found all over the Continent, in which women sing in order to attract custom. There was a low platform at one end of the room, and on it were seated three women. One of them had evidently just been accompanying her own song,—she still had an instrument of music in her hands, and was striking a few idle notes. The other two had been acting as audience. They were attired in the fantastic apparel which the women who are found in such places generally wear. An old woman was sitting knitting in a corner, whom I took to be the inevitable *patronne*. With the exception of these four the place was empty.

'They must have heard me touch the lattice, or seen it moving, for no sooner did I glance within than the three pairs of eyes on the platform were raised and fixed on mine. The old woman in the corner alone showed no consciousness of my neighbourhood. We eyed one another in silence for a second or two. Then the girl with the harp,— the instrument she was manipulating proved to be fashioned more like a harp than a guitar—called out to me,

'"*Entrez, monsieur!—Soye le bienvenu!*"

'I was a little tired. Rather curious as to whereabouts I was,—the place struck me, even at that first momentary glimpse, as hardly in the ordinary line of that kind of thing. And not unwilling to listen to a repetition of the former song, or to another sung by the same singer.

'"On condition," I replied, "that you sing me another song."

'"Ah, *monsieur*, with the greatest pleasure in the world I will sing you twenty."

'She was almost, if not quite, as good as her word. She entertained me with song after song. I may safely say that I have seldom if ever heard melody more enchanting. All languages seemed to be the same to her. She sang in French and Italian, German and English,—in tongues with which I was unfamiliar. It was in these Eastern harmonies that she was most successful. They were indescribably weird and thrilling, and she delivered them with a verve and sweetness which was amazing. I sat at one of the little tables with which the room was dotted, listening entranced.

'Time passed more rapidly than I supposed. While she sang I sipped the liquor with which the old woman had supplied me. So enthralled was I by the display of the girl's astonishing gifts that I did not notice what it was I was drinking. Looking back I can only surmise that it was some poisonous concoction of the creature's own. That one small glass had on me the strangest effect. I was still weak from the fever which I had only just succeeded in shaking off, and that, no doubt, had something to do with the result. But, as I continued to sit, I was conscious that I was sinking into a lethargic condition, against which I was incapable of struggling.

'After a while the original performer ceased her efforts, and, her companions taking her place, she came and joined me at the little table. Looking at my watch I was surprised to perceive the lateness of the hour. I rose to leave. She caught me by the wrist.

'"Do not go," she said;—she spoke English of a sort, and with the queerest accent. "All is well with you. Rest awhile."

'You will smile,—I should smile, perhaps, were I the listener instead of you, but it is the simple truth that her touch had on me what I can only describe as a magnetic influence. As her fingers closed upon my wrist, I felt as powerless in her grasp as if she held me with bands of steel. What seemed an invitation was virtually a command. I had to stay whether I would or wouldn't. She called for more liquor, and at what again was really her command I drank of it. I do not think that after she touched my wrist I uttered a word. She did all the talking. And, while she talked, she kept her eyes fixed on my face. Those eyes of hers! They were a devil's. I can positively affirm that they had on me a diabolical effect. They robbed me of my consciousness, of my power of volition, of my capacity to think,—they made me as wax in her hands. My last recollection of that fatal night is of her sitting in front of me, bending over the table, stroking my wrist with her extended fingers, staring at me with her awful eyes. After that, a curtain seems to descend. There comes a period of oblivion.'

Mr. Lessingham ceased. His manner was calm and self-contained enough; but, in spite of that I could see that the mere recollection of the things which he told me moved his nature to its foundations. There was eloquence in the drawn lines about his mouth, and in the strained expression of his eyes.

So far his tale was sufficiently commonplace. Places such as the one which he described abound in the Cairo of today; and many are the Englishmen who have entered them to their exceeding bitter cost. With that keen intuition which has done him yeoman's service in the political arena, Mr. Lessingham at once perceived the direction my thoughts were taking.

'You have heard this tale before?—No doubt. And often. The traps are many, and the fools and the unwary are not a few. The singularity of my experience is still to come. You must forgive me if I seem to stumble in the telling. I am anxious to present my case as baldly, and with as little appearance of exaggeration as possible. I say with as little appearance, for some appearance of exaggeration I fear is unavoidable. My case is so unique, and so out of the common run of our everyday experience, that the plainest possible statement must smack of the sensational.

'As, I fancy, you have guessed, when understanding returned to me, I found myself in an apartment with which I was unfamiliar. I was lying, undressed, on a heap of rugs in a corner of a low-pitched room which was furnished in a fashion which, when I grasped the details, filled me with amazement. By my side knelt the Woman of the Songs. Leaning over, she wooed my mouth with kisses. I cannot describe to you the sense of horror and of loathing with which the contact of her lips oppressed me. There was about her something so unnatural, so inhuman, that I believe even then I could have destroyed her with as little sense of moral turpitude as if she had been some noxious insect.

'"Where am I?" I exclaimed.

'"You are with the children of Isis," she replied. What she meant I did not know, and do not to this hour. "You are in the hands of the great goddess,—of the mother of men."

'"How did I come here?"

'"By the loving kindness of the great mother."

'I do not, of course, pretend to give you the exact text of her words, but they were to that effect.

'Half raising myself on the heap of rugs, I gazed about me,—and was astounded at what I saw.

'The place in which I was, though the reverse of lofty, was of considerable size,—I could not conceive whereabouts it could be. The walls and roof were of bare stone,—as though the whole had been hewed out of the solid rock. It seemed to be some sort of temple, and was redolent with the most extraordinary odour. An altar stood about the centre, fashioned out of a single block of stone. On it a fire burned with a faint blue flame,—the fumes which rose from it were no doubt chiefly responsible for the prevailing perfumes. Behind it was a huge bronze figure, more than life size. It was in a sitting posture, and represented a woman. Although it resembled no portrayal of her I have seen either before or since, I came afterwards to understand that it was meant for Isis. On the idol's brow was poised a beetle. That the creature was alive seemed clear, for, as I looked at it, it opened and shut its wings.

'If the one on the forehead of the goddess was the only live beetle which the place contained, it was not the only representation. It was modelled in the solid stone of the roof, and depicted in flaming colours on hangings which here and there were hung against the walls. Wherever the eye turned it rested on a scarab. The effect was bewildering. It was as though one saw things through the distorted glamour of a nightmare. I asked myself if I were not still dreaming; if my appearance of consciousness were not after all a mere delusion; if I had really regained my senses.

'And, here, Mr. Champnell, I wish to point out, and to emphasise the fact, that I am not prepared to positively affirm what portion of my adventures in that extraordinary, and horrible place, was actuality, and what the product of a feverish imagination. Had I been persuaded that all I thought I saw, I really did see, I should have opened my lips long ago, let the consequences to myself have been what they might. But there is the crux. The happenings were of such an incredible character, and my condition was such an abnormal one,—I was never really myself from the first moment to the last—that I have hesitated, and still do hesitate, to assert where, precisely, fiction ended and fact began.

'With some misty notion of testing my actual condition I endeavoured to get off the heap of rugs on which I reclined. As I did so the woman at my side laid her hand against my chest, lightly. But, had her gentle pressure been the equivalent of a ton of iron, it could not have been more effectual. I collapsed, sank back upon the rugs, and lay there, panting for breath, wondering if I had crossed the border line which divides madness from sanity.

'"Let me get up!—let me go!" I gasped.

'"Nay," she murmured, "stay with me yet awhile, O my beloved."

'And again she kissed me.'

Once more Mr. Lessingham paused. An involuntary shudder went all over him. In spite of the evidently great effort which he was making to retain his self-control his features were contorted by an anguished spasm. For some seconds he seemed at a loss to find words to enable him to continue.

When he did go on, his voice was harsh and strained.

'I am altogether incapable of even hinting to you the nauseous nature of that woman's kisses. They filled me with an indescribable repulsion. I look back at them with a feeling of physical, mental, and moral horror, across an interval of twenty years. The most dreadful part of it was that I was wholly incapable of offering even the faintest resistance to her caresses. I lay there like a log. She did with me as she would, and in dumb agony I endured.'

He took his handkerchief from his pocket, and, although the day was cool, with it he wiped the perspiration from his brow.

'To dwell in detail on what occurred during my involuntary sojourn in that fearful place is beyond my power. I cannot even venture to attempt it. The attempt, were it made, would be futile, and, to me, painful beyond measure. I seem to have seen all that happened as in a glass darkly,—with about it all an element of unreality. As I have already remarked, the things which revealed themselves, dimly, to my perception, seemed too bizarre, too hideous, to be true.

'It was only afterwards, when I was in a position to compare dates, that I was enabled to determine what had been the length of my imprisonment. It appears that I was in that horrible den more than two months,—two unspeakable months. And the whole time there were comings and goings, a phantasmagoric array of eerie figures continually passed to and fro before my hazy eyes. What I judge to have been religious services took place; in which the altar, the bronze image, and the beetle on its brow, figure largely. Not only were they conducted with a bewildering confusion of mysterious rites, but, if my memory is in the least degree trustworthy, they were orgies of nameless horrors. I seem to have seen things take place at them at the mere thought of which the brain reels and trembles.

'Indeed it is in connection with the cult of the obscene deity to whom these wretched creatures paid their scandalous vows that my most awful memories seem to have been associated. It may have been—I hope it was, a mirage born of my half delirious state, but it seemed to me that they offered human sacrifices.'

When Mr. Lessingham said this, I pricked up my ears. For reasons of my own, which will immediately transpire, I had been wondering if he would make any reference to a human sacrifice. He noted my display of interest,—but misapprehended the cause.

'I see you start, I do not wonder. But I repeat that unless I was the victim of some extraordinary species of double sight—in which case the whole business would resolve itself into the fabric of a dream, and I should indeed thank God!—I saw, on more than one occasion, a human sacrifice offered on that stone altar, presumably to the grim image which looked down on it. And, unless I err, in each case the sacrificial object was a woman, stripped to the skin, as white as you or I,—and before they burned her they subjected her to every variety of outrage of which even the minds of demons could conceive. More than once since then I have seemed to hear the shrieks of the victims ringing through the air, mingled with the triumphant cries of her frenzied murderers, and the music of their harps.

'It was the cumulative horrors of such a scene which gave me the strength, or the courage, or the madness, I know not which it was, to burst the bonds which bound me, and which, even in the bursting, made of me, even to this hour, a haunted man.

'There had been a sacrifice,—unless, as I have repeatedly observed, the whole was nothing but a dream. A woman—a young and lovely Englishwoman, if I could believe the evidence of my own eyes, had been outraged, and burnt alive, while I lay there helpless, looking on. The business was concluded. The ashes of the victim had been consumed by the participants. The worshippers had departed. I was left alone with the woman of the songs, who apparently acted as the guardian of that worse than slaughterhouse. She was, as usual after such an orgie, rather a devil than a human being, drunk with an insensate frenzy, delirious with inhuman longings. As she approached to offer to me her loathed caresses, I was on a sudden conscious of something which I had not felt before when in her company. It was as though something had slipped away from me,—some weight which had oppressed me, some bond by which I had been bound. I was aroused, all at once, to a sense of freedom; to a knowledge that the blood which coursed through my veins was after all my own, that I was master of my own honour.

'I can only suppose that through all those weeks she had kept me there in a state of mesmeric stupor. That, taking advantage of the weakness which the fever had left behind, by the exercise of her diabolical arts, she had not allowed me to pass out of a condition of hypnotic trance. Now, for some reason, the cord was loosed. Possibly her absorption in her religious duties had caused her to forget to tighten it. Anyhow, as she approached me, she approached a man, and one who, for the first time for many a day, was his own man. She herself seemed wholly unconscious of anything of the kind. As she drew nearer to me, and nearer, she appeared to be entirely oblivious of the fact that I was anything but the fibreless, emasculated creature which, up to that moment, she had made of me.

'But she knew it when she touched me,—when she stooped to press her lips to mine. At that instant the accumulating rage which had been smouldering in my breast through all those leaden torturing hours, sprang into flame. Leaping off my couch of rugs, I flung my hands about her throat,—and then she knew I was awake. Then she strove to tighten the cord which she had suffered to become unduly loose. Her baleful eyes were fixed on mine. I knew that she was putting out her utmost force to trick me of my manhood. But I fought with her like one possessed, and I conquered—in a fashion. I compressed her throat with my two hands as with an iron vice. I knew that I was struggling for more than life, that the odds were all against me, that I was staking my all upon the casting of a die,—I stuck at nothing which could make me victor.

'Tighter and tighter my pressure grew,—I did not stay to think if I was killing her—till on a sudden—'

Mr. Lessingham stopped. He stared with fixed, glassy eyes, as if the whole was being re-enacted in front of him. His voice faltered. I thought he would break down. But, with an effort, he continued.

'On a sudden, I felt her slipping from between my fingers. Without the slightest warning, in an instant she had vanished, and where, not a moment before, she herself had been, I found myself confronting a monstrous beetle,—a huge, writhing creation of some wild nightmare.

'At first the creature stood as high as I did. But, as I stared at it, in stupefied amazement,—as you may easily imagine,—the thing dwindled while I gazed. I did not stop to see how far the process of dwindling continued,—a stark raving madman for the nonce, I fled as if all the fiends in hell were at my heels.'

Chapter 3: After Twenty Years

'How I reached the open air I cannot tell you,—I do not know. I have a confused recollection of rushing through vaulted passages, through endless corridors, of trampling over people who tried to arrest my passage,—and the rest is blank.

'When I again came to myself I was lying in the house of an American missionary named Clements. I had been found, at early dawn, stark naked, in a Cairo street, and picked up for dead. Judging from appearances I must have wandered for miles, all through the night. Whence I had come, or whither I was going, none could tell,—I could not tell myself. For weeks I hovered between life and death. The kindness of Mr. and Mrs. Clements was not to be measured by words. I was brought to their house a penniless, helpless, battered stranger, and they gave me all they had to offer, without money and without price,—with no expectation of an earthly reward.

'Let no one pretend that there is no Christian charity under the sun. The debt I owed that man and woman I was never able to repay.

Before I was properly myself again, and in a position to offer some adequate testimony of the gratitude I felt, Mrs. Clements was dead, drowned during an excursion on the Nile' and her husband had departed on a missionary expedition into Central Africa, from which he never returned.

'Although, in a measure, my physical health returned, for months after I had left the roof of my hospitable hosts, I was in a state of semi-imbecility. I suffered from a species of aphasia. For days together I was speechless, and could remember nothing,—not even my own name. And, when that stage had passed, and I began to move more freely among my fellows, for years I was but a wreck of my former self. I was visited, at all hours of the day and night, by frightful—I know not whether to call them visions, they were real enough to me, but since they were visible to no one but myself, perhaps that is the word which best describes them. Their presence invariably plunged me into a state of abject terror, against which I was unable to even make a show of fighting. To such an extent did they embitter my existence, that I voluntarily placed myself under the treatment of an expert in mental pathology. For a considerable period of time I was under his constant supervision, but the visitations were as inexplicable to him as they were to me.

'By degrees, however, they became rarer and rarer, until at last I flattered myself that I had once more become as other men. After an interval, to make sure, I devoted myself to politics. Thenceforward I have lived, as they phrase it, in the public eye. Private life, in any peculiar sense of the term, I have had none.'

Mr. Lessingham ceased. His tale was not uninteresting, and, to say the least of it, was curious. But I still was at a loss to understand what it had to do with me, or what was the purport of his presence in my room. Since he remained silent, as if the matter, so far as he was concerned, was at an end, I told him so.

'I presume, Mr. Lessingham, that all this is but a prelude to the play. At present I do not see where it is that I come in.'

Still for some seconds he was silent. When he spoke his voice was grave and sombre, as if he were burdened by a weight of woe.

'Unfortunately, as you put it, all this has been but a prelude to the play. Were it not so I should not now stand in such pressing want of the services of a confidential agent,—that is, of an experienced man of the world, who has been endowed by nature with phenomenal perceptive faculties, and in whose capacity and honour I can place the completest confidence.'

I smiled,—the compliment was a pointed one.

'I hope your estimate of me is not too high.'

'I hope not,—for my sake, as well as for your own. I have heard great things of you. If ever man stood in need of all that human skill and acumen can do for him, I certainly am he.'

His words aroused my curiosity. I was conscious of feeling more interested than heretofore.

'I will do my best for you. Man can do no more. Only give my best a trial.'

'I will. At once.'

He looked at me long and earnestly. Then, leaning forward, he said, lowering his voice perhaps unconsciously,

'The fact is, Mr. Champnell, that quite recently events have happened which threaten to bridge the chasm of twenty years, and to place me face to face with that plague spot of the past. At this moment I stand in imminent peril of becoming again the wretched thing I was when I fled from that den of all the devils. It is to guard me against this that I have come to you. I want you to unravel the tangled thread which threatens to drag me to my doom,—and, when unravelled to sunder it—forever, if God wills!—in twain.'

'Explain.'

To be frank, for the moment I thought him mad. He went on.

'Three weeks ago, when I returned late one night from a sitting in the House of Commons, I found, on my study table, a sheet of paper on which there was a representation—marvellously like!—of the creature into which, as it seemed to me, the woman of the songs was transformed as I clutched her throat between my hands. The mere sight of it brought back one of those visitations of which I have told you, and which I thought I had done with forever,—I was convulsed by an agony of fear, thrown into a state approximating to a paralysis both of mind and body.'

'But why?'

'I cannot tell you. I only know that I have never dared to allow my thoughts to recur to that last dread scene, lest the mere recurrence should drive me mad.'

'What was this you found upon your study table,—merely a drawing?'

'It was a representation, produced by what process I cannot say, which was so wonderfully, so diabolically, like the original, that for a moment I thought the thing itself was on my table.'

'Who put it there?'

'That is precisely what I wish you to find out,—what I wish you to make it your instant business to ascertain. I have found the thing, under similar circumstances, on three separate occasions, on my study table,—and each time it has had on me the same hideous effect.'

'Each time after you have returned from a late sitting in the House of Commons?'

'Exactly.'

'Where are these—what shall I call them—delineations?'

'That, again, I cannot tell you.'

'What do you mean?'

'What I say. Each time, when I recovered, the thing had vanished.'

'Sheet of paper and all?'

'Apparently,—though on that point I could not be positive. You will understand that my study table is apt to be littered with sheets of paper, and I could not absolutely determine that the thing had not stared at me from one of those. The delineation itself, to use your word, certainly had vanished.'

I began to suspect that this was a case rather for a doctor than for a man of my profession. And hinted as much.

'Don't you think it is possible, Mr. Lessingham, that you have been overworking yourself—that you have been driving your brain too hard, and that you have been the victim of an optical delusion?'

'I thought so myself; I may say that I almost hoped so. But wait till I have finished. You will find that there is no loophole in that direction.'

He appeared to be recalling events in their due order. His manner was studiously cold,—as if he were endeavouring, despite the strangeness of his story, to impress me with the literal accuracy of each syllable he uttered.

'The night before last, on returning home, I found in my study a stranger.'

'A stranger?'

'Yes.—In other words, a burglar.'

'A burglar?—I see.—Go on.'

He had paused. His demeanour was becoming odder and odder.

'On my entry he was engaged in forcing an entry into my bureau. I need hardly say that I advanced to seize him. But—I could not.'

'You could not?—How do you mean you could not?'

'I mean simply what I say. You must understand that this was no ordinary felon. Of what nationality he was I cannot tell you. He only uttered two words, and they were certainly in English, but apart from that he was dumb. He wore no covering on his head or feet. Indeed, his only garment was a long dark flowing cloak which, as it fluttered about him, revealed that his limbs were bare.'

'An unique costume for a burglar.'

'The instant I saw him I realised that he was in some way connected with that adventure in the Rue de Rabagas. What he said and did, proved it to the hilt.'

'What did he say and do?'

'As I approached to effect his capture, he pronounced aloud two words which recalled that awful scene the recollection of which always lingers in my brain, and of which I never dare to permit myself to think. Their very utterance threw me into a sort of convulsion.'

'What were the words?'

Mr. Lessingham opened his mouth,—and shut it. A marked change took place in the expression of his countenance. His eyes became fixed and staring,—resembling the glassy orbs of the somnambulist. For a moment I feared that he was going to give me an object lesson in the 'visitations' of which I had heard so much. I rose, with a view of offering him assistance. He motioned me back.

'Thank you.—It will pass away.'

His voice was dry and husky,—unlike his usual silvern tones. After an uncomfortable interval he managed to continue.

'You see for yourself, Mr. Champnell, what a miserable weakling, when this subject is broached, I still remain. I cannot utter the words the stranger uttered, I cannot even write them down. For some inscrutable reason they have on me an effect similar to that which spells and incantations had on people in tales of witchcraft.'

'I suppose, Mr. Lessingham, that there is no doubt that this mysterious stranger was not himself an optical delusion?'

'Scarcely. There is the evidence of my servants to prove the contrary.'

'Did your servants see him?'

'Some of them,—yes. Then there is the evidence of the bureau. The fellow had smashed the top right in two. When I came to examine the contents I learned that a packet of letters was missing. They were letters which I had received from Miss Lindon, a lady whom I hope to make my wife. This, also, I state to you in confidence.'

'What use would he be likely to make of them?'

'If matters stand as I fear they do, he might make a very serious misuse of them. If the object of these wretches, after all these years, is a wild revenge, they would be capable, having discovered what she is to me, of working Miss Lindon a fatal mischief,—or, at the very least, of poisoning her mind.'

'I see.—How did the thief escape,—did he, like the delineation, vanish into air?'

'He escaped by the much more prosaic method of dashing through the drawing-room window, and clambering down from the verandah into the street, where he ran right into someone's arms.'

'Into whose arms,—a constable's?'

'No; into Mr. Atherton's,—Sydney Atherton's.'

'The inventor?'

'The same.—Do you know him?'

'I do. Sydney Atherton and I are friends of a good many years' standing.—But Atherton must have seen where he came from;—and, anyhow, if he was in the state of undress which you have described, why didn't he stop him?'

'Mr. Atherton's reasons were his own. He did not stop him, and, so far as I can learn, he did not attempt to stop him. Instead, he knocked at my hall door to inform me that he had seen a man climb out of my window.'

'I happen to know that, at certain seasons, Atherton is a queer fish,—but that sounds very queer indeed.'

'The truth is, Mr. Champnell, that, if it were not for Mr. Atherton, I doubt if I should have troubled you even now. The accident of his being an acquaintance of yours makes my task easier.'

He drew his chair closer to me with an air of briskness which had been foreign to him before. For some reason, which I was unable to fathom, the introduction of Atherton's name seemed to have enlivened him. However, I was not long to remain in darkness. In half a dozen sentences he threw more light on the real cause of his visit to me than he had done in all that had gone before. His bearing, too, was more businesslike and to the point. For the first time I had some glimmerings of the politician,—alert, keen, eager,—as he is known to all the world.

'Mr. Atherton, like myself, has been a postulant for Miss Lindon's hand. Because I have succeeded where he has failed, he has chosen to be angry. It seems that he has had dealings, either with my visitor of

Tuesday night, or with some other his acquaintance, and he proposes to use what he has gleaned from him to the disadvantage of my character. I have just come from Mr. Atherton. From hints he dropped I conclude that, probably during the last few hours, he has had an interview with someone who was connected in some way with that lurid patch in my career; that this person made so-called revelations, which were nothing but a series of monstrous lies; and these so-called revelations Mr. Atherton has threatened, in so many words, to place before Miss Lindon, That is an eventuality which I wish to avoid. My own conviction is that there is at this moment in London an emissary from that den in the whilom Rue de Rabagas—for all I know it may be the Woman of the Songs herself.

'Whether the sole purport of this individual's presence is to do me injury, I am, as yet, in no position to say, but that it is proposed to work me mischief, at any rate, by the way, is plain. I believe that Mr. Atherton knows more about this person's individuality and whereabouts than he has been willing, so far, to admit. I want you, therefore, to ascertain these things on my behalf; to find out what, and where, this person is, to drag her!—or him;—out into the light of day. In short, I want you to effectually protect me from the terrorism which threatens once more to overwhelm my mental and my physical powers, —which bids fair to destroy my intellect, my career, my life, my all.'

'What reason have you for suspecting that Mr. Atherton has seen this individual of whom you speak,—has he told you so?'

'Practically,—yes.'

'I know Atherton well. In his not infrequent moments of excitement he is apt to use strong language, but it goes no further. I believe him to be the last person in the world to do anyone an intentional injustice, under any circumstances whatever. If I go to him, armed with credentials from you, when he understands the real gravity of the situation,—which it will be my business to make him do, I believe that, spontaneously, of his own accord, he will tell me as much about this mysterious individual as he knows himself.'

'Then go to him at once.'

'Good. I will. The result I will communicate to you.'

I rose from my seat. As I did so, someone rushed into the outer office with a din and a clatter. Andrews' voice, and another, became distinctly audible,—Andrews' apparently raised in vigorous expostulation. Raised, seemingly, in vain, for presently the door of my own particular sanctum was thrown open with a crash, and Mr. Sydney

Atherton himself came dashing in,—evidently conspicuously under the influence of one of those not infrequent 'moments of excitement' of which I had just been speaking.

CHAPTER 4: A BRINGER OF TIDINGS

Atherton did not wait to see who might or might not be present, but, without even pausing to take breath, he broke into full cry on the instant,—as is occasionally his wont.

'Champnell!—Thank goodness I've found you in!—I want you!—At once!—Don't stop to talk, but stick your hat on, and put your best foot forward,—I'll tell you all about it in the cab.'

I endeavoured to call his attention to Mr. Lessingham's presence,—but without success.

'My dear fellow—'

When I had got as far as that he cut me short.

'Don't "dear fellow" me!—None of your jabber! And none of your excuses either! I don't care if you've got an engagement with the Queen, you'll have to chuck it. Where's that dashed hat of yours,—or are you going without it? Don't I tell you that every second cut to waste may mean the difference between life and death?—Do you want me to drag you down to the cab by the hair of your head?'

'I will try not to constrain you to quite so drastic a resource,—and I was coming to you at once in any case. I only want to call your attention to the fact that I am not alone.—Here is Mr. Lessingham.'

In his harum-scarum haste Mr. Lessingham had gone unnoticed. Now that his observation was particularly directed to him, Atherton started, turned, and glared at my latest client in a fashion which was scarcely flattering.

'Oh!—It's you, is it?—What the deuce are you doing here?'

Before Lessingham could reply to this most unceremonious query, Atherton, rushing forward, gripped him by the arm.

'Have you seen her?'

Lessingham, not unnaturally nonplussed by the other's curious conduct, stared at him in unmistakable amazement.

'Have I seen whom?'

'Marjorie Lindon!'

'Marjorie Lindon?'

Lessingham paused. He was evidently asking himself what the inquiry meant.

'I have not seen Miss Lindon since last night. Why do you ask?'

'Then Heaven help us!—As I'm a living man I believe he, she, or it has got her!'

His words were incomprehensible enough to stand in copious need of explanation,—as Mr. Lessingham plainly thought.

'What is it that you mean, sir?'

'What I say,—I believe that that Oriental friend of yours has got her in her clutches,—if it is a "her;" goodness alone knows what the infernal conjurer's real sex may be.'

'Atherton!—Explain yourself!'

On a sudden Lessingham's tones rang out like a trumpet call.

'If damage comes to her I shall be fit to cut my throat,—and yours!'

Mr. Lessingham's next proceeding surprised me,—I imagine it surprised Atherton still more. Springing at Sydney like a tiger, he caught him by the throat.

'You—you hound! Of what wretched folly have you been guilty? If so much as a hair of her head is injured you shall repay it me ten thousandfold!—You mischief-making, intermeddling, jealous fool!'

He shook Sydney as if he had been a rat,—then flung him from him headlong on to the floor. It reminded me of nothing so much as Othello's treatment of Iago. Never had I seen a man so transformed by rage. Lessingham seemed to have positively increased in stature. As he stood glowering down at the prostrate Sydney, he might have stood for a materialistic conception of human retribution.

Sydney, I take it, was rather surprised than hurt. For a moment or two he lay quite still. Then, lifting his head, he looked up his assailant. Then, raising himself to his feet, he shook himself,—as if with a view of learning if all his bones were whole. Putting his hands up to his neck, he rubbed it, gently. And he grinned.

'By God, Lessingham, there's more in you than I thought. After all, you are a man. There's some holding power in those wrists of yours,— they've nearly broken my neck. When this business is finished, I should like to put on the gloves with you, and fight it out. You're clean wasted upon politics,—Damn it, man, give me your hand!'

Mr. Lessingham did not give him his hand. Atherton took it,—and gave it a hearty shake with both of his.

If the first paroxysm of his passion had passed, Lessingham was still sufficiently stern.

'Be so good as not to trifle, Mr. Atherton. If what you say is correct, and the wretch to whom you allude really has Miss Lindon at her mercy, then the woman I love—and whom you also pretend to love!—stands in imminent peril not only of a ghastly death, but of what is infinitely worse than death.'

'The deuce she does!' Atherton wheeled round towards me. 'Champnell, haven't you got that dashed hat of yours yet? Don't stand there like a tailor's dummy, keeping me on tenter-hooks,—move yourself! I'll tell you all about it in the cab.—And, Lessingham, if you'll come with us I'll tell you too.'

CHAPTER 5: WHAT THE TIDINGS WERE

Three in a hansom cab is not, under all circumstances, the most comfortable method of conveyance,—when one of the trio happens to be Sydney Atherton in one of his 'moments of excitement' it is distinctly the opposite; as, on that occasion, Mr. Lessingham and I both quickly found. Sometimes he sat on my knees, sometimes on Lessingham's, and frequently, when he unexpectedly stood up, and all but precipitated himself on to the horse's back, on nobody's. In the eagerness of his gesticulations, first he knocked off my hat, then he knocked off Lessingham's, then his own, then all three together,—once, his own hat rolling into the mud, he sprang into the road, without previously going through the empty form of advising the driver of his intention, to pick it up.

When he turned to speak to Lessingham, he thrust his elbow into my eye; and when he turned to speak to me, he thrust it into Lessingham's. Never, for one solitary instant, was he at rest, or either of us at ease. The wonder is that the gymnastics in which he incessantly indulged did not sufficiently attract public notice to induce a policeman to put at least a momentary period to our progress. Had speed not been of primary importance I should have insisted on the transference of the expedition to the somewhat wider limits of a four-wheeler.

His elucidation of the causes of his agitation was apparently more comprehensible to Lessingham than it was to me. I had to piece this and that together under considerable difficulties. By degrees I did arrive at something like a clear notion of what had actually taken place.

He commenced by addressing Lessingham,—and thrusting his elbow into my eye.

'Did Marjorie tell you about the fellow she found in the street?' Up went his arm to force the trap-door open overhead,—and off went my hat. 'Now then, William Henry!—let her go!—if you kill the horse I'll buy you another!'

We were already going much faster than, legally, we ought to have done,—but that, seemingly to him was not a matter of the slightest consequence. Lessingham replied to his inquiry.

'She did not.'

'You know the fellow I saw coming out of your drawing-room window?'

'Yes.'

'Well, Marjorie found him the morning after in front of her break-fast-room window—in the middle of the street. Seems he had been wandering about all night, unclothed,—in the rain and the mud, and all the rest of it,—in a condition of hypnotic trance.'

'Who is the——gentleman you are alluding to?'

'Says his name's Holt, Robert Holt.'

'Holt?—Is he an Englishman?'

'Very much so,—City quill-driver out of a shop,—stony broke absolutely! Got the chuck from the casual ward,—wouldn't let him in,—house full, and that sort of thing,—poor devil! Pretty passes you politicians bring men to!'

'Are you sure?'

'Of what?'

'Are you sure that this man, Robert Holt, is the same person whom, as you put it, you saw coming out of my drawing-room window?'

'Sure!—Of course I'm sure!—Think I didn't recognise him?— Besides, there was the man's own tale,—owned to it himself,—besides all the rest, which sent one rushing Fulham way.'

'You must remember, Mr. Atherton, that I am wholly in the dark as to what has happened. What has the man, Holt, to do with the errand on which we are bound?'

'Am I not coming to it? If you would let me tell the tale in my own way I should get there in less than no time, but you will keep on cutting in,—how the deuce do you suppose Champnell is to make head or tail of the business if you will persist in interrupting?—Mar-jorie took the beggar in,—he told his tale to her,—she sent for me— that was just now; caught me on the steps after I had been lunching with Dora Grayling. Holt re-dished his yarn—I smelt a rat—saw that a connection possibly existed between the thief who'd been playing confounded conjuring tricks off on to me and this interesting party down Fulham way—'

'What party down Fulham way?'

'This friend of Holt's—am I not telling you? There you are, you see,—won't let me finish! When Holt slipped through the window—which is the most sensible thing he seems to have done; if I'd been in his shoes I'd have slipped through forty windows!—dusky coloured charmer caught him on the hop,—doctored him—sent him out to commit burglary by deputy. I said to Holt, "Show us this agreeable little crib, young man." Holt was game—then Marjorie chipped in—she wanted to go and see it too. I said, "You'll be sorry if you do,"—that settled it! After that she'd have gone if she'd died,—I never did have a persuasive way with women. So off we toddled, Marjorie, Holt, and I, in a growler,—spotted the crib in less than no time,—invited ourselves in by the kitchen window—house seemed empty. Presently Holt became hypnotised before my eyes,—the best established case of hypnotism by suggestion I ever yet encountered—started off on a pilgrimage of one. Like an idiot I followed, leaving Marjorie to wait for me—'

'Alone?'

'Alone!—Am I not telling you?—Great Scott, Lessingham, in the House of Commons they must be hazy to think you smart! I said, "I'll send the first sane soul I meet to keep you company." As luck would have it, I never met one,—only kids, and a baker, who wouldn't leave his cart, or take it with him either. I'd covered pretty nearly two miles before I came across a peeler,—and when I did the man was cracked—and he thought me mad, or drunk, or both. By the time I'd got myself within nodding distance of being run in for obstructing the police in the execution of their duty, without inducing him to move a single one of his twenty-four-inch feet, Holt was out of sight. So, since all my pains in his direction were clean thrown away, there was nothing left for me but to scurry back to Marjorie,—so I scurried, and I found the house empty, no one there, and Marjorie gone.'

'But, I don't quite follow—'

Atherton impetuously declined to allow Mr. Lessingham to conclude.

'Of course you don't quite follow, and you'll follow still less if you will keep getting in front. I went upstairs and downstairs, inside and out—shouted myself hoarse as a crow—nothing was to be seen of Marjorie,—or heard; until, as I was coming down the stairs for about the five-and-fiftieth time, I stepped on something hard which was lying in the passage. I picked it up,—it was a ring; this ring. Its shape is not just what it was,—I'm not as light as gossamer, especially when I come jumping downstairs six at a time,—but what's left of it is here.'

Sydney held something in front of him. Mr. Lessingham wriggled to one side to enable him to see. Then he made a snatch at it.

'It's mine!'

Sydney dodged it out of his reach.

'What do you mean, it's yours?'

'It's the ring I gave Marjorie for an engagement ring. Give it me, you hound!—unless you wish me to do you violence in the cab.'

With complete disregard of the limitations of space,—or of my comfort,—Lessingham thrust him vigorously aside. Then gripping Sydney by the wrist, he seized the gaud,—Sydney yielding it just in time to save himself from being precipitated into the street. Ravished of his treasure, Sydney turned and surveyed the ravisher with something like a glance of admiration.

'Hang me, Lessingham, if I don't believe there is some warm blood in those fishlike veins of yours. Please the piper, I'll live to fight you after all,—with the bare ones, sir, as a gentleman should do.'

Lessingham seemed to pay no attention to him whatever. He was surveying the ring, which Sydney had trampled out of shape, with looks of the deepest concern.

'Marjorie's ring!—The one I gave her! Something serious must have happened to her before she would have dropped my ring, and left it lying where it fell.'

Atherton went on.

'That's it!—What has happened to her!—I'll be dashed if I know!—When it was clear that there she wasn't, I tore off to find out where she was. Came across old Lindon,—he knew nothing;—I rather fancy I startled him in the middle of Pall Mall, when I left he stared after me like one possessed, and his hat was lying in the gutter. Went home,—she wasn't there. Asked Dora Grayling,—she'd seen nothing of her. No one had seen anything of her,—she had vanished into air. Then I said to myself, "You're a first-class idiot, on my honour! While you're looking for her, like a lost sheep, the betting is that the girl's in Holt's friend's house the whole jolly time. When you were there, the chances are that she'd just stepped out for a stroll, and that now she's back again, and wondering where on earth you've gone!"

'So I made up my mind that I'd fly back and see,—because the idea of her standing on the front doorstep looking for me, while I was going off my nut looking for her, commended itself to what I call my sense of humour; and on my way it struck me that it would be the part of wisdom to pick up Champnell, because if there is a man who can be backed to find a needle in any amount of hay-stacks it is the great Augustus.—That horse has moved itself after all, because here we are. Now, cabman, don't go driving further on,—you'll have to put a girdle round the earth if you do; because you'll have to reach this point again before you get your fare.—This is the magician's house!'

CHAPTER 6: WHAT WAS HIDDEN UNDER THE FLOOR

The cab pulled up in front of a tumbledown cheap 'villa' in an unfinished cheap neighbourhood,—the whole place a living monument of the defeat of the speculative builder.

Atherton leaped out on to the grass-grown rubble which was meant for a footpath.

'I don't see Marjorie looking for me on the doorstep.'

Nor did I,—I saw nothing but what appeared to be an unoccupied ramshackle brick abomination. Suddenly Sydney gave an exclamation.

'Hullo!—The front door's closed!'

I was hard at his heels.

'What do you mean?'

'Why, when I went I left the front door open. It looks as if I've made an idiot of myself after all, and Marjorie's returned,—let's hope to goodness that I have.'

He knocked. While we waited for a response I questioned him.

'Why did you leave the door open when you went?'

'I hardly know,—I imagine that it was with some dim idea of Marjorie's being able to get in if she returned while I was absent,—but the truth is I was in such a condition of helter skelter that I am not prepared to swear that I had any reasonable reason.'

'I suppose there is no doubt that you did leave it open?'

'Absolutely none,—on that I'll stake my life.'

'Was it open when you returned from your pursuit of Holt?'

'Wide open,—I walked straight in expecting to find her waiting for me in the front room,—I was struck all of a heap when I found she wasn't there.'

'Were there any signs of a struggle?'

'None,—there were no signs of anything. Everything was just as I had left it, with the exception of the ring which I trod on in the passage, and which Lessingham has.'

'If Miss Lindon has returned, it does not look as if she were in the house at present.'

It did not,—unless silence had such meaning. Atherton had knocked loudly three times without succeeding in attracting the slightest notice from within.

'It strikes me that this is another case of seeking admission through that hospitable window at the back.'

Atherton led the way to the rear. Lessingham and I followed. There was not even an apology for a yard, still less a garden,—there was not even a fence of any sort, to serve as an enclosure, and to shut off the house from the wilderness of waste land. The kitchen window was open. I asked Sydney if he had left it so.

'I don't know,—I dare say we did; I don't fancy that either of us stood on the order of his coming.'

While he spoke, he scrambled over the sill. We followed. When he was in, he shouted at the top of his voice,

'Marjorie! Marjorie! Speak to me, Marjorie,—it is I,—Sydney!'

The words echoed through the house. Only silence answered. He led the way to the front room. Suddenly he stopped.

'Hollo!' he cried. 'The blind's down!' I had noticed, when we were outside, that the blind was down at the front room window. 'It was up when I went, that I'll swear. That someone has been here is pretty plain,—let's hope it's Marjorie.'

He had only taken a step forward into the room when he again stopped short to exclaim.

'My stars!—here's a sudden clearance!—Why, the place is empty,— everything's clean gone!'

'What do you mean?—was it furnished when you left?'

The room was empty enough then.

'Furnished?—I don't know that it was exactly what you'd call furnished,—the party who ran this establishment had a taste in upholstery which was all his own,—but there was a carpet, and a bed, and— and lots of things,—for the most part, I should have said, distinctly Eastern curiosities. They seem to have evaporated into smoke,—which may be a way which is common enough among Eastern curiosities, though it's queer to me.'

Atherton was staring about him as if he found it difficult to credit the evidence of his own eyes.

'How long ago is it since you left?'

He referred to his watch.

'Something over an hour,—possibly an hour and a half; I couldn't swear to the exact moment, but it certainly isn't more.'

'Did you notice any signs of packing up?'

'Not a sign.' Going to the window he drew up the blind,—speaking as he did so. 'The queer thing about this business is that when we first got in this blind wouldn't draw up a little bit, so, since it wouldn't go up I pulled it down, roller and all, now it draws up as easily and smoothly as if it had always been the best blind that ever lived.'

Standing at Sydney's back I saw that the cabman on his box was signalling to us with his outstretched hand. Sydney perceived him too. He threw up the sash.

'What's the matter with you?'

'Excuse me, sir, but who's the old gent?'

'What old gent?'

'Why the old gent peeping through the window of the room upstairs?'

The words were hardly out of the driver's mouth when Sydney was through the door and flying up the staircase. I followed rather more soberly,—his methods were a little too flighty for me. When I reached the landing, dashing out of the front room he rushed into the one at the back,—then through a door at the side. He came out shouting.

'What's the idiot mean!—with his old gent! I'd old gent him if I got him!—There's not a creature about the place!'

He returned into the front room,—I at his heels. That certainly was empty,—and not only empty, but it showed no traces of recent occupation. The dust lay thick upon the floor,—there was that mouldy, earthy smell which is so frequently found in apartments which have been long untenanted.

'Are you sure, Atherton, that there is no one at the back?'

'Of course I'm sure,—you can go and see for yourself if you like; do you think I'm blind? Jehu's drunk.' Throwing up the sash he addressed the driver. 'What do you mean with your old gent at the window?—what window?'

'That window, sir.'

'Go to!—you're dreaming, man!—there's no one here.'

'Begging your pardon, sir, but there was someone there not a minute ago.'

'Imagination, cabman,—the slant of the light on the glass,—or your eyesight's defective.'

'Excuse me, sir, but it's not my imagination, and my eyesight's as good as any man's in England,—and as for the slant of the light on the glass, there ain't much glass for the light to slant on. I saw him peeping through that bottom broken pane on your left hand as plainly as I see you. He must be somewhere about,—he can't have got away,—he's at the back. Ain't there a cupboard nor nothing where he could hide?'

The cabman's manner was so extremely earnest that I went myself to see. There was a cupboard on the landing, but the door of that stood wide open, and that obviously was bare. The room behind was small, and, despite the splintered glass in the window frame, stuffy. Fragments of glass kept company with the dust on the floor, together with a choice collection of stones, brickbats, and other missiles,—which not improbably were the cause of their being there. In the corner stood a cupboard,—but a momentary examination showed that that was as bare as the other. The door at the side, which Sydney had left wide open, opened on to a closet, and that was empty. I glanced up,— there was no trap door which led to the roof. No practicable nook or cranny, in which a living being could lie concealed, was anywhere at hand.

I returned to Sydney's shoulder to tell the cabman so.

'There is no place in which anyone could hide, and there is no one in either of the rooms,—you must have been mistaken, driver.'

The man waxed wroth.

'Don't tell me! How could I come to think I saw something when I didn't?'

'One's eyes are apt to play us tricks;—how could you see what wasn't there?'

'That's what I want to know. As I drove up, before you told me to stop, I saw him looking through the window,—the one at which you are. He'd got his nose glued to the broken pane, and was staring as hard as he could stare. When I pulled up, off he started,—I saw him get up off his knees, and go to the back of the room. When the gentleman took to knocking, back he came,—to the same old spot, and flopped down on his knees. I didn't know what caper you was up to,—you might be bum bailiffs for all I knew!—and I supposed that he wasn't so anxious to let you in as you might be to get inside, and that was why he didn't take no notice of your knocking, while all the while he kept a eye on what was going on. When you goes round to the back, up he gets again, and I reckoned that he was going to meet yer, and perhaps give yer a bit of his mind, and that presently I should hear a shindy, or that something would happen.

'But when you pulls up the blind downstairs, to my surprise back he come once more. He shoves his old nose right through the smash in the pane, and wags his old head at me like a chattering magpie. That didn't seem to me quite the civil thing to do,—I hadn't done no harm to him; so I gives you the office, and lets you know that he was there. But for you to say that he wasn't there, and never had been,—blimey! that cops the biscuit. If he wasn't there, all I can say is I ain't here, and my 'orse ain't here, and my cab ain't neither,—damn it!—the house ain't here, and nothing ain't!'

He settled himself on his perch with an air of the most extreme ill usage,—he had been standing up to tell his tale. That the man was serious was unmistakable. As he himself suggested, what inducement could he have had to tell a lie like that? That he believed himself to have seen what he declared he saw was plain. But, on the other hand, what could have become—in the space of fifty seconds!—of his 'old gent'?

Atherton put a question.

'What did he look like,—this old gent of yours?'

'Well, that I shouldn't hardly like to say. It wasn't much of his face I could see, only his face and his eyes,—and they wasn't pretty. He kept a thing over his head all the time, as if he didn't want too much to be seen.'

'What sort of a thing?'

'Why,—one of them cloak sort of things, like them Arab blokes used to wear what used to be at Earl's Court Exhibition,—you know!'

This piece of information seemed to interest my companions more than anything he had said before.

'A *burnoose* do you mean?'

'How am I to know what the thing's called? I ain't up in foreign languages,—'tain't likely! All I know that them Arab blokes what was at Earl's Court used to walk about in them all over the place,—sometimes they wore them over their heads, and sometimes they didn't. In fact if you'd asked me, instead of trying to make out as I sees double, or things what was only inside my own noddle, or something or other, I should have said this here old gent what I've been telling you about was a Arab bloke,—when he gets off his knees to sneak away from the window, I could see that he had his cloak thing, what was over his head, wrapped all round him.'

Mr. Lessingham turned to me, all quivering with excitement.

'I believe that what he says is true!'

'Then where can this mysterious old gentleman have got to,—can you suggest an explanation? It is strange, to say the least of it, that the cabman should be the only person to see or hear anything of him.'

'Some devil's trick has been played,—I know it, I feel it!—my instinct tells me so!'

I stared. In such a matter one hardly expects a man of Paul Lessingham's stamp to talk of 'instinct.' Atherton stared too. Then, on a sudden, he burst out,

'By the Lord, I believe the Apostle's right,—the whole place reeks to me of hanky-panky,—it did as soon as I put my nose inside. In matters of prestidigitation, Champnell, we Westerns are among the rudiments,—we've everything to learn,—Orientals leave us at the post. If their civilisation's what we're pleased to call extinct, their conjuring—when you get to know it!—is all alive oh!'

He moved towards the door. As he went he slipped, or seemed to, all but stumbling on to his knees.

'Something tripped me up,—what's this?' He was stamping on the floor with his foot. 'Here's a board loose. Come and lend me a hand, one of you fellows, to get it up. Who knows what mystery's beneath?'

I went to his aid. As he said, a board in the floor was loose. His stepping on it unawares had caused his stumble. Together we prised it out of its place,—Lessingham standing by and watching us the while. Having removed it, we peered into the cavity it disclosed.

There was something there.

'Why,' cried Atherton 'it's a woman's clothing!'

Chapter 7: The Rest of the Find

It was a woman's clothing, beyond a doubt, all thrown in anyhow,—as if the person who had placed it there had been in a desperate hurry. An entire outfit was there, shoes, stockings, body linen, corsets, and all,—even to hat, gloves, and hairpins;—these latter were mixed up with the rest of the garments in strange confusion. It seemed plain that whoever had worn those clothes had been stripped to the skin.

Lessingham and Sydney stared at me in silence as I dragged them out and laid them on the floor. The dress was at the bottom,—it was an alpaca, of a pretty shade in blue, bedecked with lace and ribbons, as is the fashion of the hour, and lined with sea-green silk. It had perhaps been a 'charming confection' once—and that a very recent one!—but now it was all soiled and creased and torn and tumbled. The two spectators made a simultaneous pounce at it as I brought it to the light.

'My God!' cried Sydney, 'it's Marjorie's!—she was wearing it when I saw her last!'

'It's Marjorie's!' gasped Lessingham,—he was clutching at the ruined costume, staring at it like a man who has just received sentence of death. 'She wore it when she was with me yesterday,—I told her how it suited her, and how pretty it was!'

There was silence,—it was an eloquent find; it spoke for itself. The two men gazed at the heap of feminine glories,—it might have been the most wonderful sight they ever had seen. Lessingham was the first to speak,—his face had all at once grown grey and haggard.

'What has happened to her?'

I replied to his question with another.

'Are you sure this is Miss Linden's dress?'

'I am sure,—and were proof needed, here it is.'

He had found the pocket, and was turning out the contents. There was a purse, which contained money and some visiting cards on which were her name and address; a small bunch of keys, with her nameplate attached; a handkerchief, with her initials in a corner. The question of ownership was placed beyond a doubt.

'You see,' said Lessingham, exhibiting the money which was in the purse, 'it is not robbery which has been attempted. Here are two ten-pound notes, and one for five, besides gold and silver,—over thirty pounds in all.'

Atherton, who had been turning over the accumulation of rubbish between the joists, proclaimed another find.

'Here are her rings, and watch, and a bracelet,—no, it certainly does not look as if theft had been an object.'

Lessingham was glowering at him with knitted brows.

'I have to thank you for this.'

Sydney was unwontedly meek.

'You are hard on me, Lessingham, harder than I deserve,—I had rather have thrown away my own life than have suffered misadventure to have come to her.'

'Yours are idle words. Had you not meddled this would not have happened. A fool works more mischief with his folly than of malice prepense. If hurt has befallen Marjorie Lindon you shall account for it to me with your life's blood.'

'Let it be so,' said Sydney. 'I am content. If hurt has come to Marjorie, God knows that I am willing enough that death should come to me.'

While they wrangled, I continued to search. A little to one side, under the flooring which was still intact, I saw something gleam. By stretching out my hand, I could just manage to reach it,—it was a long plait of woman's hair. It had been cut off at the roots,—so close to the head in one place that the scalp itself had been cut, so that the hair was clotted with blood.

They were so occupied with each other that they took no notice of me. I had to call their attention to my discovery.

'Gentlemen, I fear that I have here something which will distress you,—is not this Miss Lindon's hair?'

They recognised it on the instant. Lessingham, snatching it from my hands, pressed it to his lips.

'This is mine,—I shall at least have something.' He spoke with a grimness which was a little startling. He held the silken tresses at arm's length. 'This points to murder,—foul, cruel, causeless murder. As I live, I will devote my all,—money, time, reputation!—to gaining vengeance on the wretch who did this deed.'

Atherton chimed in.

'To that I say, Amen!' He lifted his hand. 'God is my witness!'

'It seems to me, gentlemen, that we move too fast,—to my mind it does not by any means of necessity point to murder. On the contrary, I doubt if murder has been done. Indeed, I don't mind owning that I have a theory of my own which points all the other way.'

Lessingham caught me by the sleeve.

'Mr. Champnell, tell me your theory.'

'I will, a little later. Of course it may be altogether wrong;—though I fancy it is not; I will explain my reasons when we come to talk of it. But, at present, there are things which must be done.'

'I vote for tearing up every board in the house!' cried Sydney. 'And for pulling the whole infernal place to pieces. It's a conjurer's den.—I shouldn't be surprised if cabby's old gent is staring at us all the while from some peephole of his own.'

We examined the entire house, methodically, so far as we were able, inch by inch. Not another board proved loose,—to lift those which were nailed down required tools, and those we were without. We sounded all the walls,—with the exception of the party walls they were the usual lath and plaster constructions, and showed no signs of having been tampered with. The ceilings were intact; if anything was concealed in them it must have been there some time,—the cement was old and dirty. We took the closet to pieces; examined the chimneys; peered into the kitchen oven and the copper;—in short, we pried into everything which, with the limited means at our disposal, could be pried into,—without result. At the end we found ourselves dusty, dirty, and discomfited. The cabman's 'old gent' remained as much a mystery as ever, and no further trace had been discovered of Miss Lindon.

Atherton made no effort to disguise his chagrin.

'Now what's to be done? There seems to be just nothing in the place at all, and yet that there is, and that it's the key to the whole confounded business I should be disposed to swear.'

'In that case I would suggest that you should stay and look for it. The cabman can go and look for the requisite tools, or a workman to assist you, if you like. For my part it appears to me that evidence of another sort is, for the moment, of paramount importance; and I propose to commence my search for it by making a call at the house which is over the way.'

I had observed, on our arrival, that the road only contained two houses which were in anything like a finished state,—that which we were in, and another, some fifty or sixty yards further down, on the opposite side. It was to this I referred. The twain immediately proffered their companionship.

'I will come with you,' said Mr. Lessingham.

'And I,' echoed Sydney. 'We'll leave this sweet homestead in charge of the cabman,—I'll pull it to pieces afterwards.' He went out and spoke to the driver. 'Cabby, we're going to pay a visit to the little crib over there,—you keep an eye on this one. And if you see a sign of anyone being about the place,—living, or dead, or anyhow—you give me a yell. I shall be on the lookout, and I'll be with you before you can say Jack Robinson.'

'You bet I'll yell,—I'll raise the hair right off you.' The fellow grinned. 'But I don't know if you gents are hiring me by the day,—I want to change my horse; he ought to have been in his stable a couple of hours ago.'

'Never mind your horse,—let him rest a couple of hours extra to-morrow to make up for those he has lost today. I'll take care you don't lose anything by this little job,—or your horse either.—By the way, look here,—this will be better than yelling.'

Taking a revolver out of his trousers' pocket he handed it up to the grinning driver.

'If that old gent of yours does appear, you have a pop at him,—I shall hear that easier than a yell. You can put a bullet through him if you like,—I give you my word it won't be murder.'

'I don't care if it is,' declared the cabman, handling the weapon like one who was familiar with arms of precision. 'I used to fancy my revolver shooting when I was with the colours, and if I do get a chance I'll put a shot through the old hunks, if only to prove to you that I'm no liar.'

Whether the man was in earnest or not I could not tell,—nor whether Atherton meant what he said in answer.

'If you shoot him I'll give you fifty pounds.'

'All right!' The driver laughed. 'I'll do my best to earn that fifty!'

CHAPTER 8: MISS LOUISA COLEMAN

That the house over the way was tenanted was plain to all the world,—at least one occupant sat gazing through the window of the first floor front room. An old woman in a cap,—one of those large old-fashioned caps which our grandmothers used to wear, tied with strings under the chin. It was a bow window, and as she was seated in the bay looking right in our direction she could hardly have failed to see us as we advanced,—indeed she continued to stare at us all the while with placid calmness. Yet I knocked once, twice, and yet again without the slightest notice being taken of my summons.

Sydney gave expression to his impatience in his own peculiar vein.

'Knockers in this part of the world seem intended for ornament only,—nobody seems to pay any attention to them when they're used. The old lady upstairs must be either deaf or dotty.' He went out into the road to see if she still was there. 'She's looking at me as calmly as you please,—what does she think we're doing here, I wonder; playing a tune on her front door by way of a little amusement?—Madam!' He took off his hat and waved it to her. 'Madam! might I observe that if you won't condescend to notice that we're here your front door will run the risk of being severely injured!—She don't care for me any more than if I was nothing at all,—sound another tattoo upon that knocker. Perhaps she's so deaf that nothing short of a cataclysmal up-roar will reach her auditory nerves.'

She immediately proved, however, that she was nothing of the sort. Hardly had the sounds of my further knocking died away than, throwing up the window, she thrust out her head and addressed me in a fashion which, under the circumstances, was as unexpected as it was uncalled for.

'Now, young man, you needn't be in such a hurry!'

Sydney explained.

'Pardon me, madam, it's not so much a hurry we're in as pressed for time,—this is a matter of life and death.'

She turned her attention to Sydney,—speaking with a frankness for which, I imagine, he was unprepared.

'I don't want none of your imperence, young man. I've seen you before,—you've been hanging about here the whole day long!—and I don't like the looks of you, and so I'll let you know. That's my front door, and that's my knocker,—I'll come down and open when I like, but I'm not going to be hurried, and if the knocker's so much as touched again, I won't come down at all.'

She closed the window with a bang. Sydney seemed divided between mirth and indignation.

'That's a nice old lady, on my honour,—one of the good old crusty sort. Agreeable characters this neighbourhood seems to grow,—a sojourn hereabouts should do one good. Unfortunately I don't feel disposed just now to stand and kick my heels in the road.' Again saluting the old dame by raising his hat he shouted to her at the top of his voice. 'Madam, I beg ten thousand pardons for troubling you, but this is a matter in which every second is of vital importance,—would you allow me to ask you one or two questions?'

Up went the window; out came the old lady's head.

'Now, young man, you needn't put yourself out to holler at me,—I won't be hollered at! I'll come down and open that door in five minutes by the clock on my mantelpiece, and not a moment before.'

The fiat delivered, down came the window. Sydney looked rueful,—he consulted his watch.

'I don't know what you think, Champnell, but I really doubt if this comfortable creature can tell us anything worth waiting another five minutes to hear. We mustn't let the grass grow under our feet, and time is getting on.'

I was of a different opinion,—and said so.

'I'm afraid, Atherton, that I can't agree with you. She seems to have noticed you hanging about all day; and it is at least possible that she has noticed a good deal which would be well worth our hearing. What more promising witness are we likely to find?—her house is the only one which overlooks the one we have just quitted. I am of opinion that it may not only prove well worth our while to wait five minutes, but also that it would be as well, if possible, not to offend her by the way. She's not likely to afford us the information we require if you do.'

'Good. If that's what you think I'm sure I'm willing to wait,—only it's to be hoped that that clock upon her mantelpiece moves quicker than its mistress.'

Presently, when about a minute had gone, he called to the cabman.

'Seen a sign of anything?'

The cabman shouted back.

'Ne'er a sign,—you'll hear a sound of popguns when I do.'

Those five minutes did seem long ones. But at last Sydney, from his post of vantage in the road, informed us that the old lady was moving.

'She's getting up;—she's leaving the window;—let's hope to goodness she's coming down to open the door. That's been the longest five minutes I've known.'

I could hear uncertain footsteps descending the stairs. They came along the passage. The door was opened—'on the chain.' The old lady peered at us through an aperture of about six inches.

'I don't know what you young men think you're after, but have all three of you in my house I won't. I'll have him and you'—a skinny finger was pointed to Lessingham and me; then it was directed towards Atherton—'but have him I won't. So if it's anything particular you want to say to me, you'll just tell him to go away.'

On hearing this Sydney's humility was abject. His hat was in his hand,—he bent himself double.

'Suffer me to make you a million apologies, madam, if I have in any way offended you; nothing, I assure you, could have been farther from my intention, or from my thoughts.'

'I don't want none of your apologies, and I don't want none of you neither; I don't like the looks of you, and so I tell you. Before I let anybody into my house you'll have to sling your hook.'

The door was banged in our faces. I turned to Sydney.

'The sooner you go the better it will be for us. You can wait for us over the way.'

He shrugged his shoulders, and groaned,—half in jest, half in earnest.

'If I must I suppose I must,—it's the first time I've been refused admittance to a lady's house in all my life! What have I done to deserve this thing?—If you keep me waiting long I'll tear that infernal den to pieces!'

He sauntered across the road, viciously kicking the stones as he went. The door reopened.

'Has that other young man gone?'

'He has.'

'Then now I'll let you in. Have him inside my house I won't.'

The chain was removed. Lessingham and I entered. Then the door was refastened and the chain replaced. Our hostess showed us into the front room on the ground floor; it was sparsely furnished and not too clean,—but there were chairs enough for us to sit upon; which she insisted on our occupying.

'Sit down, do,—I can't abide to see folks standing; it gives me the fidgets.'

So soon as we were seated, without any overture on our parts she plunged in medias res.

'I know what it is you've come about,—I know! You want me to tell you who it is as lives in the house over the road. Well, I can tell you,—and I dare bet a shilling that I'm about the only one who can.'

I inclined my head.

'Indeed. Is that so, madam?'

She was huffed at once.

'Don't madam me,—I can't bear none of your lip service. I'm a plain-spoken woman, that's what I am, and I like other people's tongues to be as plain as mine. My name's Miss Louisa Coleman; but I'm generally called Miss Coleman,—I'm only called Louisa by my relatives.'

Since she was apparently between seventy and eighty—and looked every year of her apparent age—I deemed that possible. Miss Coleman was evidently a character. If one was desirous of getting information out of her it would be necessary to allow her to impart it in her own manner,—to endeavour to induce her to impart it in anybody else's would be time clean wasted. We had Sydney's fate before our eyes.

She started with a sort of roundabout preamble.

'This property is mine; it was left me by my uncle, the late George Henry Jobson,—he's buried in Hammersmith Cemetery just over the way,—he left me the whole of it. It's one of the finest building sites near London, and it increases in value every year, and I'm not going to let it for another twenty, by which time the value will have more than trebled,—so if that is what you've come about, as heaps of people do,

140

you might have saved yourselves the trouble. I keep the boards standing, just to let people know that the ground is to let,—though, as I say, it won't be for another twenty years, when it'll be for the erection of high-class mansions only, same as there is in Grosvenor Square,—no shops or public houses, and none of your shanties. I live in this place just to keep an eye upon the property,—and as for the house over the way, I've never tried to let it, and it never has been let, not until a month ago, when, one morning, I had this letter. You can see it if you like.'

She handed me a greasy envelope which she ferreted out of a capacious pocket which was suspended from her waist, and which she had to lift up her skirt to reach. The envelope was addressed, in unformed characters, 'Miss Louisa Coleman, The Rhododendrons, Convolvulus Avenue, High Oaks Park, West Kensington.'—I felt, if the writer had not been of a humorous turn of mind, and drawn on his imagination, and this really was the lady's correct address, then there must be something in a name.

The letter within was written in the same straggling, characterless calligraphy,—I should have said, had I been asked offhand, that the whole thing was the composition of a servant girl. The composition was about on a par with the writing.

The undersigned would be obliged if Miss Coleman would let her emptey house. I do not know the rent but send fifty pounds. If more will send. Please address, Mohamed el Kheir, Post Office, Sligo Street, London.

It struck me as being as singular an application for a tenancy as I remembered to have encountered. When I passed it on to Lessingham, he seemed to think so too.

'This is a curious letter, Miss Coleman.'

'So I thought,—and still more so when I found the fifty pounds inside. There were five ten-pound notes, all loose, and the letter not even registered. If I had been asked what was the rent of the house, I should have said, at the most, not more than twenty pounds,—because, between you and me, it wants a good bit of doing up, and is hardly fit to live in as it stands.'

I had had sufficient evidence of the truth of this altogether apart from the landlady's frank admission.

'Why, for all he could have done to help himself I might have kept the money, and only sent him a receipt for a quarter. And some folks would have done,—but I'm not one of that sort myself, and shouldn't care to be. So I sent this here party,—I never could pronounce his name, and never shall—a receipt for a year.'

Miss Coleman paused to smooth her apron, and consider.

'Well, the receipt should have reached this here party on the Thursday morning, as it were,—I posted it on the Wednesday night, and on the Thursday, after breakfast, I thought I'd go over the way to see if there was any little thing I could do,—because there wasn't hardly a whole pane of glass in the place,—when I all but went all of a heap. When I looked across the road, blessed it the party wasn't in already,— at least as much as he ever was in, which, so far as I can make out, never has been anything particular,—though how he had got in, unless it was through a window in the middle of the night, is more than I should care to say,—there was nobody in the house when I went to bed, that I could pretty nearly take my Bible oath,—yet there was the blind up at the parlour, and, what's more, it was down, and it's been down pretty nearly ever since.

'"Well," I says to myself, "for right down imperence this beats anything,—why he's in the place before he knows if I'll let him have it. Perhaps he thinks I haven't got a word to say in the matter,—fifty pounds or no fifty pounds, I'll soon show him." So I slips on my bonnet, and I walks over the road, and I hammers at the door.

'Well, I have seen people hammering since then, many a one, and how they've kept it up has puzzled me,—for an hour, some of them,—but I was the first one as begun it. I hammers, and I hammers, and I kept on hammering, but it wasn't no more use than if I'd been hammering at a tombstone. So I starts rapping at the window, but that wasn't no use neither. So I goes round behind, and I hammers at the back door,—but there, I couldn't make anyone hear nohow. So I says to myself, "Perhaps the party as is in, ain't in, in a manner of speaking; but I'll keep an eye on the house, and when he is in I'll take care that he ain't out again before I've had a word to say."

'So I come back home, and as I said I would, I kept an eye on the house the whole of that livelong day, but never a soul went either out or in. But the next day, which it was a Friday, I got out of bed about five o'clock, to see if it was raining, through my having an idea of taking a little excursion if the weather was fine, when I see a party coming down the road. He had on one of them dirty-coloured bed-cover sort of things, and it was wrapped all over his head and round his body, like, as I have been told, them there Arabs wear,—and, indeed, I've seen them in them myself at West Brompton, when they was in the exhibition there. It was quite fine, and broad day, and I see him as plainly as I see you,—he comes skimming along at a tear of a pace, pulls up at the house over the way, opens the front door, and lets himself in.

'"So," I says to myself, "there you are. Well, Mr. Arab, or whatever, or whoever, you may be, I'll take good care that you don't go out again before you've had a word from me. I'll show you that landladies have their rights, like other Christians, in this country, however it may be in yours." So I kept an eye on the house, to see that he didn't go out again, and nobody never didn't, and between seven and eight I goes and I knocks at the door,—because I thought to myself that the earlier I was the better it might be.

'If you'll believe me, no more notice was taken of me than if I was one of the dead. I hammers, and I hammers, till my wrist was aching, I daresay I hammered twenty times,—and then I went round to the back door, and I hammers at that,—but it wasn't the least good in the world. I was that provoked to think I should be treated as if I was nothing and nobody, by a dirty foreigner, who went about in a bed-gown through the public streets, that it was all I could do to hold myself.

'I comes round to the front again, and I starts hammering at the window, with every knuckle on my hands, and I calls out, "I'm Miss Louisa Coleman, and I'm the owner of this house, and you can't deceive me,—I saw you come in, and you're in now, and if you don't come and speak to me this moment I'll have the police."

'All of a sudden, when I was least expecting it, and was hammering my very hardest at the pane, up goes the blind, and up goes the window too, and the most awful-looking creature ever I heard of, not to mention seeing, puts his head right into my face,—he was more like a hideous baboon than anything else, let alone a man. I was struck all of a heap, and plumps down on the little wall, and all but tumbles head over heels backwards, And he starts shrieking, in a sort of a kind of English, and in such a voice as I'd never heard the like,—it was like a rusty steam engine.

'"Go away! go away! I don't want you! I will not have you,—never! You have your fifty pounds,—you have your money,—that is the whole of you,—that is all you want! You come to me no more!—never!—never no more!—or you be sorry!—Go away!"

'I did go away, and that as fast as ever my legs would carry me,—

what with his looks, and what with his voice, and what with the way that he went on, I was nothing but a mass of trembling. As for answering him back, or giving him a piece of my mind, as I had meant to, I wouldn't have done it not for a thousand pounds. I don't mind confessing, between you and me, that I had to swallow four cups of tea, right straight away, before my nerves was steady.

'"Well," I says to myself, when I did feel, as it might be, a little more easy, "you never have let that house before, and now you've let it with a vengeance,—so you have. If that there new tenant of yours isn't the greatest villain that ever went unhung it must be because he's got near relations what's as bad as himself,—because two families like his I'm sure there can't be. A nice sort of Arab party to have sleeping over the road he is!"

'But after a time I cools down, as it were,—because I'm one of them sort as likes to see on both sides of a question. "After all," I says to myself, "he has paid his rent, and fifty pounds is fifty pounds,—I doubt if the whole house is worth much more, and he can't do much damage to it whatever he does."

'I shouldn't have minded, so far as that went, if he'd set fire to the place, for, between ourselves, it's insured for a good bit over its value. So I decided that I'd let things be as they were, and see how they went on. But from that hour to this I've never spoken to the man, and never wanted to, and wouldn't, not of my own free will, not for a shilling a time,—that face of his will haunt me if I live till Noah, as the saying is. I've seen him going in and out at all hours of the day and night,—that Arab party's a mystery if ever there was one,—he always goes tearing along as if he's flying for his life.

'Lots of people have come to the house, all sorts and kinds, men and women—they've been mostly women, and even little children. I've seen them hammer and hammer at that front door, but never a one have I seen let in,—or yet seen taken any notice of, and I think I may say, and yet tell no lie, that I've scarcely took my eye off the house since he's been inside it, over and over again in the middle of the night have I got up to have a look, so that I've not missed much that has took place.

'What's puzzled me is the noises that's come from the house. Sometimes for days together there's not been a sound, it might have been a house of the dead; and then, all through the night, there've been yells and screeches, squawks and screams,—I never heard nothing like it. I have thought, and more than once, that the devil himself must be in that front room, let alone all the rest of his demons.

'And as for cats!—where they've come from I can't think. I didn't use to notice hardly a cat in the neighbourhood till that there Arab party came,—there isn't much to attract them; but since he came there's been regiments. Sometimes at night there's been troops about the place, screeching like mad,—I've wished them farther, I can tell you. That Arab party must be fond of 'em. I've seen them inside the house, at the windows, upstairs and downstairs, as it seemed to me, a dozen at a time.

CHAPTER 9: WHAT MISS COLEMAN SAW THROUGH THE WINDOW

As Miss Coleman had paused, as if her narrative was approaching a conclusion, I judged it expedient to make an attempt to bring the record as quickly as possible up to date.

'I take it, Miss Coleman, that you have observed what has occurred in the house today.'

She tightened her nut-cracker jaws and glared at me disdainfully,—her dignity was ruffled.

'I'm coming to it, aren't I?—if you'll let me. If you've got no manners I'll learn you some. One doesn't like to be hurried at my time of life, young man.'

I was meekly silent;—plainly, if she was to talk, everyone else must listen.

'During the last few days there have been some queer goings on over the road,—out of the common queer, I mean, for goodness knows that they always have been queer enough. That Arab party has been flitting about like a creature possessed,—I've seen him going in and out twenty times a day. This morning—'

She paused,—to fix her eyes on Lessingham. She apparently observed his growing interest as she approached the subject which had brought us there,—and resented it.

'Don't look at me like that, young man, because I won't have it. And as for questions, I may answer questions when I'm done, but don't you dare to ask me one before, because I won't be interrupted.'

Up to then Lessingham had not spoken a word,—but it seemed as if she was endowed with the faculty of perceiving the huge volume of the words which he had left unuttered.

'This morning—as I've said already,—' she glanced at Lessingham as if she defied his contradiction—'when that Arab party came home it was just on the stroke of seven. I know what was the exact time because, when I went to the door to the milkman, my clock was striking the half hour, and I always keep it thirty minutes fast. As I was taking the milk, the man said to me, "Hollo, Miss Coleman, here's your friend coming along." "What friend?" I says,—for I ain't got no friends, as I know, round here, nor yet, I hope no enemies neither.

'And I looks round, and there was the Arab party coming tearing down the road, his bedcover thing all flying in the wind, and his arms straight out in front of him,—I never did see anyone go at such a pace. "My goodness," I says, "I wonder he don't do himself an injury." "I wonder someone else don't do him an injury," says the milkman. "The very sight of him is enough to make my milk go sour." And he picked up his pail and went away quite grumpy,—though what that Arab party's done to him is more than I can say.—I have always noticed that milkman's temper's short like his measure. I wasn't best pleased with him for speaking of that Arab party as my friend, which he never has been, and never won't be, and never could be neither.

'Five persons went to the house after the milkman was gone, and that there Arab party was safe inside,—three of them was commercials, that I know, because afterwards they came to me. But of course they none of them got no chance with that there Arab party except of hammering at his front door, which ain't what you might call a paying game, nor nice for the temper but for that I don't blame him, for if once those commercials do begin talking they'll talk for ever.

'Now I'm coming to this afternoon.'

I thought it was about time,—though for the life of me, I did not dare to hint as much.

'Well, it might have been three, or it might have been half past, anyhow it was thereabouts, when up there comes two men and a woman, which one of the men was that young man what's a friend of yours. "Oh," I says to myself, "here's something new in callers, I wonder what it is they're wanting." That young man what was a friend of yours, he starts hammering, and hammering, as the custom was with everyone who came, and, as usual, no more notice was taken of him than nothing,—though I knew that all the time the Arab party was indoors.'

At this point I felt that at all hazards I must interpose a question.

'You are sure he was indoors?'

She took it better than I feared she might.

'Of course I'm sure,—hadn't I seen him come in at seven, and he never hadn't gone out since, for I don't believe that I'd taken my eyes off the place not for two minutes together, and I'd never had a sight of him. If he wasn't indoors, where was he then?'

For the moment, so far as I was concerned, the query was unanswerable. She triumphantly continued:

'Instead of doing what most did, when they'd had enough of hammering, and going away, these three they went round to the back, and I'm blessed if they mustn't have got through the kitchen window, woman and all, for all of a sudden the blind in the front room was pulled not up, but down—dragged down it was, and there was that young man what's a friend of yours standing with it in his hand.

'"Well," I says to myself, "if that ain't cool I should like to know what is. If, when you ain't let in, you can let yourself in, and that without so much as saying by your leave, or with your leave, things is coming to a pretty pass. Wherever can that Arab party be, and whatever can he be thinking of, to let them go on like that because that he's the sort to allow a liberty to be took with him, and say nothing, I don't believe."

'Every moment I expects to hear a noise and see a row begin, but, so far as I could make out, all was quiet and there wasn't nothing of the kind. So I says to myself, "There's more in this than meets the eye, and them three parties must have right upon their side, or they wouldn't be doing what they are doing in the way they are, there'd be a shindy."

'Presently, in about five minutes, the front door opens, and a young man—not the one what's your friend, but the other—comes sailing out, and through the gate, and down the road, as stiff and upright as a grenadier,—I never see anyone walk more upright, and few as fast. At his heels comes the young man what is your friend, and it seems to me that he couldn't make out what this other was a-doing of. I says to myself, "There's been a quarrel between them two, and him as has gone has hooked it." This young man what is your friend he stood at the gate, all of a fidget, staring after the other with all his eyes, as if he couldn't think what to make of him, and the young woman, she stood on the doorstep, staring after him too.

'As the young man what had hooked it turned the corner, and was out of sight, all at once your friend he seemed to make up his mind, and he started off running as hard as he could pelt,—and the young woman was left alone. I expected, every minute, to see him come back with the other young man, and the young woman, by the way she hung about the gate, she seemed to expect it too. But no, nothing of the kind. So when, as I expect, she'd had enough of waiting, she went into the house again, and I see her pass the front room window. After a while, back she comes to the gate, and stands looking and looking, but nothing was to be seen of either of them young men. When she'd been at the gate, I daresay five minutes, back she goes into the house,—and I never saw nothing of her again.'

'You never saw anything of her again?—Are you sure she went back into the house?'

'As sure as I am that I see you.'

'I suppose that you didn't keep a constant watch upon the premises?'

'But that's just what I did do. I felt something queer was going on, and I made up my mind to see it through. And when I make up my mind to a thing like that I'm not easy to turn aside. I never moved off the chair at my bedroom window, and I never took my eyes off the house, not till you come knocking at my front door.'

'But, since the young lady is certainly not in the house at present, she must have eluded your observation, and, in some manner, have left it without your seeing her.'

'I don't believe she did, I don't see how she could have done,—there's something queer about that house, since that Arab party's been inside it. But though I didn't see her, I did see someone else.'

'Who was that?'

'A young man.'

'A young man?'

'Yes, a young man, and that's what puzzled me, and what's been puzzling me ever since, for see him go in I never did do.'

'Can you describe him?'

'Not as to the face, for he wore a dirty cloth cap pulled down right over it, and he walked so quickly that I never had a proper look. But I should know him anywhere if I saw him, if only because of his clothes and his walk.'

'What was there peculiar about his clothes and his walk?'

'Why, his clothes were that old, and torn, and dirty, that a ragman wouldn't have given a thank you for them,—and as for fit,—there wasn't none, they hung upon him like a scarecrow—he was a regular figure of fun; I should think the boys would call after him if they saw him in the street. As for his walk, he walked off just like the first young man had done, he strutted along with his shoulders back, and his head in the air, and that stiff and straight that my kitchen poker would have looked crooked beside of him.'

'Did nothing happen to attract your attention between the young lady's going back into the house and the coming out of this young man?'

Miss Coleman cogitated.

'Now you mention it there did,—though I should have forgotten all about it if you hadn't asked me,—that comes of your not letting me tell the tale in my own way. About twenty minutes after the young woman had gone in someone put up the blind in the front room, which that young man had dragged right down, I couldn't see who it was for the blind was between us, and it was about ten minutes after that that young man came marching out.'

'And then what followed?'

'Why, in about another ten minutes that Arab party himself comes scooting through the door.'

'The Arab party?'

'Yes, the Arab party! The sight of him took me clean aback. Where he'd been, and what he'd been doing with himself while them there people played hi-spy-hi about his premises I'd have given a shilling out of my pocket to have known, but there he was, as large as life, and carrying a bundle.'

'A bundle?'

'A bundle, on his head, like a muffin-man carries his tray. It was a great thing, you never would have thought he could have carried it, and it was easy to see that it was as much as he could manage; it bent him nearly double, and he went crawling along like a snail,—it took him quite a time to get to the end of the road.'

Mr. Lessingham leaped up from his seat, crying, 'Marjorie was in that bundle!'

'I doubt it,' I said.

He moved about the room distractedly, wringing his hands.

'She was! she must have been! God help us all!'

'I repeat that I doubt it. If you will be advised by me you will wait awhile before you arrive at any such conclusion.'

All at once there was a tapping at the window pane. Atherton was staring at us from without.

He shouted through the glass, 'Come out of that, you fossils!—I've news for you!'

Miss Coleman, getting up in a fluster, went hurrying to the door.

'I won't have that young man in my house. I won't have him! Don't let him dare to put his nose across my doorstep.'

I endeavoured to appease her perturbation.

'I promise you that he shall not come in, Miss Coleman. My friend here, and I, will go and speak to him outside.'

She held the front door open just wide enough to enable Lessingham and me to slip through, then she shut it after us with a bang. She evidently had a strong objection to any intrusion on Sydney's part.

Standing just without the gate he saluted us with a characteristic vigour which was scarcely flattering to our late hostess. Behind him was a constable.

'I hope you two have been mewed in with that old pussy long enough. While you've been tittle-tattling I've been doing,—listen to what this bobby's got to say.'

The constable, his thumbs thrust inside his belt, wore an indulgent smile upon his countenance. He seemed to find Sydney amusing. He spoke in a deep bass voice,—as if it issued from his boots.

'I don't know that I've got anything to say.'

It was plain that Sydney thought otherwise.

'You wait till I've given this pretty pair of gossips a lead, officer, then I'll trot you out.' He turned to us.

'After I'd poked my nose into every dashed hole in that infernal den, and been rewarded with nothing but a pain in the back for my trouble, I stood cooling my heels on the doorstep, wondering if I should fight the cabman, or get him to fight me, just to pass the time away,—for he says he can box, and he looks it,—when who should come strolling along but this magnificent example of the metropolitan constabulary.' He waved his hand towards the policeman, whose grin grew wider. 'I looked at him, and he looked at me, and then when we'd had enough of admiring each other's fine features and striking proportions, he said to me, "Has he gone?" I said, "Who?—Baxter?— or Bob Brown?" He said, "No, the Arab."

'I said, "What do you know about any Arab?" He said, "Well, I saw him in the Broadway about three-quarters of an hour ago, and then, seeing you here, and the house all open, I wondered if he had gone for good." With that I almost jumped out of my skin, though you can bet your life I never showed it. I said, "How do you know it was he?" He said, "It was him right enough, there's no doubt about that.

If you've seen him once, you're not likely to forget him." "Where was he going?" "He was talking to a cabman,—four-wheeler. He'd got a great bundle on his head,—wanted to take it inside with him. Cabman didn't seem to see it." That was enough for me,—I picked this most deserving officer up in my arms, and carried him across the road to you two fellows like a flash of lightning.'

Since the policeman was six feet three or four, and more than sufficiently broad in proportion, his scarcely seemed the kind of figure to be picked up in anybody's arms and carried like a 'flash of lightning,' which,—as his smile grew more indulgent, he himself appeared to think.

Still, even allowing for Atherton's exaggeration, the news which he had brought was sufficiently important. I questioned the constable upon my own account.

'There is my card, officer, probably, before the day is over, a charge of a very serious character will be preferred against the person who has been residing in the house over the way. In the meantime it is of the utmost importance that a watch should be kept upon his movements. I suppose you have no sort of doubt that the person you saw in the Broadway was the one in question?'

'Not a morsel. I know him as well as I do my own brother,—we all do upon this beat. He's known amongst us as the Arab. I've had my eye on him ever since he came to the place. A queer fish he is. I always have said that he's up to some game or other. I never came across one like him for flying about in all sorts of weather, at all hours of the night, always tearing along as if for his life. As I was telling this gentleman I saw him in the Broadway,—well, now it's about an hour since, perhaps a little more. I was coming on duty when I saw a crowd in front of the District Railway Station,—and there was the Arab, having a sort of argument with the cabman. He had a great bundle on his head, five or six feet long, perhaps longer. He wanted to take this great bundle with him into the cab, and the cabman, he didn't see it.'

'You didn't wait to see him drive off.'

'No,—I hadn't time. I was due at the station,—I was cutting it pretty fine as it was.'

'You didn't speak to him,—or to the cabman?'

'No, it wasn't any business of mine you understand. The whole thing just caught my eye as I was passing.'

'And you didn't take the cabman's number?'

'No, well, as far as that goes it wasn't needful. I know the cabman, his name and all about him, his stable's in Bradmore.'

I whipped out my note-book.

'Give me his address.'

'I don't know what his Christian name is, Tom, I believe, but I'm not sure. Anyhow his surname's Ellis and his address is Church Mews, St John's Road, Bradmore,—I don't know his number, but any one will tell you which is his place, if you ask for Four-Wheel Ellis,— that's the name he's known by among his pals because of his driving a four-wheeler.'

'Thank you, officer. I am obliged to you.' Two half-crowns changed hands. 'If you will keep an eye on the house and advise me at the address which you will find on my card, of anything which takes place there during the next few days, you will do me a service.'

We had clambered back into the hansom, the driver was just about to start, when the constable was struck by a sudden thought.

'One moment, sir,—blessed if I wasn't going to forget the most important bit of all. I did hear him tell Ellis where to drive him to,— he kept saying it over and over again, in that queer lingo of his. "Waterloo Railway Station, Waterloo Railway Station." "All right," said Ellis, "I'll drive you to Waterloo Railway Station right enough, only I'm not going to have that bundle of yours inside my cab. There isn't room for it, so you put it on the roof." "To Waterloo Railway Station," said the Arab, "I take my bundle with me to Waterloo Railway Station,—I take it with me." "Who says you don't take it with you?" said Ellis. "You can take it, and twenty more besides, for all I care, only you don't take it inside my cab,—put it on the roof." "I take it with me to Waterloo Railway Station," said the Arab, and there they were, wrangling and jangling, and neither seeming to be able to make out what the other was after, and the people all laughing.'

'Waterloo Railway Station,—you are sure that was what he said?'

'I'll take my oath to it, because I said to myself, when I heard it, "I wonder what you'll have to pay for that little lot, for the District Railway Station's outside the four-mile radius." As we drove off I was inclined to ask myself, a little bitterly—and perhaps unjustly—if it were not characteristic of the average London policeman to almost forget the most important part of his information,—at any rate to leave it to the last and only to bring it to the front on having his palm crossed with silver.

As the hansom bowled along we three had what occasionally approached a warm discussion.

152

'Marjorie was in that bundle,' began Lessingham, in the most lugubrious of tones, and with the most woebegone of faces.

'I doubt it,' I observed.

'She was,—I feel it,—I know it. She was either dead and mutilated, or gagged and drugged and helpless. All that remains is vengeance.'

'I repeat that I doubt it.'

Atherton struck in.

'I am bound to say, with the best will in the world to think otherwise, that I agree with Lessingham.'

'You are wrong.'

'It's all very well for you to talk in that cock-sure way, but it's easier for you to say I'm wrong than to prove it. If I am wrong, and if Lessingham's wrong, how do you explain his extraordinary insistence on taking it inside the cab with him, which the bobby describes? If there wasn't something horrible, awful in that bundle of his, of which he feared the discovery, why was he so reluctant to have it placed upon the roof?'

'There probably was something in it which he was particularly anxious should not be discovered, but I doubt if it was anything of the kind which you suggest.'

'Here is Marjorie in a house alone—nothing has been seen of her since,—her clothing, her hair, is found hidden away under the floor. This scoundrel sallies forth with a huge bundle on his head,—the bobby speaks of it being five or six feet long, or longer,—a bundle which he regards with so much solicitude that he insists on never allowing it to go, for a single instant, out of his sight and reach. What is in the thing? don't all the facts most unfortunately point in one direction?'

Mr. Lessingham covered his face with his hands, and groaned.

'I fear that Mr. Atherton is right.'

'I differ from you both.'

Sydney at once became heated.

'Then perhaps you can tell us what was in the bundle?'

'I fancy I could make a guess at the contents.'

'Oh you could, could you, then, perhaps, for our sakes, you'll make it,—and not play the oracular owl!—Lessingham and I are interested in this business, after all.'

'It contained the bearer's personal property: that, and nothing more. Stay! before you jeer at me, suffer me to finish. If I am not mistaken as to the identity of the person whom the constable describes as the

Arab, I apprehend that the contents of that bundle were of much more importance to him than if they had consisted of Miss Lindon, either dead or living. More. I am inclined to suspect that if the bundle was placed on the roof of the cab, and if the driver did meddle with it, and did find out the contents, and understand them, he would have been driven, out of hand, stark staring mad.'

Sydney was silent, as if he reflected. I imagine he perceived there was something in what I said.

'But what has become of Miss Lindon?'

'I fancy that Miss Lindon, at this moment, is—somewhere; I don't, just now, know exactly where, but I hope very shortly to be able to give you a clearer notion,—attired in a rotten, dirty pair of boots; a filthy, tattered pair of trousers; a ragged, unwashed apology for a shirt; a greasy, ancient, shapeless coat; and a frowsy peaked cloth cap.'

They stared at me, opened-eyed. Atherton was the first to speak.

'What on earth do you mean?'

'I mean that it seems to me that the facts point in the direction of my conclusions rather than yours—and that very strongly too. Miss Coleman asserts that she saw Miss London return into the house; that within a few minutes the blind was replaced at the front window; and that shortly after a young man, attired in the costume I have described, came walking out of the front door. I believe that young man was Miss Marjorie Lindon.'

Lessingham and Atherton both broke out into interrogations, with Sydney, as usual, loudest.

'But—man alive! what on earth should make her do a thing like that? Marjorie, the most retiring, modest girl on all God's earth, walk about in broad daylight, in such a costume, and for no reason at all! my dear Champnell, you are suggesting that she first of all went mad.'

'She was in a state of trance.'

'Good God!—Champnell!'

'Well?'

'Then you think that—juggling villain did get hold of her?'

'Undoubtedly. Here is my view of the case, mind it is only a hypothesis and you must take it for what it is worth. It seems to me quite clear that the Arab, as we will call the person for the sake of identification, was somewhere about the premises when you thought he wasn't.'

'But—where? We looked upstairs, and downstairs, and everywhere—where could he have been?'

'That, as at present advised, I am not prepared to say, but I think you may take it for granted that he was there. He hypnotised the man Holt, and sent him away, intending you to go after him, and so being rid of you both—'

'The deuce he did, Champnell! You write me down an ass!'

'As soon as the coast was clear he discovered himself to Miss Lindon, who, I expect, was disagreeably surprised, and hypnotised her.'

'The hound!'

'The devil!'

The first exclamation was Lessingham's, the second Sydney's.

'He then constrained her to strip herself to the skin—'

'The wretch!'

'The fiend!'

'He cut off her hair; he hid it and her clothes under the floor where we found them—where I think it probable that he had already some ancient masculine garments concealed—'

'By Jove! I shouldn't be surprised if they were Holt's. I remember the man saying that that nice joker stripped him of his duds,—and certainly when I saw him,—and when Marjorie found him!—he had absolutely nothing on but a queer sort of cloak. Can it be possible that that humorous professor of hanky-panky—may all the maledictions of the accursed alight upon his head!—can have sent Marjorie Lindon, the daintiest damsel in the land!—into the streets of London rigged out in Holt's old togs!'

'As to that, I am not able to give an authoritative opinion, but, if I understand you aright, it at least is possible. Anyhow I am disposed to think that he sent Miss Lindon after the man Holt, taking it for granted that he had eluded you.—'

'That's it. Write me down an ass again!'

'That he did elude you, you have yourself admitted.'

'That's because I stopped talking with that mutton-headed bobby,—I'd have followed the man to the ends of the earth if it hadn't been for that.'

'Precisely; the reason is immaterial, it is the fact with which we are immediately concerned. He did elude you. And I think you will find that Miss Lindon and Mr. Holt are together at this moment.'

'In men's clothing?'

'Both in men's clothing, or, rather, Miss Lindon is in a man's rags.'

'Great Potiphar! To think of Marjorie like that!'

'And where they are, the Arab is not very far off either.'

Lessingham caught me by the arm.

'And what diabolical mischief do you imagine that he proposes to do to her?'

I shirked the question.

'Whatever it is, it is our business to prevent his doing it.'

'And where do you think they have been taken?'

'That it will be our immediate business to endeavour to discover,—and here, at any rate, we are at Waterloo.'

CHAPTER 11: THE QUARRY DOUBLES

I turned towards the booking-office on the main departure platform. As I went, the chief platform inspector, George Bellingham, with whom I had some acquaintance, came out of his office. I stopped him.

'Mr. Bellingham, will you be so good as to step with me to the booking-office, and instruct the clerk in charge to answer one or two questions which I wish to put to him. I will explain to you afterwards what is their exact import, but you know me sufficiently to be able to believe me when I say that they refer to a matter in which every moment is of the first importance.'

He turned and accompanied us into the interior of the booking-case.

'To which of the clerks, Mr. Champnell, do you wish to put your questions?'

'To the one who issues third-class tickets to Southampton.'

Bellingham beckoned to a man who was counting a heap of money, and apparently seeking to make it tally with the entries in a huge ledger which lay open before him,—he was a short, slightly-built young fellow, with a pleasant face and smiling eyes.

'Mr. Stone, this gentleman wishes to ask you one or two questions.'

'I am at his service.'

I put my questions.

'I want to know, Mr. Stone, if, in the course of the day, you have issued any tickets to a person dressed in Arab costume?'

His reply was prompt.

'I have—by the last train, the 7.25,—three singles.'

Three singles! Then my instinct had told me rightly.

'Can you describe the person?'

Mr. Stone's eyes twinkled.

'I don't know that I can, except in a general way,—he was uncommonly old and uncommonly ugly, and he had a pair of the most extraordinary eyes I ever saw,—they gave me a sort of all-overish feeling when I saw them glaring at me through the pigeon hole. But I can tell you one thing about him, he had a great bundle on his head, which he steadied with one hand, and as it bulged out in all directions it's presence didn't make him popular with other people who wanted tickets too.'

Undoubtedly this was our man.

'You are sure he asked for three tickets?'

'Certain. He said three tickets to Southampton; laid down the exact fare,—nineteen and six—and held up three fingers—like that. Three nasty looking fingers they were, with nails as long as talons.'

'You didn't see who were his companions?'

'I didn't,—I didn't try to look. I gave him his tickets and off he went,—with the people grumbling at him because that bundle of his kept getting in their way.'

Bellingham touched me on the arm.

'I can tell you about the Arab of whom Mr. Stone speaks. My attention was called to him by his insisting on taking his bundle with him into the carriage,—it was an enormous thing, he could hardly squeeze it through the door; it occupied the entire seat. But as there weren't as many passengers as usual, and he wouldn't or couldn't be made to understand that his precious bundle would be safe in the luggage van along with the rest of the luggage, and as he wasn't the sort of person you could argue with to any advantage, I had him put into an empty compartment, bundle and all.'

'Was he alone then?'

'I thought so at the time, he said nothing about having more than one ticket, or any companions, but just before the train started two other men—English men—got into his compartment; and as I came down the platform, the ticket inspector at the barrier informed me that these two men were with him, because he held tickets for the three, which, as he was a foreigner, and they seemed English, struck the inspector as odd.'

'Could you describe the two men?'

'I couldn't, not particularly, but the man who had charge of the barrier might. I was at the other end of the train when they got in. All I noticed was that one seemed to be a commonplace looking individual and that the other was dressed like a tramp, all rags and tatters, a disreputable looking object he appeared to be.'

'That,' I said to myself, 'was Miss Marjorie Lindon, the lovely daughter of a famous house; the wife-elect of a coming statesman.'

To Bellingham I remarked aloud:

'I want you to strain a point, Mr. Bellingham, and to do me a service which I assure you you shall never have any cause to regret. I want you to wire instructions down the line to detain this Arab and his companions and to keep them in custody until the receipt of further instructions. They are not wanted by the police as yet, but they will be as soon as I am able to give certain information to the authorities at Scotland Yard,—and wanted very badly. But, as you will perceive for yourself, until I am able to give that information every moment is important.—Where's the Station Superintendent?'

'He's gone. At present I'm in charge.'

'Then will you do this for me? I repeat that you shall never have any reason to regret it.'

'I will if you'll accept all responsibility.'

'I'll do that with the greatest pleasure.'

Bellingham looked at his watch.

'It's about twenty minutes to nine. The train's scheduled for Basingstoke at 9.6. If we wire to Basingstoke at once they ought to be ready for them when they come.'

'Good!'

The wire was sent.

We were shown into Bellingham's office to await results Lessingham paced agitatedly to and fro; he seemed to have reached the limits of his self-control, and to be in a condition in which movement of some sort was an absolute necessity. The mercurial Sydney, on the contrary, leaned back in a chair, his legs stretched out in front of him, his hands thrust deep into his trouser pockets, and stared at Lessingham, as if he found relief to his feelings in watching his companion's restlessness. I, for my part, drew up as full a *précis* of the case as I deemed advisable, and as time permitted, which I despatched by one of the company's police to Scotland Yard.

Then I turned to my associates.

'Now, gentlemen, it's past dinner time. We may have a journey in front of us. If you take my advice you'll have something to eat.'

Lessingham shook his head.

'I want nothing.'

'Nor I,' echoed Sydney.

I started up.

'You must pardon my saying nonsense, but surely you of all men, Mr.. Lessingham, should be aware that you will not improve the situation by rendering yourself incapable of seeing it through. Come and dine.'

I haled them off with me, willy-nilly, to the refreshment room, I dined,—after a fashion; Mr. Lessingham swallowed with difficulty, a plate of soup; Sydney nibbled at a plate of the most unpromising looking 'chicken and ham,'—he proved, indeed, more intractable than Lessingham, and was not to be persuaded to tackle anything easier of digestion.

I was just about to take cheese after chop when Bellingham came hastening in, in his hand an open telegram.

'The birds have flown,' he cried.

'Flown!—How?'

In reply he gave me the telegram. I glanced at it. It ran:

'Persons described not in the train. Guard says they got out at Vauxhall. Have wired Vauxhall to advise you.'

'That's a level-headed chap,' said Bellingham. 'The man who sent that telegram. His wiring to Vauxhall should save us a lot of time,—we ought to hear from there directly. Hollo! what's this? I shouldn't be surprised if this is it.'

As he spoke a porter entered,—he handed an envelope to Bellingham. We all three kept our eyes fixed on the inspector's face as he opened it. When he perceived the contents he gave an exclamation of surprise.

'This Arab of yours, and his two friends, seem rather a curious lot, Mr. Champnell.'

He passed the paper on to me. It took the form of a report. Lessingham and Sydney, regardless of forms and ceremonies, leaned over my shoulder as I read it.

'Passengers by 7.30 Southampton, on arrival of train, complained of noises coming from a compartment in coach 8964. Stated that there had been shrieks and yells ever since the train left Waterloo, as if someone was being murdered. An Arab and two Englishmen got out of the compartment in question, apparently the party referred to in wire just to hand from Basingstoke. All three declared that there was nothing the matter. That they had been shouting for fun. Arab gave up three third singles for Southampton, saying, in reply to questions, that they had changed their minds, and did not want to go any farther. As there were no signs of a struggle or of violence, nor, apparently, any definite cause for detention, they were allowed to pass.

'They took a four-wheeler, No. 09435. The Arab and one man went inside, and the other man on the box. They asked to be driven to Commercial Road, Limehouse. The cab has since returned. Driver says he put the three men down, at their request, in Commercial Road, at the corner of Sutcliffe Street, near the East India Docks. They walked up Sutcliffe Street, the Englishmen in front, and the Arab behind, took the first turning to the right, and after that he saw nothing of them.

'The driver further states that all the way the Englishman inside, who was so ragged and dirty that he was reluctant to carry him, kept up a sort of wailing noise which so attracted his attention that he twice got off his box to see what was the matter, and each time he said it was nothing. The cabman is of opinion that both the Englishmen were of weak intellect. We were of the same impression here. They said nothing, except at the seeming instigation of the Arab, but when spoken to stared and gaped like lunatics.

'It may be mentioned that the Arab had with him an enormous bundle, which he persisted, in spite of all remonstrances, on taking with him inside the cab.'

As soon as I had mastered the contents of the report, and perceived what I believed to be—unknown to the writer himself—its hideous inner meaning, I turned to Bellingham.

'With your permission, Mr. Bellingham, I will keep this communication,—it will be safe in my hands, you will be able to get a copy, and it may be necessary that I should have the original to show to the police. If any inquiries are made for me from Scotland Yard, tell them that I have gone to the Commercial Road, and that I will report my movements from Limehouse Police Station.'

In another minute we were once more traversing the streets of London,—three in a hansom cab.

Chapter 12: The Murder at Mrs. 'Enderson's

It is something of a drive from Waterloo to Limehouse,—it seems longer when all your nerves are tingling with anxiety to reach your journey's end; and the cab I had hit upon proved to be not the fastest I might have chosen. For some time after our start, we were silent. Each was occupied with his own thoughts.

Then Lessingham, who was sitting at my side, said to me,

'Mr. Champnell, you have that report.'

'I have.'

'Will you let me see it once more?'

I gave it to him. He read it once, twice,—and I fancy yet again. I purposely avoided looking at him as he did so. Yet all the while I was conscious of his pallid cheeks, the twitched muscles of his mouth, the feverish glitter of his eyes,—this Leader of Men, whose predominate characteristic in the House of Commons was immobility, was rapidly approximating to the condition of a hysterical woman. The mental strain which he had been recently undergoing was proving too much for his physical strength. This disappearance of the woman he loved bade fair to be the final straw. I felt convinced that unless something was done quickly to relieve the strain upon his mind he was nearer to a state of complete mental and moral collapse than he himself imagined.

Had he been under my orders I should have commanded him to at once return home, and not to think; but conscious that, as things were, such a direction would be simply futile, I decided to do something else instead. Feeling that suspense was for him the worst possible form of suffering I resolved to explain, so far as I was able, precisely what it was I feared, and how I proposed to prevent it.

Presently there came the question for which I had been waiting, in a harsh, broken voice which no one who had heard him speak on a public platform, or in the House of Commons, would have recognised as his.

'Mr. Champnell,—who do you think this person is of whom the report from Vauxhall Station speaks as being all in rags and tatters?'

He knew perfectly well,—but I understood the mental attitude which induced him to prefer that the information should seem to come from me.

'I hope that it will prove to be Miss Lindon.'

'Hope!' He gave a sort of gasp.

'Yes, hope,—because if it is I think it possible, nay probable, that within a few hours you will have her again enfolded in your arms.'

'Pray God that it may be so! pray God!—pray the good God!'

I did not dare to look round for, from the tremor which was in his tone, I was persuaded that in the speaker's eyes were tears. Atherton continued silent. He was leaning half out of the cab, staring straight ahead, as if he saw in front a young girl's face, from which he could not remove his glance, and which beckoned him on.

After a while Lessingham spoke again, as if half to himself and half

161

to me.

'This mention of the shrieks on the railway, and of the wailing noise in the cab,—what must this wretch have done to her? How my darling must have suffered!'

That was a theme on which I myself scarcely ventured to allow my thoughts to rest. The notion of a gently-nurtured girl being at the mercy of that fiend incarnate, possessed—as I believed that so-called Arab to be possessed—of all the paraphernalia of horror and of dread, was one which caused me tangible shrinkings of the body. Whence had come those shrieks and yells, of which the writer of the report spoke, which had caused the Arab's fellow-passengers to think that murder was being done? What unimaginable agony had caused them? what speechless torture? And the 'wailing noise,' which had induced the prosaic, indurated London cabman to get twice off his box to see what was the matter, what anguish had been provocative of that?

The helpless girl who had already endured so much, endured, perhaps, that to which death would have been preferred!—shut up in that rattling, jolting box on wheels, alone with that diabolical Asiatic, with the enormous bundle, which was but the lurking place of nameless terrors,—what might she not, while being borne through the heart of civilised London, have been made to suffer? What had she not been made to suffer to have kept up that continued 'wailing noise'?

It was not a theme on which it was wise to permit one's thoughts to linger,—and particularly was it clear that it was one from which Lessingham's thoughts should have been kept as far as possible away.

'Come, Mr. Lessingham, neither you nor I will do himself any good by permitting his reflections to flow in a morbid channel. Let us talk of something else. By the way, weren't you due to speak in the House tonight?'

'Due!—Yes, I was due,—but what does it matter?'

'But have you acquainted no one with the cause of your non-attendance?'

'Acquaint!—whom should I acquaint?'

'My good sir! Listen to me, Mr. Lessingham. Let me entreat you very earnestly, to follow my advice. Call another cab,—or take this! and go at once to the House. It is not too late. Play the man, deliver the speech you have undertaken to deliver, perform your political duties. By coming with me you will be a hindrance rather than a help, and you may do your reputation an injury from which it never may recover. Do as I counsel you, and I will undertake to do my very utmost to let you have good news by the time your speech is finished.'

He turned on me with a bitterness for which I was unprepared.

'If I were to go down to the House, and try to speak in the state in which I am now, they would laugh at me, I should be ruined.'

'Do you not run an equally great risk of being ruined by staying away?'

He gripped me by the arm.

'Mr. Champnell, do you know that I am on the verge of madness? Do you know that as I am sitting here by your side I am living in a dual world? I am going on and on to catch that—that fiend, and I am back again in that Egyptian den, upon that couch of rugs, with the Woman of the Songs beside me, and Marjorie is being torn and tortured, and burnt before my eyes! God help me! Her shrieks are ringing in my ears!'

He did not speak loudly, but his voice was none the less impressive on that account. I endeavoured my hardest to be stern.

'I confess that you disappoint me, Mr. Lessingham. I have always understood that you were a man of unusual strength; you appear instead, to be a man of extraordinary weakness; with an imagination so ill-governed that its ebullitions remind me of nothing so much as feminine hysterics, Your wild language is not warranted by circumstances. I repeat that I think it quite possible that by tomorrow morning she will be returned to you.'

'Yes,—but how? as the Marjorie I have known, as I saw her last,—or how?'

That was the question which I had already asked myself, in what condition would she be when we had succeeded in snatching her from her captor's grip? It was a question to which I had refused to supply an answer. To him I lied by implication.

'Let us hope that, with the exception of being a trifle scared, she will be as sound and hale and hearty as even in her life.'

'Do you yourself believe that she'll be like that,—untouched, unchanged, unstained?'

Then I lied right out,—it seemed to me necessary to calm his growing excitement.

'I do.'

'You don't!'

'Mr. Lessingham!'

'Do you think that I can't see your face and read in it the same thoughts which trouble me? As a man of honour do you care to deny that when Marjorie Lindon is restored to me,—if she ever is!—you fear she will be but the mere soiled husk of the Marjorie whom I knew and loved?'

'Even supposing that there may be a modicum of truth in what you say,—which I am far from being disposed to admit—what good purpose do you propose to serve by talking in such a strain?'

'None,—no good purpose,—unless it be the desire of looking the truth in the face. For, Mr. Champnell, you must not seek to play with me the hypocrite, nor try to hide things from me as if I were a child. If my life is ruined—it is ruined,—let me know it, and look the knowledge in the face. That, to me, is to play the man.'

I was silent.

The wild tale he had told me of that Cairene inferno, oddly enough—yet why oddly, for the world is all coincidence!—had thrown a flood of light on certain events which had happened some three years previously and which ever since had remained shrouded in mystery. The conduct of the business afterwards came into my hands,—and briefly, what had occurred was this:

Three persons,—two sisters and their brother, who was younger than themselves, members of a decent English family, were going on a trip round the world. They were young, adventurous, and—not to put too fine a point on it—foolhardy. The evening after their arrival in Cairo, by way of what is called 'a lark,' in spite of the protestations of people who were better informed than themselves, they insisted on going, alone, for a ramble through the native quarter.

They went,—but they never returned. Or, rather the two girls never returned. After an interval the young man was found again,—what was left of him. A fuss was made when there were no signs of their reappearance, but as there were no relations, nor even friends of theirs, but only casual acquaintances on board the ship by which they had travelled, perhaps not so great a fuss as might have been was made. Anyhow, nothing was discovered. Their widowed mother, alone in England, wondering bow it was that beyond the receipt of a brief wire, acquainting her with their arrival at Cairo, she had heard nothing further of their wanderings, placed herself in communication with the diplomatic people over there,—to learn that, to all appearances, her three children had vanished from off the face of the earth.

Then a fuss was made,—with a vengeance. So far as one can judge the whole town and neighbourhood was turned pretty well upside down. But nothing came of it,—so far as any results were concerned,

164

the authorities might just as well have left the mystery of their vanishment alone. It continued where it was in spite of them.

However, some three months afterwards a youth was brought to the British Embassy by a party of friendly Arabs who asserted that they had found him naked and nearly dying in some remote spot in the Wady Haifa desert. It was the brother of the two lost girls. He was as nearly dying as he very well could be without being actually dead when they brought him to the Embassy,—and in a state of indescribable mutilation. He seemed to rally for a time under careful treatment, but he never again uttered a coherent word. It was only from his delirious ravings that any idea was formed of what had really occurred.

Shorthand notes were taken of some of the utterances of his delirium. Afterwards they were submitted to me. I remembered the substance of them quite well, and when Mr. Lessingham began to tell me of his own hideous experiences they came back to me more clearly still. Had I laid those notes before him I have little doubt but that he would have immediately perceived that seventeen years after the adventure which had left such an indelible scar upon his own life, this youth—he was little more than a boy—had seen the things which he had seen, and suffered the nameless agonies and degradations which he had suffered.

The young man was perpetually raving about some indescribable den of horror which was own brother to Lessingham's temple and about some female monster, whom he regarded with such fear and horror that every allusion he made to her was followed by a convulsive paroxysm which taxed all the ingenuity of his medical attendants to bring him out of. He frequently called upon his sisters by name, speaking of them in a manner which inevitably suggested that he had been an unwilling and helpless witness of hideous tortures which they had undergone; and then he would rise in bed, screaming, 'They're burning them! they're burning them! Devils! devils!' And at those times it required all the strength of those who were in attendance to restrain his maddened frenzy.

The youth died in one of these fits of great preternatural excitement, without, as I have previously written, having given utterance to one single coherent word, and by some of those who were best able to judge it was held to have been a mercy that he did die without having been restored to consciousness. And, presently, tales began to be whispered, about some idolatrous sect, which was stated to have its headquarters somewhere in the interior of the country—some located it in this neighbourhood, and some in that—which was stated to still practise, and to always have practised, in unbroken historical continuity, the debased, unclean, mystic, and bloody rites, of a form of idolatry which had had its birth in a period of the world's story which was so remote, that to all intents and purposes it might be described as pre-historic.

While the ferment was still at its height, a man came to the British Embassy who said that he was a member of a tribe which had its habitat on the banks of the White Nile. He asserted that he was in association with this very idolatrous sect,—though he denied that he was one of the actual sectaries. He did admit, however, that he had assisted more than once at their orgies, and declared that it was their constant practice to offer young women as sacrifices—preferably white Christian women, with a special preference, if they could get them, to young English women. He vowed that he himself had seen with his own eyes, English girls burnt alive. The description which he gave of what preceded and followed these foul murders appalled those who listened. He finally wound up by offering, on payment of a stipulated sum of money, to guide a troop of soldiers to this den of demons, so that they should arrive there at a moment when it was filled with worshippers, who were preparing to participate in an orgie which was to take place during the next few days.

His offer was conditionally accepted. He was confined in an apartment with one man on guard inside and another on guard outside the room. That night the sentinel without was startled by hearing a great noise and frightful screams issuing from the chamber in which the native was interned. He summoned assistance. The door was opened. The soldier on guard within was stark, staring mad,—he died within a few months, a gibbering maniac to the end. The native was dead. The window, which was a very small one, was securely fastened inside and strongly barred without. There was nothing to show by what means entry had been gained. Yet it was the general opinion of those who saw the corpse that the man had been destroyed by some wild beast. A photograph was taken of the body after death, a copy of which is still in my possession. In it are distinctly shown lacerations about the neck and the lower portion of the abdomen, as if they had been produced by the claws of some huge and ferocious animal. The skull is splintered in half-a-dozen places, and the face is torn to rags.

That was more than three years ago. The whole business has remained as great a mystery as ever. But my attention has once or twice

166

been caught by trifling incidents, which have caused me to more than suspect that the wild tale told by that murdered native had in it at least the elements of truth; and which have even led me to wonder if the trade in kidnapping was not being carried on to this very hour, and if women of my own flesh and blood were not still being offered up on that infernal altar. And now, here was Paul Lessingham, a man of world-wide reputation, of great intellect, of undoubted honour, who had come to me with a wholly unconscious verification of all my worst suspicions!

That the creature spoken of as an Arab,—and who was probably no more an Arab than I was, and whose name was certainly not Mohamed el Kheir!—was an emissary from that den of demons, I had no doubt. What was the exact purport of the creature's presence in England was another question, Possibly part of the intention was the destruction of Paul Lessingham, body, soul and spirit; possibly another part was the procuration of fresh victims for that long-drawn-out holocaust. That this latter object explained the disappearance of Miss Lindon I felt persuaded. That she was designed by the personification of evil who was her captor, to suffer all the horrors at which the stories pointed, and then to be burned alive, amidst the triumphant yells of the attendant demons, I was certain. That the wretch, aware that the pursuit was in full cry, was tearing, twisting, doubling, and would stick at nothing which would facilitate the smuggling of the victim out of England, was clear.

My interest in the quest was already far other than a merely professional one. The blood in my veins tingled at the thought of such a woman as Miss Lindon being in the power of such a monster. I may assuredly claim that throughout the whole business I was urged forward by no thought of fee or of reward. To have had a share in rescuing that unfortunate girl, and in the destruction of her noxious persecutor, would have been reward enough for me.

One is not always, even in strictly professional matters, influenced by strictly professional instincts.

The cab slowed. A voice descended through the trap door.

'This is Commercial Road, sir,—what part of it do you want?'

'Drive me to Limehouse Police Station.'

We were driven there. I made my way to the usual inspector behind the usual pigeon-hole.

'My name is Champnell. Have you received any communication from Scotland Yard tonight having reference to a matter in which I

167

am interested?'

'Do you mean about the Arab? We received a telephonic message about half an hour ago.'

'Since communicating with Scotland Yard this has come to hand from the authorities at Vauxhall Station. Can you tell me if anything has been seen of the person in question by the men of your division?'

I handed the inspector the 'report.' His reply was laconic.

'I will inquire.'

He passed through a door into an inner room and the 'report' went with him.

'Beg pardon, sir, but was that a Harab you was a-talking about to the Hinspector?'

The speaker was a gentleman unmistakably of the gutter-snipe class. He was seated on a form. Close at hand hovered a policeman whose special duty it seemed to be to keep an eye upon his movements.

'Why do you ask?'

'I beg your pardon, sir, but I saw a Harab myself about a hour ago,—leastways he looked like as if he was a Harab.'

'What sort of a looking person was he?'

'I can't 'ardly tell you that, sir, because I didn't never have a proper look at him,—but I know he had a bloomin' great bundle on 'is 'ead. ... It was like this, 'ere. I was comin' round the corner, as he was passin', I never see 'im till I was right atop of 'im, so that I haccidentally run agin 'im,—my heye! didn't 'e give me a downer! I was down on the back of my 'ead in the middle of the road before I knew where I was and 'e was at the other end of the street. If 'e 'adn't knocked me more'n 'arf silly I'd been after 'im, sharp,—I tell you! and hasked 'im what 'e thought 'e was a-doin' of, but afore my senses was back agin 'e was out o' sight,—clean!'

'You are sure he had a bundle on his head?'

'I noticed it most particular.'

'How long ago do you say this was? and where?'

'About a hour ago,—perhaps more, perhaps less.'

'Was he alone?'

'It seemed to me as if a cove was a-follerin' 'im, leastways there was a bloke as was a-keepin' close at 'is 'eels,—though I don't know what 'is little game was, I'm sure. Ask the pleesman—he knows, he knows everything the pleesman do.'

168

I turned to the 'pleesman.'

'Who is this man?'

The 'pleesman' put his hands behind his back, and threw out his chest. His manner was distinctly affable.

'Well,—he's being detained upon suspicion. He's given us an address at which to make inquiries, and inquiries are being made. I shouldn't pay too much attention to what he says if I were you. I don't suppose he'd be particular about a lie or two.'

This frank expression of opinion re-aroused the indignation of the gentleman on the form.

'There you hare! at it again! That's just like you peelers,—you're all the same! What do you know about me?—Nuffink! This gen'leman ain't got no call to believe me, not as I knows on,—it's all the same to me if 'e do or don't, but it's trewth what I'm sayin', all the same.'

At this point the inspector re-appeared at the pigeon-hole. He cut short the flow of eloquence.

'Now then, not so much noise outside there!' He addressed me. 'None of our men have seen anything of the person you're inquiring for, so far as we're aware. But, if you like, I will place a man at your disposal, and he will go round with you, and you will be able to make your own inquiries.'

A capless, wildly excited young ragamuffin came dashing in at the street door. He gasped out, as clearly as he could for the speed which he had made:

'There's been murder done, Mr. Pleesman,—a Harab's killed a bloke.'

'Mr. Pleesman' gripped him by the shoulder.

'What's that?'

The youngster put up his arm, and ducked his head, instinctively, as if to ward off a blow.

'Leave me alone! I don't want none of your 'andling!—I ain't done nuffink to you! I tell you 'e 'as!'

The inspector spoke through the pigeon-hole.

'He has what, my lad? What do you say has happened?'

'There's been murder done—it's right enough!—there 'as!—up at Mrs. 'Enderson's, in Paradise Place,—a Harab's been and killed a bloke!'

CHAPTER 13: THE MAN WHO WAS MURDERED

The inspector spoke to me.

'If what the boy says is correct it sounds as if the person whom you are seeking may have had a finger in the pie.'

I was of the same opinion, as, apparently, were Lessingham and Sidney, Atherton collared the youth by the shoulder which Mr. Pleesman had left disengaged.

'What sort of looking bloke is it who's been murdered?'

'I dunno! I 'aven't seen 'im! Mrs. 'Enderson, she says to me! "'Gustus Barley," she says, "a bloke's been murdered. That there Harab what I chucked out 'alf a hour ago been and murdered 'im, and left 'im behind up in my back room. You run as 'ard as you can tear and tell them there dratted pleese what's so fond of shovin' their dirty noses into respectable people's 'ouses." So I comes and tells yer. That's all I knows about it.'

We went four in the hansom which had been waiting in the street to Mrs. Henderson's in Paradise Place,—the inspector and we three. 'Mr. Pleesman' and ''Gustus Barley' followed on foot. The inspector was explanatory.

'Mrs. Henderson keeps a sort of lodging-house,—a "Sailors' Home" she calls it, but no one could call it sweet. It doesn't bear the best of characters, and if you asked me what I thought of it, I should say in plain English that it was a disorderly house.'

Paradise Place proved to be within three or four hundred yards of the Station House. So far as could be seen in the dark it consisted of a row of houses of considerable dimensions,—and also of considerable antiquity. They opened on to two or three stone steps which led directly into the street. At one of the doors stood an old lady with a shawl drawn over her head. This was Mrs. Henderson. She greeted us with garrulous volubility.

'So you 'ave come, 'ave you? I thought you never was a-comin' that I did.' She recognised the inspector. 'It's you, Mr. Phillips, is it?' Perceiving us, she drew a little back 'Who's them 'ere parties? They ain't coppers?'

Mr. Phillips dismissed her inquiry, curtly.

'Never you mind who they are. What's this about someone being murdered.'

'Ssh!' The old lady glanced round. 'Don't you speak so loud, Mr. Phillips. No one don't know nothing about it as yet. The parties what's in my 'ouse is most respectable,—most! and they couldn't abide the notion of there being police about the place.'

'We quite believe that, Mrs. Henderson.'

The inspector's tone was grim.

Mrs. Henderson led the way up a staircase which would have been distinctly the better for repairs. It was necessary to pick one's way as one went, and as the light was defective stumbles were not infrequent.

Our guide paused outside a door on the topmost landing. From some mysterious recess in her apparel she produced a key.

'It's in 'ere. I locked the door so that nothing mightn't be disturbed. I knows 'ow particular you pleesmen is.'

She turned the key. We all went in—we, this time, in front, and she behind.

A candle was guttering on a broken and dilapidated single wash-hand stand. A small iron bedstead stood by its side, the clothes on which were all tumbled and tossed. There was a rush-seated chair with a hole in the seat,—and that, with the exception of one or two chipped pieces of stoneware, and a small round mirror which was hung on a nail against the wall, seemed to be all that the room contained. I could see nothing in the shape of a murdered man. Nor, it appeared, could the Inspector either.

'What's the meaning of this, Mrs. Henderson? I don't see anything here.'

'It's be'ind the bed, Mr. Phillips. I left 'im just where I found 'im, I wouldn't 'ave touched 'im not for nothing, nor yet 'ave let nobody else 'ave touched 'im neither, because, as I say, I know 'ow particular you pleesmen is.'

We all four went hastily forward. Atherton and I went to the head of the bed, Lessingham and the inspector, leaning right across the bed, peeped over the side. There, on the floor in the space which was between the bed and the wall, lay the murdered man.

At sight of him an exclamation burst from Sydney's lips.

'It's Holt!'

'Thank God!' cried Lessingham. 'It isn't Marjorie!'

The relief in his tone was unmistakable. That the one was gone was plainly nothing to him in comparison with the fact that the other was left.

Thrusting the bed more into the centre of the room I knelt down beside the man on the floor. A more deplorable spectacle than he presented I have seldom witnessed. He was decently clad in a grey tweed suit, white hat, collar and necktie, and it was perhaps that fact which made his extreme attenuation the more conspicuous. I doubt if there was an ounce of flesh on the whole of his body. His cheeks and the sockets of his eyes were hollow. The skin was drawn tightly over his cheek bones,—the bones themselves were staring through. Even his nose was wasted, so that nothing but a ridge of cartilage remained. I put my arm beneath his shoulder and raised him from the floor; no resistance was offered by the body's gravity,—he was as light as a little child.

'I doubt,' I said, 'if this man has been murdered. It looks to me like a case of starvation, or exhaustion,—possibly a combination of both.'

'What's that on his neck?' asked the inspector,—he was kneeling at my side.

He referred to two abrasions of the skin,—one on either side of the man's neck.

'They look to me like scratches. They seem pretty deep, but I don't think they're sufficient in themselves to cause death.'

'They might be, joined to an already weakened constitution. Is there anything in his pockets?—let's lift him on to the bed.'

We lifted him on to the bed,—a featherweight he was to lift. While the Inspector was examining his pockets—to find them empty—a tall man with a big black beard came bustling in. He proved to be Dr Glossop, the local police surgeon, who had been sent for before our quitting the Station House.

His first pronouncement, made as soon as he commenced his examination, was, under the circumstances, sufficiently startling.

'I don't believe the man's dead. Why didn't you send for me directly you found him?'

The question was put to Mrs. Henderson.

'Well, Dr Glossop, I wouldn't touch 'im myself, and I wouldn't 'ave 'im touched by no one else, because, as I've said afore, I know 'ow particular them pleesmen is.'

'Then in that case, if he does die you'll have had a hand in murdering him,—that's all'

The lady sniggered. 'Of course Dr Glossop, we all knows that you'll always 'ave your joke.'

'You'll find it a joke if you have to hang, as you ought to, you—' The doctor said what he did say to himself, under his breath. I doubt if it was flattering to Mrs. Henderson. 'Have you got any brandy in the house?'

'We've got everythink in the 'ouse for them as likes to pay for it,—everythink.' Then, suddenly remembering that the police were present, and that hers were not exactly licensed premises, 'Leastways we can send out for it for them parties as gives us the money, being, as is well known, always willing to oblige.'

'Then send for some,—to the tap downstairs, if that's the nearest! If this man dies before you've brought it I'll have you locked up as sure as you're a living woman.'

The arrival of the brandy was not long delayed,—but the man on the bed had regained consciousness before it came. Opening his eyes he looked up at the doctor bending over him.

'Hollo, my man! that's more like the time of day! How are you feeling?'

The patient stared hazily up at the doctor, as if his sense of perception was not yet completely restored,—as if this big bearded man was something altogether strange. Atherton bent down beside the doctor.

'I'm glad to see you looking better, Mr. Holt. You know me don't you? I've been running about after you all day long.'

'You are—you are—' The man's eyes closed, as if the effort at recollection exhausted him. He kept them closed as he continued to speak.

'I know who you are. You are—the gentleman.'

'Yes, that's it, I'm the gentleman,—name of Atherton.—Miss Lindon's friend. And I daresay you're feeling pretty well done up, and in want of something to eat and drink,—here's some brandy for you.'

The doctor had some in a tumbler. He raised the patient's head, allowing it to trickle down his throat. The man swallowed it mechanically, motionless, as if unconscious what it was that he was doing. His cheeks flushed, the passing glow of colour caused their condition of extraordinary, and, indeed, extravagant attenuation, to be more prominent than ever. The doctor laid him back upon the bed, feeling his pulse with one hand, while he stood and regarded him in silence.

Then, turning to the inspector, he said to him in an undertone;

'If you want him to make a statement he'll have to make it now, he's going fast. You won't be able to get much out of him,—he's too far gone, and I shouldn't bustle him, but get what you can.'

The Inspector came to the front, a notebook in his hand.

'I understand from this gentleman—' signifying Atherton—'that your name's Robert Holt. I'm an Inspector of police, and I want you to tell me what has brought you into this condition. Has anyone been assaulting you?'

Holt, opening his eyes, glanced up at the speaker mistily, as if he could not see him clearly,—still less understand what it was that he was saying. Sydney, stooping over him, endeavoured to explain.

'The Inspector wants to know how you got here, has anyone been doing anything to you? Has anyone been hurting you?'

The man's eyelids were partially closed. Then they opened wider and wider. His mouth opened too. On his skeleton features there came a look of panic fear. He was evidently struggling to speak. At last words came.

'The beetle!' He stopped. Then, after an effort, spoke again. 'The beetle!'

'What's he mean?' asked the Inspector.

'I think I understand,' Sydney answered; then turning again to the man in the bed. 'Yes, I hear what you say,—the beetle. Well, has the beetle done anything to you?'

'It took me by the throat!'

'Is that the meaning of the marks upon your neck?'

'The beetle killed me.'

The lids closed. The man relapsed into a state of lethargy. The inspector was puzzled;—and said so.

'What's he mean about a beetle?'

Atherton replied.

'I think I understand what he means,—and my friends do too. We'll explain afterwards. In the meantime I think I'd better get as much out of him as I can,—while there's time.'

'Yes,' said the doctor, his hand upon the patient's pulse, 'while there's time. There isn't much—only seconds.'

Sydney endeavoured to rouse the man from his stupor.

'You've been with Miss Lindon all the afternoon and evening, haven't you, Mr. Holt?'

Atherton had reached a chord in the man's consciousness. His lips moved,—in painful articulation.

'Yes—all the afternoon—and evening—God help me!'

'I hope God will help you my poor fellow; you've been in need of His help if ever man was. Miss Lindon is disguised in your old clothes, isn't she?'

'Yes,—in my old clothes. My God!'

'And where is Miss Lindon now?'

The man had been speaking with his eyes closed. Now he opened them, wide; there came into them the former staring horror. He became possessed by uncontrollable agitation,—half raising himself in

174

bed. Words came from his quivering lips as if they were only drawn from him by the force of his anguish.

'The beetle's going to kill Miss Lindon.'

A momentary paroxysm seemed to shake the very foundations of his being. His whole frame quivered. He fell back on to the bed,—ominously. The doctor examined him in silence—while we too were still.

'This time he's gone for good, there'll be no conjuring him back again.'

I felt a sudden pressure on my arm, and found that Lessingham was clutching me with probably unconscious violence. The muscles of his face were twitching. He trembled. I turned to the doctor.

'Doctor, if there is any of that brandy left will you let me have it for my friend?'

Lessingham disposed of the remainder of the 'shillings worth.' I rather fancy it saved us from a scene.

The Inspector was speaking to the woman of the house.

'Now, Mrs. Henderson, perhaps you'll tell us what all this means. Who is this man, and how did he come in here, and who came in with him, and what do you know about it altogether? If you've got anything to say, say it, only you'd better be careful, because it's my duty to warn you that anything you do say may be used against you.'

Chapter 14: All That Mrs 'Enderson Knew

Mrs. Henderson put her hands under her apron and smirked.

'Well, Mr. Phillips, it do sound strange to 'ear you talkin' to me like that. Anybody'd think I'd done something as I didn't ought to 'a' done to 'ear you going on. As for what's 'appened, I'll tell you all I know with the greatest willingness on earth. And as for bein' careful, there ain't no call for you to tell me to be that, for that I always am, as by now you ought to know.'

'Yes,—I do know. Is that all you have to say?'

'Rilly, Mr. Phillips, what a man you are for catching people up, you rilly are. O' course that ain't all I've got to say,—ain't I just a-comin' to it?'

'Then come.'

'If you presses me so you'll muddle of me up, and then if I do 'appen to make a herror, you'll say I'm a liar, when goodness knows there ain't no more truthful woman not in Limehouse.'

Words plainly trembled on the inspector's lips,—which he refrained from uttering. Mrs. Henderson cast her eyes upwards, as if she sought for inspiration from the filthy ceiling.

'So far as I can swear it might 'ave been a hour ago, or it might 'ave been a hour and a quarter, or it might 'ave been a hour and twenty minutes—'

'We're not particular as to the seconds.'

'When I 'ears a knockin' at my front door, and when I comes to open it, there was a Harab party, with a great bundle on 'is 'ead, bigger nor 'isself, and two other parties along with him. This Harab party says, in that queer foreign way them Harab parties 'as of talkin', "A room for the night, a room." Now I don't much care for foreigners, and never did, especially them Harabs, which their 'abits ain't my own,—so I as much 'ints the same. But this 'ere Harab party, he didn't seem to quite foller of my meaning, for all he done was to say as he said afore, "A room for the night, a room." And he shoves a couple of 'arf crowns into my 'and. Now it's always been a motter o' mine, that money is money, and one man's money is as good as another man's. So, not wishing to be disagreeable—which other people would have taken 'em if I 'adn't, I shows 'em up 'ere. I'd been downstairs it might 'ave been 'arf a hour, when I 'ears a shindy a-coming from this room—'

'What sort of a shindy?'

'Yelling and shrieking—oh my gracious, it was enough to set your blood all curdled,—for ear-piercingness I never did 'ear nothing like it. We do 'ave troublesome parties in 'ere, like they do elsewhere, but I never did 'ear nothing like that before. I stood it for about a minute, but it kep' on, and kep' on, and every moment I expected as the other parties as was in the 'ouse would be complainin', so up I comes and I thumps at the door, and it seemed that thump I might for all the notice that was took of me.'

'Did the noise keep on?'

'Keep on! I should think it did keep on! Lord love you! shriek after shriek, I expected to see the roof took off.'

'Were there any other noises? For instance, were there any sounds of struggling, or of blows?'

'There weren't no sounds except of the party hollering.'

'One party only?'

'One party only. As I says afore, shriek after shriek,—when you put your ear to the panel there was a noise like some other party blubbering, but that weren't nothing, as for the hollering you wouldn't have thought that nothing what you might call 'umin could 'ave kep' up such a screechin'. I thumps and thumps and at last when I did think that I should 'ave to 'ave the door broke down, the Harab says to me from inside, "Go away! I pay for the room! go away!" I did think that pretty good, I tell you that. So I says, "Pay for the room or not pay for the room, you didn't pay to make that shindy!" And what's more I says, "If I 'ear it again," I says, "out you goes! And if you don't go quiet I'll 'ave somebody in as'll pretty quickly make you!"'

'Then was there silence?'

'So to speak there was,—only there was this sound as if some party was a-blubbering, and another sound as if a party was a-panting for his breath.'

'Then what happened?'

'Seeing that, so to speak, all was quiet, down I went again. And in another quarter of a hour, or it might 'ave been twenty minutes, I went to the front door to get a mouthful of hair. And Mrs. Barker, what lives over the road, at No. 24, she comes to me and says, "That there Arab party of yours didn't stop long." I looks at 'er, "I don't quite foller you," I says,—which I didn't. "I saw him come in," she says, "and then, a few minutes back, I see 'im go again, with a great bundle on 'is 'ead he couldn't 'ardly stagger under!" "Oh," I says, "that's news to me, I didn't know 'e'd gone, nor see him neither—" which I didn't. So, up I comes again, and, sure enough, the door was open, and it seems to me that the room was empty, till I come upon this pore young man what was lying be'ind the bed,'

There was a growl from the doctor.

'If you'd had any sense, and sent for me at once, he might have been alive at this moment.'

''Ow was I to know that, Dr Glossop? I couldn't tell. My finding 'im there murdered was quite enough for me. So I runs downstairs, and I nips 'old of 'Gustus Barley, what was leaning against the wall, and I says to him, "'Gustus Barley, run to the station as fast as you can and tell 'em that a man's been murdered,—that Harab's been and killed a bloke." And that's all I know about it, and I couldn't tell you no more, Mr. Phillips, not if you was to keep on asking me questions not for hours and hours'

'Then you think it was this man'—with a motion towards the bed—'who was shrieking?'

'To tell you the truth, Mr. Phillips, about that I don't 'ardly know what to think. If you 'ad asked me I should 'ave said it was a woman. I ought to know a woman's holler when I 'ear it, if any one does, I've

177

'eard enough of 'em in my time, goodness knows. And I should 'ave said that only a woman could 'ave hollered like that and only 'er when she was raving mad. But there weren't no woman with him. There was only this man what's murdered, and the other man,—and as for the other man I will say this, that 'e 'adn't got twopennyworth of clothes to cover 'im. But, Mr. Phillips, howsomever that may be, that's the last Harab I'll 'ave under my roof, no matter what they pays, and you may mark my words I'll 'ave no more.'

Mrs. Henderson, once more glancing upward, as if she imagined herself to have made some declaration of a religious nature, shook her head with much solemnity.

Chapter 15: The Sudden Stopping

As we were leaving the house a constable gave the inspector a note. Having read it he passed it to me. It was from the local office.

> Message received that an Arab with a big bundle on his head has been noticed loitering about the neighbourhood of St Pancras Station. He seemed to be accompanied by a young man who had the appearance of a tramp. Young man seemed ill. They appeared to be waiting for a train, probably to the North. Shall I advise detention?

I scribbled on the flyleaf of the note.

> Have them detained. If they have gone by train have a special in readiness.

In a minute we were again in the cab. I endeavoured to persuade Lessingham and Atherton to allow me to conduct the pursuit alone,—in vain. I had no fear of Atherton's succumbing, but I was afraid for Lessingham. What was more almost than the expectation of his collapse was the fact that his looks and manner, his whole bearing, so eloquent of the agony and agitation of his mind, was beginning to tell upon my nerves. A catastrophe of some sort I foresaw. Of the curtain's fall upon one tragedy we had just been witnesses. That there was worse—much worse, to follow I did not doubt. Optimistic anticipations were out of the question,—that the creature we were chasing would relinquish the prey uninjured, no one, after what we had seen and heard, could by any possibility suppose. Should a necessity suddenly arise for prompt and immediate action, that Lessingham would prove a hindrance rather than a help I felt persuaded.

But since moments were precious, and Lessingham was not to be persuaded to allow the matter to proceed without him, all that remained was to make the best of his presence.

The great arch of St Pancras was in darkness. An occasional light seemed to make the darkness still more visible. The station seemed deserted. I thought, at first, that there was not a soul about the place, that our errand was in vain, that the only thing for us to do was to drive to the police station and to pursue our inquiries there. But as we turned towards the booking-office, our footsteps ringing out clearly through the silence and the night, a door opened, a light shone out from the room within, and a voice inquired:

'Who's that?'

'My name's Champnell. Has a message been received from me from the Limehouse Police Station?'

'Step this way.'

We stepped that way,—into a snug enough office, of which one of the railway inspectors was apparently in charge. He was a big man, with a fair beard. He looked me up and down, as if doubtfully. Lessingham he recognised at once. He took off his cap to him.

'Mr. Lessingham, I believe?'

'I am Mr. Lessingham. Have you any news for me?'

I fancy, by his looks,—that the official was struck by the pallor of the speaker's face,—and by his tremulous voice.

'I am instructed to give certain information to a Mr. Augustus Champnell.'

'I am Mr. Champnell. What's your information?'

'With reference to the Arab about whom you have been making inquiries. A foreigner, dressed like an Arab, with a great bundle on his head, took two single thirds for Hull by the midnight express.'

'Was he alone?'

'It is believed that he was accompanied by a young man of very disreputable appearance. They were not together at the booking-office, but they had been seen together previously. A minute or so after the Arab had entered the train this young man got into the same compartment—they were in the front waggon.'

'Why were they not detained?'

'We had no authority to detain them, nor any reason, until your message was received a few minutes ago we at this station were not aware that inquiries were being made for them.'

'You say he booked to Hull,—does the train run through to Hull?'

'No—it doesn't go to Hull at all. Part of it's the Liverpool and Manchester Express, and part of it's for Carlisle. It divides at Derby. The man you're looking for will change either at Sheffield or at Cudworth Junction and go on to Hull by the first train in the morning. There's a local service.'

I looked at my watch.

'You say the train left at midnight. It's now nearly five-and-twenty past. Where's it now?'

'Nearing St Albans, it's due there 12.35.'

'Would there be time for a wire to reach St Albans?'

'Hardly,—and anyhow there'll only be enough railway officials about the place to receive and despatch the train. They'll be fully occupied with their ordinary duties. There won't be time to get the police there.'

'You could wire to St Albans to inquire if they were still in the train?'

'That could be done,—certainly. I'll have it done at once if you like.

'Then where's the next stoppage?'

'Well, they're at Luton at 12.51. But that's another case of St Albans. You see there won't be much more than twenty minutes by the time you've got your wire off, and I don't expect there'll be many people awake at Luton. At these country places sometimes there's a policeman hanging about the station to see the express go through, but, on the other hand, very often there isn't, and if there isn't, probably at this time of night it'll take a good bit of time to get the police on the premises. I tell you what I should advise.'

'What's that?'

'The train is due at Bedford at 1.29—send your wire there. There ought to be plenty of people about at Bedford, and anyhow there'll be time to get the police to the station.'

'Very good. I instructed them to tell you to have a special ready,—have you got one?'

'There's an engine with steam up in the shed,—we'll have all ready for you in less than ten minutes. And I tell you what,—you'll have about fifty minutes before the train is due at Bedford. It's a fifty mile run. With luck you ought to get there pretty nearly as soon as the express does.—Shall I tell them to get ready?'

'At once.'

While he issued directions through a telephone to what, I presume, was the engine shed, I drew up a couple of telegrams. Having completed his orders he turned to me.

'They're coming out of the siding now—they'll be ready in less than ten minutes. I'll see that the line's kept clear. Have you got those wires?'

'Here is one,—this is for Bedford.'

It ran:

Arrest the Arab who is in train due at 1.29. When leaving St Pancras he was in a third-class compartment in front waggon. He has a large bundle, which detain. He took two third singles for Hull. Also detain his companion, who is dressed like a tramp. This is a young lady whom the Arab has disguised and kidnapped while in a condition of hypnotic trance. Let her have medical assistance and be taken to a hotel. All expenses will be paid on the arrival of the undersigned who is following by special train. As the Arab will probably be very violent a sufficient force of police should be in waiting.

Augustus Champnell.

'And this is the other. It is probably too late to be of any use at St Albans,—but send it there, and also to Luton.'

Is Arab with companion in train which left St Pancras at 13.0? If so, do not let them get out till train reaches Bedford, where instructions are being wired for arrest.

The inspector rapidly scanned them both.

'They ought to do your business, I should think. Come along with me—I'll have them sent at once, and we'll see if your train's ready.'

The train was not ready,—nor was it ready within the prescribed ten minutes. There was some hitch, I fancy, about a saloon. Finally we had to be content with an ordinary old-fashioned first-class carriage. The delay, however, was not altogether time lost. Just as the engine with its solitary coach was approaching the platform someone came running up with an envelope in his hand.

'Telegram from St Albans.'

I tore it open. It was brief and to the point.

Arab with companion was in train when it left here. Am wiring Luton.

'That's all right. Now unless something wholly unforeseen takes

181

place, we ought to have them.'

That unforeseen!

I went forward with the Inspector and the guard of our train to exchange a few final words with the driver. The inspector explained what instructions he had given.

'I've told the driver not to spare his coal but to take you into Bedford within five minutes after the arrival of the express. He says he thinks that he can do it.'

The driver leaned over his engine, rubbing his hands with the usual oily rag. He was a short, wiry man with grey hair and a grizzled moustache, with about him that bearing of semi-humorous, frank-faced resolution which one notes about engine-drivers as a class.

'We ought to do it, the gradients are against us, but it's a clear night and there's no wind. The only thing that will stop us will be if there's any shunting on the road, or any luggage trains; of course, if we are blocked, we are blocked, but the Inspector says he'll clear the way for us.'

'Yes,' said the inspector, 'I'll clear the way. I've wired down the road already.'

Atherton broke in.

'Driver, if you get us into Bedford within five minutes of the arrival of the mail there'll be a five-pound note to divide between your mate and you.'

The driver grinned.

'We'll get you there in time, sir, if we have to go clear through the shunters. It isn't often we get a chance of a five-pound note for a run to Bedford, and we'll do our best to earn it.'

The fireman waved his hand in the rear.

'That's right, sir!' he cried. 'We'll have to trouble you for that five-pound note.'

So soon as we were clear of the station it began to seem probable that, as the fireman put it, Atherton would be 'troubled.' Journeying in a train which consists of a single carriage attached to an engine which is flying at topmost speed is a very different business from being an occupant of an ordinary train which is travelling at ordinary express rates. I had discovered that for myself before. That night it was impressed on me more than ever. A tyro—or even a nervous 'season'— might have been excused for expecting at every moment we were going to be derailed. It was hard to believe that the carriage had any springs,—it rocked and swung, and jogged and jolted.

Of smooth travelling had we none. Talking was out of the question;—and for that, I, personally, was grateful. Quite apart from the difficulty we experienced in keeping our seats—and when every moment our position was being altered and we were jerked backwards and forwards up and down, this way and that, that was a business which required care,—the noise was deafening. It was as though we were being pursued by a legion of shrieking, bellowing, raging demons.

'George!' shrieked Atherton, 'he does mean to earn that fiver. I hope I'll be alive to pay it him!'

He was only at the other end of the carriage, but though I could see by the distortion of his visage that he was shouting at the top of his voice,—and he has a voice,—I only caught here and there a word or two of what he was saying. I had to make sense of the whole.

Lessingham's contortions were a study. Few of that large multitude of persons who are acquainted with him only by means of the portraits which have appeared in the illustrated papers, would then have recognised the rising statesman. Yet I believe that few things could have better fallen in with his mood than that wild travelling. He might have been almost shaken to pieces,—but the very severity of the shaking served to divert his thoughts from the one dread topic which threatened to absorb them to the exclusion of all else beside. Then there was the tonic influence of the element of risk. The pick-me-up effect of a spice of peril. Actual danger there quite probably was none; but there very really seemed to be.

And one thing was absolutely certain, that if we did come to smash while going at that speed we should come to as everlasting smash as the heart of man could by any possibility desire. It is probable that the knowledge that this was so warmed the blood in Lessingham's veins. At any rate as—to use what in this case, was simply a form of speech—I sat and watched him, it seemed to me that he was getting a firmer hold of the strength which had all but escaped him, and that with every jog and jolt he was becoming more and more of a man.

On and on we went dashing, clashing, smashing, roaring, rumbling. Atherton, who had been endeavouring to peer through the window, strained his lungs again in the effort to make himself audible.

'Where the devil are we?'

Looking at my watch I screamed back at him.

'It's nearly one, so I suppose we're somewhere in the neighbourhood of Luton.—Hollo! What's the matter?'

That something was the matter seemed certain. There was a shrill whistle from the engine. In a second we were conscious—almost too conscious—of the application of the Westinghouse brake. Of all the jolting that was ever jolted! the mere reverberation of the carriage threatened to resolve our bodies into their component parts. Feeling what we felt then helped us to realise the retardatory force which that vacuum brake must be exerting,—it did not seem at all surprising that the train should have been brought to an almost instant stand-still.

Simultaneously all three of us were on our feet. I let down my window and Atherton let down his,—he shouting out,

'I should think that inspector's wire hasn't had its proper effect, looks as if we're blocked—or else we've stopped at Luton. It can't be Bedford.'

It wasn't Bedford—so much seemed clear. Though at first from my window I could make out nothing. I was feeling more than a trifle dazed,—there was a singing in my ears,—the sudden darkness was impenetrable. Then I became conscious that the guard was opening the door of his compartment. He stood on the step for a moment, seeming to hesitate. Then, with a lamp in his hand, he descended on to the line.

'What's the matter?' I asked.

'Don't know, sir. Seems as if there was something on the road. What's up there?'

This was to the man on the engine. The fireman replied:

'Someone in front there's waving a red light like mad,—lucky I caught sight of him, we should have been clean on top of him in another moment. Looks as if there was something wrong. Here he comes.'

As my eyes grew more accustomed to the darkness I became aware that someone was making what haste he could along the six-foot way, swinging a red light as he came. Our guard advanced to meet him, shouting as he went:

'What's the matter! Who's that?'

A voice replied,

'My God! Is that George Hewett. I thought you were coming right on top of us!'

Our guard again.

'What! Jim Branson! What the devil are you doing here, what's wrong? I thought you were on the twelve out, we're chasing you.'

'Are you? Then you've caught us. Thank God for it!—We're a

wreck.'

I had already opened the carriage door. With that we all three clambered out on to the line.

Chapter 16: The Contents of the Third-Class Carriage

I moved to the stranger who was holding the lamp. He was in official uniform.

'Are you the guard of the 12.0 out from St Pancras?'

'I am.'

'Where's your train? What's happened?'

'As for where it is, there it is, right in front of you, what's left of it. As to what's happened, why, we're wrecked.'

'What do you mean by you're wrecked?'

'Some heavy loaded trucks broke loose from a goods in front and came running down the hill on top of us.'

'How long ago was it?'

'Not ten minutes. I was just starting off down the road to the signal box, it's a good two miles away, when I saw you coming. My God! I thought there was going to be another smash.'

'Much damage done?'

'Seems to me as if we're all smashed up. As far as I can make out they're matchboxed up in front. I feel as if I was all broken up inside of me. I've been in the service going on for thirty years, and this is the first accident I've been in.'

It was too dark to see the man's face, but judging from his tone he was either crying or very near to it.

Our guard turned and shouted back to our engine,

'You'd better go back to the box and let 'em know!'

'All right!' came echoing back.

The special immediately commenced retreating, whistling continually as it went. All the country side must have heard the engine shrieking, and all who did hear must have understood that on the line something was seriously wrong.

The smashed train was all in darkness, the force of the collision had put out all the carriage lamps. Here was a flickering candle, there the glimmer of a match, these were all the lights which shone upon the scene. People were piling up debris by the side of the line, for the purpose of making a fire,—more for illumination than for warmth.

Many of the passengers had succeeded in freeing themselves, and were moving hither and thither about the line. But the majority appeared to be still imprisoned. The carriage doors were jammed. Without the necessary tools it was impossible to open them. Every step we took our ears were saluted by piteous cries. Men, women, children, appealed to us for help.

'Open the door, sir!' 'In the name of God, sir, open the door!'

Over and over again, in all sorts of tones, with all degrees of violence, the supplication was repeated.

The guards vainly endeavoured to appease the, in many cases, half-frenzied creatures.

'All right, sir! If you'll only wait a minute or two, madam! We can't get the doors open without tools, a special train's just started off to get them. If you'll only have patience there'll be plenty of help for everyone of you directly. You'll be quite safe in there, if you'll only keep still.'

But that was just what they found it most difficult to do—keep still!

In the front of the train all was chaos. The trucks which had done the mischief—there were afterwards shown to be six of them, together with two guards' vans—appeared to have been laden with bags of Portland cement. The bags had burst, and everything was covered with what seemed gritty dust. The air was full of the stuff, it got into our eyes, half blinding us. The engine of the express had turned a complete somersault. It vomited forth smoke, and steam, and flames,—every moment it seemed as if the woodwork of the carriages immediately behind and beneath would catch fire.

The front coaches were, as the guard had put it, 'match-boxed.' They were nothing but a heap of debris,—telescoped into one another in a state of apparently inextricable confusion. It was broad daylight before access was gained to what had once been the interiors. The condition of the first third-class compartment revealed an extraordinary state of things.

Scattered all over it were pieces of what looked like partially burnt rags, and fragments of silk and linen. I have those fragments now. Experts have assured me that they are actually neither of silk nor linen! but of some material—animal rather than vegetable—with which they are wholly unacquainted. On the cushions and woodwork—especially on the woodwork of the floor—were huge blotches,—stains of some sort. When first noticed they were damp, and gave out a most unpleasant smell. One of the pieces of woodwork is yet in my possession,—with the stain still on it. Experts have pronounced upon it too,—with the result that opinions are divided. Some maintain that the stain was produced by human blood, which had been subjected to a great heat, and, so to speak, parboiled.

Others declare that it is the blood of some wild animal,—possibly of some creature of the cat species. Yet others affirm that it is not blood at all, but merely paint. While a fourth describes it as—I quote the written opinion which lies in front of me—'caused apparently by a deposit of some sort of viscid matter, probably the excretion of some variety of lizard.'

In a corner of the carriage was the body of what seemed a young man costumed like a tramp. It was Marjorie Lindon.

So far as a most careful search revealed, that was all the compartment contained.

CHAPTER 17: THE CONCLUSION OF THE MATTER

It is several years since I bore my part in the events which I have rapidly sketched,—or I should not have felt justified in giving them publicity. Exactly how many years, for reasons which should be sufficiently obvious, I must decline to say.

Marjorie Lindon still lives. The spark of life which was left in her, when she was extricated from among the debris of the wrecked express, was fanned again into flame. Her restoration was, however, not merely an affair of weeks or months, it was a matter of years. I believe that, even after her physical powers were completely restored—in itself a tedious task—she was for something like three years under medical supervision as a lunatic. But all that skill and money could do was done, and in course of time—the great healer—the results were entirely satisfactory.

Her father is dead,—and has left her in possession of the family estates. She is married to the individual who, in these pages, has been known as Paul Lessingham. Were his real name divulged she would be recognised as the popular and universally reverenced wife of one of the greatest statesmen the age has seen.

Nothing has been said to her about the fateful day on which she was—consciously or unconsciously—paraded through London in the tattered masculine habiliments of a vagabond. She herself has never once alluded to it. With the return of reason the affair seems to have passed from her memory as wholly as if it had never been, which, although she may not know it, is not the least cause she has for thankfulness. Therefore what actually transpired will never, in all human probability, be certainly known and particularly what precisely occurred in the railway carriage during that dreadful moment of sudden passing from life unto death. What became of the creature who all but did her to death; who he was—if it was a 'he,' which is extremely doubtful; whence he came; whither he went; what was the purport of his presence here,—to this hour these things are puzzles.

Paul Lessingham has not since been troubled by his old tormentor. He has ceased to be a haunted man. None the less he continues to have what seems to be a constitutional disrelish for the subject of beetles, nor can he himself be induced to speak of them. Should they be mentioned in a general conversation, should he be unable to immediately bring about a change of theme, he will, if possible, get up and leave the room. More, on this point he and his wife are one.

The fact may not be generally known, but it is so. Also I have reason to believe that there still are moments in which he harks back, with something like physical shrinking, to that awful nightmare of the past, and in which he prays God, that as it is distant from him now so may it be kept far off from him forever.

Before closing, one matter may be casually mentioned. The tale has never been told, but I have unimpeachable authority for its authenticity.

During the recent expeditionary advance towards Dongola, a body of native troops which was encamped at a remote spot in the desert was aroused one night by what seemed to be the sound of a loud explosion. The next morning, at a distance of about a couple of miles from the camp, a huge hole was discovered in the ground,—as if blasting operations, on an enormous scale, had recently been carried on. In the hole itself, and round about it, were found fragments of what seemed bodies; credible witnesses have assured me that they were bodies neither of men nor women, but of creatures of some monstrous growth. I prefer to believe, since no scientific examination of the remains took place, that these witnesses ignorantly, though innocently, erred.

One thing is sure. Numerous pieces, both of stone and of metal, were seen, which went far to suggest that some curious subterranean building had been blown up by the force of the explosion. Especially were there portions of moulded metal which seemed to belong to what must have been an immense bronze statue. There were picked up also, more than a dozen replicas in bronze of the whilom sacred *scarabaeus*.

That the den of demons described by Paul Lessingham, had, that night, at last come to an end, and that these things which lay scattered, here and there, on that treeless plain, were the evidences of its final destruction, is not a hypothesis which I should care to advance with any degree of certainty. But, putting this and that together, the facts seem to point that way,—and it is a consummation devoutly to be desired.

By-the-bye, Sydney Atherton has married Miss Dora Grayling. Her wealth has made him one of the richest men in England. She began, the story goes, by loving him immensely; I can answer for the fact that he has ended by loving her as much. Their devotion to each other contradicts the pessimistic nonsense which supposes that every marriage must be of necessity a failure. He continues his career of an inventor. His investigations into the subject of aerial flight, which have brought the flying machine within the range of practical politics, are on everybody's tongue.

The best man at Atherton's wedding was Percy Woodville, now the Earl of Barnes. Within six months afterwards he married one of Mrs. Atherton's bridesmaids.

It was never certainly shown how Robert Holt came to his end. At the inquest the coroner's jury was content to return a verdict of 'Died of exhaustion.' He lies buried in Kensal Green Cemetery, under a handsome tombstone, the cost of which, had he had it in his pockets, might have indefinitely prolonged his days.

It should be mentioned that that portion of this strange history which purports to be The Surprising Narration of Robert Holt was compiled from the statements which Holt made to Atherton, and to Miss Lindon, as she then was, when, a mud-stained, shattered derelict he lay at the lady's father's house.

Miss Linden's contribution towards the elucidation of the mystery was written with her own hand. After her physical strength had come back to her, and, while mentally, she still hovered between the darkness and the light, her one relaxation was writing. Although she would never speak of what she had written, it was found that her theme was always the same. She confided to pen and paper what she would not speak of with her lips. She told, and re-told, and re-told again, the story of her love, and of her tribulation so far as it is contained in the present volume. Her MSS. invariably began and ended at the same point. They have all of them been destroyed, with one exception. That exception is herein placed before the reader.

On the subject of the Mystery of the Beetle I do not propose to pronounce a confident opinion. Atherton and I have talked it over many and many a time, and at the end we have got no 'forrarder.' So far as I am personally concerned, experience has taught me that there are indeed more things in heaven and earth than are dreamed of in our philosophy, and I am quite prepared to believe that the so-called Beetle, which others saw, but I never, was—or is, for it cannot be certainly shown that the thing is not still existing—a creature born neither of God nor man.

The Spectre House

Gelett Burgess

Mr. Enoch Gerrish's paper on "*The Customs and Costumes of Ardent Spirits*" had ended at last, amid a babel of applause from the members of the Psychical Research Society. No one had listened, however; they applauded because he had finished. For an hour and twenty minutes Mr. Gerrish had kept them from their annual dinner.

They were sorry they had re-elected him president.

The dinner began, but to Mr. Gerrish's floating fancy it never really ended. He ate on and on, abstractedly, and from time to time he lifted a glass and drank, without taking off his eyes from the bunch of celery in front of him.

He was thinking.

It was not the stuffed grouse, nor the *leberwurst*, nor the mince pie, nor the Burgundy, nor even the bunch of celery that induced Mr. Gerrish's hypnosis. To his mind this dinner was out of place at a meeting of such an important and intellectual society. He was thinking of his next paper, which was to be upon the "*Materialisation and Dematerialisation of Inanimate Objects.*"

If the members had known that he was already thinking of another paper, he would have been very much put out.

At long intervals, his mind, swimming laboriously through the mazes of his forthcoming argument, rose, as one might say, to the surface of things, and he heard, as if borne from miles away, a song at the other end of the table. He was occasionally hit unaware by a flying jest which exploded in inane laughter.

His mind was on other things, though, he still passed his plate mechanically for a fourth helping of pie. An impressive company of empty bottles assembled beside his plate. He ate and drank like a machine which someone had started and had forgotten to stop.

The dinner did not end ; but the scene changed, somehow, as in a dream—suddenly, much as a woman changes the subject of a conversation, and with even less reason.

He found himself in the street, walking.

He kept in the middle of the street and counted his steps, skipping hundreds without noticing it. He was well into the millions when he reached No. 45 Taylor Street. He walked upstairs backward so as not to wake the baby, crawled through the transom into his room, and disrobed.

He got into a Harveyized nightshirt, stiff and brittle, and polished as an ostrich egg, and went to bed. His shirt creaked when he breathed, and he fancied he was still walking, so he kept on counting.

Suddenly he sat up and looked about him, for the candle was burning. He was in bed at No. 45 Taylor Street. But this house had burned down last March! He was sure of that, for he had escaped down a ladder with great difficulty, carrying a pitcher of cold water carefully. The crowd had laughed at him, but he had explained to them his reasons for saving the pitcher, which was, so he said, a last present from his dying mother. The crowd had not believed this.

How, then, could he be in No. 45 Taylor Street if the house had been burned down? Or had it burned up? There was the hole in the plastering where he had tried to look through the wall after the last dinner of the society. The pattern of the wall-paper, too, made faces at him, as it always did after he had over-eaten.

The house, then, had been materialised!

He reached for the pencil and paper which he always kept at the head of his bed in case an idea or a ghost ever occurred to him. He would make a note of this to use as a *datum* for his next essay. But the paper and pencil were not there. They never were there when he needed them. He got up and looked out of the window. It was almost morning. A milkwagon was passing. From the next house came the sound of snorting and a housemaid rattling at the kitchen stove. He turned back to go to bed.

There was hardly room enough left to sleep in.

The walls had grown translucent and as through a mist he saw in the back yard his dog smelling at the dust-bin. Through blurred, jelly-like walls on either side he saw the windows of the adjoining houses. His own house was fast fading away. The whole front wall, bathed in the rays of the rising sun, had already disappeared ! The ceiling had vanished.

With a sudden access of light the entire building melted away and was gone from sight. He could not see the floor though he felt the hard boards still under his feet, and he even ran an invisible sliver into his great toe, removing it with difficulty. He groped his way, as if he were in the dark, feeling for the bed. He found it first with his left shin, and lay down, pulling the covers over him, in the same futile way that an ostrich endeavours to hide itself by putting its head in the sand.

The blankets were invisible to the naked eye and useless to protect him from espionage, but they kept him warm.

Mr. Gerrish lay in bed feeling very silly, watching the city awake. He dared not attempt to cross the floor, for fear of falling downstairs or out of the window. Walking had been difficult enough that night when the house was visible. What would it be when the floor was gone? It made him giddy to think of it.

He was imprisoned in the atmosphere like a bird in a cage, sixty feet from the pavement. He felt like a fish in a glass aquarium, except that he could not swim.

The window next door was opened and the shade drawn. A house-maid put out her hand to see if it were raining. Then she looked up into the sky and saw Mr. Gerrish. Did she think it was raining middle-aged gentlemen in night-shirts? For a long time she could not remove her eyes ; she was fascinated by the sight.

She must have thought he was a belated angel who had missed the last train to Paradise.

To Mr. Gerrish's relief, she vanished, but soon reappeared with the cook. The two did not leave the window till all was over.

A policeman next entered the theatre of Mr. Gerrish's misery. The mortified but high-minded gentleman watched through his toes as the officer walked down the street. When he reached Mr. Gerrish's great toe he stopped and looked up at the cook and the housemaid. From these his eyes slowly travelled across the intervening space till they reached the figure of a gentleman in scant attire—alone in the air!

"I say, you!" yelled the policeman, "come down out of that! It's agin' the law to sleep out-of-doors!"

Mr. Gerrish waved his hand, feebly, in mild expo-deprecation. What was the use of trying to explain the situation? Who would be-lieve that he was in his own house, in his own room, lying on his own bed, and was at heart as modest as a spinster He would like nothing better than to be removed or have the house returned.

The policeman began to throw stones at him, but only succeeded in breaking a window. He heard the crash, but saw nothing. It was not till he had broken his own pate against the spectre house that he realized the unique but illegal situation.

By this time a large crowd had gathered. The cook and the housemaid had not once taken their eyes from Mr. Gerrish ; he could feel them staring when his back was turned. The policeman rang in a fire alarm and telephoned for the sergeant.

After this things went more merrily.

Ladders were brought and leaned against the invisible house, seemingly supported by nothing; no one dared ascend. Men with axes hacked at the walls, for the door, wherever it was, was locked. A regiment of volunteers was called out to keep the mob in check. The mayor of the city appeared and read the Riot Act from the top of a four-wheeled cab. Mr. Gerrish watched all this through half-closed eyelids; he felt the mortifying situation keenly, and pretended to be asleep to hide his embarrassment.

At last, after recklessly mounting a ladder, a fool of a policeman rushed in where this angel in a night-shirt had feared to tread. He grabbed Mr. Gerrish in his arms, and after bumping both heads against innumerable obstacles, bore him to the ground amidst the cheers of the now delirious populace.

When Mr. Gerrish finally dared to open his eyes and release his grip from the policeman's neck, everyone had vanished except the cook and the housemaid; the house had reappeared as good as new, absolutely opaque in the early dawn.

He saw the big black number "45," but it was not like the house from which he had made such a sensational exit.

Then he remembered that No. 45 Taylor Street had been rebuilt after the fire in March.

"See here," said the policeman, winking at the housemaid, "you'd better git back to bed, or you'll catch cold. I caught you just in time."

Mr. Gerrish read 14,000 words on the "*Materialisation and Dematerialisation of Inanimate Objects*" at the next dinner of the Psychical Research Society, but no one listened.

Flaxman Low:
The Story of Saddler's Croft

by E. and H. Heron

(pseud. for Katherine and Hesketh Prichard)

Although Flaxman Low has devoted his life to the study of psychical phenomena, he has always been most earnest in warning persons who feel inclined to dabble in spiritualism, without any serious motive for doing so, of the mischief and danger accruing to the rash experimenter.

Extremely few persons are sufficiently masters of themselves to permit of their calling in the vast unknown forces outside ordinary human knowledge for mere purposes of amusement.

In support of this warning the following extraordinary story is laid before our readers.

★★★★★★

Deep in the forest land of Sussex, close by an unfrequented road, stands a low half-timbered house, that is only separated from the roadway by a rough stone wall and a few flower borders.

The front is covered with ivy, and looks out between two conical trees upon the passers-by. The windows are many of them diamond-paned, and an unpretentious white gate leads up to the front door. It is a quaint, quiet spot, with an old-world suggestion about it which appealed strongly to pretty Sadie Corcoran as she drove with her husband along the lane. The Corcorans were Americans, and had to the full the American liking for things ancient. Saddler's Croft struck them both as ideal, and when they found out that it was much more roomy and comfortable than it looked from the road, and also that it had large lawns and grounds attached to it, they decided at once on taking it for a year or two.

When they mentioned the project to Phil Strewd, their host, and an old friend of Corcoran, he did not favour it. Much as he should have liked to have them for neighbours, he thought that Saddler's Croft had too many unpleasant traditions connected with it. Besides, it had lain empty for three years, as the last occupants were spiritualists of some sort, and the place was said to be haunted. But Mrs. Corcoran was not to be put off, and declared that a flavour of ghostliness was all that Saddler's Croft required to make it absolutely the most attractive residence in Europe.

The Corcorans moved in about October, but it was not till the following July that Flaxman Low met Mr. Strewd on the Victoria platform.

"I'm glad you're coming down to Andy Corcoran's," Strewd began. "You must remember him? I introduced you to him at the club a couple of years ago. He's an awfully decent fellow, and an old friend of mine. He once went with an Arctic expedition, and has crossed Greenland or San Josef's Land on snowshoes or something. I've got the book about it at home. So you can size him up for yourself. He's now married to a very pretty woman, and they have taken a house in my part of the world.

"I didn't want them to rent Saddler's Croft, for it had a bad name some years ago. Some of your psychical folk used to live there. They made a sort of Greek temple at the back, where they used to have queer goings on, so I'm told. A Greek was living with them called Agapoulos, who was the arch-priest of their sect, or whatever it was. Ultimately Agapoulos died on a moonlight night in the temple, in the middle of their rites. After that his friends left, but, of course, people said he haunted the place. I never saw anything myself, but a young sailor, home on leave about that time, swore he'd catch the ghost, and he was found next morning on the temple steps. He was past telling us what had happened, or what he had seen, for he was dead. I'll never forget his face. It was horrible!"

"And since then?"

"After that the place would not let, although the talk of the ghost being seen died away until quite lately. I suppose the old caretaker went to bed early, and avoided trouble that way. But during the last few months Corcoran has seen it repeatedly himself, and—in fact, things seem to be going on very strangely. What with Mrs. Corcoran wild on studying psychology, as she calls it—"

"So Mrs. Corcoran has a turn that way?"

"Yes, since young Sinclair came home from Ceylon about five months ago. I must tell you he was very thick with Agapoulos in former times, and people said he used to join in all the ruffianism at Saddler's Croft. You'll see the rest for yourself. You are asked down ostensibly to please Mrs. Corcoran, but Andy hopes you may help him to clear up the mystery."

Flaxman Low found Corcoran a tall, thin, nervy American of the best type; while his wife was as pretty and as charming as we have grown accustomed to expect an American girl to be.

"I suppose," Corcoran began, "that Phil has been giving you all the gossip about this house? I was entirely sceptical once; but now—do you believe in midsummer madness?"

"I believe there often is a deep truth hidden in common beliefs and superstitions. But let me hear more."

"I'll tell you what happened not twenty-four hours ago. Everything has been working up to it for the last three months, but it came to a head last night, and I immediately wired for you. I had been sitting in my smoking-room rather late reading. I put out the lamp and was just about to go to bed when the brilliance of the moonlight struck me, and I put my head through the window to look over the lawn. Directly I heard chanting of a most unusual character from the direction of the temple, which lies at the back of that plantation. Then one voice, a beautiful tenor, detached itself from the rest, and seemed to approach the house. As it came nearer I saw my wife cross the grass to the plantation with a wavering, uncertain gait. I ran after her, for I believed she was walking in her sleep; but before I could reach her a man came out of the grass alley at the other side of the lawn.

"I saw them go away together down the alley towards the temple, but I could not stir, the moonbeams seemed to be penetrating my brain, my feet were chained, the wildest and most hideous thoughts seemed rocking—I can use no other term—in my head. I made an effort, and ran round by another way, and met them on the temple steps. I had strength left to grasp at the man—remember I saw him plainly, with his dark, Greek face—but he turned aside and leapt into the underwood, leaving in my hand only the button from the back of his coat.

"Now comes the incomprehensible part. Sadie, without seeing me, or so it appeared, glided away again towards the house; but I was determined to find the man who had eluded me. The moonlight poured upon my head; I felt it like an absolute touch. The chanting grew louder, and drowned every other recollection. I forgot Sadie, I forgot all but the delicious sounds, and I—I, a nineteenth-century, hard-headed Yankee—hammered at those accursed doors to be allowed to enter. Then, like a dream, the singing was behind me and around me—someone came, or so I thought, and pushed me gently in. The moon was pouring through the end window; there were many people. In the morning I found myself lying on the floor of the temple, and all about me the dust was undisturbed but for the mark of my own single footstep and the spot where I had fallen. You may say it was all a dream, Low, but I tell you some infernal power hangs about that building."

"From what you tell me," said Flaxman Low, "I can almost undertake to say that Mrs. Corcoran is at present nearly, if not quite, ignorant of the horrible experience you remember. In her case the emotions of wonder and curiosity have probably alone been worked upon as in a dream."

"I believe in her absolutely," exclaimed Corcoran, "but this power swamps all resistance. I have another strange circumstance to add. On coming to myself I found the button still in my hand. I have since had the opportunity of fitting it to its right position in the coat of a man who is a pretty constant visitor here," the American's lips tightened, "a young Sinclair, who does tea-planting in Ceylon when he has the health for it, but is just now at home to recruit. He is the son of a neighbouring squire, and in every particular of face and figure unlike the handsome Greek I saw that night."

"Have you spoken to him on the subject?"

"Yes; I showed him the button, and told him I had found it near the temple. He took the news very curiously. He did not look confused or guilty, but simply scared out of his senses. He offered no explanation, but made a hasty excuse, and left us. My wife looked on with the most perfect indifference, and offered no remark."

"Has Mrs. Corcoran appeared to be very languid of late?" asked Low.

"Yes, I have noticed that."

"Judging from the effect produced by the chanting upon you, I should say that you were something of a musician?" said Low irrelevantly.

"Yes," replied the other, astonished.

"Then, this evening, when I am talking with Mrs. Corcoran, will you reproduce the melody you heard on that night?"

Corcoran agreed, and the conversation ended with a request on the part of Mr. Low to be permitted to make the acquaintance of Mrs. Corcoran, and further, to be given the opportunity of talking to her alone.

Sadie Corcoran received him with effusion.

"O Mr. Low, I'm just perfectly delighted to see you! I'm looking forward to the most lovely spiritual talks. It's such fun! You know I was in quite a psychical set before I married, but afterwards I dropped it, because Andy has some effete old prejudices."

Flaxman Low inquired how it happened that her interest had revived.

"It is the air of this dear old place," she replied, with a more serious expression. "I always found the subject very attractive, and lately we have made the acquaintance of a Mr. Sinclair, who is a——" she checked herself with an odd look, "who knows all about it."

"How does he advise you to experiment?" asked Mr. Low. "Have you ever tried sleeping with the moonlight on your face?"

She flushed, and looked startled.

"Yes, Mr. Sinclair told me that the spiritualists who formerly lived in this house believed that by doing so you could put yourself into communication with—other intelligences. It makes one dream," she added, "such strange dreams."

"Are they pleasant dreams?" asked Flaxman Low gravely.

"Not now, but by and by he assures me that they will be."

"But you must think of your dreams all day long, or the moonlight will not affect you so readily on the next occasion, and you are obliged to repeat a certain formula? Is it not so?"

She admitted it was, and added: "But Mr. Sinclair says that if I persevere I shall soon pass through the zone of the bad spirits and enter the circle of the good. So I choose to go on. It is all so wonderful and exciting. Oh, here is Mr. Sinclair! I'm sure you will find many interesting things to talk over." The drawing-room lay at the back of the house, and overlooked a strip of lawn shut in on the further side by a thick plantation of larches. Directly opposite to the French window, where they were seated, a grass alley which had been cut through the plantation gave a glimpse of turf and forest land beyond. From this alley now emerged a young man in riding-breeches, who walked moodily across the lawn with his eyes on the ground. In a few minutes Flaxman Low understood that young Sinclair had a pronounced admiration for his hostess, the reckless, headstrong admiration with which a weak-willed man of strong emotions often deceives himself and the woman he loves. He was manifestly in wretched health and equally wretched spirits, a combination that greatly impaired the very ordinary type of English good-looks which he represented.

While the three had tea together Mrs. Corcoran made some attempt to lead up to the subject of spiritualism, but Sinclair avoided it, and soon Mrs. Corcoran lost her vivacity, which gave place to a well-marked languor, a condition that Low shortly grew to connect with Sinclair's presence.

Presently she left them, and the two men went outside and walked up and down smoking for a while till Flaxman Low turned down the path between the larches. Sinclair hung back.

"You'll find it stuffy down there," he said, with curved nostrils.

"I rather wanted to see what building that roof over the trees belongs to," replied Low.

With manifest reluctance Sinclair went on beside him. Another turn at right angles brought them into the path leading up to the little temple, which Low found was solidly built of stone. In shape it was oblong, with a pillared Ionic *façade*. The trees stood closely round it, and it contained only one window, now void of glass, set high in the further end of the building. Low asked a question.

"It was a summer-house made by the people who lived here formerly," replied Sinclair, with brusqueness. "Let's get away. It's beastly damp."

"It is an odd kind of summer-house. It looks more like—" Low checked himself. "Can we go inside?" He went up the low steps and tried the door, which yielded readily, and he entered to look round.

The walls had once been ornamented with designs in black and some glittering pigment, while at the upper end a *dais* nearly four feet high stood under the arched window, the whole giving the vague impression of a church. One or two peculiarities of structure and decoration struck Low.

He turned sharply on Sinclair.

"What was this place used for?"

But Sinclair was staring round with a white, working face; his glance seemed to trace out the half-obliterated devices upon the walls, and then rested on the *dais*. A sort of convulsion passed over his features, as his head was jerked forward, rather as if pushed by some unseen force than by his own will, while, at the same time, he brought his hand to his mouth, and kissed it. Then with a strange, prolonged cry he rushed headlong out of the temple, and appeared no more at Saddler's Croft that day.

The afternoon was still and warm with brooding thunderstorm, but at night the sky cleared.

Now it happened that Andy Corcoran was, amongst many other good things, an accomplished musician, and, while Flaxman Low and Mrs. Corcoran talked at intervals by the open French window, he sat down at the piano and played a weird melody. Mrs. Corcoran broke off in the middle of a sentence, and soon she began swaying gently to the rhythm of the music, and presently she was singing. Suddenly, Corcoran dropped his hand on the notes with a crash. His wife sprang from her chair.

"Andy! Where are you? Where are you?" And in a moment she had thrown herself, sobbing hysterically, into his arms, while he begged her to tell him what troubled her.

"It was that music. Oh, don't play it any more! I liked it at first, and then all at once it seemed to terrify me!" He led her back towards the light.

"Where did you learn that song, Sadie? Tell me."

She lifted her clear eyes to his.

"I don't know! I can't remember, but it is like a dreadful memory! Never play it again! Promise me!"

"Of course not, darling."

By midnight the moon sailed broad and bright above the house. Flaxman Low and the American were together in the smoking-room. The room was in darkness. Low sat in the shadow of the open window, while Corcoran waited behind him in the gloom. The shade of the larches lay in a black line along the grass, the air was still and heavy, not a leaf moved. From his position, Low could see the dark masses of the forest stretching away into the dimness over the undulating country. The scene was very lovely, very lonely, and very sad.

A little trill of bells within the room rang the half-hour after midnight, and scarcely had the sound ceased when from outside came another—a long cadenced wailing chant of voices in unison that rose and fell faint and far off but with one distinct note, the same that Low had heard in Sinclair's beast-like cry earlier in the day.

After the chanting died away, there followed a long sullen interval, broken at last by a sound of singing, but so vague and dim that it might have been some elusive air throbbing within the brain. Slowly it grew louder and nearer. It was the melody Sadie had begged never to hear again, and it was sung by a tenor voice, vibrating and beautiful.

Low felt Corcoran's hand grip his shoulder, when out upon the grass Sadie, a slim figure in trailing white, appeared advancing with uncertain steps towards the alley of the larches. The next moment the singer came forward from the shadows to meet her. It was not Sinclair, but a much more remarkable-looking personage. He stopped and raised his face to the moon, a face of an extraordinary perfection of beauty such as Flaxman Low had never seen before. But the great dark eyes, the full powerfully moulded features, had one attribute in common with Sinclair's face, they wore the same look of a profound and infinite unhappiness.

"Come." Corcoran gripped Flaxman Low's shoulder. "She is sleep-walking. We will see who it is this time."

When they reached the lawn the couple had disappeared. Corcoran leading, the two men ran along under the shadow of the house, and so by another path to the back of the temple.

The empty window glowed in the light of the moon, and the hum of a subdued chanting floated out amongst the silent trees. The sound seized upon the brain like a whiff of opium, and a thousand unbidden thoughts ran through Flaxman Low's mind. But his mental condition was as much under his control as his bodily movements. Pulling himself together he ran on. Sadie Corcoran and her companion were mounting the steps under the pillars. The girl held back, as if drawn forward against her will; her eyes were blank and open, and she moved slowly.

Then Corcoran dashed out of the shadow.

What occurred next Mr. Low does not know, for he hurried Mrs. Corcoran away towards the house, holding her arm gently. She yielded to his touch, and went silently beside him to the drawing-room, where he guided her to a couch. She lay down upon it like a tired child, and closed her eyes without a word.

After a while Flaxman Low went out again to look for Corcoran. The temple was dark and silent, and there was no one to be seen. He groped his way through the long grass towards the back of the building. He had not gone far when he stumbled over something soft that moved and groaned. Low lit a match, for it was impossible to see anything in the gloom under the trees. To his horror he found the American at his feet, beaten and battered almost beyond recognition.

The first thing next morning Mr. Strewd received a note from Flaxman Low asking him to come over at once. He arrived in the course of the forenoon, and listened to an account of Corcoran's adventures during the night, with an air of dismay.

"So it's come at last!" he remarked, "I'd no idea Sinclair was such a bruiser."

"Sinclair? What do you suppose Sinclair had to do with it?"

"Oh, come now, Low, what's the good of that? Why, my man told me this morning when I was shaving that Sinclair went home some time last night all covered in blood. I'd half a guess at what had happened then."

"But I tell you I saw the man with whom Corcoran fought. He was an extraordinarily handsome man with a Greek face."

Strewd whistled.

"By George, Low, you let your imagination run away with you," he said, shaking his head.

"That's all nonsense, you know."

"We must try to find out if it is," said Low.

"Will you come over tonight and stay with me? There will be a full moon."

"Yes, and it has affected all your brains! Here's Mrs. Corcoran full of surprise over her husband's condition! You don't suppose that's genuine?"

"I know it is genuine," replied Low quietly. "Bring your Kodak with you when you come, will you?"

The day was long, languorous, and heavy; the thunderstorm had not yet broken, but once again the night rose cloudless. Flaxman Low decided to watch alone near the temple while Strewd remained on the alert in the house, ready to give his help if it should be needed.

The hush of the night, the smell of the dewy larches, the silvery light with its bewildering beauty creeping from point to point as the moon rose, all the pure influences of nature, seemed to Low more powerful, more effective, than he had ever before felt them to be. Forcing his mind to dwell on ordinary subjects, he waited. Midnight passed, and then began indistinct sounds, shuffling footsteps, murmurings, and laughter, but all faint and evasive. Gradually the tumultuous thoughts he had experienced on the previous evening began to run riot in his brain.

When the singing began he does not know. It was only by an immense effort of will that he was able to throw off the trance that was stealing over him, holding him prisoner—how nearly a willing prisoner he shudders to remember. But habits of self-control have been Low's only shield in many a dangerous hour. They came to his aid now. He moved out in front of the temple just in time to see Sadie pass within the temple door. Waiting only a moment to make quite sure of his senses, and concentrating his will on the single desire of saving her, he followed. He says he was conscious of a crowd of persons at either side; he knew without looking that the pictures on the wall glowed and lived again.

Through the high window opposite him a broad white shaft of light fell, and immediately under it, on the *dais*, stood the man whom Mr. Low in his heart now called Agapoulos. Supreme in its beauty and its sadness that beautiful face looked across the bowed heads of those present into the eyes of Mr. Flaxman Low. Slowly, very slowly, as a narrow lane opened up before him amongst the figures of the crowd, Low advanced towards the *daïs*. The man's smile seemed to draw him on; he stretched out his hand as Flaxman Low approached. And Low was conscious of a longing to clasp it even though that might mean perdition.

At the last moment, when it seemed to him he could resist no longer, he became aware of the white-clad figure of Sadie beside him. She also was looking up at the beautiful face with a wild gaze. Low hesitated no longer. He was now within two feet of the *dais*. He swung back his left hand and dealt a smashing half-arm blow at the figure. The man staggered with a very human groan, and then fell face forward on the *dais*. A whirlwind of dust seemed to rise and obscure the moonlight; there was a wild sense of motion and flight, a subdued sibilant murmur like the noise of a swarm of bats in commotion, and then Flaxman Low heard Phil Strewd's loud voice at the door, and he shouted to him to come.

"What has happened?" said Strewd, as he helped to raise the fallen man. "Why, whom have we got here? Good heavens, Low, it is Agapoulos! I remember him well!"

"Leave him there in the moonlight. Take Mrs. Corcoran away and hurry back with the Kodak. There is no time to lose before the moon leaves this window."

The moonlight was full and strong, the exposure prolonged and steady, so that when afterwards Flaxman Low came to develop the film—but we are anticipating, for the night and its revelations were not over yet. The two men waited through the dark hour that precedes the dawn, intending when daylight came to remove their prisoner elsewhere. They sat on the edge of the *dais* side by side, Strewd at Low's request holding the hand of the unconscious man, and talked till the light came.

"I think it's about time to move him now," suggested Strewd, looking round at the wounded man behind him. As he did so, he sprang to his feet with a shout.

"What's this, Low? I've gone mad, I think! Look here!"

Flaxman Low bent over the pale, unconscious face. It bore no longer the impress of that exquisite Greek beauty they had seen an hour earlier; it only showed to their astonished gaze the haggard outlines of young Sinclair.

Some days later Strewd rubbed the back of his head energetically with a broad hand, and surmised aloud.

"This is a strange world, my masters," and he looked across the cool shady bedroom at Andy Corcoran's bandaged head.

"And the other world's stranger, I guess," put in the American drily, "if we may judge by the sample of the supernatural we have lately had.

"You know I hold that there is no such thing as the supernatural; all is natural," said Flaxman Low. "We need more light, more knowledge. As there is a well-defined break in the notes of the human voice, so there is a break between what we call natural and supernatural. But the notes of the upper register correspond with those in the lower scale; in like manner, by drawing upon our experience of things we know and see, we should be able to form accurate hypotheses with regard to things which, while clearly pertaining to us, have so far been regarded as mysteries."

"I doubt if any theory will touch this mystery," Strewd objected. "I have questioned Sinclair, and noted down his answers as you asked me, Low. Here they are."

"No, thank you. Will you compare my theory with what he has told you? In the first place, Agapoulos was, I fancy, one of a clique calling themselves Dianists, who desired to revive the ancient worship of the moon. That I easily gathered from the symbol of the moon in front of the temple and from the half-defaced devices on the walls inside. Then I perceived that Sinclair, when we were standing before the *dais*, almost unconsciously used the gesture of the moon worshippers. The chant we heard was the lament for Adonis. I could multiply evidences, but there is no need to do so. The fact also tells that the place is haunted on moonlight nights only."

"Sinclair's confession corroborates all this," said Strewd at this point.

Corcoran turned irritably on his couch.

"Moon-worship was not exactly the nicest form of idolatry," he said in a weary tone; "but I can't see how that accounts for the awkward fact that a man who not only looks like Agapoulos, but was caught, and even photographed as Agapoulos, turns out at the end of an hour or so, during which there was no chance of substituting one for the other, to be another person of an entirely different appearance. Add to this that Agapoulos is dead and Sinclair is living, and we have an array of facts that drive one to suspect that common-sense and reason are delusions. Go on, Low."

"The substitution, as you call it, of Agapoulos for Sinclair is one of the most marked and best attested cases of obsession with which I have personally come into contact," answered Flaxman Low. "You will notice that during Sinclair's absence in Ceylon nothing was seen of the ghost—on his return it again appeared."

"What is obsession? I know what it is supposed to be, but—" Corcoran stopped.

"I should call it in this case as nearly as possible an instance of spiritual hypnotism. We know there is such a thing as human hypnotism; why should not a disembodied spirit have similar powers? Sinclair has been obsessed by the spirit of Agapoulos; he not only yielded to his influence in the man's lifetime, but sought it again after his death. I don't profess to claim any great knowledge of the subject, but I do know that terrible results have come about from similar practices. Sinclair, for his own reasons, invited the control of a spirit, and, having no inherent powers of resistance, he became its slave. Agapoulos must have possessed extraordinary will-force; his soul actually dominated Sinclair's. Thus not only the mental attributes of Sinclair but even his bodily appearance became modified to the likeness of the Greek. Sinclair himself probably looked upon his experiences as a series of vivid dreams induced by dwelling on certain thoughts and using certain formulae, until this morning when his condition proved to him that they were real enough."

"That is perhaps all very well so far as it goes," put in Strewd, "but I fail to understand how a seedy, weakly chap like Sinclair could punish my friend Andy here, as we must suppose he has done, if we accept your ideas, Low."

"You are aware that under abnormal conditions, such as may be observed in the insane, a quite extraordinary reserve of latent strength is frequently called out from apparently weak persons. So Sinclair's usual powers were largely reinforced by abnormal influences."

"I have another question to ask, Low," said Corcoran. "Can you explain the strange attraction and influence the temple possessed over all of us, and especially over my wife?"

"I think so. Mrs. Corcoran, through a desire for amusement and excitement, placed herself in a degree of communication with the spiritual world during sleep. Remember, the Greek lived here, and the thoughts and emotions of individuals remain in the aura of places closely associated with them. Personally, I do not doubt that Agapoulos is a strong and living intelligence, and those persons who frequent the vicinity of the temple are readily placed in rapport with his wandering spirit by means of this aura. To use common words, evil influences haunt the temple."

"But this is intolerable. What can we do?"

"Leave Saddler's Croft, and persuade Mrs. Corcoran to have no more to do with spiritism. As for Sinclair, I will see him. He has opened what may be called the doors of life. It will be a hard task to close them again, and to become his own master. But it may be done."

Sister Maddelena

Ralph Adams Cram

Across the valley of the Oreto from Monreale, on the slopes of the mountains just above the little village of Parco, lies the old convent of Sta. Catarina. From the cloister terrace at Monreale you can see its pale walls and the slim campanile of its chapel rising from the crowded citron and mulberry orchards that flourish, rank and wild, no longer cared for by pious and loving hands. From the rough road that climbs the mountains to Assunto, the convent is invisible, a gnarled and ragged olive grove intervening, and a spur of cliffs as well, while from Palermo one sees only the speck of white, flashing in the sun, indistinguishable from the many similar gleams of desert monastery or pauper village.

Partly because of this seclusion, partly by reason of its extreme beauty, partly, it may be, because the present owners are more than charming and gracious in their pressing hospitality, Sta. Catarina seems to preserve an element of the poetic, almost magical; and as I drove with the Cavaliere Valguanera one evening in March out of Palermo, along the garden valley of the Oreto, then up the mountain side where the warm light of the spring sunset swept across from Monreale, lying golden and mellow on the luxuriant growth of figs, and olives, and orange-trees, and fantastic cacti, and so up to where the path of the convent swung off to the right round a dizzy point of cliff that reached out gaunt and gray from the olives below,—as I drove thus in the balmy air, and saw of a sudden a vision of creamy walls and orange roofs, draped in fantastic festoons of roses, with a single curving palm-tree stuck black and feathery against the gold sunset, it is hardly to be wondered at that I should slip into a mood of visionary enjoyment, looking for a time on the whole thing as the misty phantasm of a summer dream.

The *Cavaliere* had introduced himself to us,—Tom Rendel and me,—one morning soon after we reached Palermo, when, in the first bewilderment of architects in this paradise of art and colour, we were working nobly at our sketches in that dream of delight, the Capella Palatina. He was himself an amateur archæologist, he told us, and passionately devoted to his island; so he felt impelled to speak to any one whom he saw appreciating the almost—and in a way fortunately— unknown beauties of Palermo. In a little time we were fully acquainted, and talking like the oldest friends. Of course he knew acquaintances of Rendel's,—someone always does: this time they were officers on the tubby U. S. S. *Quinebaug*, that, during the summer of 1888, was trying to uphold the maritime honour of the United States in European waters.

Luckily for us, one of the officers was a kind of cousin of Rendel's, and came from Baltimore as well, so, as he had visited at the *Cavaliere's* place, we were soon invited to do the same. It was in this way that, with the luck that attends Rendel wherever he goes, we came to see something of domestic life in Italy, and that I found myself involved in another of those adventures for which I naturally sought so little.

I wonder if there is any other place in Sicily so faultless as Sta. Catarina? Taormina is a paradise, an epitome of all that is beautiful in Italy,—Venice excepted. Girgenti is a solemn epic, with its golden temples between the sea and hills. Cefalù is wild and strange, and Monreale a vision out of a fairy tale; but Sta. Catarina!—

Fancy a convent of creamy stone and rose-red brick perched on a ledge of rock midway between earth and heaven, the cliff falling almost sheer to the valley two hundred feet and more, the mountain rising behind straight towards the sky; all the rocks covered with cactus and dwarf fig-trees, the convent draped in smothering roses, and in front a terrace with a fountain in the midst; and then—nothing— between you and the sapphire sea, six miles away. Below stretches the Eden valley, the Concha d'Oro, gold-green fig orchards alternating with smoke-blue olives, the mountains rising on either hand and sinking undulously away towards the bay where, like a magic city of ivory and nacre, Palermo lies guarded by the twin mountains, Monte Pellegrino and Capo Zafferano, arid rocks like dull amethysts, rose in sunlight, violet in shadow: lions *couchant*, guarding the sleeping town.

Seen as we saw it for the first time that hot evening in March, with the golden lambent light pouring down through the valley, making it in verity a "shell of gold," sitting in Indian chairs on the terrace, with the perfume of roses and jasmines all around us, the valley of the Ore-to, Palermo, Sta. Catarina, Monreale,—all were but parts of a dreamy vision, like the heavenly city of Sir Percivale, to attain which he passed across the golden bridge that burned after him as he vanished in the intolerable light of the Beatific Vision.

It was all so unreal, so phantasmal, that I was not surprised in the least when, late in the evening after the ladies had gone to their rooms, and the *Cavaliere*, Tom, and I were stretched out in chairs on the terrace, smoking lazily under the multitudinous stars, the *Cavaliere* said, "There is something I really must tell you both before you go to bed, so that you may be spared any unnecessary alarm."

"You are going to say that the place is haunted," said Rendel, feeling vaguely on the floor beside him for his glass of Amaro: "thank you; it is all it needs."

The *Cavaliere* smiled a little: "Yes, that is just it. Sta. Catarina is really haunted; and much as my reason revolts against the idea as superstitious and savouring of priestcraft, yet I must acknowledge I see no way of avoiding the admission. I do not presume to offer any explanations, I only state the fact; and the fact is that tonight one or other of you will, in all human—or unhuman—probability, receive a visit from Sister Maddelena. You need not be in the least afraid, the apparition is perfectly gentle and harmless; and, moreover, having seen it once, you will never see it again. No one sees the ghost, or whatever it is, but once, and that usually the first night he spends in the house. I myself saw the thing eight—nine years ago, when I first bought the place from the Marchese di Muxaro; all my people have seen it, nearly all my guests, so I think you may as well be prepared."

"Then tell us what to expect," I said; "what kind of a ghost is this nocturnal visitor?"

"It is simple enough. Sometime tonight you will suddenly awake and see before you a Carmelite nun who will look fixedly at you, say distinctly and very sadly, 'I cannot sleep,' and then vanish. That is all, it is hardly worth speaking of, only some people are terribly frightened if they are visited unwarned by strange apparitions; so I tell you this that you may be prepared."

"This was a Carmelite convent, then?" I said.

"Yes; it was suppressed after the unification of Italy, and given to the House of Muxaro; but the family died out, and I bought it. There is a story about the ghostly nun, who was only a novice, and even that unwillingly, which gives an interest to an otherwise very common-

212

place and uninteresting ghost."

"I beg that you will tell it us," cried Rendel.

"There is a storm coming," I added. "See, the lightning is flashing already up among the mountains at the head of the valley; if the story is tragic, as it must be, now is just the time for it. You will tell it, will you not?"

The *Cavaliere* smiled that slow, cryptic smile of his that was so unfathomable.

"As you say, there is a shower coming, and as we have fierce tempests here, we might not sleep; so perhaps we may as well sit up a little longer, and I will tell you the story."

The air was utterly still, hot and oppressive; the rich, sick odour of the oranges just bursting into bloom came up from the valley in a gently rising tide. The sky, thick with stars, seemed mirrored in the rich foliage below, so numerous were the glow-worms under the still trees, and the fireflies that gleamed in the hot air. Lightning flashed fitfully from the darkening west; but as yet no thunder broke the heavy silence.

The *Cavaliere* lighted another cigar, and pulled a cushion under his head so that he could look down to the distant lights of the city. "This is the story," he said.

"Once upon a time, late in the last century, the Duca di Castiglione was attached to the court of Charles III., King of the Two Sicilies, down at Palermo. They tell me he was very ambitious, and, not content with marrying his son to one of the ladies of the House of Tuscany, had betrothed his only daughter, Rosalia, to Prince Antonio, a cousin of the king. His whole life was wrapped up in the fame of his family, and he quite forgot all domestic affection in his madness for dynastic glory. His son was a worthy scion, cold and proud; but Rosalia was, according to legend, utterly the reverse,—a passionate, beautiful girl, wilful and headstrong, and careless of her family and the world.

"The time had nearly come for her to marry Prince Antonio, a typical *roué* of the Spanish court, when, through the treachery of a servant, the duke discovered that his daughter was in love with a young military officer whose name I don't remember, and that an elopement had been planned to take place the next night. The fury and dismay of the old autocrat passed belief; he saw in a flash the downfall of all his hopes of family aggrandizement through union with the royal house, and, knowing well the spirit of his daughter, despaired of ever bringing her to subjection.

213

"Nevertheless, he attacked her unmercifully, and, by bullying and threats, by imprisonment, and even bodily chastisement, he tried to break her spirit and bend her to his indomitable will. Through his power at court he had the lover sent away to the mainland, and for more than a year he held his daughter closely imprisoned in his palace on the Toledo,—that one, you may remember, on the right, just beyond the *Via del Collegio dei Gesuiti*, with the beautiful iron-work grilles at all the windows, and the painted frieze.

"But nothing could move her, nothing bend her stubborn will; and at last, furious at the girl he could not govern, Castiglione sent her to this convent, then one of the few houses of barefoot Carmelite nuns in Italy. He stipulated that she should take the name of Maddelena, that he should never hear of her again, and that she should be held an absolute prisoner in this conventual castle.

"Rosalia—or Sister Maddelena, as she was now—believed her lover dead, for her father had given her good proofs of this, and she believed him; nevertheless she refused to marry another, and seized upon the convent life as a blessed relief from the tyranny of her maniacal father.

"She lived here for four or five years; her name was forgotten at court and in her father's palace. Rosalia di Castiglione was dead, and only Sister Maddelena lived, a Carmelite nun, in her place.

"In 1798 Ferdinand IV. found himself driven from his throne on the mainland, his kingdom divided, and he himself forced to flee to Sicily. With him came the lover of the dead Rosalia, now high in military honour. He on his part had thought Rosalia dead, and it was only by accident that he found that she still lived, a Carmelite nun.

"Then began the second act of the romance that until then had been only sadly commonplace, but now became dark and tragic. Michele—Michele Biscari,—that was his name; I remember now— haunted the region of the convent, striving to communicate with Sister Maddelena; and at last, from the cliffs over us, up there among the citrons—you will see by the next flash of lightning—he saw her in the great cloister, recognized her in her white habit, found her the same dark and splendid beauty of six years before, only made more beautiful by her white habit and her rigid life.

"By and by he found a day when she was alone, and tossed a ring to her as she stood in the midst of the cloister. She looked up, saw him, and from that moment lived only to love him in life as she had loved his memory in the death she had thought had overtaken him.

"With the utmost craft they arranged their plans together. They could not speak, for a word would have aroused the other inmates of the convent. They could make signs only when Sister Maddelena was alone. Michele could throw notes to her from the cliff,—a feat demanding a strong arm, as you will see, if you measure the distance with your eye,—and she could drop replies from the window over the cliff, which he picked up at the bottom.

"Finally he succeeded in casting into the cloister a coil of light rope. The girl fastened it to the bars of one of the windows, and—so great is the madness of love—Biscari actually climbed the rope from the valley to the window of the cell, a distance of almost two hundred feet, with but three little craggy resting-places in all that height. For nearly a month these nocturnal visits were undiscovered, and Michele had almost completed his arrangements for carrying the girl from Sta. Catarina and away to Spain, when unfortunately one of the sisters, suspecting some mystery, from the changed face of Sister Maddelena, began investigating, and at length discovered the rope neatly coiled up by the nun's window, and hidden under some clinging vines.

"She instantly told the Mother Superior; and together they watched from a window in the crypt of the chapel,—the only place, as you will see tomorrow, from which one could see the window of Sister Maddelena's cell. They saw the figure of Michele daringly ascending the slim rope; watched hour after hour, the Sister remaining while the Superior went to say the hours in the chapel, at each of which Sister Maddelena was present; and at last, at prime, just as the sun was rising, they saw the figure slip down the rope, watched the rope drawn up and concealed, and knew that Sister Maddelena was in their hands for vengeance and punishment,—a criminal.

"The next day, by the order of the Mother Superior, Sister Maddelena was imprisoned in one of the cells under the chapel, charged with her guilt, and commanded to make full and complete confession. But not a word would she say, although they offered her forgiveness if she would tell the name of her lover. At last the Superior told her that after this fashion would they act the coming night: she herself would be placed in the crypt, tied in front of the window, her mouth gagged; that the rope would be lowered, and the lover allowed to approach even to the sill of her window, and at that moment the rope would be cut, and before her eyes her lover would be dashed to death on the ragged cliffs.

"The plan was feasible, and Sister Maddelena knew that the Mother was perfectly capable of carrying it out. Her stubborn spirit was broken, and in the only way possible; she begged for mercy, for the sparing of her lover. The Mother Superior was deaf at first; at last she said, 'It is your life or his. I will spare him on condition that you sacrifice your own life.' Sister Maddelena accepted the terms joyfully, wrote a last farewell to Michele, fastened the note to the rope, and with her own hands cut the rope and saw it fall coiling down to the valley bed far below.

"Then she silently prepared for death; and at midnight, while her lover was wandering, mad with the horror of impotent fear, around the white walls of the convent, Sister Maddelena, for love of Michele, gave up her life. How, was never known. That she was indeed dead was only a suspicion, for when Biscari finally compelled the civil authorities to enter the convent, claiming that murder had been done there, they found no sign. Sister Maddelena had been sent to the parent house of the barefoot Carmelites at Avila in Spain, so the Superior stated, because of her incorrigible contumacy.

"The old Duke of Castiglione refused to stir hand or foot in the matter, and Michele, after fruitless attempts to prove that the Superior of Sta. Catarina had caused the death, was forced to leave Sicily. He sought in Spain for very long; but no sign of the girl was to be found, and at last he died, exhausted with suffering and sorrow.

"Even the name of Sister Maddelena was forgotten, and it was not until the convents were suppressed, and this house came into the hands of the Muxaros, that her story was remembered. It was then that the ghost began to appear; and, an explanation being necessary, the story, or legend, was obtained from one of the nuns who still lived after the suppression. I think the fact—for it is a fact—of the ghost rather goes to prove that Michele was right, and that poor Rosalia gave her life a sacrifice for love,—whether in accordance with the terms of the legend or not, I cannot say. One or the other of you will probably see her tonight. You might ask her for the facts. Well, that is all the story of Sister Maddelena, known in the world as Rosalia di Castiglione. Do you like it?"

"It is admirable," said Rendel, enthusiastically. "But I fancy I should rather look on it simply as a story, and not as a warning of what is going to happen. I don't much fancy real ghosts myself."

"But the poor Sister is quite harmless;" and Valguanera rose, stretching himself. "My servants say she wants a mass said over her, or something of that kind; but I haven't much love for such priestly hocus-pocus,—I beg your pardon" (turning to me), "I had forgotten that you were a Catholic: forgive my rudeness."

"My dear *Cavaliere*, I beg you not to apologize. I am sorry you cannot see things as I do; but don't for a moment think I am hypersensitive."

"I have an excuse,—perhaps you will say only an explanation; but I live where I see all the absurdities and corruptions of the church."

"Perhaps you let the accidents blind you to the essentials; but do not let us quarrel tonight,—see, the storm is close on us. Shall we go in?"

The stars were blotted out through nearly all the sky; low, thunderous clouds, massed at the head of the valley, were sweeping over so close that they seemed to brush the black pines on the mountain above us. To the south and east the storm-clouds had shut down almost to the sea, leaving a space of black sky where the moon in its last quarter was rising just to the left of Monte Pellegrino,—a black silhouette against the pallid moonlight. The rosy lightning flashed almost incessantly, and through the fitful darkness came the sound of bells across the valley, the rushing torrent below, and the dull roar of the approaching rain, with a deep organ point of solemn thunder through it all.

We fled indoors from the coming tempest, and taking our candles, said "goodnight," and sought each his respective room.

My own was in the southern part of the old convent, giving on the terrace we had just quitted, and about over the main doorway. The rushing storm, as it swept down the valley with the swelling torrent beneath, was very fascinating, and after wrapping myself in a dressing-gown I stood for some time by the deeply embrasured window, watching the blazing lightning and the beating rain whirled by fitful gusts of wind around the spurs of the mountains. Gradually the violence of the shower seemed to decrease, and I threw myself down on my bed in the hot air, wondering if I really was to experience the ghostly visit the *Cavaliere* so confidently predicted.

I had thought out the whole matter to my own satisfaction, and fancied I knew exactly what I should do, in case Sister Maddelena came to visit me. The story touched me: the thought of the poor faithful girl who sacrificed herself for her lover,—himself, very likely, quite unworthy,—and who now could never sleep for reason of her unquiet soul, sent out into the storm of eternity without spiritual aid or counsel. I could not sleep; for the still vivid lightning, the crowding thoughts of the dead nun, and the shivering anticipation of my possible visitation, made slumber quite out of the question.

No suspicion of sleepiness had visited me, when, perhaps an hour after midnight, came a sudden vivid flash of lightning, and, as my dazzled eyes began to regain the power of sight, I saw her as plainly as in life,—a tall figure, shrouded in the white habit of the Carmelites, her head bent, her hands clasped before her. In another flash of lightning she slowly raised her head and looked at me long and earnestly. She was very beautiful, like the Virgin of Beltraffio in the National Gallery,—more beautiful than I had supposed possible, her deep, passionate eyes very tender and pitiful in their pleading, beseeching glance. I hardly think I was frightened, or even startled, but lay looking steadily at her as she stood in the beating lightning.

Then she breathed, rather than articulated, with a voice that almost brought tears, so infinitely sad and sorrowful was it, "I cannot sleep!" and the liquid eyes grew more pitiful and questioning as bright tears fell from them down the pale dark face.

The figure began to move slowly towards the door, its eyes fixed on mine with a look that was weary and almost agonized. I leaped from the bed and stood waiting. A look of utter gratitude swept over the face, and, turning, the figure passed through the doorway.

Out into the shadow of the corridor it moved, like a drift of pallid storm-cloud, and I followed, all natural and instinctive fear or nervousness quite blotted out by the part I felt I was to play in giving rest to a tortured soul. The corridors were velvet black; but the pale figure floated before me always, an unerring guide, now but a thin mist on the utter night, now white and clear in the bluish lightning through some window or doorway.

Down the stairway into the lower hall, across the refectory, where the great *frescoed* crucifixion flared into sudden clearness under the fitful lightning, out into the silent cloister.

It was very dark. I stumbled along the heaving bricks, now guiding myself by a hand on the whitewashed wall, now by a touch on a column wet with the storm. From all the eaves the rain was dripping on to the pebbles at the foot of the arcade: a pigeon, startled from the capital where it was sleeping, beat its way into the cloister close. Still the white thing drifted before me to the farther side of the court, then along the cloister at right angles, and paused before one of the many doorways that led to the cells.

A sudden blaze of fierce lightning, the last now of the fleeting trail of storm, leaped around us, and in the vivid light I saw the white face turned again with the look of overwhelming desire, of beseeching *pathos*, that had choked my throat with an involuntary sob when first I saw Sister Maddelena. In the brief interval that ensued after the flash, and before the roaring thunder burst like the crash of battle over the trembling convent, I heard again the sorrowful words, "I cannot sleep," come from the impenetrable darkness. And when the lightning came again, the white figure was gone.

I wandered around the courtyard, searching in vain for Sister Maddelena, even until the moonlight broke through the torn and sweeping fringes of the storm. I tried the door where the white figure vanished: it was locked; but I had found what I sought, and, carefully noting its location, went back to my room, but not to sleep.

In the morning the *Cavaliere* asked Rendel and me which of us had seen the ghost, and I told him my story; then I asked him to grant me permission to sift the thing to the bottom; and he courteously gave the whole matter into my charge, promising that he would consent to anything.

I could hardly wait to finish breakfast; but no sooner was this done than, forgetting my morning pipe, I started with Rendel and the *Cavaliere* to investigate.

"I am sure there is nothing in that cell," said Valguanera, when we came in front of the door I had marked. "It is curious that you should have chosen the door of the very cell that tradition assigns to Sister Maddelena; but I have often examined that room myself, and I am sure that there is no chance for anything to be concealed. In fact, I had the floor taken up once, soon after I came here, knowing the room was that of the mysterious Sister, and thinking that there, if anywhere, the monastic crime would have taken place; still, we will go in, if you like."

He unlocked the door, and we entered, one of us, at all events, with a beating heart. The cell was very small, hardly eight feet square. There certainly seemed no opportunity for concealing a body in the tiny place; and although I sounded the floor and walls, all gave a solid, heavy answer,—the unmistakable sound of masonry.

For the innocence of the floor the *Cavaliere* answered. He had, he said, had it all removed, even to the curving surfaces of the vault below; yet somewhere in this room the body of the murdered girl was concealed,—of this I was certain. But where? There seemed no answer; and I was compelled to give up the search for the moment, somewhat to the amusement of Valguanera, who had watched curiously to see if I could solve the mystery.

But I could not forget the subject, and towards noon started on another tour of investigation. I procured the keys from the *Cavaliere*, and examined the cells adjoining; they were apparently the same, each with its window opposite the door, and nothing—Stay, were they the same? I hastened into the suspected cell; it was as I thought: this cell, being on the corner, could have had two windows, yet only one was visible, and that to the left, at right angles with the doorway. Was it imagination? As I sounded the wall opposite the door, where the other window should be, I fancied that the sound was a trifle less solid and dull. I was becoming excited. I dashed back to the cell on the right, and, forcing open the little window, thrust my head out.

It was found at last! In the smooth surface of the yellow wall was a rough space, following approximately the shape of the other cell windows, not plastered like the rest of the wall, but showing the shapes of bricks through its thick coatings of whitewash. I turned with a gasp of excitement and satisfaction: yes, the embrasure of the wall was deep enough; what a wall it was!—four feet at least, and the opening of the window reached to the floor, though the window itself was hardly three feet square. I felt absolutely certain that the secret was solved, and called the *Cavaliere* and Rendel, too excited to give them an explanation of my theories.

They must have thought me mad when I suddenly began scraping away at the solid wall in front of the door; but in a few minutes they understood what I was about, for under the coatings of paint and plaster appeared the original bricks; and as my architectural knowledge had led me rightly, the space I had cleared was directly over a vertical joint between firm, workmanlike masonry on one hand, and rough amateurish work on the other, bricks laid anyway, and without order or science.

Rendel seized a pick, and was about to assail the rude wall, when I stopped him.

"Let us be careful," I said; "who knows what we may find?" So we set to work digging out the mortar around a brick at about the level of our eyes.

How hard the mortar had become! But a brick yielded at last, and with trembling fingers I detached it. Darkness within, yet beyond question there was a cavity there, not a solid wall; and with infinite care we removed another brick. Still the hole was too small to admit enough light from the dimly illuminated cell. With a chisel we pried at the sides of a large block of masonry, perhaps eight bricks in size. It moved, and we softly slid it from its bed.

Valguanera, who was standing watching us as we lowered the bricks to the floor, gave a sudden cry, a cry like that of a frightened woman,—terrible, coming from him. Yet there was cause.

Framed by the ragged opening of the bricks, hardly seen in the dim light, was a face, an ivory image, more beautiful than any antique bust, but drawn and distorted by unspeakable agony: the lovely mouth half open, as though gasping for breath; the eyes cast upward; and below, slim chiselled hands crossed on the breast, but clutching the folds of the white Carmelite habit, torture and agony visible in every tense muscle, fighting against the determination of the rigid pose.

We stood there breathless, staring at the pitiful sight, fascinated, bewitched. So this was the secret. With fiendish ingenuity, the rigid ecclesiastics had blocked up the window, then forced the beautiful creature to stand in the alcove, while with remorseless hands and iron hearts they had shut her into a living tomb. I had read of such things in romance; but to find the verity here, before my eyes—

Steps came down the cloister, and with a simultaneous thought we sprang to the door and closed it behind us. The room was sacred; that awful sight was not for curious eyes. The gardener was coming to ask some trivial question of Valguanera. The *Cavaliere* cut him short. "Pietro, go down to Parco and ask Padre Stefano to come here at once." (I thanked him with a glance.) "Stay!" He turned to me: "*Signore*, it is already two o'clock and too late for mass, is it not?"

I nodded.

Valguanera thought a moment, then he said, "Bring two horses; the *Signor Americano* will go with you,—do you understand?" Then, turning to me, "You will go, will you not? I think you can explain matters to Padre Stefano better than I."

"Of course I will go, more than gladly." So it happened that after a hasty luncheon I wound down the mountain to Parco, found Padre Stefano, explained my errand to him, found him intensely eager and sympathetic, and by five o'clock had him back at the convent with all that was necessary for the resting of the soul of the dead girl.

In the warm twilight, with the last light of the sunset pouring into the little cell through the window where almost a century ago Rosalia had for the last time said farewell to her lover, we gathered together to speed her tortured soul on its journey, so long delayed. Nothing was omitted; all the needful offices of the church were said by Padre Stefano, while the light in the window died away, and the flickering flames of the candles carried by two of the acolytes from San Francesco threw fitful flashes of pallid light into the dark recess where the white face had prayed to Heaven for a hundred years.

Finally, the *Padre* took the *asperge* from the hands of one of the *acolytes*, and with a sign of the cross in benediction while he chanted the *Asperges*, gently sprinkled the holy water on the upturned face. Instantly the whole vision crumbled to dust, the face was gone, and where once the candlelight had flickered on the perfect semblance of the girl dead so very long, it now fell only on the rough bricks which closed the window, bricks laid with frozen hearts by pitiless hands.

But our task was not done yet. It had been arranged that Padre Stefano should remain at the convent all night, and that as soon as midnight made it possible he should say the first mass for the repose of the girl's soul. We sat on the terrace talking over the strange events of the last crowded hours, and I noted with satisfaction that the *Cavaliere* no longer spoke of the church with that hardness, which had hurt me so often. It is true that the *Padre* was with us nearly all the time; but not only was Valguanera courteous, he was almost sympathetic; and I wondered if it might not prove that more than one soul benefited by the untoward events of the day.

With the aid of the astonished and delighted servants, and no little help as well from Signora Valguanera, I fitted up the long cold Altar in the chapel, and by midnight we had the gloomy sanctuary beautiful with flowers and candles. It was a curiously solemn service, in the first hour of the new day, in the midst of blazing candles and the thick incense, the odour of the opening orange-blooms drifting up in the fresh morning air, and mingling with the incense smoke and the perfume of flowers within.

Many prayers were said that night for the soul of the dead girl, and I think many afterwards; for after the benediction I remained for a little time in my place, and when I rose from my knees and went towards the chapel door, I saw a figure kneeling still, and, with a start, recognized the form of the *Cavaliere*. I smiled with quiet satisfaction and gratitude, and went away softly, content with the chain of events that now seemed finished.

The next day the alcove was again walled up, for the precious dust could not be gathered together for transportation to consecrated ground; so I went down to the little cemetery at Parco for a basket of earth, which we cast in over the ashes of Sister Maddelena.

By and by, when Rendel and I went away, with great regret, Valguanera came down to Palermo with us; and the last act that we performed in Sicily was assisting him to order a tablet of marble, whereon was carved this simple inscription:—

Here Lies The Body Of
Rosalia Di Castiglioni,
Called
Sister Maddelena.
Her Soul
Is With Him Who Gave It.

To this I added in thought:—

"*Let him that is without sin among you cast the first stone.*"

Aylmer Vance: The Invader

Alice & Claude Askew

'What a wonderful moonlight night!' The words broke slowly from Aylmer Vance's lips, then he turned and looked at me strangely.

We were fellow-guests at the same little inn in Surrey, and we had just made our way out of the hot, stuffy parlour into a cool and perfumed garden.

'Does the moonlight ever affect you?' Vance asked. 'Does a night like this fill you with vague longings? Do you yearn to discover die secret of the universe—to know more than is good for man to know—perhaps to peer into the future?'

I nodded.

'Yes,' I answered slowly, then I turned to my companion. 'You have made a pretty deep study of spiritual phenomena, haven't you, Vance? I wish you would tell me something about the various experiences that have befallen you during the years you have been investigating on behalf of the "Ghost Circle".'

Vance shook his head. 'No, no,' he answered hurriedly. 'You wouldn't really be interested, Dexter. You are a level-headed barrister, my friend. You don't believe in spooks.'

'You're wrong there,' I retorted. The subject interests me profoundly, and tonight is just the night for a ghost story. There's a white, witching moon in the heavens—the pine trees look weird in the distance—and hark how the wind is sighing amongst their branches!'

Aylmer Vance smiled. He was a curious-looking man, tall and lean in build, with a pale but distinctly interesting face. His eyes were a bright blue, very sharp and keen, and he had long thin hands. There was a certain hardness about him—a chill austerity—but his voice, in strange contrast to his manner, was rich and flexible, and I had already fallen under the spell of his arresting personality.

We had first met at a dinner party in London about two months ago—a men's dinner—and I had been very interested in Aylmer Vance at the time. He had been pointed out to me as a ghost-seer. I had been told that ghost-hunting was his cult. And now, as luck would have it, we had tumbled across each other again, for we were both staying at the same little inn in Surrey. I had come down that day for some pike fishing, but I could not make out what had induced Aylmer Vance to spend a week at the Magpie Inn. But there he was, anyway.

We had recognised each other, dined by mutual consent at the same little round table, and now as we stood in the garden smoking our cigarettes I hoped that our acquaintance would end by developing into a friendship—a real friendship. But I had been told that Vance rarely made friends—that he lived a very solitary and self-contained life. He was quite well-off, and owned an old Georgian house situated somewhere in Essex, but he was not often in England. He was a great traveller—a born wanderer—and, needless to say, a bachelor.

'If you're really interested I don't mind telling you about three or four strange experiences that have befallen me during the years I have devoted to the investigation of spiritual phenomena.'

Aylmer Vance threw away his cigarette as he spoke. A queer look came over his face.

'I have certainly had some amazing adventures,' he continued. 'I have come across all sorts and conditions of men. I have been the means of detecting several instances of fraud and imposition on the part of so-called "mediums"—also of proving that natural causes are often responsible for the "haunting" that is supposed to go on in various houses. But I must admit that I have been absolutely baffled once or twice—unable to account for what I have seen with my own eyes, heard with my own ears.'

Vance paused and put a long thin hand upon my arm.

'Let us go and sit in the summer-house at the end of the garden, and I will tell you what happened about six years ago to two dear friends of mine—Annie Sinclair and her husband—for never have I been more impressed than by the Sinclair tragedy. In fact, it was the Sinclair affair that first induced me to take an interest in psychical research. The whole episode was so wrapped in mystery that even now I cannot explain it to myself. I am still in the dark as to what actually occurred.'

A curious, very intent note stole in Aylmer Vance's voice as he said the last words. A faraway look came into his eyes.

'Yes, I will tell you what happened to the Sinclairs,' he repeated. 'My story will certainly prove to you, if it proves nothing else, how dangerous it is to meddle with forces of which we know little.'

Still keeping his hand on my shoulder, he led me in the direction of the summer-house, which stood just at the bottom of the garden, and I remember how pungent the scent of the pines was—how overpoweringly pungent—and the wind made a queer rustling and sobbing amongst the branches of the pine trees—a low, monotonous moaning.

We settled ourselves down in the summer-house and I lit a cigarette. The moonlight was particularly brilliant that evening, I remember. It illuminated the whole garden. But the pine woods looked strangely blurred and black in the distance, and I felt rather eerie. Still I wished my companion would begin his story. I was sure it would be worth listening to.

'George Sinclair was my greatest friend when we were up at Oxford together,' Vance began, 'and after we left Magdalen we kept up our friendship, seeing each other constantly. Then I went abroad—for two or three years. When I came back to England George had a great piece of news for me. He had just got engaged to be married to a Scotch girl. Her name was Annie Riddell.

'I went up to Scotland for the wedding. In fact, I was George's best man, and I'm bound to confess that I envied him his bride, for Annie looked a young goddess on her wedding day. She was tall and fair—rather a large woman, with a beautiful placid face and very sweet blue eyes; there was immense repose about her. George was just the opposite—very restless and excitable, dark, thin, and rather undersized; but they were crazily in love with each other, these two—as much in love as any man and woman could be, I think, and when I went to stay with them about six months later at George's place down in Wiltshire it was really delightful—in these days of matrimonial discontent—to see how fond a man and his wife could be of each other; not but what Annie gave away a little too much to George, I thought.

'She hardly appeared to have a will of her own—whatever he said was her law; but then George, for his part, was absolutely devoted to Annie. He thought her the most beautiful and perfect creature on God's earth—he worshipped her openly all day long, and Annie accepted her husband's homage with a bland serenity. If she hadn't been so beautiful I expect I should have thought her a dull woman, for she certainly lacked ideas, but she was so good to look at that one really hardly wanted to maintain a long conversation with her; you could stare at Annie for hours just as you could stare at a beautiful picture, and with the same pleasure.'

Vance paused for a minute. He seemed to be looking right into the pine wood, then he suddenly turned to me with one of his quick movements.

'Yes, they were intensely happy, those two, for the first three or four years of their married life—extraordinarily happy—but they began to be a bit disappointed by-and-by when no babies came—not that it made any difference to their love for each other. Their mutual sorrow knit them more closely together, if anything; but George, having no children to interest himself in, took it into his head to go in for occult research.

'The subject had always fascinated him, even from his boyhood, and then one day, as ill-luck would have it, George's attention was directed to the fact that he had a barrow on his property, by an archaeological friend of his who happened to be staying with the Sinclairs at Grey Towers. You know what I mean by a barrow, don't you?—one of those old British burial places of which there are still a few to be found in England.

'Well, George, egged on by his friend, started to dig up the barrow, and his efforts were rewarded, for he found two heavy gold armlets in it, and you cannot imagine how excited George got over this find. He had a theory that these armlets had belonged to some Druid priestess, and he took them to a medium, who spun him no end of a yarn about the woman who had once worn them; but she wasn't a priestess at all, the medium declared; she was a British princess, a very beautiful but jealous, black-hearted woman who had had a strange love affair and had been murdered by her lover.

'George drank in this yarn eagerly, and then what must the silly fool of a medium do but tell him that he possessed occult powers himself, and that Annie—who, needless to say, had always accompanied George on his visits to the medium—beautiful, quiet, meditative Annie, would make a very fine trance subject.

'Of course George, on hearing this, determined to exert his gifts, and Annie, who had always been like wax in his hands since the day of their marriage, went off obligingly enough into trances whenever he wanted her to. I don't think she was at all interested herself in occult subjects—at least not at the start, though she pretended to take an interest in them for George's sake, but she soon got frightened. She realised, being a sensible woman, that a certain amount of danger must always attend occult studies.

'Besides, she didn't like to feel—at least so she told me one day—that the spirits of dead men and dead women were talking through her to George, for Annie honestly believed that when she went off into one of her queer trances, she really became the vehicle of communication between the quick and the dead. She never doubted her own powers in that respect, but she was afraid of them.

'The whole thing began to prey on her after a time—to get upon her nerves, but George couldn't see this—or wouldn't see it. Evening after evening he insisted on putting Annie into a trance—he was never tired of experimenting with her. He didn't seem to realise that these experiments might have a disastrous effect upon his wife's health—that it might shatter Annie's entire system. He believed that in time the secrets of the other world would be revealed through her instrumentality—that a link would at last be established between the spirit world and our world.'

Vance paused. He threw away his cigarette—he drew a deep breath.

'Mark you, I don't blame George very much. He was an explorer into realms unknown, and, just like any other explorer, he was ready to sacrifice even his nearest and dearest, and I believe Annie's trances were quite genuine. I don't think for one instant she could have invented the things she said; besides, she wasn't that sort of woman—neither was she an hysterical subject.'

'So you think these trances were genuine?' I remarked.

'I do,' Vance replied. He bent forward and frowned and frowned; I thought how pale his face looked in the moonlight—how ghastly white. I noticed how tightly his hands were clenched; it was evident that the relating of this tale caused him deep emotion. 'I must own that I became profoundly interested myself in Annie's strange trances after a time, especially when the spirit of the British princess to whom the gold armlets found in the barrow had originally belonged began to take possession of Annie when she went off into her trances and talk through her mouth—and a mighty lot the princess had to say, too—queer, strange talk.

'She told us that she regretted most passionately that she was dead—that she longed to be alive again, walking the earth. She admitted that she was one of those restless, tormented spirits who, in psychical parlance, are known as "earth-bound spirits"—that all her desires were material, and she told George with brazen effrontery later on that she had fallen in love with him and that she would like to remain in possession of his wife's body—in fact, to take Annie's place in his life, and her language was plain and unvarnished, I can assure you—distinctly primitive. It gave me quite a shock to hear such words proceeding from Annie's lips, unconscious though she was, poor girl, of what the spirit who possessed her body for the time being was saying.'

Vance stirred in his seat—his lips twitched. He looked paler than I had thought it possible for a man to be.

'After the second or third *séance*, absorbing and interesting though they were, I got a bit uneasy in my mind. The whole thing struck me as horrible—repulsive, this dead woman invoking George in the most passionate language and having the audacity to suggest that she should try and keep Annie's gentle spirit out of its own tenement -continue to inhabit Annie's body. I said as much to George. I told him that I thought the *séances* had better stop, but he wouldn't listen to me; he was far too interested—far too keen on continuing his experiments.

'A fortnight later Annie spoke to him herself, however, and declined to go into any more trances. She declared that it had been a difficult matter to eject the princess's spirit after the last *séance*—that quite a fight had taken place between her own soul and the dead woman's soul, and that she was unwilling to run the risk of such a conflict again.

'"I assure you, George, I feel quite frightened," Annie exclaimed, "I am convinced that the princess wants to get possession of me. She'd like to live again in my body, and she's so strong—she's so frightfully strong—that it's difficult to drive her away after the trance is over—when I want to wake up—when you tell me to wake up."

'George laughed at this. He thought Annie was talking very foolishly, but he was seriously annoyed with her all the same for wanting to stop the *séances*—he insisted that they should continue—he was absolutely determined to proceed with his investigations.

'Well, Annie held out for a long time, but she gave way in the end. She was the sweetest woman on earth, I think, and though she made no secret of the fact that she simply loathed being put into a trance, George only laughed at her and finally got her to sit again, but Annie kept saying she would only sit once more. I don't know whether George believed that she would stick to her word, but anyway he asked me to go down to Grey Towers to be present at this last *séance*, but I couldn't go, so those two were just left to themselves and George's devil tricks.'

Vance rose abruptly to his feet. He looked very lean and haggard; the Sinclair tragedy seemed to have become his tragedy as well.

'Even now, after all these years, Dexter, I turn sick when I think of what happened down at Grey Towers. You see, I heard all about it afterwards—from George.'

Vance walked to the summer-house door. His thin face worked painfully. He kept clenching and unclenching his hands.

'They sat on a Saturday night—that is what George told me, for I had the whole story later on from his lips. He put Annie into a trance at once—Annie very nervous and unwilling—and after a bit the British woman came and took possession of her as usual. To make the connecting link as strong as he could, George had insisted that Annie should wear the gold bracelets dug up from the barrow, and so with these heavy links upon her arms, these relics from a barbarous past, Annie sat in her husband's study, a passive agent to what happened; but she repeated before the *séance* began what she had already said before.

'She told George that this would be the last time she would ever allow him to put her into a trance—that the coming back into her body was so difficult. She said just before she went off that she really would not sit again—that he mustn't ask her to, and that speech may have precipitated matters, of course, for I bet you the British woman knew that Annie meant what she said, and so she was aware that she would never again have the chance of speaking through Annie's lips—clothing her naked soul in Annie's body, and she determined to pit her strength against Annie's—to fight for what she wanted.'

'But what happened?' I interrupted eagerly. 'Did Mrs Sinclair find some difficulty in getting out of her trance? Did her heart fail suddenly—did she die that night?'

'I wish she had—I wish to God she had,' Vance answered bitterly. 'But worse—far worse—befell Annie. The British she-devil having taken complete possession of Annie's body absolutely refused to budge, for when George endeavoured to wake Annie up from her trance another woman—a passionate, primitive woman—stared at him out of his wife's eyes, and he knew that what Annie had feared had come to pass. A new tenant had taken up its habitation in her body—a tenant who refused to quit. There, Dexter, can you imagine a more grim and terrible situation; can you?'

Vance turned to me and put a hand upon my arm. I could feel how his fingers shook.

'I don't suppose you believe my story—it sounds pretty incredible—I don't think I believe it myself; but George swore to me that he knew Annie's gentle loving spirit couldn't get back into her body—that the British woman wouldn't turn out. Why, he declared that Annie's face changed before his eyes—that a devilish expression came into it, and to add to the sickening horror of the whole scene, the woman who called herself his wife began to make violent love to him—fierce, unrestrained love, and he had to suffer her hot, burning kisses; he couldn't tear himself away from her arms, and presently the woman demanded food and drink and ate ravenously, and then she began to croon and sing to herself, and George swore that he seemed to hear people singing outside the house, answering her—the low murmur of innumerable voices. It was just like a nightmare—an awful nightmare.

'It was hours that night before the woman fell asleep, and she gripped George's hand in her sleep—she held on to him as if she would never let him go, and when she woke up at dawn she began to sing to herself, some queer outlandish chant, and she sang as she brushed her hair, the wonderful pale gold hair that had always been one of Annie's greatest charms, and George, lying in bed, shivered, and lay there shivering and shaking, watching a beautiful woman combing her beautiful hair, but afraid of her—afraid.'

Vance hesitated, then he gave a queer hoarse laugh.

'I know what you're thinking. You are telling yourself that in all probability Annie Sinclair had got into a queer mental condition, thanks to all the *séances* that her husband had been insisting on, and that would account for her changed looks and manner—the singular way she was behaving—and no doubt George was feeling a bit queer and shaky himself—as nervous as a cat—frightened of his crazy wife, the wife who was apparently going off her head. That's the rational view to take of the situation isn't it—the most feasible view?'

'I don't altogether agree with you,' I retorted. 'We know that there have been several authenticated cases of demoniacal possessions.' I hesitated, then added, not looking at Vance as I addressed him, 'Did you see Mrs Sinclair after the—the *séance*?'

'Yes, I went straight down to Grey Towers on the receipt of an urgent telegram from George, and I felt when I met Annie as though I was meeting a stranger—and a strange woman who was always on her guard, but I dared not admit as much to George. I pretended that there was nothing amiss. Good Lord, man, what else could I do? But I was conscious all the time that some evil spirit had taken up its habitation in Annie's beautiful body—a wicked, baneful spirit—and the leer in Annie's eyes made me feel sick—I could hardly bear to look at her, and such a cruel smile played about her lips. She watched George just as a cat watches a mouse, and her hands were never still—those dreadful restless hands of hers. She walked with a stride, not as Annie used to walk, and her clothes seemed to hang on her awkwardly—Annie's clothes.'

Vance sat down again on the seat by my side. He was breathing hard; I could see that little beads of perspiration had broken out on his forehead, and he shivered, for all that it was such a hot evening.

'Wasn't it horrible, Dexter?' he whispered hoarsely. 'Wasn't it horrible? You see, George and I were absolutely certain that Annie's body had been possessed by a she-devil, and we knew that Annie's soul—her sweet, gentle, loving soul—was trying its hardest to get back to its earthly habitation, only the intruder wouldn't go, and we both knew that she was trying to come back to us and that she just couldn't; and we were aware—tragically aware—that as so often happens in this world, evil was conquering goodness. But the awful reflection, from George's point of view, was that he had deliberately played into evil's hands—that he himself had brought this terrible thing to pass—that it was his work—his.'

'Good Lord—how ghastly for the poor chap!' I muttered the words low, half under my breath. Listening to Vance it was impossible to disbelieve the story he was telling me—he spoke with such extraordinary conviction; then I leaned forward eagerly. 'Go on, Vance—what was the end of it all?'

'The end.' Vance drew a deep breath. 'Well, it wasn't a pretty end, Dexter.' He rose to his feet again; he looked absolutely livid in the moonlight. 'I stayed at Grey Towers for about a week—I simply couldn't have borne to remain there another day, for that creature—that thing who inhabited Annie's body—was beginning to show herself in her true colours. It was a barbaric woman whom George had for a wife now—a woman who loved cruelty for cruelty's sake. Why, she half killed George's dog one day because the poor brute wouldn't come to her when she called it—and can you wonder? She beat the dog with a stick till George got hold of her by the wrists and dragged her off to her own room, and I don't know what passed between them there—I don't even like to think of it, but I honestly believe that George beat her—beat her as she had beaten the dog, for when she came down she looked cowed. But she killed a bird the next day—Annie's pet canary—walked up to the cage, took the bird out and wrung its neck deliberately, and all because its singing annoyed her. Can you wonder that I came away from Grey Towers that afternoon?—And yet perhaps I ought to have stayed for George's sake—for Annie's.'

Vance folded his arms. He drew another deep, half-sobbing breath.

'I heard from George a fortnight later. He told me that things were going from bad to worse—that the woman—for that was how he referred to her—had ridden Annie's favourite mare pretty well to death—that the servants had all given notice at Grey Towers, explaining that they couldn't understand the strange change that had come over their mistress—her ugly ways.

'Then George went on to say in his letter that he intended to put the woman into a trance that night and try and eject the evil spirit out of Annie's body, but I knew, even as I read George's letter—something seemed to tell me—that the woman would never consent to be put into a trance. She would be too clever for that—too cunning. And I was right, for two days later I got another letter from George—a letter in which he explained that the woman refused to sit.

'She was becoming wilder and more barbaric than ever, he added. A curious atmosphere seemed to hang over Grey Towers—an atmosphere of evil—and he could hear strange sounds at night. The whole house seemed to be full of mutterings and rumblings. There had been a terrible thunderstorm the day before, and the storm seemed to have broken directly over Grey Towers, and the woman had stood by the window laughing at the storm. He had been obliged to send his two dogs away, they kept up such an incessant howling; and he was left with hardly a servant in the house. The neighbours seemed to realise that something strange was happening and stopped calling. He felt forsaken by God and man.'

Vance paused.

'I ought to have gone straight back to Grey Towers on receipt of that letter, Dexter—hurried to my poor friend at once—but I didn't—I just didn't. I wrote to George, however, a long letter, and I suggested that it mightn't be a bad thing if he called in a certain famous psychic investigator to his aid, who might be able to exorcise the evil spirit that had taken up its habitation in Annie's body. But George wouldn't do this. Perhaps he was shy of making his story public. Perhaps he hoped to conquer by himself.

'What he did was to remove himself and the woman from Grey

Towers. He rented a little cottage at Dartmoor and he and the woman went down there by themselves, and then I suppose the fight began—the long fight between George and the woman—for you may be certain that day after day—night after night—he tried his level best to throw her into a trance. But the woman refused to let herself go—to be conquered—and you can imagine, can you not, Annie's spirit hovering vaguely in the background—a silent witness of what was going on—an anguished witness.

'They could keep no servants at the cottage. A village woman came in in the morning and did the cleaning and what simple cooking was required. And so the days passed—the long sultry midsummer days—and George ceased to write to me. He left me in the dark as to what was going on.'

Vance sank down on his seat again. He covered his face with his hands—those long, thin nervous hands of his.

'I couldn't stand George's silence, not knowing what was happening, and at last I determined to go down to Dartmoor. I wrote to George announcing I was coming, and asked if he could either put me up at the cottage or take a room for me in the village. But George wired back to me and told me not to come.

You can do no good, (so the telegram ran) No-one can do us any good. Leave us alone, please.

'So I left them alone. I—I left them alone.'

A long silence fell, a silence I dared not break. I could hear the wind shaking and rustling the branches of the pine trees, keeping up a dull moaning. I could smell the sharp pungent scent of the pines.

The moon suddenly went in behind a cloud, and Aylmer Vance and I were alone in the darkness, and I was glad that the moon had hid her face. I did not want to look at Vance at that moment, and I felt sure that he did not want to look at me.

'You wish to hear the end of the story, Dexter?'

'Yes, I do.'

'Well, two days after I got that telegram from George I was sitting in the smoking-room of my club, when I suddenly heard some newsboys running down the street, and they were shouting out at the top of their shrill cockney voices:"'Orrible murder at Dartmoor—'orrible murder at Dartmoor", and I knew at once what had happened.

'I went out and bought a paper and I read that a gentleman—a Mr George Sinclair, who had recently rented a small cottage on Dartmoor—had murdered his wife the night before—had stuck a knife into her heart as they sat alone in their little cottage parlour, and had blown out his brains a few hours later—shot himself just when the dawn was breaking.

'The romantic part of the murder from the journalistic point of view consisted in the fact that the murderer, after killing his victim, had carried the dead woman's body up to their bedroom, dressed the corpse in a rich white satin gown, combed out her long fair hair, lit any amount of candles, and arranged them round the bed, and had then gone out into the little garden and picked nearly every flower, strewing these flowers over the dead woman, piling them in great scented masses at her feet; and there was no motive for the crime—so the newspapers informed their readers. Oh, they made capital enough, did those newspaper johnnies, out of the Sinclair mystery, I can assure you. They fairly revelled in it for days. And they didn't know—not a clever chap amongst them—that I could have told them the true history of the crime if I had chosen to unlock my lips. But I didn't.

'I went straight down to Dartmoor, however, and I said goodbye to George and I said goodbye to Annie. Lovely and pleasant they had been in their lives till that devil woman came between diem, and in their deaths they were not divided.

'They were buried on the same day. The jury, of course, brought in a verdict of "temporary insanity" in George's case. I wish they could have slept in the same grave, but popular sentiment forbade that. The murderer and his victim couldn't lie together; for the public didn't know that it was not his wife whom George Sinclair had stabbed through the breast on a warm midsummer night—that it was a strange woman, a woman who belonged to the Stone Age.'

Vance paused, then gave another of his odd, mirthless laughs. He let his hands drip from his face.

'Queer yarn, mine, isn't it, Dexter—a bit hard to swallow? I don't ask you to believe it—to credit it. George Sinclair and myself may both have been the victims of a terrible delusion. The constant sitting at *séances* may have effected a deterioration in Annie's character, which we wrongly attributed to demoniacal possession, or of course overwrought nerves would account for die hysterical rages into which she threw herself at times. It is quite on the cards that the Sinclair affair was no case of demoniacal possession. But it was a tragedy for all that, wasn't it—a ghastly tragedy?'

'The most ghastly tragedy,' I repeated. The moon came out at that moment, and as I looked at Aylmer Vance our eyes met. I bent forward and laid an impulsive hand upon his arm. 'You do believe, don't you?' I whispered hoarsely. 'You do believe that the dead woman's spirit—the spirit of the British woman—had got hold of Annie Sinclair's body? You feel as I feel—that George did right when he killed the woman whom the world believed to be Annie Sinclair?'

'I don't know—I can't say,' Vance answered. 'But I am certain of one thing'—that George Sinclair and his wife would be alive today if George had not persuaded Annie to go in for those ghastly sittings—if he had left that barrow undisturbed—for it does not do to meddle with the burial places of the primitive dead. It's an unwise proceeding to have anything to do with an earth-bound soul—a soul whose desires are all of the earth, earthy. And Annie knew this, mark you, and felt it. She was wiser in her generation than George, but just because she was sweet and gentle—'

He paused, and did not finish his sentence. But he drew his hand hurriedly across his eyes, and I realised—the knowledge suddenly came to me—that in his own quiet, reserved way Aylmer Vance had loved his friend's wife, the woman who belonged heart and soul to her husband.

We walked out of the summer-house. The pine woods looked as dark and mysterious as ever. I was conscious that Nature guarded innumerable secrets from man—secrets which she was loath to give up.

My grasp tightened on Vance's arm.

'Vance,' I whispered, 'have you ever seen a ghost with your own eyes—a visitant from the other world?'

'Have I?' Vance smiled—a curious smile. 'I will tell you about a little ghost whom I once had the pleasure of meeting, tomorrow night if you feel inclined to stay on at the inn and have another day's pike fishing. Yes, I will tell you where I met Lady Green-Sleeves. And there's nothing tragic about this story, Dexter. It was merely a singular experience—a romantic episode.'

The Telepather
Henry A. Hering

A middle-aged New Yorker jeweller, without any Art training,
is painting exquisite pictures under the telepathic influence of
a deceased artist.—*Daily Paper.*

'Mr Psyche,' said the caller, 'I have come for your assistance. My
name is Banwell. I am a bookseller in Pitt Alley, Cornhill.' Psyche the
occultist bowed, for literature appealed to him.

'Will you kindly step this way, Mr Banwell?' he asked politely.

'Do you remember the name of Aylmer Lupton?' asked Mr Banwell as he sat down in the consulting room.

'I seem to know it,' said the occultist. 'A poet, I believe?'

'He was a painter—an Associate of the Royal Academy,' Mr Banwell replied. 'He was a man of singular fascination, as those people
often are,' he added regretfully. 'It seems scarcely credible to me now,
but I lent him money, a great deal of money, on very little security. I
lent him five thousand pounds, and now he is dead.'

'You have my sincere sympathy,' said Mr Psyche.

'Thank you. His house and his insurance policies were mortgaged
to me, and he has left me his furniture and what pictures he had on
hand; but all these don't tot up to more than a couple of thousands.
He still owes me three thousand pounds, and I must have the money,
Mr Psyche. I can't afford to lose it.'

'But how can you get money from a dead man ?' asked Psyche.

'That is precisely what I came here to learn,' said the bookseller,
'and I am sure you can help me. You may have come across Lupton's
ghost in the way of business, and I should very much like to be placed
in communication with it, if you have. He could put me up to a soft
thing somewhere, I'm sure—a gold mine, for instance. He must know
of things we are quite ignorant of here, for he is certainly under a great

obligation to me.'

'We have not come across Mr Lupton's ghost as yet,' said Mr Psyche gravely. 'In fact, I may tell you our ghost department is not what is used to be. People are indifferent to apparitions nowadays, in this country, at any rate, and ghosts are so sensitive that they don't go where they are not wanted—consequently we see very little of them. I rarely have an application from one. They do better in the Colonies. In Australian and Canadian upcountry districts they are much in demand, I believe. You see the evenings are long and dull there, and people are glad to have a little excitement. But if by any chance I do hear of Mr Lupton's ghost, I will try to arrange an appointment for you.'

'But,' said the bookseller, getting up and pacing the room, I want something definite, and that at once. You surely must be able to communicate with the departed in the regular way of business. You have a medium ?'

'We have several,' Mr Psyche replied, 'and they are at your service; but mediums are only good when they are fresh and impressionable. Two years at the business seems quite enough to exhaust their powers, with the result that they colour their communications with their own individuality. Frankly, I am disappointed with the recent working of my mediums.'

Mr Psyche was hardly himself that day. Once he had had the monopoly of the occult market, but now competition was keen, and the trend of prices was downward. Moreover, duties were threatened on sundry of his importations, and as they might fairly be scheduled under the head of luxuries, he knew the toll would be heavy. A parcel of novelties, too, had just gone down in the Dead Sea. Therefore he had some cause for depression. Suddenly his face cleared. 'This is not a case for a medium,' he said. 'It is one for my Telepather.'

'Ah,' said Mr Banwell, "Who's he?"

'It isn't a man; it's a machine,' explained Mr Psyche, 'a machine invented by an adept in Thibet for establishing communication with the spirits of the departed. The unreliability of mediums is recognised even in the Home of Occultism, and this machine is intended to do their work and do it more perfectly. I have only recently acquired it, and as yet have not made use of its services, since the communications desired by my clients with their departed friends have been of a purely sentimental character, and for this purpose a medium is quite able to satisfy them. But you have an important business matter to discuss, so I shall be happy to place my Telepather at your disposal. Come this way, please.'

Mr Psyche led the bookseller along a dark and narrow passage, and at the end unlocked the door of a small room. On a table in the centre was a box about two feet square. The occultist took off the cover with extreme care, and exposed to view a very curious-looking machine. It was like no other machine that Mr Banwell had ever seen. It was a medley of wheels and drums, and from a central cylinder projected a tangle of wires, the extremities of which fell loosely down when the cover was removed. Two strands coated with green silk ended in metal holders. There were dials on which were mysterious markings, six drums, and six funnelled orifices pointing in as many directions.

Mr Banwell examined it with much interest. 'How does the thing work ?' he asked.

'I can't explain its mechanism,' said Mr Psyche, 'but all you have to do is to grasp these handles, and concentrate your thoughts on the person with whom you wish to communicate. It is necessary for the success of the experiment to have surroundings in harmony with the person sought. In your case the Telepather ought to be put in the studio of the dead artist, where his personality will still be the dominating influence. The room in which he worked will yet contain remnants of his psychic aura, and this will place the instrument in touch with him. Armed with that clue it will track him on the psychic plane pretty much as a bloodhound traces a criminal on this. The success of the experiment, however, depends chiefly on the intensity of your concentration on the subject. I gather that will not be-wanting?'

'Lupton owes me £3,000,' said Mr Banwell, 'and I need it badly. I can concentrate intensely on that thought without the slightest effort.'

'Good,' said the occultist, rubbing his hands together. 'You say the house is in your possession ?'

'It is. I am trying to let it furnished, but at present no one is in it.'

'Good again,' said Psyche. 'As a rule I let my manager superintend such matters, but as I wish to have personal experience of the working of the Telepather I will conduct the experiment myself. We can start at once if it suits you. There is a preliminary fee,' he added.

'How much ?' inquired Mr Banwell.

Psyche reflected. 'I will only charge you five guineas. If you get into contact with Mr Lupton there will be an additional twenty guineas to pay, and if you get your money back, a further sum of one hundred guineas. For the latter fee I will also include a communication to another departed friend.'

Mr Banwell pulled out his purse. 'Here is your preliminary fee,' he said, handing over the money. 'I shan't trouble any other friend with a communication. Mr Lupton is the only dead man I hanker after, but I want him badly.'

Two hours after they drove up to the house on Muswell Hill lately occupied by Aylmer Lupton the artist, and Mr Psyche himself carried the Telepather into the studio. This was a lame apartment with a good light, comfortably and even luxuriously furnished. There were rich rugs and draperies, bronzes and casts. There was a fine baronial fireplace and an oak gallery Two or three large easels and a quantity of canvases sketchbooks portfolios, colour-boxes, palettes and brushes testified to the industry of the deceased artist.

Psyche remarked on the luxury of the place. 'It was paid for in my money' said Mr Banwell. 'And you should see my own room' he added bitterly. 'Over the shop—horse-hair and antimacassars. The contrast with this won't bear thinking of.'

'We have all got to learn from sad experience, and I myself once lost as much as you through an Italian nobleman' said Mr Psyche gently, as he placed the Telepather on a side table and removed the cover. 'Now will you kindly pull up a chair, sit down, and take hold of the two metal holders? Grasp them tightly, as you would the handles of an ordinary electric battery. Concentrate your thoughts for all you are worth on Aylmer Lupton—on the promises he made—on the money he owes you.'

Mr Banwell sat down and gripped the holders. 'I will leave you, said Psyche, 'so that my individuality shall not be a disturbing influence.'

Half an hour later he returned. 'Any results?' he asked.

'None whatever,' said Mr Banwell gloomily

'Don't be discouraged' said the occultist. 'The instrument may still be charged with the personality of the last user. Concentrate. Concentrate. This is generally difficult and in your case I fancy the thought of the money may be stronger than that of the man himself. I find poetry a great' help in concentration—even the mechanical repetition of it I have out down a few lines on the situation which may be of some use,' modestly producing a piece of paper from which he read:

Aylmer Lupton, artist rare,
Aylmer Lupton, A.R.A.

I am Banwell calling you,
Answer make without delay.

Golden pounds you owe to me,
Thousands three of them there are,
Let me have my thousands back
Or I'll haunt you, near or far.

'Don't you think the last line a bit strong?' said Banwell.

'You can't put it strong enough with spirits,' explained Mr Psyche. 'They'll hedge if at all possible, but if they see you're in earnest they'll come to terms. There's nothing a spirit dislikes so much as someone from down here following it, and the best way to deal with Lupton is to let him know we mean business. Ah!'

The exclamation was caused by a convulsive movement of one of the wires. A tremor ran along its length. It lifted itself drowsily, and commenced to paw the air with its feelers. A tremor ran down the second wire, and then it, too, raised itself and waved slowly in the air.

'Bravo, bravo,' cried Mr Psyche. 'Concentrate! Concentrate! The Telepather is moving!'

Another strand rose, and still another, till at last all the wires were in motion. Gradually their movements increased in rapidity. Now the first one was whirling round, licking the air to the left, to the right, above and below. Gradually the others quickened their action, and soon all the wires were lashing round in every direction, like so many angry snakes.

'Concentrate! Concentrate!' repeated Psyche, as he put the verses in front of Mr Banwell, who repeated:

Aylmer Lupton, artist rare,
Aylmer Lupton, A.R.A.
I am Banwell calling you,
Answer make without delay.

The whirling of the wires increased, and from the Telepather came a gurgling sound as if the machine were waking to a living intensity. Its antennae shot out madly. They flicked Banwell in the face and across his hands. Still he hung on to the metal holders and recited Mr Psyche's verses.

Suddenly a change came over the wires. From moving in all directions, one by one they assumed a common course. One by one they turned to the same quarter—towards the big light of the room.

'Good, good,' said Mr Psyche, rubbing his hands. 'They're tracking him.' He consulted a compass on his watch-chain. 'He's gone north. They're after him, and they'll find him. I'll leave you to work it out with the Telepather.'

When he came back the wires were interlocked and rigid. They were fixed at an angle of forty-five degrees, pointing direct to the window. Mr Banwell was showing signs of exhaustion.

'That will do for the present,' said Psyche. "We've got into communication, and that's a fine day's work. It's equal to my most sanguine expectations.'

'That's all very well,' said Banwell, 'but I don't see any particular results.'

'My dear sir,' protested Mr Psyche, 'these things are not worked like trade. You can't pay your money, and get what you want over the counter, so to speak. The Telepather has obviously tracked its object, and most probably will have delivered your message. Mr Lupton's ghost will be surprised and annoyed, and possibly frightened at being followed, and will be inclined to do something for you, if only to get rid of you. We shall have to give it no rest till it sends a satisfactory reply. But we have probably done enough for today. I will leave the instrument with you on the understanding that you are not to touch it till I come in the morning, when we will repeat the communication. I suggest that you pass as much time as possible in this room. Take your meals here if you can, and above all, sleep here.'

With this, Mr Psyche departed for Soho. The day waned, and darkness finally settled on Muswell Hill. No one could have guessed that anything unusual was occurring there. Milkmen, postmen, and lamplighters went their customary rounds. People came home. Meals were eaten. Some men made love: others made strife—just as in any other suburb of London that night. Then lights were extinguished one by one, and Muswell Hill became inert. On a studio floor, Banwell, the bookseller of Pitt Court, Cornhill, slept and snored; but on a table the Telepather still reared its mystic wires to the north.

On the following day when Mr Psyche returned, the bookseller opened the door with palette and paint-brushes in hand.

'Ah, Mr Banwell,' said the occultist, 'I did not know you were an artist.'

'I didn't know it myself,' said Banwell sheepishly, 'but as I had nothing to do I thought I might as well pass the time painting. What do you think of the result?' he asked, pointing to a picture on an easel.

Mr Psyche looked at it critically. 'It's very good,' he said at last. 'But surely you have not done all that?'

'Not all,' Banwell replied, 'but I did the cardinal and the lady.'

'Hum, I congratulate you,' said Mr Psyche. 'For a bookseller I think it wonderful. But now to business, for I must get back by noon. Have you had any communication from Mr Lupton?'

'None whatever,' said Banwell.

'Perhaps not directly—but indirectly? Don't you feel different in any way? How do your thoughts run?'

'I feel all right,' said Mr Banwell. 'In fact, now I come to think of it, I feel especially right. My brain is clearer than usual—or is it my eyes that are so? I see things differently, somehow. The world looks pleasanter and more vivid. I can see pictures everywhere—I can even see one in you. You don't know what a picture you make with that shiny hat of yours against the drapery. You're positively chic. Hold on a minute.'

He took up a sketch-block and a crayon, and began to draw—to draw rapidly. His hand moved across the paper in a businesslike manner. In five minutes he scrawled a signature, and presented the block with a flourish to Psyche.

The occultist looked at it. 'Wonderful!' he exclaimed. 'You're an artist.'

Mr Banwell looked extremely gratified. 'I think you're right,' he said. 'I never knew it before, but now I feel I am one. It must be my surroundings that have brought it out.'

'It's more than that,' replied Mr Psyche solemnly. 'Look at the writing on the wall.'

The bookseller looked round. 'I spoke metaphorically,' said Psyche, returning the block. 'Look at the name you've put to your sketch.'

'Why, I've signed it "Aylmer Lupton!"' exclaimed Banwell. 'I don't know how I came to do it.'

'I congratulate you; I congratulate myself on the entire success of the experiment,' said Mr Psyche with a little pomp and circumstance. 'It is most gratifying.'

'I don't follow you,' said Banwell. 'Please explain.'

'Explain? Your own handwriting explains,' replied Mr Psyche, pointing to the drawing. 'This is Lupton's answer. He can't put your money down for you, and he doesn't see his way to allocate you an actual gold mine; but he can work out his own individuality through you. In other words, he can make you paint his pictures for him. I've inquired about him, and find his work is in great demand. You can satisfy that demand. There's your gold mine for you. This is really fine. The Telepather has more than fulfilled its warranty, and I shall now feel justified in ordering the few additional parts suggested by the adept in Thibet—and another machine as well.'

In his professional gratification Mr Psyche paced the room, rubbing his hands joyfully. Suddenly he stopped.

'As the machine is here,' he said, 'you'd better have another hour at it. That will serve to clinch matters and keep Lupton up to the scratch if he has any intention of hedging.'

Once more Mr Banwell sat down and grasped the handles of the Telepather. A happy contented buzz came from the machine, and a happy, contented smile covered the bookseller's face. Mr Psyche went into the garden, and when he again entered the room Banwell had left the machine and was standing before another easel with a new canvas in front of him, sketching an outline with masterly strokes.

'I could not help it,' he explained apologetically. 'The impulse was too strong.'

Mr Psyche fitted the top to his Telepather. 'A complete success. Most satisfactory,' he said. I shall give my mediums notice to leave when I get back to the shop. I expect there'll be another outcry about the displacement of labour by machinery, but it can't be helped. The Telepather will do the work much better and more economically. Perhaps you'll let me have my further fee now,' he continued to Banwell—'twenty guineas according to our agreement, since communication has been established with Mr Lupton.'

Banwell nodded, pulled out his cheque-book and made out a cheque for the amount.

'One word of advice,' said the occultist, as he folded it up and put it in his pocket-book. 'From my long experience I suggest that you do not altogether neglect your bookselling business. Art is all very well in its way, but a snug little shop is probably more dependable in the long run.'

Mr Banwell waved his brush disdainfully. "When I think of the years I've wasted in trade,' he said, 'I'm ashamed of myself.' Then he turned to his easel again.

Mr Psyche watched him for a few minutes, and then put on his hat. He took up the Telepather, and left the artist at his work.

A month passed. In all that time, Mr Banwell, despite the warning of the occultist, only paid one visit to his shop. On that occasion he wore a wide-brimmed felt hat and a velvet jacket. A black cravat tied in a bunching bow adorned his neck, and there was a little uncertainty as to the existence of a collar. At first the assistant left in charge of the shop did not recognise him.

'Oh, good-morning, sir,' he gasped at length, as the identity of the caller dawned upon him. 'Glad to see you, sir, at last. There's a great deal to talk about. You didn't let me know what to reply to W. H. Smith and Son, and I'm afraid they've gone to law. Then there's that matter of Britton's to settle, and Motte writes that—'

'Don't worry me with such sordid trifles, Dufton,' said Mr Banwell. 'I'm not in a mood to attend to them. I want a nice present for a lady.'

'For a lady, sir!' said the assistant with marked surprise, for Mr Banwell had hitherto been regarded as an avoider of the sex.

'For a lady,' repeated the bookseller. 'You wouldn't expect me to buy one for a canary, would you? What can you recommend?'

'Here's a new edition of the late Lord Tennyson, sir,' said the assistant, 'but perhaps the *edition de luxe* of Ella Wheeler Wilcox would suit better,' pointing to a fair array of volumes in an artistic case.

'Hum,' reflected Mr Banwell, glancing from one to the other of the proffered wares. 'The *edition de luxe* of Miss Wilcox will do,' he said at last. 'Book it to me—Banwell, Muswell Hill—you have the address. Oh, and Dufton, I ought to tell you I'm giving up the shop as soon as I can. If you hear of a likely purchaser let me know, but don't worry me with details. I can't bear too many crude facts. I'm living in another atmosphere.'

With this and a jaunty nod, Mr Banwell swept out of the shop.

The assistant stared after him, and then went to the door and watched him out of sight. 'Oh, he's dotty,' he said when he came back. 'Clean dotty. I've run straight, so far, but this temptation is more than I can stand. I will not be responsible for the consequences. "A nice present for a lady!" Oh, golly!'

When Mr Psyche called at Muswell Hill a fortnight later, he was ushered into the drawing-room, and, a few minutes later, an astonishing figure entered. It was a comely lady of the Georgian period, with hooped dress, powdered hair and patches.

I beg your pardon,' said Mr Psyche as this apparition sat down. 'I came to see Mr Banwell. Is he at home?'

'He is,' replied the lady, 'and, what's more, he's likely to be for some time ahead. He's my husband,' she exclaimed.

'Indeed!' exclaimed Mr Psyche. 'I didn't know he was a married man.'

'He didn't know it himself a week ago,' said the lady with much cheerfulness. 'We were married last Thursday. I'm glad you've called. We've had a lot of talk durin' our 'oneymoon, and he's told me a cock-an'-bull tale about you and a machine or an animal called a telepanther. I say, is Banny all there?' and she tapped her head significantly.

'I look upon him as a very intelligent tradesman,' replied Psyche.

'And an artist,' added Mrs Banwell.

'Certainly an artist. Taking him all round, I should say his present mental equipment is far above the ordinary.'

'I'm a model,' continued the lady. 'I sat for Aylmer Lupton, and when I called the other week I found Banny here instead. I bowled him over straight away at my first sittin'. Lucky he fell in with me, for I can look after him. Some others I won't name would just have bled him dry. Well, I fancy I know somethin' about Art, and Banny's pictures are just as good as Lupton's. I can't tell one from t'other.'

'I should expect that to be the case,' said Mr Psyche. 'They're worth two 'undred apiece.'

'Very gratifying,' murmured the occultist. 'They are. And he's got orders for as many as he can bring. He does one a week.'

'I am glad to hear it. There is a little account I have against your husband for one hundred guineas which I shall now be justified in presenting,' said Mr Psyche, unbuttoning his coat and producing a paper from his pocket.

The lady ignored his movements. 'Two 'undred a week is ten thousand four 'undred a year,' she said.

'All about that,' admitted Mr Psyche, 'but you must make allowances for wear and tear—I mean holidays or illnesses. A man cannot work like a machine.'

'Banny does. He works just like a machine. Directly he's finished one canvas he takes up another.'

'Remarkable,' said Mr Psyche.

'I shall keep him up to it,' said the lady. 'Ten thousand a year! Think of that! The old country isn't played out when a little snip of a chap like Banny can make ten thousand a year.'

'The country is far from being played out, madam,' said Mr Psyche, who was in an optimistic frame of mind that day. 'I was never one of those who regarded the outlook in that light. In my business, although we have undoubtedly lost ground in some directions, such as ghosts and apparitions generally, yet in others—psychic thought and clair-voyancy, for instance—we have more than held our own. I could give you some statistics conclusively proving that we are still far ahead of our nearest competitors in these respects.'

'My hat!' exclaimed the lady. 'How you do talk. Well, you can't see Banny today. He's paintin', and I must get back now. I'm sittin' for Mary Antoinette.'

'At any rate, I suppose he can give me a cheque for this,' said Mr Psyche, tendering his account.

'It's a lot o' money,' Mrs Banwell remarked as she looked at the document. 'Shall I tell him you'll settle for eighty quid, spot cash?'

'The agreement was for a hundred guineas—not quids,' said Mr Psyche stiffly, 'so I am afraid I cannot reduce the amount. Whatever income Mr Banwell is now making from art is undoubtedly owing to my services, so if there were any alteration in my honorarium I should expect an increase rather than a decrease in the amount.'

'You do talk,' said the lady admiringly. 'It's as good as a recitation. Well, I'll have a word with Banny.'

Ten minutes later Mr Psyche left the house on Muswell Hill the richer by one hundred guineas.

Weeks, and even months passed, and the incident had become but a pleasing memory to the occultist, when one day he received a tel-egram: 'Bring Telepather at once. Same terms. Waiting.—Banwell.'

Somewhat surprised by the urgency of the message Mr Psyche proceeded to Muswell Hill. Banwell, red-eyed and dishevelled, met him in the doorway. Behind him with folded arms and puckered lips loomed his wife.

'What's the matter?' inquired Mr Psyche.

'I can't paint,' said Banwell.

'He can't even draw,' snapped the lady.

'Dear me, how's that?' inquired the occultist.

Banwell shook his head lugubriously. 'I finished a Lupton last week, as good as any I've done, and it went to my usual customer for £200. Since then I've tried to start another, but I can't think of a subject, and I can't even draw a cow. Come and look at my attempts.'

Mr Psyche looked at them. They were puerile efforts, suitable for a person of no artistic gifts whatever. 'You certainly can't draw cows,' said Mr Psyche at last.

'And what's more, I don't want to,' Banwell rasped. 'I don't know what I'm doing here at all. I don't feel at home in this place. I wanted to go to business this morning, but Maria wouldn't let me. She insisted on sending that wire for you to come.'

'And now you've got here, you'd better get to work,' said the lady. 'I understand you'll want a fiver in advance,' handing over a banknote.

'Guineas, madam,' said Mr Psyche. 'Thank you,' as a further five shillings were produced. 'Now I propose to repeat what I did before with such excellent results. Our previous experiment was so eminently successful that there is hardly room to doubt the result of this. If Mr Banwell will kindly sit down and concentrate his thoughts on Mr Lupton, and say the poetry I composed, no doubt all will turn out well and he'll start painting again as merrily as ever. The connection will probably require renewing from time to time. I blame myself for not having foreseen this.'

Mr Banwell sat down and grasped the handles.

'Now concentrate,' said Psyche.

'And no foolin',' added Mrs Banwell.

Psyche glanced doubtfully at the lady. 'Perhaps, madam,' he said, 'we may be looked upon by the shade of Mr Lupton as disturbing influences, and it would therefore be wiser for us to leave the room.'

When the occultist returned in half-an-hour or so, Banwell was still holding the metal handles, but the wires, instead of frisking merrily around, still drooped listlessly.

'There are no results,' said Banwell, throwing down the handles, 'and what's more, there won't be any. Lupton's chucked me. I feel it in my bones.'

'Strange,' reflected Mr Psyche. 'You were doing so well, and you seemed to be working in such perfect unison. What object can he have in leaving you in the lurch like this?'

Banwell shook his head despondently. 'I don't know,' he said.

'Stop!' exclaimed Psyche. 'How much have you made out of your paintings?'

'She has it down,' replied Banwell. 'Maria, Maria,' he called out, 'what do the sales tot up to?'

'Two thousand eight hundred pounds, ten shillings,' said Mrs Banwell, entering the room with account-book in hand. 'And there's that sale of Saturday to add to it. That makes three thousand pounds, ten shillings.'

'Ah!' said Mr Psyche. 'Now I see it. Isn't that the precise sum Lupton owed you? Ten shillings over, I believe. He has settled his account with you. He's not going to do more, and injustice you can't expect it. I'm afraid you've painted your last picture, Mr Banwell.'

'What!' exclaimed Mrs Banwell. 'Have I only married a bookseller?'

'A man with £3,000 ready money, a house and furniture, and a snug little business in the City,' remarked Mr Psyche, with some severity.

'I married a painter making ten thousand a year,' said the lady bitterly. 'Banwell of Pitt Alley only makes six 'undred—and not always that. He's a shopman, too.'

'Madam,' retorted Mr Psyche, 'you are ungrateful. Mr Banwell's occupation is as honourable, if not as dazzling as a painter's, and is far more solid in the long run. You have both of you cause for congratulation. You have not only got your money back, Mr Banwell, but you have found a wife.'

'You're right there,' said the lady. 'He's found a wife who will look after him, and see he doesn't fool his money away again. Put on your hat, Banny, and we'll go down to the shop. I've run it since I sacked your man on our weddin'-day, and it's not doin' badly. If I don't make it 'um, I'll know why.'

Mrs Banwell did indeed make things hum. Sometimes as he dances to the tune she calls, Mr Banwell regrets his experiment in occultism, but his rapidly increasing wealth reconciles him, on the whole, to the situation.

On Bank Holidays it is his custom to go to the Tate Gallery, where he stands before a couple of paintings signed 'Aylmer Lupton', and marvels how he did them

What Was It?

Fitz-James O'Brien

It is, I confess, with considerable diffidence that I approach the strange narrative which I am about to relate. The events which I purpose detailing are of so extraordinary a character that I am quite prepared to meet with an unusual amount of incredulity and scorn. I accept all such beforehand. I have, I trust, the literary courage to face unbelief. I have, after mature consideration resolved to narrate, in as simple and straightforward a manner as I can compass, some facts that passed under my observation, in the month of July last, and which, in the annals of the mysteries of physical science, are wholly unparalleled.

I live at No. — Twenty-sixth Street, in New York. The house is in some respects a curious one. It has enjoyed for the last two years the reputation of being haunted. It is a large and stately residence, surrounded by what was once a garden, but which is now only a green enclosure used for bleaching clothes. The dry basin of what has been a fountain, and a few fruit trees ragged and unpruned, indicate that this spot in past days was a pleasant, shady retreat, filled with fruits and flowers and the sweet murmur of waters.

The house is very spacious. A hall of noble size leads to a large spiral staircase winding through its centre, while the various apartments are of imposing dimensions. It was built some fifteen or twenty years since by Mr. A——, the well-known New York merchant, who five years ago threw the commercial world into convulsions by a stupendous bank fraud. Mr. A——, as everyone knows, escaped to Europe, and died not long after, of a broken heart. Almost immediately after the news of his decease reached this country and was verified, the report spread in Twenty-sixth Street that No. — was haunted. Legal measures had dispossessed the widow of its former owner, and it was inhabited merely by a caretaker and his wife, placed there by the house agent into whose hands it had passed for the purposes of renting or sale.

These people declared that they were troubled with unnatural noises. Doors were opened without any visible agency. The remnants of furniture scattered through the various rooms were, during the night, piled one upon the other by unknown hands. Invisible feet passed up and down the stairs in broad daylight, accompanied by the rustle of unseen silk dresses, and the gliding of viewless hands along the massive balusters. The caretaker and his wife declared they would live there no longer. The house agent laughed, dismissed them, and put others in their place. The noises and supernatural manifestations continued. The neighbourhood caught up the story, and the house remained untenanted for three years. Several persons negotiated for it; but, somehow, always before the bargain was closed they heard the unpleasant rumours and declined to treat any further.

It was in this state of things that my landlady, who at that time kept a boarding-house in Bleecker Street, and who wished to move further up town, conceived the bold idea of renting No. — Twenty-sixth Street. Happening to have in her house rather a plucky and philo-sophical set of boarders, she laid her scheme before us, stating can-didly everything she had heard respecting the ghostly qualities of the establishment to which she wished to remove us. With the exception of two timid persons,—a sea-captain and a returned Californian, who immediately gave notice that they would leave,—all of Mrs. Moffat's guests declared that they would accompany her in her chivalric incur-sion into the abode of spirits.

Our removal was effected in the month of May, and we were charmed with our new residence. The portion of Twenty-sixth Street where our house is situated, between Seventh and Eighth Avenues, is one of the pleasantest localities in New York. The gardens back of the houses, running down nearly to the Hudson, form, in the summer time, a perfect avenue of verdure. The air is pure and invigorating, sweeping, as it does, straight across the river from the Weehawken heights, and even the ragged garden which surrounded the house, although displaying on washing days rather too much clothesline, still gave us a piece of greensward to look at, and a cool retreat in the sum-mer evenings, where we smoked our cigars in the dusk, and watched the fireflies flashing their dark lanterns in the long grass.

Of course we had no sooner established ourselves at No. — than we began to expect ghosts. We absolutely awaited their advent with eagerness. Our dinner conversation was supernatural. One of the boarders, who had purchased Mrs. Crowe's *Night Side of Nature* for his own private delectation, was regarded as a public enemy by the entire household for not having bought twenty copies. The man led a life of supreme wretchedness while he was reading this volume.

A system of espionage was established, of which he was the victim. If he incautiously laid the book down for an instant and left the room, it was immediately seized and read aloud in secret places to a select few. I found myself a person of immense importance, it having leaked out that I was tolerably well versed in the history of supernaturalism, and had once written a story the foundation of which was a ghost. If a table or a wainscot panel happened to warp when we were assembled in the large drawing-room, there was an instant silence, and everyone was prepared for an immediate clanking of chains and a spectral form.

After a month of psychological excitement, it was with the utmost dissatisfaction that we were forced to acknowledge that nothing in the remotest degree approaching the supernatural had manifested itself. Once the black butler asseverated that his candle had been blown out by some invisible agency while he was undressing himself for the night; but as I had more than once discovered this coloured gentleman in a condition when one candle must have appeared to him like two, thought it possible that, by going a step further in his potations, he might have reversed this phenomenon, and seen no candle at all where he ought to have beheld one.

Things were in this state when an accident took place so awful and inexplicable in its character that my reason fairly reels at the bare memory of the occurrence. It was the tenth of July. After dinner was over I repaired, with my friend Dr. Hammond, to the garden to smoke my evening pipe. Independent of certain mental sympathies which existed between the doctor and myself, we were linked together by a vice. We both smoked opium. We knew each other's secret, and respected it. We enjoyed together that wonderful expansion of thought, that marvellous intensifying of the perceptive faculties, that boundless feeling of existence when we seem to have points of contact with the whole universe,—in short, that unimaginable spiritual bliss, which I would not surrender for a throne, and which I hope you, reader, will never—never taste.

Those hours of opium happiness which the doctor and I spent

together in secret were regulated with a scientific accuracy. We did not blindly smoke the drug of paradise, and leave our dreams to chance. While smoking, we carefully steered our conversation through the brightest and calmest channels of thought. We talked of the East, and endeavoured to recall the magical panorama of its glowing scenery. We criticised the most sensuous poets,—those who painted life ruddy with health, brimming with passion, happy in the possession of youth and strength and beauty. If we talked of Shakespeare's *Tempest*, we lingered over Ariel, and avoided Caliban. Like the Guebers, we turned our faces to the East, and saw only the sunny side of the world.

This skilful colouring of our train of thought produced in our subsequent visions a corresponding tone. The splendours of Arabian fairyland dyed our dreams. We paced the narrow strip of grass with the tread and port of kings. The song of the *rana arborea*, while he clung to the bark of the ragged plum-tree, sounded like the strains of divine musicians. Houses, walls, and streets melted like rain clouds, and *vistas* of unimaginable glory stretched away before us. It was a rapturous companionship. We enjoyed the vast delight more perfectly because, even in our most ecstatic moments, we were conscious of each other's presence. Our pleasures, while individual, were still twin, vibrating and moving in musical accord.

On the evening in question, the tenth of July, the doctor and myself drifted into an unusually metaphysical mood. We lit our large *meerschaums*, filled with fine Turkish tobacco, in the core of which burned a little black nut of opium, that, like the nut in the fairy tale, held within its narrow limits wonders beyond the reach of kings; we paced to and fro, conversing. A strange perversity dominated the currents of our thought. They would *not* flow through the sun-lit channels into which we strove to divert them. For some unaccountable reason, they constantly diverged into dark and lonesome beds, where a continual gloom brooded. It was in vain that, after our old fashion, we flung ourselves on the shores of the East, and talked of its gay bazaars, of the splendours of the time of Haroun, of *harems* and golden palaces.

Black *afreets* continually arose from the depths of our talk, and expanded, like the one the fisherman released from the copper vessel, until they blotted everything bright from our vision. Insensibly, we yielded to the occult force that swayed us, and indulged in gloomy speculation. We had talked some time upon the proneness of the human mind to mysticism, and the almost universal love of the terrible, when Hammond suddenly said to me. "What do you consider to be

253

the greatest element of terror?"

The question puzzled me. That many things were terrible, I knew. Stumbling over a corpse in the dark; beholding, as I once did, a woman floating down a deep and rapid river, with wildly lifted arms, and awful, upturned face, uttering, as she drifted, shrieks that rent one's heart while we, spectators, stood frozen at a window which overhung the river at a height of sixty feet, unable to make the slightest effort to save her, but dumbly watching her last supreme agony and her disappearance. A shattered wreck, with no life visible, encountered floating listlessly on the ocean, is a terrible object, for it suggests a huge terror, the proportions of which are veiled. But it now struck me, for the first time, that there must be one great and ruling embodiment of fear,—a King of Terrors, to which all others must succumb. What might it be? To what train of circumstances would it owe its existence?

"I confess, Hammond," I replied to my friend, "I never considered the subject before. That there must be one Something more terrible than any other thing, I feel. I cannot attempt, however, even the most vague definition."

"I am somewhat like you, Harry," he answered. "I feel my capacity to experience a terror greater than anything yet conceived by the human mind;—something combining in fearful and unnatural amalgamation hitherto supposed incompatible elements. The calling of the voices in Brockden Brown's novel of *Wieland* is awful; so is the picture of the Dweller of the Threshold, in Bulwer's *Zanoni*; but," he added, shaking his head gloomily, "there is something more horrible still than those."

"Look here, Hammond," I rejoined, "let us drop this kind of talk, for Heaven's sake! We shall suffer for it, depend on it."

"I don't know what's the matter with me tonight," he replied, "but my brain is running upon all sorts of weird and awful thoughts. I feel as if I could write a story like Hoffman, tonight, if I were only master of a literary style."

"Well, if we are going to be Hoffmanesque in our talk, I'm off to bed. Opium and nightmares should never be brought together. How sultry it is! Goodnight, Hammond."

"Goodnight, Harry. Pleasant dreams to you."

"To you, gloomy wretch, *afreets*, ghouls, and enchanters."

We parted, and each sought his respective chamber. I undressed quickly and got into bed, taking with me, according to my usual custom, a book, over which I generally read myself to sleep. I opened the volume as soon as I had laid my head upon the pillow, and instantly flung it to the other side of the room. It was Goudon's *History of Monsters,*—a curious French work, which I had lately imported from Paris, but which, in the state of mind I had then reached, was anything but an agreeable companion. I resolved to go to sleep at once; so, turning down my gas until nothing but a little blue point of light glimmered on the top of the tube, I composed myself to rest.

The room was in total darkness. The atom of gas that still remained alight did not illuminate a distance of three inches round the burner. I desperately drew my arm across my eyes, as if to shut out even the darkness, and tried to think of nothing. It was in vain. The confounded themes touched on by Hammond in the garden kept obtruding themselves on my brain. I battled against them. I erected ramparts of would-be blackness of intellect to keep them out. They still crowded upon me. While I was lying still as a corpse, hoping that by a perfect physical inaction I should hasten mental repose, an awful incident occurred. A *something* dropped, as it seemed, from the ceiling, plumb upon my chest, and the next instant I felt two bony hands encircling my throat, endeavouring to choke me.

I am no coward, and am possessed of considerable physical strength. The suddenness of the attack, instead of stunning me, strung every nerve to its highest tension. My body acted from instinct, before my brain had time to realize the terrors of my position. In an instant I wound two muscular arms around the creature, and squeezed it, with all the strength of despair, against my chest. In a few seconds the bony hands that had fastened on my throat loosened their hold, and I was free to breathe once more. Then commenced a struggle of awful intensity. Immersed in the most profound darkness, totally ignorant of the nature of the Thing by which I was so suddenly attacked, finding my grasp slipping every moment, by reason, it seemed to me, of the entire nakedness of my assailant, bitten with sharp teeth in the shoulder, neck, and chest, having every moment to protect my throat against a pair of sinewy, agile hands, which my utmost efforts could not confine,—these were a combination of circumstances to combat which required all the strength, skill, and courage that I possessed.

At last, after a silent, deadly, exhausting struggle, I got my assailant under by a series of incredible efforts of strength. Once pinned, with my knee on what I made out to be its chest, I knew that I was victor. I rested for a moment to breathe. I heard the creature beneath me panting in the darkness, and felt the violent throbbing of a heart. It was apparently as exhausted as I was; that was one comfort. At this moment I remembered that I usually placed under my pillow, before going to bed, a large yellow silk pocket handkerchief. I felt for it instantly; it was there. In a few seconds more I had, after a fashion, pinioned the creature's arms.

I now felt tolerably secure. There was nothing more to be done but to turn on the gas, and, having first seen what my midnight assailant was like, arouse the household. I will confess to being actuated by a certain pride in not giving the alarm before; I wished to make the capture alone and unaided.

Never losing my hold for an instant, I slipped from the bed to the floor, dragging my captive with me. I had but a few steps to make to reach the gas-burner; these I made with the greatest caution, holding the creature in a grip like a vice. At last I got within arm's length of the tiny speck of blue light which told me where the gas-burner lay. Quick as lightning I released my grasp with one hand and let on the full flood of light. Then I turned to look at my captive.

I cannot even attempt to give any definition of my sensations the instant after I turned on the gas. I suppose I must have shrieked with terror, for in less than a minute afterward my room was crowded with the inmates of the house. I shudder now as I think of that awful moment. *I saw nothing!* Yes; I had one arm firmly clasped round a breathing, panting, corporeal shape, my other hand gripped with all its strength a throat as warm, as apparently fleshy, as my own; and yet, with this living substance in my grasp, with its body pressed against my own, and all in the bright glare of a large jet of gas, I absolutely beheld nothing! Not even an outline,—a vapour!

I do not, even at this hour, realise the situation in which I found myself. I cannot recall the astounding incident thoroughly. Imagination in vain tries to compass the awful paradox.

It breathed. I felt its warm breath upon my cheek. It struggled fiercely. It had hands. They clutched me. Its skin was smooth, like my own. There it lay, pressed close up against me, solid as stone,—and yet utterly invisible !

I wonder that I did not faint or go mad on the instant. Some wonderful instinct must have sustained me ; for, absolutely, in place of loosening my hold on the terrible Enigma, I seemed to gain an additional strength in my moment of horror, and tightened my grasp with such wonderful force that I felt the creature shivering with agony.

Just then Hammond entered my room at the head of the household. As soon as he beheld my face—which, I suppose, must have been an awful sight to look at—he hastened forward, crying, "Great heaven, Harry! what has happened?"

"Hammond! Hammond!" I cried, "come here. Oh, this is awful! I have been attacked in bed by something or other, which I have hold of; but I can't see it,—I can't see it!"

Hammond, doubtless struck by the unfeigned horror expressed in my countenance, made one or two steps forward with an anxious yet puzzled expression. A very audible titter burst from the remainder of my visitors. This suppressed laughter made me furious. To laugh at a human being in my position! It was the worst species of cruelty. *Now*, I can understand why the appearance of a man struggling violently, as it would seem, with an airy nothing, and calling for assistance against a vision, should have appeared ludicrous. *Then*, so great was my rage against the mocking crowd that had I the power I would have stricken them dead where they stood.

"Hammond! Hammond!" I cried again, despairingly, "for God's sake come to me. I can hold the—the thing but a short while longer. It is overpowering me. Help me! Help me!"

"Harry," whispered Hammond, approaching me, "you have been smoking too much opium."

"I swear to you, Hammond, that this is no vision," I answered, in the same low tone. "Don't you see how it shakes my whole frame with its struggles? If you don't believe me, convince yourself. Feel it,—touch it."

Hammond advanced and laid his hand in the spot I indicated. A wild cry of horror burst from him. He had felt it!

In a moment he had discovered somewhere in my room a long piece of cord, and was the next instant winding it and knotting it about the body of the unseen being that I clasped in my arms.

"Harry," he said, in a hoarse, agitated voice, for, though he preserved his presence of mind, he was deeply moved, "Harry, it's all safe now. You may let go, old fellow, if you're tired. The Thing can't move."

I was utterly exhausted, and I gladly loosed my hold.

Hammond stood holding the ends of the cord that bound the Invisible, twisted round his hand, while before him, self-supporting as it were, he beheld a rope laced and interlaced, and stretching tightly around a vacant space. I never saw a man look so thoroughly stricken with awe. Nevertheless his face expressed all the courage and deter-mination which I knew him to possess. His lips, although white, were set firmly, and one could perceive at a glance that, although stricken with fear, he was not daunted.

The confusion that ensued among the guests of the house who were witnesses of this extraordinary scene between Hammond and myself,—who beheld the pantomime of binding this struggling Something,—who beheld me almost sinking from physical exhaustion when my task of jailer was over, the confusion and terror that took possession of the bystanders, when they saw all this, was beyond description. The weaker ones fled from the apartment. The few who remained clustered near the door and could not be induced to approach Hammond and his *charge*. Still incredulity broke out through their terror. They had not the courage to satisfy themselves, and yet they doubted. It was in vain that I begged of some of the men to come near and convince themselves by touch of the existence in that room of a living being which was invisible. They were incredulous, but did not dare to undeceive themselves. How could a solid, living, breathing body be invisible, they asked. My reply was this. I gave a sign to Hammond, and both of us—conquering our fearful repugnance to touch the invisible creature—lifted it from the ground, manacled as it was, and took it to my bed. Its weight was about that of a boy of fourteen.

"Now my friends," I said, as Hammond and myself held the creature suspended over the bed, "I can give you self-evident proof that here is a solid, ponderable body, which, nevertheless, you cannot see. Be good enough to watch the surface of the bed attentively."

I was astonished at my own courage in treating this strange event so calmly; but I had recovered from my first terror, and felt a sort of scientific pride in the affair, which dominated every other feeling.

The eyes of the bystanders were immediately fixed on my bed. At a given signal Hammond and I let the creature fall. There was a dull sound of a heavy body alighting on a soft mass. The timbers of the bed creaked. A deep impression marked itself distinctly on the pillow, and on the bed itself. The crowd who witnessed this gave a low cry, and rushed from the room. Hammond and I were left alone with our *mystery*.

We remained silent for some time, listening to the low, irregular breathing of the creature on the bed, and watching the rustle of the bedclothes as it impotently struggled to free itself from confinement. Then Hammond spoke.

"Harry, this is awful."

"Ay, awful."

"But not unaccountable."

"Not unaccountable! What do you mean? Such a thing has never occurred since the birth of the world. I know not what to think, Hammond. God grant that I am not mad, and that this is not an insane fantasy!"

"Let us reason a little, Harry. Here is a solid body which we touch, but which we cannot see. The fact is so unusual that it strikes us with terror. Is there no parallel, though, for such a phenomenon? Take a piece of pure glass. It is tangible and transparent. A certain chemical coarseness is all that prevents its being so entirely transparent as to be totally invisible. It is not *theoretically impossible*, mind you, to make a glass which shall not reflect a single ray of light,—a glass so pure and homogeneous in its atoms that the rays from the sun will pass through it as they do through the air, refracted but not reflected. We do not see the air, and yet we feel it."

"That's all very well, Hammond, but these are inanimate substances. Glass does not breathe, air does not breathe. *This* thing has a heart that palpitates,—a will that moves it,—lungs that play, and inspire and respire."

"You forget the phenomena of which we have so often heard of late," answered the doctor, gravely. "At the meetings called 'spirit circles,' invisible hands have been thrust into the hands of those persons round the table,—warm, fleshly hands that seemed to pulsate with mortal life."

"What? Do you think, then, that this thing is—"

"I don't know what it is," was the solemn reply; "but please the gods I will, with your assistance, thoroughly investigate it."

We watched together, smoking many pipes, all night long, by the bedside of the unearthly being that tossed and panted until it was apparently wearied out. Then we learned by the low, regular breathing that it slept.

The next morning the house was all astir. The boarders congregated on the landing outside my room, and Hammond and myself were lions. We had to answer a thousand questions as to the state of our extraordinary prisoner, for as yet not one person in the house except ourselves could be induced to set foot in the apartment.

The creature was awake. This was evidenced by the convulsive manner in which the bedclothes were moved in its efforts to escape. There was something truly terrible in beholding, as it were, those second-hand indications of the terrible writhings and agonised struggles for liberty which themselves were invisible.

Hammond and myself had racked our brains during the long night to discover some means by which we might realize the shape and general appearance of the Enigma. As well as we could make out by passing our hands over the creature's form, its outlines and lineaments were human. There was a mouth; a round, smooth head without hair; a nose, which, however, was little elevated above the cheeks; and its hands and feet felt like those of a boy. At first we thought of placing the being on a smooth surface and tracing its outlines with chalk, as shoemakers trace the outline of the foot. This plan was given up as being of no value. Such an outline would give not the slightest idea of its conformation.

A happy thought struck me. We would take a cast of it in plaster of Paris. This would give us the solid figure, and satisfy all our wishes. But how to do it? The movements of the creature would disturb the setting of the plastic covering, and distort the mould. Another thought. Why not give it chloroform? It had respiratory organs,—that was evident by its breathing. Once reduced to a state of insensibility, we could do with it what we would. Doctor X—— was sent for; and after the worthy physician had recovered from the first shock of amazement, he proceeded to administer the chloroform. In three minutes afterward we were enabled to remove the fetters from the creature's body, and a modeller was busily engaged in covering the invisible form with the moist clay.

In five minutes more we had a mould, and before evening a rough facsimile of the Mystery. It was shaped like a man—distorted, uncouth, and horrible, but still a man. It was small, not over four feet and some inches in height, and its limbs revealed a muscular development that was unparalleled. Its face surpassed in hideousness anything I had ever seen. Gustav Doré, or Callot, or Tony Johannot, never conceived anything so horrible. There is a face in one of the latter's illustrations to *Un Voyage où il vous plaira,* which somewhat approaches the countenance of this creature, but does not equal it. It was the physiognomy of what I should fancy a ghoul might be. It looked as if it was capable of feeding on human flesh.

Having satisfied our curiosity, and bound every one in the house to secrecy, it became a question what was to be done with our Enigma? It was impossible that we should keep such a horror in our house; it was equally impossible that such an awful being should be let loose upon the world. I confess that I would have gladly voted for the creature's destruction. But who would shoulder the responsibility? Who would undertake the execution of this horrible semblance of a human being? Day after day this question was deliberated gravely. The boarders all left the house. Mrs. Moffat was in despair, and threatened Hammond and myself with all sorts of legal penalties if we did not remove the Horror. Our answer was, "We will go if you like, but we decline taking this creature with us. Remove it yourself if you please. It appeared in your house. On you the responsibility rests." To this there was, of course, no answer. Mrs. Moffat could not obtain for love or money a person who would even approach the Mystery.

The most singular part of the affair was that we were entirely ignorant of what the creature habitually fed on. Everything in the way of nutriment that we could think of was placed before it, but was never touched. It was awful to stand by, day after day, and see the clothes toss, and hear the hard breathing, and know that it was starving.

Ten, twelve days, a fortnight passed, and it still lived. The pulsations of the heart, however, were daily growing fainter, and had now nearly ceased. It was evident that the creature was dying for want of sustenance. While this terrible life-struggle was going on, I felt miserable. I could not. sleep. Horrible as the creature was, it was pitiful to think of the pangs it was suffering.

At last it died. Hammond and I found it cold and stiff one morning in the bed. The heart had ceased to beat, the lungs to inspire. We hastened to bury it in the garden. It was a strange funeral, the dropping of that viewless corpse into the damp hole. The cast of its form I gave to Doctor X——, who keeps it in his museum in Tenth Street.

As I am on the eve of a long journey from which I may not return, I have drawn up this narrative of an event the most singular that has ever come to my knowledge.

The Mystery of the Circular Chamber

L. T. Meade and Robert Eustace

INTRODUCTION

It so happened that the circumstances of fate allowed me to follow my own bent in the choice of a profession. From my earliest youth the weird, the mysterious had an irresistible fascination for me. Having private means, I resolved to follow my unique inclinations, and I am now well known to all my friends as a professional exposer of ghosts, and one who can clear away the mysteries of most haunted houses. Up to the present I have never had cause to regret my choice, but at the same time I cannot too strongly advise any one who thinks of following my example to hesitate before engaging himself in tasks that entail time, expense, thankless labour, often ridicule, and not seldom great personal danger. To explain, by the application of science, phenomena attributed to spiritual agencies has been the work of my life. I have, naturally, gone through strange difficulties in accomplishing my mission. I propose in these pages to relate the histories of certain queer events, enveloped at first in mystery, and apparently dark with portent, but, nevertheless, when grappled with in the true spirit of science, capable of explanation.

One day in late September I received the following letter from my lawyer:—

My Dear Bell,—

I shall esteem it a favour if you can make it convenient to call upon me at ten o'clock tomorrow morning on a matter of extreme privacy.

At the appointed hour I was shown into Mr. Edgcombe's private room. I had known him for years—we were, in fact, old friends—and I was startled now by the look of worry, not to say anxiety, on his usu-

262

ally serene features.

"You are the very man I want, Bell," he cried. "Sit down; I have a great deal to say to you. There is a mystery of a very grave nature which I hope you may solve for me. It is in connection with a house said to be haunted."

He fixed his bright eyes on my face as he spoke. I sat perfectly silent, waiting for him to continue.

"In the first place," he resumed, "I must ask you to regard the matter as confidential."

"Certainly," I answered.

"You know," he went on, "that I have often laughed at your special hobby, but it occurred to me yesterday that the experiences you have lived through may enable you to give me valuable assistance in this difficulty."

"I will do my best for you, Edgcombe," I replied.

He lay back in his chair, folding his hands.

"The case is briefly as follows," he began. "It is connected with the family of the Wentworths. The only son, Archibald, the artist, has just died under most extraordinary circumstances. He was, as you probably know, one of the most promising water-colour painters of the younger school, and his pictures in this year's Academy met with universal praise. He was the heir to the Wentworth estates, and his death has caused a complication of claims from a member of a collateral branch of the family, who, when the present squire dies, is entitled to the money. This man has spent the greater part of his life in Australia, is badly off, and evidently belongs to a rowdy set. He has been to see me two or three times, and I must say frankly that I am not taken with his appearance."

"Had he anything to do with the death?" I interrupted.

"Nothing whatever, as you will quickly perceive. Wentworth has been accustomed from time to time to go alone on sketching tours to different parts of the country. He has tramped about on foot, and visited odd, out-of-the-way nooks searching for subjects. He never took much money with him, and always travelled as an apparently poor man. A month ago he started off alone on one of these tours. He had a handsome commission from Barlow & Co., picture-dealers in the Strand. He was to paint certain parts of the River Merran; and although he certainly did not need money, he seemed glad of an object for a good ramble. He parted with his family in the best of health and spirits, and wrote to them from time to time; but a week ago they heard the news that he had died suddenly at an inn on the Merran. There was, of course, an inquest and an autopsy. Dr. Miles Gordon, the Wentworths' consulting physician, was telegraphed for, and was present at the post-mortem examination. He is absolutely puzzled to account for the death. The medical examination showed Wentworth to be in apparently perfect health at the time. There was no lesion to be discovered upon which to base a different opinion, all the organs being healthy.

"Neither was there any trace of poison, nor marks of violence. The coroner's verdict was that Wentworth died of syncope, which, as you know perhaps, is a synonym for an unknown cause. The inn where he died is a very lonely one, and has the reputation of being haunted. The landlord seems to bear a bad character, although nothing has ever been proved against him. But a young girl who lives at the inn gave evidence which at first startled every one. She said at the inquest that she had earnestly warned Wentworth not to sleep in the haunted room. She had scarcely told the coroner so before she fell to the floor in an epileptic fit. When she came to herself she was sullen and silent, and nothing more could be extracted from her. The old man, the innkeeper, explained that the girl was half-witted, but he did not attempt to deny that the house had the reputation of being haunted, and said that he had himself begged Wentworth not to put up there. Well, that is about the whole of the story. The coroner's inquest seems to deny the evidence of foul play, but I have my very strong suspicions. What I want you to do is to ascertain if they are correct. Will you undertake the case?"

"I will certainly do so," I replied. "Please let me have any further particulars, and a written document to show, in case of need, that I am acting under your directions."

Edgcombe agreed to this, and I soon afterwards took my leave. The case had the features of an interesting problem, and I hoped that I should prove successful in solving it.

That evening I made my plans carefully. I would go into ——shire early on the following morning, assuming for my purpose the character of an amateur photographer. Having got all necessary particulars from Edgcombe, I made a careful mental map of my operations. First of all I would visit a little village of the name of Harkhurst, and put up at the inn, the Crown and Thistle. Here Wentworth had spent a fortnight when he first started on his commission to make drawings of the River Merran. I thought it likely that I should obtain some information there. Circumstances must guide me as to my further steps, but my intention was to proceed from Harkhurst to the Castle Inn, which was situated about six miles further up the river. This was the inn where the tragedy had occurred.

Towards evening on the following day I arrived at Harkhurst. When my carriage drew up at the Crown and Thistle, the landlady was standing in the doorway. She was a buxom-looking dame, with a kindly face. I asked for a bed.

"Certainly, sir," she answered. She turned with me into the little inn, and taking me upstairs, showed me a small room, quite clean and comfortable, looking out on the yard. I said it would do capitally, and she hurried downstairs to prepare my supper. After this meal, which proved to be excellent, I determined to visit the landlord in the bar. I found him chatty and communicative.

"This is a lonely place," he said; "we don't often have a soul staying with us for a month at a time." As he spoke he walked to the door, and I followed him. The shades of night were beginning to fall, but the picturesqueness of the little hamlet could not but commend itself to me.

"And yet it is a lovely spot," I said. "I should have thought tourists would have thronged to it. It is at least an ideal place for photographers."

"You are right there, sir," replied the man; "and although we don't often have company to stay in the inn, now and then we have a stray artist. It's not three weeks back," he continued, "that we had a gentleman like you, sir, only a bit younger, to stay with us for a week or two. He was an artist, and drew from morning till night—ah, poor fellow!"

"Why do you say that?" I asked.

"I have good cause, sir. Here, wife," continued the landlord, looking over his shoulder at Mrs. Johnson, the landlady, who now appeared on the scene, "this gentleman has been asking me questions about our visitor, Mr. Wentworth, but perhaps we ought not to inflict such a dismal story upon him tonight."

"Pray do," I said; "what you have already hinted at arouses my curiosity. Why should you pity Mr. Wentworth?"

"He is dead, sir," said the landlady, in a solemn voice. I gave a pretended start, and she continued,—

"And it was all his own fault. Ah, dear! it makes me almost cry to think of it. He was as nice a gentleman as I ever set eyes on, and so strong, hearty, and pleasant. Well, sir, everything went well until one day he said to me, 'I am about to leave you, Mrs. Johnson. I am going to a little place called the Castle Inn, further up the Merran.'

"'The Castle Inn!' I cried. 'No, Mr. Wentworth, that you won't, not if you value your life.'

"'And why not?' he said, looking at me with as merry blue eyes as you ever saw in anybody's head. 'Why should I not visit the Castle Inn? I have a commission to make some drawings of that special bend of the river.'

"'Well, then, sir,' I answered, 'if that is the case, you'll just have a horse and trap from here and drive over as often as you want to. For the Castle Inn ain't a fit place for a Christian to put up at.'

"'What do you mean?' he asked of me.

"'It is said to be haunted, sir, and what does happen in that house the Lord only knows, but there's not been a visitor at the inn for some years, not since Bailiff Holt came by his death.'

"'Came by his death?' he asked. 'And how was that?'

"'God knows, but I don't,' I answered. 'At the coroner's inquest it was said that he died from syncope, whatever that means, but the folks round here said it was fright.' Mr. Wentworth just laughed at me. He didn't mind a word I said, and the next day, sir, he was off, carrying his belongings with him."

"Well, and what happened?" I asked, seeing that she paused.

"What happened, sir? Just what I expected. Two days afterwards came the news of his death. Poor young gentleman! He died in the very room where Holt had breathed his last; and, oh, if there wasn't a fuss and to-do, for it turned out that, although he seemed quite poor to us, with little or no money, he was no end of a swell, and had rich relations, and big estates coming to him; and, of course, there was a coroner's inquest and all the rest, and great doctors came down from London, and our Dr. Stanmore, who lives down the street, was sent for, and though they did all they could, and examined him, as it were, with a microscope, they could find no cause for death, and so they give it out that it was syncope, just as they did in the case of poor Holt. But, sir, it wasn't; it was fright, sheer fright. The place is haunted. It's a mysterious, dreadful house, and I only hope you won't have nothing to do with it."

She added a few more words and presently left us.

"That's a strange story," I said, turning to Johnson; "your wife has excited my curiosity. I should much like to get further particulars."

"There don't seem to be anything more to tell, sir," replied Johnson. "It's true what the wife says, that the Castle Inn has a bad name. It's not the first, no, nor the second, death that has occurred there."

"You mentioned your village doctor; do you think he could enlighten me on the subject?"

"I am sure he would do his best, sir. He lives only six doors away, in a red house. Maybe you wouldn't mind stepping down the street and speaking to him?"

"You are sure he would not think it a liberty?"

"Not he, sir; he'll be only too pleased to exchange a word with someone outside this sleepy little place."

"Then I'll call on him," I answered, and taking up my hat I strolled down the street. I was lucky in finding Dr. Stanmore at home, and the moment I saw his face I determined to take him into my confidence.

"The fact is this," I said, when he had shaken hands with me, "I should not dream of taking this liberty did I not feel certain that you could help me."

"And in what way?" he asked, not stiffly, but with a keen, inquiring, interested glance.

"I have been sent down from London to inquire into the Wentworth mystery," I said.

"Is that so?" he said, with a start. Then he continued gravely: "I fear you have come on a wild-goose chase. There was nothing discovered at the autopsy to account for the death. There were no marks on the body, and all the organs were healthy. I met Wentworth often while he was staying here, and he was as hearty and strong-looking a young man as I have ever come across."

"But the Castle Inn has a bad reputation," I said.

"That is true; the people here are afraid of it. It is said to be haunted. But really, sir, you and I need not trouble ourselves about stupid reports of that sort. Old Bindloss, the landlord, has lived there for years, and there has never been anything proved against him."

"Is he alone?"

"No; his wife and a grandchild live there also."

"A grandchild?" I said. "Did not this girl give some startling evidence at the inquest?"

"Nothing of any consequence," replied Dr. Stanmore; "she only repeated what Bindloss had already said himself—that the house was haunted, and that she had asked Wentworth not to sleep in the room."

"Has anything ever been done to explain the reason why this room is said to be haunted?" I continued.

"Not that I know of. Rats are probably at the bottom of it."

"But have not there been other deaths in the house?"

"That is true."

"How many?"

"Well, I have myself attended no less than three similar inquests."

"And what was the verdict of the jury?"

"In each case the verdict was death from syncope."

"Which means, cause unknown," I said, jumping impatiently to my feet. "I wonder, Dr. Stanmore, that you are satisfied to leave the matter in such a state."

"And, pray, what can I do?" he inquired. "I am asked to examine a body. I find all the organs in perfect health; I cannot trace the least appearance of violence, nor can I detect poison. What other evidence can I honestly give?"

"I can only say that I should not be satisfied," I replied. "I now wish to add that I have come down from London determined to solve this mystery. I shall myself put up at the Castle Inn."

"Well?" said Dr. Stanmore.

"And sleep in the haunted room."

"Of course you don't believe in the ghost."

"No; but I believe in foul play. Now, Dr. Stanmore, will you help me?"

"Most certainly, if I can. What do you wish me to do?"

"This—I shall go to the Castle Inn tomorrow. If at the end of three days I do not return here, will you go in search of me, and at the same time post this letter to Mr. Edgcombe, my London lawyer?"

"If you do not appear in three days I'll kick up no end of a row," said Dr. Stanmore, "and, of course, post your letter."

Soon afterwards I shook hands with the doctor and left him.

After an early dinner on the following day, I parted with my good-natured landlord and his wife, and with my knapsack and kodak strapped over my shoulders, started on my way. I took care to tell no one that I was going to the Castle Inn, and for this purpose doubled back through a wood, and so found the right road. The sun was nearly setting when at last I approached a broken-down signpost, on which, in half-obliterated characters, I could read the words, "To the Castle Inn." I found myself now at the entrance of a small lane, which was evidently little frequented, as it was considerably grass-grown. From where I stood I could catch no sight of any habitation, but just at that moment a low, somewhat inconsequent laugh fell upon my ears. I turned quickly and saw a pretty girl, with bright eyes and a childish face, gazing at me with interest. I had little doubt that she was old Bindloss's grand-daughter.

"Will you kindly tell me," I asked, "if this is the way to the Castle Inn?"

My remark evidently startled her. She made a bound forward, seized me by my hand, and tried to push me away from the entrance to the lane into the high road.

"Go away!" she cried; "we have no beds fit for gentlemen at the Castle Inn. Go! go!" she continued, and she pointed up the winding road. Her eyes were now blazing in her head, but I noticed that her lips trembled, and that very little would cause her to burst into tears.

"But I am tired and footsore," I answered. "I should like to put up at the inn for the night."

"Don't!" she repeated; "they'll put you into a room with a ghost. Don't go; 'tain't a place for gentlemen." Here she burst not into tears, but into a fit of high, shrill, almost idiotic laughter. She suddenly clapped one of her hands to her forehead, and, turning, flew almost as fast as the wind down the narrow lane and out of sight.

I followed her quickly. I did not believe that the girl was quite as mad as she seemed, but I had little doubt that she had something extraordinary weighing on her mind.

At the next turn I came in view of the inn. It was a queer-looking old place, and I stopped for a moment to look at it.

The house was entirely built of stone. There were two storeys to the centre part, which was square, and at the four corners stood four round towers. The house was built right on the river, just below a large mill-pond. I walked up to the door and pounded on it with my stick. It was shut, and looked as inhospitable as the rest of the place. After a moment's delay it was opened two or three inches, and the surly face of an old woman peeped out.

"And what may you be wanting?" she asked.

"A bed for the night," I replied; "can you accommodate me?"

She glanced suspiciously first at me and then at my camera.

"You are an artist, I make no doubt," she said, "and we don't want no more of them here."

She was about to slam the door in my face, but I pushed my foot between it and the lintel.

"I am easily pleased," I said; "can you not give me some sort of bed for the night?"

"You had best have nothing to do with us," she answered. "You go off to Harkhurst; they can put you up at the Crown and Thistle."

"I have just come from there," I answered. "As a matter of fact, I could not walk another mile."

"We don't want visitors at the Castle Inn," she continued. Here she peered forward and looked into my face. "You had best be off," she repeated; "they say the place is haunted."

I uttered a laugh.

"You don't expect me to believe that?" I said. She glanced at me from head to foot. Her face was ominously grave.

"You had best know all, sir," she said, after a pause. "Something happens in this house, and no living soul knows what it is, for they who have seen it have never yet survived to tell the tale. It's not more than a week back that a young gentleman came here. He was like you, bold as brass, and he too wanted a bed, and would take no denial. I told him plain, and so did my man, that the place was haunted. He didn't mind no more than you mind. Well, he slept in the only room we have got for guests, and he—he *died there*."

"What did he die of?" I asked.

"Fright," was the answer, brief and laconic. "Now do you want to come or not?"

"Yes; I don't believe in ghosts. I want the bed, and I am determined to have it."

The woman flung the door wide open.

"Don't say as I ain't warned you," she cried. "Come in, if you must." She led me into the kitchen, where a fire burned sullenly on the hearth.

"Sit you down, and I'll send for Bindloss," she said. "I can only promise to give you a bed if Bindloss agrees. Liz, come along here this minute."

A quick young step was heard in the passage, and the pretty girl whom I had seen at the top of the lane entered. Her eyes sought my face, her lips moved as if to say something, but no sound issued from them.

"Go and find your granddad," said the old woman. "Tell him there is a gentleman here that wants a bed. Ask him what's to be done."

The girl favoured me with a long and peculiar glance, then turning on her heel she left the room. As soon as she did so the old woman

270

peered forward and looked curiously at me.

"I'm sorry you are staying," she said; "don't forget as I warned you. Remember, this ain't a proper inn at all. Once it was a mill, but that was afore Bindloss's day and mine. Gents would come in the summer and put up for the fishing, but then the story of the ghost got abroad, and lately we have no visitors to speak of, only an odd one now and then who ain't wanted—no, he ain't wanted. You see, there was three deaths here. Yes"—she held up one of her skinny hands and began to count on her fingers—"yes, three up to the present; three, that's it. Ah, here comes Bindloss."

A shuffling step was heard in the passage, and an old man, bent with age, and wearing a long white beard, entered the room.

"We has no beds for strangers," he said, speaking in an aggressive and loud tone. "Hasn't the wife said so? We don't let out beds here."

"As that is the case, you have no right to have that signpost at the end of the lane," I retorted. "I am not in a mood to walk eight miles for a shelter in a country I know nothing about. Cannot you put me up somehow?"

"I have told the gentleman everything, Sam," said the wife. "He is just for all the world like young Mr. Wentworth, and not a bit frightened."

The old landlord came up and faced me.

"Look you here," he said, "you stay on at your peril. I don't want you, nor do the wife. Now is it 'yes' or 'no'?"

"It is 'yes,'" I said.

"There's only one room you can sleep in."

"One room is sufficient."

"It's the one Mr. Wentworth died in. Hadn't you best take up your traps and be off?"

"No, I shall stay."

"Then there's no more to be said."

"Run, Liz," said the woman, "and light the fire in the parlour."

The girl left the room, and the woman, taking up a candle, said she would take me to the chamber where I was to sleep. She led me down a long and narrow passage, and then, opening a door, down two steps into the most extraordinary-looking room I had ever seen. The walls were completely circular, covered with a paper of a staring grotesque pattern. A small iron bedstead projected into the middle of the floor, which was uncarpeted except for a slip of matting beside it. A cheap deal wash-hand-stand, a couple of chairs, and a small table with a blurred looking-glass stood against the wall beneath a deep embrasure, in which there was a window. This was evidently a room in one of the circular towers. I had never seen less inviting quarters.

"Your supper will be ready directly, sir," said the woman, and placing the candle on the little table, she left me.

The place felt damp and draughty, and the flame of the candle flickered about, causing the tallow to gutter to one side. There was no fireplace in the room, and above, the walls converged to a point, giving the whole place the appearance of an enormous extinguisher. I made a hurried and necessarily limited toilet, and went into the parlour. I was standing by the fire, which was burning badly, when the door opened, and the girl Liz came in, bearing a tray in her hand. She laid the tray on the table and came up softly to me.

"Fools come to this house," she said, "and you are one."

"Pray let me have my supper, and don't talk," I replied. "I am tired and hungry, and want to go to bed."

Liz stood perfectly still for a moment.

"'Tain't worth it," she said; then, in a meditative voice, "no, 'tain't worth it. But I'll say no more. Folks will never be warned!"

Her grandmother's voice calling her caused her to bound from the room.

My supper proved better than I had expected, and, having finished it, I strolled into the kitchen, anxious to have a further talk with the old man. He was seated alone by the fire, a great mastiff lying at his feet.

"Can you tell me why the house is supposed to be haunted?" I asked suddenly, stooping down to speak to him.

"How should I know?" he cried hoarsely. "The wife and me have been here twenty years, and never seen nor heard anything, but for certain folks *do* die in the house. It's mortal unpleasant for me, for the doctors come along, and the coroner, and there's an inquest and no end of fuss. The folks die, although no one has ever laid a finger on 'em; the doctors can't prove why they are dead, but dead they be. Well, there ain't no use saying more. You are here, and maybe you'll pass the one night all right."

"I shall go to bed at once," I said, "but I should like some candles. Can you supply me?"

The man turned and looked at his wife, who at that moment entered the kitchen. She went to the dresser, opened a wooden box, and taking out three or four tallow candles, put them into my hand.

I rose, simulating a yawn.

"Goodnight, sir," said the old man; "goodnight; I wish you well."

A moment later I had entered my bedroom, and having shut the door, proceeded to give it a careful examination. As far as I could make out, there was no entrance to the room except by the door, which was shaped to fit the circular walls. I noticed, however, that there was an unaccountable draught, and this I at last discovered came from below the oak wainscoting of the wall. I could not in any way account for the draught, but it existed to an unpleasant extent. The bed, I further saw, was somewhat peculiar; it had no castors on the four legs, which were let down about half an inch into sockets provided for them in the wooden floor.

This discovery excited my suspicions still further. It was evident that the bed was intended to remain in a particular position. I saw that it directly faced the little window sunk deep into the thick wall, so that any one in bed would look directly at the window. I examined my watch, found that it was past eleven, and placing both the candles on a tiny table near the bed, I lay down without undressing. I was on the alert to catch the slightest noise, but the hours dragged on and nothing occurred. In the house all was silence, and outside the splashing and churning of the water falling over the wheel came distinctly to my ears.

I lay awake all night, but as morning dawned fell into an uneasy sleep. I awoke to see the broad daylight streaming in at the small window.

Making a hasty toilet, I went out for a walk, and presently came in to breakfast. It had been laid for me in the big kitchen, and the old man was seated by the hearth.

"Well," said the woman, "I hope you slept comfortable, sir."

I answered in the affirmative, and now perceived that old Bindloss and his wife were in the humour to be agreeable. They said that if I was satisfied with the room I might spend another night at the inn. I told them that I had a great many photographs to take, and would be much obliged for the permission. As I spoke I looked round for the girl, Liz. She was nowhere to be seen.

"Where is your granddaughter?" I asked of the old woman.

"She has gone away for the day," was the reply. "It's too much for Liz to see strangers. She gets excited, and then the fits come on."

"What sort of fits?"

"I can't tell what they are called, but they're bad, and weaken her, poor thing! Liz ought never to be excited." Here Bindloss gave his wife a warning glance; she lowered her eyes, and going across to the range, began to stir the contents of something in a saucepan.

That afternoon I borrowed some lines from Bindloss, and, taking an old boat which was moored to the bank of the mill-pond, set off under the pretence of fishing for pike. The weather was perfect for the time of year.

Waiting my opportunity, I brought the boat up to land on the bank that dammed up the stream, and getting out walked along it in the direction of the mill-wheel, over which the water was now rushing.

As I observed it from this side of the bank, I saw that the tower in which my room was placed must at one time have been part of the mill itself, and I further noticed that the masonry was comparatively new, showing that alterations must have taken place when the house was abandoned as a mill and was turned into an inn. I clambered down the side of the wheel, holding on to the beams, which were green and slippery, and peered through the paddles.

As I was making my examination, a voice suddenly startled me.

"What are you doing down there?"

I looked up; old Bindloss was standing on the bank looking down at me. He was alone, and his face was contorted with a queer mixture of fear and passion. I hastily hoisted myself up, and stood beside him.

"What are you poking about down there for?" he said, pushing his ugly old face into mine as he spoke. "You fool! if you had fallen you would have been drowned. No one could swim a stroke in that mill-race. And then there would have been another death, and all the old fuss over again! Look here, sir, will you have the goodness to get out of the place? I don't want you here any more."

"I intend to leave tomorrow morning," I answered in a pacifying voice, "and I am really very much obliged to you for warning me about the mill."

"You had best not go near it again," he said in a menacing voice, and then he turned hastily away. I watched him as he climbed up a steep bank and disappeared from view. He was going in the opposite direction from the house. Seizing the opportunity of his absence, I once more approached the mill. Was it possible that Wentworth had been hurled into it? But had this been the case there would have been signs and marks on the body. Having reached the wheel, I clambered boldly down. It was now getting dusk, but I could see that a prolongation of the axle entered the wall of the tower. The fittings were also in wonderfully good order, and the bolt that held the great wheel only required to be drawn out to set it in motion.

That evening during supper I thought very hard. I perceived that Bindloss was angry, also that he was suspicious and alarmed. I saw plainly that the only way to really discover what had been done to Wentworth was to cause the old ruffian to try similar means to get rid of me. This was a dangerous expedient, but I felt desperate, and my curiosity as well as interest were keenly aroused. Having finished my supper, I went into the passage preparatory to going into the kitchen. I had on felt slippers, and my footfall made no noise. As I approached the door I heard Bindloss saying to his wife,—

"He's been poking about the mill-wheel; I wish he would make himself scarce."

"Oh, he can't find out anything," was the reply. "You keep quiet, Bindloss; he'll be off in the morning."

"That's as maybe," was the answer, and then there came a harsh and very disagreeable laugh. I waited for a moment, and then entered the kitchen. Bindloss was alone now; he was bending over the fire, smoking.

"I shall leave early in the morning," I said, "so please have my bill ready for me." I then seated myself near him, drawing up my chair close to the blaze. He looked as if he resented this, but said nothing.

"I am very curious about the deaths which occur in this house," I said, after a pause. "How many did you say there were?"

"That is nothing to you," he answered. "We never wanted you here; you can go when you please."

"I shall go tomorrow morning, but I wish to say something now."

"And what may that be?"

"I don't believe in that story about the place being haunted."

"Oh, you don't, don't you?" He dropped his pipe, and his glittering eyes gazed at me with a mixture of anger and ill-concealed alarm.

"No," I paused, then I said slowly and emphatically, "I went back to the mill even after your warning, and——"

"What?" he cried, starting to his feet.

"Nothing," I answered; "only I don't believe in the ghost."

His face turned not only white but livid. I left him without another word. I saw that his suspicions had been much strengthened by my words. This I intended. To induce the ruffian to do his worst was the only way to wring his secret from him.

My hideous room looked exactly as it had done on the previous evening. The grotesque pattern on the walls seemed to start out in bold relief. Some of the ugly lines seemed at that moment, to my imagination, almost to take human shape, to convert themselves into ogre-like faces, and to grin at me. Was I too daring? Was it wrong of me to risk my life in this manner? I was terribly tired, and, curious as it may seem, my greatest fear at that crucial moment was the dread that I might fall asleep. I had spent two nights with scarcely any repose, and felt that at any moment, notwithstanding all my efforts, slumber might visit me. In order to give Bindloss full opportunity for carrying out his scheme, it was necessary for me to get into bed, and even to feign sleep. In my present exhausted condition the pretence of slumber would easily lapse into the reality.

This risk, however, which really was a very grave one, must be run. Without undressing I got into bed, pulling the bed-clothes well over me. In my hand I held my revolver. I deliberately put out the candles, and then lay motionless, waiting for events. The house was quiet as the grave—there was not a stir, and gradually my nerves, excited as they were, began to calm down. As I had fully expected, overpowering sleepiness seized me, and, notwithstanding every effort, I found myself drifting away into the land of dreams. I began to wish that whatever apparition was to appear would do so at once and get it over. Gradually but surely I seemed to pass from all memory of my present world, and to live in a strange and terrible phantasmagoria. In that state I slept, in that state also I dreamt, and dreamt horribly.

I thought that I was dancing a waltz with an enormously tall woman. She towered above me, clasping me in her arms, and began to whirl me round and round at a giddy speed. I could hear the crashing music of a distant band. Faster and faster, round and round some great empty hall was I whirled. I knew that I was losing my senses, and screamed to her to stop and let me go. Suddenly there was a terrible crash close to me. Good God! I found myself awake, but—I was still moving. Where was I? Where was I going? I leapt up on the bed, only to reel and fall heavily backwards upon the floor. What was the matter? Why was I sliding, sliding? Had I suddenly gone mad, or was I still suffering from some hideous nightmare? I tried to move, to stagger to my feet.

Then by slow degrees my senses began to return, and I knew where I was. I was in the circular room, the room where Wentworth had died; but what was happening to me I could not divine. I only knew that I was being whirled round and round at a velocity that was every moment increasing. By the moonlight that struggled in through the window I saw that the floor and the bed upon it was revolving, but the table was lying on its side, and its fall must have awakened me.

I could not see any other furniture in the room. By what mysterious manner had it been removed? Making a great effort, I crawled to the centre of this awful chamber, and, seizing the foot of the bed, struggled to my feet. Here I knew there would be less motion, and I could just manage to see the outline of the door. I had taken the precaution to slip the revolver into my pocket, and I still felt that if human agency appeared, I had a chance of selling my life dearly; but surely the horror I was passing through was invented by no living man! As the floor of the room revolved in the direction of the door I made a dash for it, but was carried swiftly past, and again fell heavily. When I came round again I made a frantic effort to cling to one of the steps, but in vain; the head of the bedstead caught me as it flew round, and tore my arms away. In another moment I believe I should have gone raving mad with terror. My head felt as if it would burst; I found it impossible to think consecutively. The only idea which really possessed me was a mad wish to escape from this hideous place. I struggled to the bedstead, and dragging the legs from their sockets, pulled it into the middle of the room away from the wall. With this out of the way, I managed at last to reach the door in safety.

The moment my hand grasped the handle I leapt upon the little step and tried to wrench the door open. It was locked, locked from without; it defied my every effort. I had only just standing room for my feet. Below me the floor of the room was still racing round with terrible speed. I dared scarcely look at it, for the giddiness in my head increased each moment. The next instant a soft footstep was distinctly audible, and I saw a gleam of light through a chink of the door. I heard a hand fumbling at the lock, the door was slowly opened outwards, and I saw the face of Bindloss.

For a moment he did not perceive me, for I was crouching down on the step, and the next instant with all my force I flung myself upon him. He uttered a yell of terror. The lantern he carried dropped and went out, but I had gripped him round the neck with my fingers, driving them deep down into his lean, sinewy throat. With frantic speed I pulled him along the passage up to a window, through which the moonlight was shining. Here I released my hold of his throat, but immediately covered him with my revolver.

"Down on your knees, or you are a dead man!" I cried. "Confess everything, or I shoot you through the heart."

"I FLUNG MYSELF UPON HIM."

His courage had evidently forsaken him; he began to whimper and cry bitterly.

"Spare my life," he screamed. "I will tell everything, only spare my life."

"Be quick about it," I said; "I am in no humour to be merciful. Out with the truth."

I was listening anxiously for the wife's step, but except for the low hum of machinery and the splashing of the water I heard nothing.

"Speak," I said, giving the old man a shake. His lips trembled, his words came out falteringly.

"It was Wentworth's doing," he panted.

"Wentworth? Not the murdered man?" I cried.

"No, no, his cousin. The ruffian who has been the curse of my life. Owing to that last death he inherits the property. He is the real owner of the mill, and he invented the revolving floor. There were deaths— oh yes, oh yes. It was so easy, and I wanted the money. The police never suspected, nor did the doctors. Wentworth was bitter hard on me, and I got into his power." Here he choked and sobbed. "I am a miserable old man, sir," he gasped.

"So you killed your victims for the sake of money?" I said, grasping him by the shoulder.

"Yes," he said, "yes. The bailiff had twenty pounds all in gold; no one ever knew. I took it and was able to satisfy Wentworth for a bit."

"And what about Archibald Wentworth?"

"That was *his* doing, and I was to be paid."

"And now finally you wanted to get rid of me?"

"Yes; for you suspected."

As I spoke I perceived by the ghastly light of the moon another door near. I opened it and saw that it was the entrance to a small dark lumber room. I pushed the old man in, turned the key in the lock, and ran downstairs. The wife was still unaccountably absent. I opened the front door, and trembling, exhausted, drenched in perspiration, found myself in the open air. Every nerve was shaken. At that terrible moment I was not in the least master of myself. My one desire was to fly from the hideous place. I had just reached the little gate when a hand, light as a feather, touched my arm. I looked up; the girl Liz stood before me.

"You are saved," she said; "thank God! I tried all I could to stop the wheel. See, I am drenched to the skin; I could not manage it. But at least I locked Granny up. She's in the kitchen, sound asleep. She drank a lot of gin."

"Where were you all day yesterday?" I asked.

"Locked up in a room in the further tower, but I managed to squeeze through the window, although it half killed me. I knew if you stayed that they would try it on tonight. Thank God you are saved."

"Well, don't keep me now," I said; "I have been saved as by a miracle. You are a good girl; I am much obliged to you. You must tell me another time how you manage to live through all these horrors."

"Ain't I all but mad?" was her pathetic reply. "Oh, my God, what I suffer!" She pressed her hand to her face; the look in her eyes was terrible. But I could not wait now to talk to her further. I hastily left the place.

How I reached Harkhurst I can never tell, but early in the morning I found myself there. I went straight to Dr. Stanmore's house, and having got him up, I communicated my story. He and I together immediately visited the superintendent of police. Having told my exciting tale, we took a trap and all three returned to the Castle Inn. We were back there before eight o'clock on the following morning. But as the police officer expected, the place was empty. Bindloss had been rescued from the dark closet, and he and his wife and the girl Liz had all flown. The doctor, the police officer, and I, all went up to the circular room. We then descended to the basement, and after a careful examination we discovered a low door, through which we crept; we then found ourselves in a dark vault, which was full of machinery.

By the light of a lantern we examined it. Here we saw an explanation of the whole trick. The shaft of the mill-wheel which was let through the wall of the tower was *continuous as the axle of a vertical cogged wheel*, and by a multiplication action turned a large horizontal wheel into which a vertical shaft descended. This shaft was let into the centre of four crossbeams, supporting the floor of the room in which I had slept. All round the circular edge of the floor was a steel rim which turned in a circular socket. It needed but a touch to set this hideous apparatus in motion.

The police immediately started in pursuit of Bindloss, and I returned to London. That evening Edgcombe and I visited Dr. Miles Gordon. Hard-headed old physician that he was, he was literally aghast when I told him my story. He explained to me that a man placed in the position in which I was when the floor began to move would by means of centrifugal force suffer from enormous congestion of the brain. In fact, the revolving floor would induce an artificial condition of apoplexy. If the victim were drugged or even only sleeping heavily, and the floor began to move slowly, insensibility would almost immediately be induced, which would soon pass into coma and death, and a post-mortem examination some hours afterwards would show no cause for death, as the brain would appear perfectly healthy, the blood having again left it.

From the presence of Dr. Miles Gordon, Edgcombe and I went to Scotland Yard, and the whole affair was put into the hands of the London detective force. With the clue which I had almost sacrificed my life to furnish, they quickly did the rest. Wentworth was arrested, and under pressure was induced to make a full confession, but old Bindloss had already told me the gist of the story. Wentworth's father had owned the mill, had got into trouble with the law, and changed his name. In fact, he had spent five years in penal servitude. He then went to Australia and made money. He died when his son was a young man. This youth inherited all the father's vices. He came home, visited the mill, and, being of a mechanical turn of mind, invented the revolving floor. He changed the mill into an inn, put Bindloss, one of his "pals," into possession with the full intention of murdering unwary travellers from time to time for their money.

The police, however, wanted him for a forged bill, and he thought it best to fly. Bindloss was left in full possession. Worried by Wentworth, who had him in his power for a grave crime committed years ago, he himself on two occasions murdered a victim in the circular room. Meanwhile several unexpected deaths had taken place in the older branch of the Wentworth family, and Archibald Wentworth alone stood between his cousin and the great estates. Wentworth came home, and with the aid of Bindloss got Archibald into his power. The young artist slept in the fatal room, and his death was the result. At this moment Wentworth and Bindloss are committed for trial at the Old Bailey, and there is no doubt what the result will be.

The ghost mystery in connection with the Castle Inn has, of course, been explained away forever.

The Haunted Homestead

Henry William Herbert

THE MURDER

There are few wilder spots on earth, than the deep wooded gorge through which the waters of the mad Ashuelot rush northward from the pellucid lakelets, embosomed in the eastern spurs of the great Alleghany chain, whence it starts rash and rapid—meet emblem of ambitious man—upon its brief career of foam and fury. The hills— mountains, in bold abruptness, if not by actual height entitled to the name—sinking precipitous and sheer, to the bed of the chafing river, which, in the course of ages, has scarped and channelled their rude sides, and cleft the living granite a hundred fathom down, have left scant space below for a wild road, here hewn or blasted through strata of the eternal rock, there reared upon abutments of rough logs, and traversing some five times in each mile of distance, the devious torrent, as it wheels off in arrowy angles from side to side of its stern channel.

Above, so perpendicularly do the cliffs ascend, that the huge pines, which shoot out from each rift and crevice of their seamed flanks, far overhang the path, dropping their scaly cones into the boiling caldrons of the stream, and almost interlacing their black boughs; so that midsummer's noon scarce pours a wintry twilight into the damp and cavernous ravine, while a November's eve lowers darker than a starless midnight. Even now, when the hand of enterprise has dotted the whole circumjacent region with prosperous (arms and thriving villages, it is a desolate and gloomy pass; but in the years immediately succeeding the war of the independence—when, for unnumbered miles, the land around was clothed in its primeval garniture of forest—when but two tiny hamlets, Keene and Fitzwilliam, had been late-founded on the mountain track, at that time the sole thoroughfare between the young states of New Hampshire and Vermont, with scarce a human habitation in all the dreary miles that intervened between those infant settlements, it was indeed as fearful, ay, and as perilous a route as ever struck dismay into the bosom of lone traveller.

Those were rude days and stern! those were days that, in truth, and in more modes than one, tried—shrewdly tried—men's souls! War had, indeed, passed over—but many of its worst attributes and adjuncts still harassed the unsettled land. Traffic had been well nigh abolished—the culture of the earth had been neglected—want, bitter want, pervaded the whole country—the minds of men, long-used to violence and strife and rapine, slowly resumed their calm and governed tenor—disbanded soldiers, the outcasts of the patriot forces, broken and desperate characters, roamed singly or in bands, without resources or employment, through every state of the new union; nor had the Indian, undismayed by the weak government of the scarce-formed republic, ceased from his late-indulged career of massacre and havoc.

Such was the period—such the nature of the times—when on a lowering and fitful evening toward the last days of October, a mounted traveller was seen to pass the sandhills, which form the jaws of the gorge on the southern side, on his way northward, to Vermont; wherein large tracts of fertile land were offered by the government for saw, at rates which tempted many to become purchasers and settlers in that romantic district. The sun had set already when he rode past the door of the one lowly tavern which then, as for the most part is the case in all new settlements, was the chief building of Fitzwilliam.

A heavy mass of dark grey clouds, surging up slowly from the west, had occupied, at least, one half of the fast-darkening .firmament; broad gouts of rain fell one by one at distant intervals; and the deep melancholy sough of the west wind wailed through the dismal gorge of the Ashuelot in sure foreboding of the near tempest. The landlord of that humble hostelry stood in his lowly doorway, and warned the lated wayfarer to light down for the night, and take the morning with him for his guide through the wild pass that lay before him; but he who was thus timely warned, shook his head only in reply, and asking, in his turn, the distance to Hartley's Hawknest tavern, learned that six miles, of dangerous wild road, yet intervened between him and his destined harbour.

For half a minute it seemed as though he doubted, for he drew in his rein and gazed with an inquiring glance toward the threatening heavens; at all events, his hesitation, if such it were, soon ended, he doubled the cape of his short horseman's cloak closer about his neck, touched his horse lightly with the spur, and cantered moderately onward.

He was a tall and slight, though sinewy figure, with something in his air, and in the practised grace wherewith he sat and wheeled his horse, that spoke of military service—nor did his dress, although not strictly martial, belie the supposition; the square-topped cap of otterskin, the braided loops and frogs on his hussar-like cloak, the leathern breeches, and high boots, equipped with long brass spurs, were by no means dissimilar to the accoutrements of sundry among the regiments of continental horse, disbanded at the termination of the war, although divested of the lace and coloured facings, which would have made them strictly uniform. The animal, moreover, which be rode, had evidently been subjected to the manege, for be was well upon his haunches, with the arched neck and light mouth, champing on the bit, that speak so certainly the well-trained charger—his saddle, too, equipped with holsters at the bow, and a small valise at the cantle, was covered with a handsome bear-skin; while the bridle, with its nosebag, its cavesson, and brass-scaled frontlet, had yet more certainly been decorated so for no pacific purpose.

Darker, and darker yet, frowned the dull skies above him, as threading the black pass, with no guide save the chafing roar of the vexed waters, and the white glistening of their tortured spray, he hastened onward; and now the wind, which had long sobbed and moaned among the giant pines, that lent a heavier gloom to the dark twilight road, raved out in savage gusts, whirling away the smaller branches, like straws, in their mad dalliance; the rain, at every lull, plashing upon the slippery rocks—the thunder crashing and roaring at the zenith, and the pale fires of heaven flashing in ghostly sheets across the narrow stripe of sky, which alone showed between the wood-fringed cliffs glooming on either hand, five hundred feet aloft.

Yet not for rain or storm did the good charger flinch, or the bold rider curb him. With his head bowed upon his breast, his rein relaxed and free, and his foot firm in the stirrup, as confident in the high qualities of his generous steed, fleetly and fearlessly he galloped onward; turn after turn of the stern glen he doubled—bridge after bridge clattered beneath his thundering stride—mile after mile was won—and now, as he wheeled round the base of a huge rocky buttress—from which the stream, rebutted by its massy weight, swept off in a wide reach to the right hand, while on the left the hills receded somewhat from its brink, leaving a sylvan amphitheatre of a few acres circuit—the lights of the small wayside inn, known, in those days, to all who traversed the frontiers of the neighbour states, as Hartley's Hawknest, glanced cheerfully upon the traveller's eyes.

It was a long, low, log-built tenement, with several latticed windows looking toward the river which it faced, the upper story projecting so far as to constitute a rugged sort of galleried *piazza*. A glorious weeping elm, that loveliest of forest trees, stood at the southern end; its drooping foliage, sere, now, and changed from its rich verdure, overshadowing many a yard of ground, and its gigantic trunk, garnished with rings and staples, whereto were fastened, as the stranger galloped up, two or three sorry-looking, ill-conditioned horses, meanly caparisoned with straw-stuffed pads and hempen halters, wailing the leisure of their masters, who were employed—as many a snatch of vulgar song, and many a burst of dissonant harsh laughter pealing into the bosom of the night, betokened—in rude debauchery within. A rudely-fashioned spout of timber discharged a stream of limpid water into a huge stone cistern, whence it leaped with a merry murmur, and ran gurgling down a pebbled channel to join the river in the bottom—and beyond this, a long range of sheds and stabling stood out at a right angle to the tavern.

Pausing before the open shed, the stranger saw, with no small feelings of annoyance, that the whole length of its unpinned and sordid manger was occupied by a large drove of horses; while, by the stamp of hoofs within, and muscling sounds as of beasts busy with their provender, he readily guessed that the stables, also, were completely crowded. Linking his panting charger, therefore, to one of the hooks in the elm-tree, and throwing his own cloak across its croupe, he stepped across the threshold into, the thronged and smoky bar-room. The inn, as he had but too surely augured, was crowded to the utmost—a drove of horses, on their way southward from Vermont, had come in that same evening, their drivers having engaged every bed and pallet in the house—a dozen farmers of, the neighbourhood, scared from proceeding on their homeward routes by the terrific aspect of the night, had occupied the little parlour—the very bar-room floor was strewn with buffaloes and blankets, whereon reposed a dozen sturdy forms, seemingly undisturbed by the obscene and stormy revelling of several of their comrades, who had preferred a night-long drinking bout to a hard couch and uncertain slumbers.

There needed scarce a question to ascertain that not a spot remained where he could spread his cloak; nor, which weighed most with him, a shed, however lowly, wherein to stable his good horse. Nothing remained, then, but to procure a feed of oats for the worn animal, some slight refreshment for himself, and to proceed, as best he might, to Keene, still twelve miles distant, with the worst portions of the road yet to be overcome. No long space did it take the youth, for he was young and eminently handsome; and, as the lights displayed his lithe and active symmetry, set off by a close frock of forest green, edged in accordance with the fashion of the day, by a thin cord of gold, none who looked on him could fail to discover the gentleman of birth and breeding in every feature of his face, in every gesture of his active frame.

And eagerly and keenly did many an eye of those who revelled round him, of those who seemed to slumber, scan his whole form, and dress, and bearing. Several gaunt, wolfish-looking men, muffled in belted blanket coats, bearded and grim and hideous, proffered him their revolting hospitality, and would fain, as it seemed, have entered into converse with hint; but while offending none by anything of haughtiness or of direct avoidance, he yet withdrew himself from their company, and sat wrapped in his own meditations until the voice of the landlord summoned him to the scant meal, which he discussed in haste, and standing; this ended, he drew forth his purse to pay his reckoning; nor was it 'till he noted the quick and fiery glances which shot from many an eye, dwelt gloatingly upon the silken network, through which gleamed many a golden coin, that he became aware of his imprudence in drawing out so large a sum, as he had thus unwittingly displayed before so doubtful an assemblage.

Nor did the consequences of his error fail to stand visibly before him, when sundry of the bystanders offered to yield their places to the stranger, should he prefer to tarry; and one, a tall, dark-visaged, gloomy-looking man, wearing a long and formidable butcher-knife in his buff belt, and holding a tall rifle in his hand, announced his intention to ride some three miles on the way toward Keene, forthwith, to the spot where his own homeward path branched off from the main road, tendered his services and company, as a guide well acquainted with the pass; and even offered him a night's lodging in his own cabin. While thus addressed, the stranger was aware of a shrewd meaning look which the landlord cast toward him as he handed him his change; but seeing no mode whereby to avoid the man's society, and feeling that he should more easily be able to defend himself if assailed, against a person by his side, than against one who might, unseen, waylay him, he was contented with declining the night's lodging, and courteously accepted his assistance as a guide.

The wind had quite sank as he again mounted his recruited charger, and the storm had swept over; yet was the road as dark as a wolf's mouth through the ravine, which narrowed more and more as they proceeded farther, and was even more obscured by the precipitous hills and overhanging foliage. Slowly they journeyed on, compelled to spare their speed by the deep channels and huge stones which broke the surface of the path; and close and various were the questionings to which the traveller was subjected by his acute, although, untutored guide. Acute, however, as he was, he had met, in the stranger, his full match; for, seemingly responding to each query with perfect and accommodating frankness, he yet contrived to say no word which should give any clue to his intentions or his destination; so that when they had reached the spot where their paths separated, the countryman knew nothing more than when they had set forth, of his companion's views or business.

"Well, sir," he said, speaking in better language than might have been expected from his appearance and demeanour, "well, sir, since you will not accept my humble hospitality, I wish you a goodnight. We shall most likely never meet again—if so, I wish you well, sir. I, too, have been a soldier—mind, when you reach the; next bridge, directly you have passed it, you take the right hand path; a little brook you'll have to ford, and it may be a thought high from this rain; but you will find it safe and a good bottom! No! no!" he added, as the traveller would have slipped a guinea into the hand he had extended—"no! no! I have done you no service; I will take no reward! Goodnight!"

"Goodnight, and thanks!" returned the other—and they parted! The traveller, in half repentant thought, blaming himself with generous self-reproach for the suspicious fears he had half entertained of his guide's good faith, and, for the moment, well nigh regretting that he had not accompanied the other to his hospitable home. But thoughts like these were soon absorbed in the necessity of looking to the guidance of his horse among the various difficulties of darkness and an unknown road—and now he reached the first bridge, and the cross track by which he was directed to proceed. Yet, though he had forgot no syllable of his instructions, he hesitated for the left hand was evidently the most travelled route, and that, by which he had been told to journey, seemed but a narrow and occasional bye path. He hesitated, and while he stood there, a wild whooping cry rang on his ear; a melancholy, long-protracted wail, followed. by the quick flapping of wide wings.

As the first sound burst on his ear, the horseman started, and half turned in his saddle, thrusting his hand, meantime, into his ready holsters—but as the final notes were followed by the heavy rash of pinions on the night wind—"Why, what a timorous fool am I," he muttered, "to be thus scared by the chance clamour of a silly fowl! Well! Well! 'tis of a piece with my late doubts," and setting spurs to his reluctant horse—reluctant to turn into that bye path—he trotted forward. A few steps brought him to a small gloomy hollow—the bed of the brooklet mentioned by the farmer—now swollen by the late storm into the semblance of a wintry torrent, brawling among loose stones, and at a few yards' distance from the ford dashing a sheet of broad white foam over a rocky ridge into the fierce Ashuelot. The trees grew close down to the brink on either hand, o'er canoping the dismal ford—the water was as black as Acheron!

The traveller drew in his rein, and steered his charger cautiously down the steep bank, when, as his fore feet touched the merge, a heavy blow was dealt him from behind, with a huge bludgeon, bowing him to the horse's neck.

Before be could recover, a second followed, truly aimed at the juncture of the spine and scull; a flash of myriad sparks streamed through his reeling eyes—his brain spun round and round—and, with a heavy sullen splash, he fell into the shallow poor—a strong hand wheeled the charger round, and a smart blow upon the quarters, sent him in full career over the self-same road which he had lately traversed under the guidance of a master's hand. The freshness of the water laving his forehead, lent, for a moment, a new life to the wounded traveller—he sprang to his feet, and grappled at the throat of his unseen assailant! Just at that point of time, a single sheeted flash, the last faint glimmering of the retreated storm, played for a moment on the sky—he recognised by that feint glimmer the dark visage and the gloomy scowl—he marked the glitter of the long butcher-knife, too late to parry its home thrust. One cry on God for mercy! one long, sick thrilling gasp! one fluttering shudder of the convulsed and lifeless limbs! and his heart's blood was mingled with the turbulent stream—and he lay at the feet of his destroyer, a mere clod in the valley.

It was now long past midnight, and—though the storm, which had so fiercely raved through the dim gorge of the Ashuelot, had spent in fury hours ago—the clouds yet hung heavy and low in grey and ghostlike wreaths along the mountain sides; the stars were all unseen in their high-places; the moon, hid in her vacant interlunar cave, offered no gracious rays to the belated traveller. The lights, however, of the Hawknest, glimmering through its narrow casement, poured their long lines of yellow lustre into the bosom of the darkness, while, from within, the loud laugh of the revellers proclaimed that sleep, that night, held no uninterrupted sway over the inmates of the wayside tavern.

The scene in the small bar-room, was much the same as it has been described at a period some hours earlier on the same dismal night. The landlord, his avarice contending with his natural love of rest, scarce half awake, sat nodding in the bar; eight or nine men, in various postures of uneasy sleep, cumbered the unswept floor, wrapped up in blanket coats and buffalo robes; while five or six, their fellows, sat round a dirty pine table, playing at cards with a pack, the figures on which were all but invisible through the deep coat of filth and grease that covered them—and occasionally calling for some compound of the various fiery mixtures, which had already half-besotted their dull intellects.

Such was the scene, and such the occupation of the casual inmates who that night filled the Hawknest tavern; when, suddenly, in the midst of a profound silence, which had endured for many minutes, unbroken, except by the fluttering sound of the cards, thrown heedlessly upon the board, the hiccough of the waking—or the heavy snore of the sleeping—drunkard!—suddenly there was heard a crash—a thundering crash, that made the walls of the low cottage reel, and the glasses positively jingle on the table?—a crash, that simultaneously aroused all bands—some from their heavy slumbers, others from their engrossing game, to sudden terror and amazement! It seemed as if some ponderous weight had fallen on the floor ef the room overhead. With anxious eager eyes they gazed into each other's faces, speechlessly waiting for some repetition of the sound! "What's that in the devil's name?" asked one, pot valour mingling strangely with amazement in his blank features—"What's in the chamber overhead?"

"Nothing" replied the landlord, who appeared the most thoroughly dismayed of all the company—"there's nothing in it now, nor hasn't been these ten yean!"

"The chimney's fallen, then—that's it, boys! that's it, I'll be sworn, so you hadn't need look scart! The chimney's been shook by the wind, Jackson, and so it's jest now fell, and frightened all of us most out of our wits."

This explanation, plausible as it seemed at first sight, was eagerly admitted by the party, anxious to adopt any reasoning that might efface their fast-growing superstition—but as the speaker ceased—while two or three of the boldest were in the act of moving toward the door as if to ascertain the truth of his suggestion, a strange, wild, wailing sound was heard, as it were, of the west wind rising after a lull. There was, however, in its tone, something more thrilling and less earthly than ever was marked in the cadences of the most furious gale that swept over earth or ocean. Wilder it waxed and wilder—louder and louder every instant, till it was no less difficult to catch the import of words spoken in that sheltered bar-room, than it had been upon a frigate's forecastle.

"God—what a hurricane!" cried one, and rushed to the door which opened directly on the road; but, as it yielded to his touch, no furious gust broke in—the air without was calm and motionless—not a twig quivered on the lofty elm, not a cloud stirred from its stance along the rocky flanks of the ravine, not a breath stirred the pendulous vane upon the gable—still that shrill, tremulous, rocking sound rang through the chambers of the tavern; and in an instant, every inmate of its walls, women, and men, and children, half dressed, and pale, and trembling—as if ague-stricken—rushed down the creaking stairs, seeking for safety in companionship, and ere five minutes had elapsed, all were collected on the little space of greensward that sloped toward the east from the road downward to the river.

Still the wild sound wailed on—and more than one of the stout woodsmen, their minds already half familiarised to that which had appalled them at the first, more from its suddenness than from any other cause, were rallying their scattered senses—when the tones rose yet shriller and more piercing, and changed, as it were, by magic, into a burst of the most fiendish and unnatural laughter; while two or three of the upper casements flow violently open, as if forced from within by some power which they could not resist.

Upon the instant, actuated by some strange impulse which he could not himself have well explained, he who had been, from the first, the boldest of the party, levelled his rifle at the central window, and drew the trigger without uttering a word—the powder flashed in the pan, vivid and keen the stream of living flame burst from the muzzle, but the report, if such there were, was drowned in a yell that pealed from the same window, so horribly sustained, so long, so agonized, that the blood curdled in the stout hearts, while several of the women swooned outright, or fell into hysterics; and the continued outcries of the terrified children lasted long after the sounds, which had excited them, subsided into total silence—for with that awful and heart-rending shriek, the terrible disturbance ended. Some time elapsed without the utterance of a word—the distant lightning flickered across the dark horizon—the bat came flitting on his leathern wings around the eaves and angles of the low inn—the whip-poor-will was heard chanting his oft-repeated melancholy chant down in the thickets by the waterside, and the far rushing of the turbulent Ashuelot rose with a soothing murmur upon the silent night.

By slow degrees the pallid and awe-stricken group recovered from their deep dismay—Dirk Ericson, the woodsman, who had discharged his rifle as fearlessly against the powers of air as though it had been against the breast of mortal foe—Dirk was a sturdy borderer from the frontiers of New York, who had learned soldiership and woodcraft under the kindred guidance of Mad Anthony—Dirk Ericson was the first to enter the walls of the haunted dwelling, for such all now believed, closely escorted, however, by two sturdy brothers, Asa and Enoch Allen, sons of the soil, and natives of the wild gorge, through which they had so often chased the red-deer, or trapped the savage catamount.

They entered, slowly, indeed, and guardedly—and with the muzzles of their true rifles lowered, and their knives loosened in the sheath as if to meet the onset of beings like themselves —but well nigh fearlessly—for theirs were mountain-bred, tough hearts, which—the first sudden start passed over—feared neither man nor devil. They entered, but no sign or sight was there that showed of peril—the lights stood there unsnuffed, capped with large fiery fungusses, but burning quietly away—the glasses were untouched upon the board as when the revellers left them—the blankets of the sleepers lay undisturbed upon the dusty boards.

"Nothing here, boys," cried the undaunted Dirk. "Let's see if the devil's upstairs yet! I a'n't afeared on him, boys, no how!" and snatching up a light, he rushed with a quick step, as though half doubtful of his own resolution, up the frail, clattering staircase. There, the large open space immediately above the bar-room, from which the other chambers opened, was, indeed, absolutely empty—there was no particle of furniture which could have fallen! No! not a billet of a wood, nor a stray brick! nor, in short, any symptom of the bygone disturbance, except a few chips of plaster, which had been broken from the wall by Dirk's unerring bullet, and now lay scattered on the floor. They searched the house from the garret to the cellar, and found no living thing, and heard no sound, but of their own making. They joined the group upon the green, and as they told of their fruitless search, the courage of all present rose! And soon it was agreed, that no one had been in the least degree alarmed; and it was almost doubted by some among the number, whether there had, indeed, been any sounds, but what might be accounted for on natural causes.

While they were yet in anxious conversation, another sound came from a distance on their ears, but this time, it was one to which all there were well accustomed—the hard tramp of a horse, apparently at a full gallop down the pass from the northward.

"Here comes a late traveller," cried mine host. "Bustle, lads, bustle—best not be caught out here-a-ways, like a lot of scart chickens—jump, there, you Peleg Young, and fetch the lanthorn."

Some of the party, as he spoke, turned inward, and betook themselves to a renewal of their potations as to some solace for the troubles they had undergone; while others, Ericson and his confederate hunters among the number, lingered to greet or gaze at the newcomer. Nearer and nearer came the hard clanging tramp—and now Dirk shook his head.

"There is no bridle on that beast," he said—"leastwise if there be bridle, there a'n't no hand to steer it. Hark! how wildlike it clatters down yon stony pitch—now it has started off the road upon the turf—and now—it's a shodden hoof, too—see how it strike the fire on the hillside: There a'n't no rider there, or else my name's not Dirk."

Even as he spoke—bridled and saddled, but with his bridle flying loose, embossed with foam, reeking with sweat, and splashed with soil and clay of every hue and texture, a noble horse dashed at full speed into the very centre of the group, and stopping short with a couple of small, sudden plunges, and a wild whinny, stood perfectly quiet, and suffered Dirk to catch him by the bridle without any attempt at flight or resistance.

"Why, it's the traveller's horse," he cried, almost upon the instant—"the stranger gentleman's—that stopped in jest to supper, and rode on with black Cornelius Heyer. Here's a queer go, now! something's gone wrong, I reckon—show a light here!"

"The horse has come down, Dirk, in the rough road; and the traveller's pitched off, I guess; we'll have him here to-rights," said Asa Allen.

"You're out this time, boy," answered the woodman; "this beast harnt been down this night, any ways," as he examined his knees by the light of the winking lanthorn, "and the stranger warn't the last to pitch off, if he had. That chap was an old dragooner, and a Virginian too, I reckon. This bridle's broke, too—and see here, this long, thick wheal upon his flank—the traveller hadn't no whip with him—and the blow what made this, was struck from behind, by a man on foot—see, it slants downward, forward and downward, tapering off to the front end! There's been foul play here, anywise! Take hold of his head, Asa—and give me the light, you Peleg, till I look over his accoutrements. Pistols both in the holsters—that looks cur'ous, and—this here cover's been pulled open, though, and in hurry, too, for the loop's broke—both loaded! Ha! here's a drop of blood—jest one drop on the pummel. The traveller's had foul play, boys—he has, no question of it!"

"And what we heerd, was sent to tell us on't!" replied another."

"Fast doubt it was," said Dirk, "and we'll hear more of it, if we don't stir ourselves, and search out this unnat'ral murder, The task's fell upon us, boys; and we have got jest to keep mighty straight, and obey orders! Who'll go along with me—you, Asa, and you, Enoch, I count upon—you'll stick to old Dirk's tracks, I know—who else?"

"I will, and I, and I," responded several voices of the rough borderers, who had again assembled at this new cause of excitement, and who were, perhaps, less alarmed at the prospect of a tramp through the woods, and even a skirmish with mortal enemies, than of pat-sing the remainder of the night in that haunted homestead. Rifles were hunted up and loaded; pouches and horns and wood-knives slung .or belted; horses were saddled; and in less than half an hour, eight hardy woodmen were in their stirrups, ready to follow old Dirk Ericson wherever he might guide them.

"Well, Dirk, what's the fix now? how'll we set to, to find him?"

"Why, he set out from here, you see, with black Cornelius," answered the veteran, "and no one else has travelled up since they two quit, so we can take their track to where they parted; and so see, if it be, as Cornelius quit at his own turn; and if he did, two on us can jest ride up and see if he's in bed, and tell him how it's chanced; and the rest on us follow up the stranger's track to where the mischief has fell out. We'll hunt it out, I reckon—leastwise, if I lose the trail on't, there must be e'en a most plaguy snarl in't."

No more was said—the plan was evidently good—two or three lanthorns were provided; and having ascertained the tracks of the two horses—the noble charger of the stranger, and the mean gasson of the farmer—easily visible in the deep mud which lay in every hollow of the route, the little band got under way in silence. Their progress was, of course, slow and guarded, for it was absolutely necessary to pause from time to time, and survey the ground; so to make sure that they had not o'errun the scent—but still at every halt, their caution was rewarded, for, in each muddy spot, the double trail was clearly visible. They reached the well known turning, and, much to the relief of all concerned, in the night search, the farmer's hoof-track diverged from that of his companion, wheeling directly homeward; they could see even where the horses of the two had pawed and poached the ground, while they had held brief parley ere they parted.

"Now, then," said Dirk, "so far, our course is clear! but now comes all the snarl on't. Well, we must see to't how we can best. Asa and Enoch, hear to me, boys—follow up Heyer's track clear to the eend on't—and take note of every stop and turn on't; and if he but gone home, creep up quite quiet to the windows, and see if he's in bed, or how. But don't you rouse him, no how—and when he's fairly lodged, the one on you set right down where you can watch the door, and let the tother come down to the road by the back track, past Lupton's branch, and so keep up the main road till he overtakes us. Take a light with you, boys, and keep a bright look out! The rest come on with me."

So perfect was the confidence of the whole party, in the old hunter's deep sagacity, that not a question was asked, much less an opinion given in opposition to his orders. Away rode the detachment, and on moved the main body—their work becoming, at every step, more difficult and intricate, since, having now no clue, at all, they were compelled to ascertain the trail, foot by foot. Much time had been spent, therefore, before they reached the second turning of the road close to the bridge, under which Lupton's branch fell into the main river. Here, as we know already, the hapless rider had quitted the true path; and here our company, for the first time, overshot the scent—for, nothing doubting that the trail lay right onward the road, from the fork upward to the bridge, being so hard, and of a soil so rocky as to give no note of any footmarks—they galloped forward to the next muddy bottom, when, pausing to look for the guiding track, they found, at once, that it had not passed further.

"Here's the snarl, boys! here's the snarl," shouted Dirk. "Down, every one on you; we must e'en hunt it out by inches. You, Andry Hewson, hold all the horses—Spencer and Young get forrard with the lights, and hold them low down to the airth, I tell you!"

His orders were obeyed implicitly; and in a short time the result was the discovery of the horse-track turning away on the other side of the bridge, into the blind and unused bye-path.

"There's deviltry in this," muttered the crafty veteran. "Dark as it was, there still was light enough to show the main track—and neither horse nor man would turn off into this devil's hole, unless they had been told to. It's no use mounting, boys, I tell you—the trouble's been hard by here, now I tell you!"

They made the trail good to the branch, the last tracks being of the hind feet on the very marge of the turbulent stream—they crossed it, but no footprint had deranged one pebble on the verge! "Try back, once more," cried Dirk, "try back—this is the very spot!" and in a few more moments the sod spurned up, where the startled charger had wheeled round in terror as his master fell, revealed another secret of the dark mystery. Every stone was now turned, every leaf or branch removed that might have been disposed to cover the assassin's tracks, but all in vain! A little dam of stones was now run out into the stream, under old Ericson's direction, so as to turn the waters into a channel somewhat different from their wonted course; a narrow stripe of mud was thus exposed to sight, which had, of late, been covered by the foamy ripples, and there, the very spot whereon the traveller's corpse had fallen, with a large footprint by the side of it, was rendered clear to every eye! Beyond this, and one splash of blood close to the water's edge, all clue was lost.

The morning dawned while they were yet busy with the search, and the broad sun came out, banishing every shadow, and revealing every secret of sweet nature, but no light does his radiance cast on this dread mystery. The woods were searched for miles around—the waters of the wild Ashuelot were dragged for leagues of distance—all to no purpose! No spot of soil had been disturbed—the pools and shallows gave up no dead.

While they were yet employed about the ford, one of the young allies returned with the tidings that Heyer's trail ran straight home—

that his horse had been turned out into its wonted pasture—that the door was unlocked, and a light burning in the chamber, which showed the man calmly reclining on his bed in the undisturbed slumbers of apparent innocence.

With this all clue was lost; and, save that night after night the same hellish disturbance resounded through the chambers of the tavern, till the inhabitants, fairly unable to endure the terrors of this nightly uproar, abandoned it to solitude and ruin, the very story of the hapless traveller might well have been forgotten even on the very scene of his murder.

THE REVELATION

Days, weeks, and months rolled on—and still, as we have said, night after night the fearful din, the crash succeeded by those fiendish yells and that appalling laughter, rang through the haunted chambers of the Hawknest Tavern. For a brief space the inmates strove to maintain their dwelling despite these awful visitations—but brief indeed was that space! For guest by guest, the old familiar customers fell off, deserting their accustomed stations by the glowing hearth in winter, or on the cool and shadowy stoop in the warm summer evenings. So widely did the terrors spread of the mysterious and unearthly sounds, which now clothed with a novel-horror the dark pass of the Ashuelot, that travellers began to shun the route entirely, preferring a circuitous and more fatiguing road to one whereon the Spirits of the Dead held, as it was almost universally believed, nocturnally their hellish orgies. The few and humble wayfarers who still held to the wonted path, hurried along, as the Spanish tourist has it, with beard on shoulder, stealing at every turn a fearful glance around them making no halt nor tarrying on their journey, and shunning the pass altogether, save when the sun rode high in heaven.

The consequences of this change were sad in the extreme to Hartley—his occupation gone, his customers departed, his old friends gazing on him with doubtful and suspicious eyes, poverty staring in his face, driven forth from his home at last by the overwhelming awe of those dread noises—he and his family were suddenly reduced from moderate affluence and comfort to the extremity of sordid want. A little cabin framed of rude logs received them, a miserable hut, which had been raised for temporary occupation only, within a gunshot of the fatal bridge whereby the hapless traveller had fallen, involving in his ruin the innocent family of him who warned and would have succoured him.

Game at this time abounded in the wild woods around, and by his rifle only did the unhappy landlord now support his once rich and respected household.

It is the way of this world to judge ever by result—and before long men who had known him from his cradle, and known his probity and worth, began to shrink from him, as one on whom the judgment of an offended Providence had weighed too visibly—whom punishment divine had marked out as a sinner of no small degree. They shrank from him at market, they drew aside from his contaminating touch even in the house of prayer-all shunned him, all with the exception of one man believed him guilty—guilty of that too, which by no possibility, he could have committed—the murder of that youth who died at two miles distance, while Hartley was employed before the eyes of many in his own crowded bar-room. The man—the only man who drew yet closer, to his side, who to the limit of his own scanty means assisted him, was Dirk, the hunter, while he who spoke the loudest in suspicious hints, and dark insinuations—who was he but the murderer!

Two years had passed, and now inseparable friends, Hartley and Dirk roved over the rude mountains side by side—there was no rock ribbed summit which their adventurous feet had not mounted ; no glen so deep but had resounded to the crack of their true rifles. Not a beast of the hills, nor a fowl of the air, but ministered to their support; and, though avoided by the neighbours as a spot, guilt-stricken and accursed, the little hut of Hartley was once again the scene of humble comfort, and of content at least, if not of happiness. The peltry, conveyed by old Dirk to the nearest market, sold or exchanged, yielded the foreign luxuries of clothing, groceries and liquor—the flesh of the deer, the hare, or the ruffled grouse simmered as temptingly on gridiron or stewpan, and tasted full as well, as veal or mutton.

The little garden plot tended by Hartley's eldest, a fine lad now rising towards manhood, was rich with many a succulent root and savoury herb. All prospered—poorly indeed, but hopefully and humbly!—all prospered save the man ! No soothing of his anxious wife, no sparkling merriment of his loved children, no consolation cheery and bold of his bluff fellow could chase the now habitual gloom from Hartley's honest brow. To be suspected had sank, like the iron of the psalmist, into his very soul. To be condemned of men, no error ever proved against him—to be shunned like the haggard wolf—pointed by every finger in execration and contempt.

Two years had passed—and the same time, which had cast down the innocent from the goodwill of men, from the communion of his fellows, from wealth and happiness and comfort, had raised the real murderer to affluence and respect and honour. For many months after the perpetration of his crime, be had pursued his ordinary avocations of the hard-working occupant of a small mountain farm; but when he found that suspicion had cast no glimpse toward him but had on the contrary fixed steadfastly upon another, he gave out that a rich uncle had died suddenly far off in Massachusetts, had journeyed thitherward, been absent several weeks, and returned rich in cattle, moveables and money, his wealthy kinsman's heir. The mountain farm, which had been mortgaged heavily, was cleared from all encumbrance.

A new and handsome dwelling-house erected on a knoll o'erlooking proudly what was now called the Bridge of Blood, and Hartley's low-browed cabin. Gardens stretched down in pretty terraced slopes to the brink of the arrowy stream; orchards were planted in the rear; fine barns and out-houses erected, among which stood now desolate and fast decaying the former homestead—the very hovel through the unshuttered lattices of which the Allens' had looked for and witnessed the feigned slumbers of the foul assassin.

Two years, as has been said, had passed; when one tempestuous evening old Dirk who still, as he would boast at times, feared neither man nor devil—set forth on his return from Fitzwilliam, whither he had come in the morning with a large pack of beaver. In driving a hard bargain with a pedlar for his peltry, hour of daylight after hour had slipped away unheeded, and supper was announced before the terms of sale were finally concluded—despite his wish to get home early, the veteran hunter could not refuse the invitation to "*sit* by," and it was eight o'clock before he started homeward—his pack supplied him with broadcloth and fifty things beside, in lieu of its furred peltry, his trusty rifle balanced upon his shoulder, and his heart fortified, had that been needful, by a good stirrup cup of right Jamaica.

Then as will often happen when men are most in haste, accident after accident befell him; none indeed very serious, or even trouble-some, but still sufficient to delay him on his route, so that his practised eye read clearly from the position of the stars which blinked forth now and then from their dim canopy of storm that midnight was at hand ere be reached the old Hawknest.

"Well! well," be muttered to himself as he approached its lonely and decaying walls—"well! well, I've heern it afore now, and I guess it wont be the death of me, if I should hear it once again!"

Just then the winds rose high and swept the storm-clouds clear athwart the skies, and left them bright and sparkling with their ten thousand lamps of living fire.—"Ha!" he exclaimed as he looked up—"I reckon its full time for 't now," and as he spoke he stood and gazed with a strange sense of curiosity and wonder not altogether unmixed, it is true, with a sort of half-pleasing apprehension. The windows, where the glass was yet entire, reflected back the quiet radiance of the moon—the doorway, wide open—for the door fallen inwards hung by one rusted hinge—showed cavernous and dark in the calm gleamy light—a bright wind whispered in the branches of the huge cluster, and a small thread of water from the horse-trough gurgled along its pebbly channel with a sweet peaceful murmur. The hunter's wonderment increased as he stood gazing at the tranquil scene, and be determined after a little hesitation to sit down by the streamlet's edge and wait to satisfy himself whether the fearful sounds still haunted the old tavern, or whether they indeed as be now half surmised had ceased forever.

No sooner was his resolution taken than he began to act on it—a moment's search sufficed to find a moss-grown seat of rack, another and his huge limbs were outstretched by the marge of the tinkling runnel, while with an eye as tranquil and as serene a brow, as though he were anticipating some long-promised pleasure, be waited the repetition of the mysterious sounds which had so long driven from those mouldering walls all human occupants. In vain however did be wait, for the moon set, and the stars twinkled and went out, and amber clouds clothed the eastern firmament and day burst forth in its glory and no more fearful noise than the air murmuring in the branches, and the rill gurgling down to meet the noisier river, and the shrill accent of the katydid and cricket, the melancholy wailing of the whip-poor-will, or the far whooping of the answered owl fell on the hunter's ear. Cheery of bean he started up as the day dawned and hurried homeward with glad tidings—the Hawknest was no longer haunted!

On the next night at about nine o'clock a light was shining from the casement of the old bar-room, whence no light had flashed gladness on the traveller's eyes for many a weary month. Two men sat by the old round table on which lay, ready to each hand two ponderous rifles, a watch, some food and liquor, and last not least a copy of the *Testament*! They were old Dirk, the hunter, and his comrade, Hartley, who had returned to pass the night in that spot, and satisfy themselves fully that the disturbance was at rest forever. It needs not to rehearse what passed that night—suffice it that no sound nor sight occurred, save the accustomed rural noises of the neighbourhood; and that some two hours before daylight, they left the place convinced and joyfully on their route homeward.

Homeward they walked in glad and joyous converse, 'till on a sudden as they reached a little height commanding from a distance a view of ——'s new house and farm buildings, their eyes were suddenly attracted by an appearance of bright dancing lights—as of the *aurora borealis*—flashing and streaming heavenward from a focus situated as it seemed in the rear of the new-planted orchards. Strange were the sights indeed, flashes of vivid flame upleaping suddenly from earth and then a long dark interval and then a glimmering glow pervading the whole circuit of the homestead.

Believing that a fire had burst out suddenly among the outbuildings the veterans dashed forward with the wind and nerve that hunters can alone possess. They scaled the rocky height, dashed through the muddy hollow, reached the spot and there from the old house, now desolate and quite deserted, they saw these fearful flashes bursting at every instant. Through every chink and cranny of the door, the walls, the shutters, streamed the deep crimson glare, along the roof tree danced meteoric balls, of an unearthly pallid lustre on either gable that permanently fixed a globe of lurid fire.

"Fire! Fire!" shouted Dirk—"Fire! halloa! halloa! Hans! the old house is a fire!" And with the words he rushed against the door and striking it with the sole of his foot broke every bar and fastening and drove it inwards, but within all was dark!—deep—solid—pitchy blackness.

Hartley and Dirk stared for a moment blankly each in the other's face, but the next they were met by ——, asking them with a volley of fierce imprecations what they intended by waking up his household thus with a false alarm.

"False alarm!" answered Dirk; "why had you seen it, I guess you'd not ha' thought it so false anyhow, why man, the whole air was alight with it."

"Pshaw! you're drunk both on you," returned the other. "You've brought your gammon to the wrong place, my men. Don't you see all's dark and quiet here, as honest men's homes ought to be. What are you arter I'd pleased be to know this time o'night!"

300

"That's neither here nor there," responded Dirk, "we saw a fire up here-a-ways and we come neighbourlike to tell you on't."

"Well! where's the fire now, I'd like to be showed, then I'll think as how you meant honestly, and that's more too I tell you than all would, leastwise all men as knowed you, Hartley."

While these words had been passing, the party had been moving rapidly from the outbuildings, all walking fast under considerable excitement of their feelings toward the house, when suddenly Dirk turned about and instantly pointing toward the old homestead replied "There 'tis!"—and sure enough there the self-same appearances were visible! The red flames glaring out from every crack and cranny, the lurid flashes streaming high into air above the roof tree—the incandescent globes sitting on either gable. "There 'tis!—what d'ye say now?"

"Pshaw! stuff," replied the other, "is that all?" and entered the house instantly slamming the door violently after him.

"Is that all?—then he's used to it," muttered the other—"come aways, Hartley, come aways now I tell ye!—Blood will out!—Blood will out, man, and here I'm on the track on't now I tell you!"

Home they returned that night, and laid their plans in secret—the seventh day afterward—during the nights of all that seven, Hartley and Dirk watched undisturbed in the tavern, while the two Allens' lay in wait around the murderer's homestead, and every night beheld those wild and ominous flashes—the seventh day afterward a busy crowd were hard at work, masons and carpenters, about the ruined Hawknest. Hammers were clanging, saws were whistling and grating, and above all the merry hum of light, free hearted labor rose on the morning air. On the tenth day the family returned to take possession, the old sign was hung out, the old bar was replenished with its accustomed bottles, and oil things fell again into their ordinary course.

Meanwhile night after night, the Allens' and old Dirk hung round —— buildings, and still the hellish lights were seen glancing and flashing bright and clearly visible for many a mile around, and still no note was taken by —— or any of his household. The autumn passed away—winter came on cold, cheerless, and severe; and the old Hawknest tavern once again re-established with all its pristine comforts, travellers once more turned their steps along the wonted road; old friends too, as prosperity returned, returned with many a greeting—men wondered how they could have doubted or for a moment thought ill of kind, good neighbour Hartley.

As these events took place, rumour, and public talk were busy with
——! With the descent of Hartley's star, to borrow the astronomer's
jargon, his had arisen gloriously—now Hartley was again in the as-
cendant; and his correspondingly declined! No fear however—no
dark anticipation appeared to cloud his days—his nights, despite those
fearful sights, were seemingly all fearless. Still the spies lay around him,
they listened at his fastened doors, they peeped in through his guarded casements, and ere long murmurs went through the mouths how
——— and his wife strove fiercely, how no peace was in that household, how no prosperity had followed those ill-gotten gains.

One night old Dirk, with his two comrades, lay there as was their
wont, marking their destined prey, that night more terribly than ever
the furious flames arose, and sounds unheard before—the same wild
yells and bursts of fiendish laughter which had driven Hartley from
his Hawknest, rang round the gleaming buildings! That night more
bitterly than ever rose from within the dwelling house the voices
of contention and strife. The shrill notes of the terrified and angry
wife, pealed piercingly into the ears, while the deep imprecations of
. the man, answered like muttering thunder. At length the door burst
open—lantern in hand ——— rushed forth. "By G—," he cried, "this
night shall finish it, or finish me!" And it did both!

Straight he rushed to the desolate building, entered it, and again
after brief stay rushed forth as if beneath the goad of Orestes' furies—
clashed back into his own dwelling—and within ten minutes' time, a
volume of fierce *real* flame burst out of every crack and cranny—the
shingled walls blazed out, the thatch flared torch-like heavenward—
the rafters smouldered and cracked, and leaped out into living flame,
and all glowed like a tenfold furnace, and rushed earthward and was
dark. The Haunted Homestead was no more upon the earth!

With that night ceased all sights or sounds unearthly, but still suspicion ceased not. Ceased not—nay it waxed ten times wilder, more
rife, more stirring than before! Men muttered secretly no longer, but
spoke aloud their doubts—almost their certainty. Meantime winter
wore onward—Christmas was passed, and February's snows had covered the whole face of nature. It was a dark and starless night—the
wonted party were assembled in the old bar room, when there arrived
a stronger, a tall, dark, handsome, military-looking man, on whom
scarce had Dirk's eyes and Hartley's fallen ere a quick meaning glance
was interchanged between them. The likeness struck both on the instant, strange likeness to the murdered traveller.

With his accustomed depth of wild sagacity, the veteran hunter turned, without noticing apparently the stranger, on the occurrences which had so strangely agitated the inmates of that house and valley. Ere long the stranger's face gave token of anxiety and wonder, and one word led to others, and questions answered brought but fresh questions, until it came out that the man before them had at a period corresponding to that of the commencement of our tale lost his only brother—one whose demeanour and appearance agreed in all particulars with the description given by the woodmen of the unhappy traveller, who had fallen.

It was resolved on the next morning to probe the mystery to the utmost. An appointment was made instantly for an early hour on the following day, when the two Allens, Dirk, and Hartley, professed their readiness to guide their new friend to the scene of the murder. But as the woodmen departed one or two noticed that the night had changed—that it was mild and soft, and the snow sloppy under foot, and all predicted confidently that the slight snow would be gone on the morrow.

And so in truth it was, morn came, and the whole earth was bare, and the soft western wind swept with a mild low sigh over the woody hills. Scarce had the morning dawned, ere they were on the ground—and lo! wonder of wonders—on one spot, exactly on the site of the burnt building a little space of snow lay still—there was none else for miles around—precisely in the form of a man's body.

"He's there," cried Dirk exultingly, "he's there!—when there's a ground thaw the snow always lies over a buried log or any thing that checks the rising heat—he's there. Get axes, boys, and you'll see as I tell's true!"

Axes and crows were brought, the earth was upturned, and there! there! under the very spot whereon the murderer's bed had stood the night he slept so calmly—there lay a human skeleton—a few shreds of green cloth, bordered with narrow cords of gold, a pair of horse-man's pistols, rusted and green with mould. The stranger seized them "Oh, God!" he cried, "my brother's—oh! my brother's!"

The tale is told—for it boots not to dwell upon the murderer's seizure—his agony—confession and despair. Enough the Hawknest tavern still invites the weary travellers to enter its low portal—and Hartley's name in this, third generation, is blazoned on the time-worn signpost, while near the Bridge of Blood a heap of shattered ruins are still pointed out, where stood the *Haunted Homestead.*

LEONAUR

ALSO FROM LEONAUR

AVAILABLE IN SOFTCOVER OR HARDCOVER WITH DUST JACKET

MR MUKERJI'S GHOSTS *by S. Mukerji*—Supernatural tales from the British Raj period by India's Ghost story collector.

KIPLINGS GHOSTS *by Rudyard Kipling*—Twelve stories of Ghosts, Hauntings, Curses, Werewolves & Magic.

THE COLLECTED SUPERNATURAL AND WEIRD FICTION OF WASHINGTON IRVING: VOLUME 1 *by Washington Irving*—Including one novel 'A History of New York', and nine short stories of the Strange and Unusual.

THE COLLECTED SUPERNATURAL AND WEIRD FICTION OF WASHINGTON IRVING: VOLUME 2 *by Washington Irving*—Including three novelettes 'The Legend of the Sleepy Hollow', 'Dolph Heyliger', 'The Adventure of the Black Fisherman' and thirty-two short stories of the Strange and Unusual.

THE COLLECTED SUPERNATURAL AND WEIRD FICTION OF JOHN KENDRICK BANGS: VOLUME 1 *by John Kendrick Bangs*—Including one novel 'Toppleton's Client or A Spirit in Exile', and ten short stories of the Strange and Unusual.

THE COLLECTED SUPERNATURAL AND WEIRD FICTION OF JOHN KENDRICK BANGS: VOLUME 2 *by John Kendrick Bangs*—Including four novellas 'A House-Boat on the Styx', 'The Pursuit of the House-Boat', 'The Enchanted Typewriter' and 'Mr. Munchausen' of the Strange and Unusual.

THE COLLECTED SUPERNATURAL AND WEIRD FICTION OF JOHN KENDRICK BANGS: VOLUME 3 *by John Kendrick Bangs*—Including twor novellas 'Olympian Nights', 'Roger Camerden: A Strange Story', and ten short stories of the Strange and Unusual.

THE COLLECTED SUPERNATURAL AND WEIRD FICTION OF MARY SHELLEY: VOLUME 1 *by Mary Shelley*—Including one novel 'Frankenstein or the Modern Prometheus', and fourteen short stories of the Strange and Unusual.

THE COLLECTED SUPERNATURAL AND WEIRD FICTION OF MARY SHELLEY: VOLUME 2 *by Mary Shelley*—Including one novel 'The Last Man', and three short stories of the Strange and Unusual.

THE COLLECTED SUPERNATURAL AND WEIRD FICTION OF AMELIA B. EDWARDS *by Amelia B. Edwards*—Contains two novelettes 'Monsieur Maurice', and 'The Discovery of the Treasure Isles', one ballad 'A Legend of Boisguilbert' and seventeen short stories to cill the blood.

LEONAUR

ALSO FROM LEONAUR

AVAILABLE IN SOFTCOVER OR HARDCOVER WITH DUST JACKET

THE COLLECTED SCIENCE FICTION AND FANTASY OF STANLEY G. WEINBAUM 1—INTERPLANETARY ODYSSEYS *by Stanley G. Weinbaum*—Classic Tales of Interplanetary Adventure Including: A Martian Odyssey, its Sequel Valley of Dreams, the Complete 'Ham' Hammond Stories and Others.

THE COLLECTED SCIENCE FICTION AND FANTASY OF STANLEY G. WEINBAUM 2—OTHER EARTHS *by Stanley G. Weinbaum*—Classic Futuristic Tales Including: *Dawn of Flame* & its Sequel The Black Flame, plus The Revolution of 1960 & Others.

THE COLLECTED SCIENCE FICTION AND FANTASY OF STANLEY G. WEINBAUM 3—STRANGE GENIUS *by Stanley G. Weinbaum*—Classic Tales of the Human Mind at Work Including the Complete Novel The New Adam, the 'van Manderpootz' Stories and Others.

THE COLLECTED SCIENCE FICTION AND FANTASY OF STANLEY G. WEINBAUM 4—THE BLACK HEART *by Stanley G. Weinbaum*—Classic Strange Tales Including: the Complete Novel The Dark Other, Plus Proteus Island and Others.

THE COLLECTED SCIENCE FICTION & FANTASY OF JACK LONDON 1—BEFORE ADAM & OTHER STORIES *by Jack London*—included in this Volume Before Adam The Scarlet Plague A Relic of the Pliocene When the World Was Young The Red One Planchette A Thousand Deaths Goliah A Curious Fragment The Rejuvenation of Major Rathbone.

THE COLLECTED SCIENCE FICTION & FANTASY OF JACK LONDON 2—THE IRON HEEL & OTHER STORIES *by Jack London*—included in this Volume The Iron Heel The Enemy of All the World The Shadow and the Flash The Strength of the Strong The Unparalleled Invasion The Dream of Debs.

THE COLLECTED SCIENCE FICTION & FANTASY OF JACK LONDON 3—THE STAR ROVER & OTHER STORIES *by Jack London*—included in this Volume The Star Rover The Minions of Midas The Eternity of Forms The Man With the Gash.

THE CRETAN TEAT *by Brian Aldiss*—The Cretan Teat is a wry and comic novel that interweaves its own fiction with an inner fiction about the discovery of a Byzantine painting of the Mother of the Blessed Virgin Mary suckling the infant Jesus and a fake ikon that becomes an instrument of Nemesis.